A Paramount Picture.   *The Canary Murder Case.*

" A MAN WAS HIDDEN IN THIS CLOSET WHEN THE CANARY
WAS KILLED," DECLARED PHILO VANCE.

THE "CANARY" MURDER CASE

A PHILO VANCE STORY

BY

S. S. VAN DINE

**ILLUSTRATED WITH SCENES
FROM THE PARAMOUNT PHOTOPLAY**

GROSSET & DUNLAP
PUBLISHERS   NEW YORK

INTRODUCTORY

For many years I was the personal attorney and constant companion of Mr. Philo Vance; and this period covered the four years during which Mr. John F.-X. Markham, Vance's closest friend, was District Attorney of New York. As a result it was my privilege to be a spectator of what I believe was the most amazing series of criminal cases that ever passed before the eyes of a young lawyer. Indeed, the grim dramas I witnessed during that period constitute one of the most astonishing secret documents in American police history.

Of these dramas Vance was the central character. By an analytical and interpretative process which, as far as I know, has never before been applied to criminal activities, he succeeded in solving many of the important crimes on which both the police and the District Attorney's office had hopelessly fallen down.

Due to my peculiar relations with Vance it happened that not only did I participate in all the cases with which he was connected, but I was also present at most of the informal discussions concerning them which took place between him and the District Attorney; and, being of methodical temperament, I kept a complete record of them. It is fortunate that I performed this gratuitous labor of accumulation and transcription, for now that circumstances have rendered possible my making the cases public, I am able to present them in full detail and with all their various sidelights and succeeding steps.

In another volume—"The Benson Murder Case" —I have related how Vance happened to become involved in criminal investigation, and have also set forth the unique analytic methods of crime detection by which he solved the problem of Alvin Benson's mysterious murder.

The present chronicle has to do with Vance's solution of the brutal murder of Margaret Odell—a *cause célèbre* which came to be known as the "Canary" murder. The strangeness, the daring, the seeming impenetrability of the crime marked it as one of the most singular and astonishing cases in New York's police annals; and had it not been for Philo Vance's participation in its solution, I firmly believe it would have remained one of the great unsolved mysteries of this country.

S. S. VAN DINE.

New York.

CONTENTS

CHARACTERS OF THE BOOK

PHILO VANCE

JOHN F.-X. MARKHAM
District Attorney of New York County.

MARGARET ODELL (THE "CANARY")
Famous Broadway beauty and ex-*Follies* girl, who was mysteriously murdered in her apartment.

AMY GIBSON
Margaret Odell's maid.

CHARLES CLEAVER
A man-about-town.

KENNETH SPOTSWOODE
A manufacturer.

LOUIS MANNIX
An importer.

DR. AMBROISE LINDQUIST
A fashionable neurologist.

TONY SKEEL
A professional burglar.

WILLIAM ELMER JESSUP
Telephone operator.

HARRY SPIVELY
Telephone operator.

ALYS LA FOSSE
A musical-comedy actress.

WILEY ALLEN
A gambler.

POTTS
A street-cleaner.

AMOS FEATHERGILL
  Assistant District Attorney.
WILLIAM M. MORAN
  Commanding Officer of the Detective Bureau.
ERNEST HEATH
  Sergeant of the Homicide Bureau.
SNITKIN
  Detective of the Homicide Bureau.
GUILFOYLE
  Detective of the Homicide Bureau.
BURKE
  Detective of the Homicide Bureau.
TRACY
  Detective assigned to District Attorney's office.
DEPUTY-INSPECTOR CONRAD BRENNER
  Burglar-tools expert.
CAPTAIN DUBOIS
  Finger-print expert.
DETECTIVE BELLAMY
  Finger-print expert.
PETER QUACKENBUSH
  Official photographer.
DR. DOREMUS
  Medical Examiner.
SWACKER
  Secretary to the District Attorney.
CURRIE
  Vance's valet.

CHAPTER I

In the offices of the Homicide Bureau of the Detective Division of the New York Police Department, on the third floor of the Police Headquarters building in Center Street, there is a large steel filing cabinet; and within it, among thousands of others of its kind, there reposes a small green index-card on which is typed: *"ODELL, MARGARET. 184 West 71st Street. Sept. 10. Murder: Strangled about 11 p. m. Apartment ransacked. Jewelry stolen. Body found by Amy Gibson, maid."*

Here, in a few commonplace words, is the bleak, unadorned statement of one of the most astonishing crimes in the police annals of this country—a crime so contradictory, so baffling, so ingenious, so unique, that for many days the best minds of the Police Department and the District Attorney's office were completely at a loss as to even a method of approach. Each line of investigation only tended to prove that Margaret Odell could not possibly have been murdered. And yet, huddled on the great silken davenport in her living-room lay the girl's strangled body, giving the lie to so grotesque a conclusion.

The true story of this crime, as it eventually came to light after a disheartening period of utter darkness and confusion, revealed many strange and bizarre ramifications, many dark recesses of man's

1

unexplored nature, and the uncanny subtlety of a human mind sharpened by desperate and tragic despair. And it also revealed a hidden page of passional melodrama which, in its essence and organisms, was no less romantic and fascinating than that vivid, theatrical section of the *Comédie Humaine* which deals with the fabulous love of Baron Nucingen for Esther van Gobseck, and with the unhappy Torpille's tragic death.

Margaret Odell was a product of the bohemian *demi-monde* of Broadway—a scintillant figure who seemed somehow to typify the gaudy and spurious romance of transient gaiety. For nearly two years before her death she had been the most conspicuous and, in a sense, popular figure of the city's night life. In our grandparents' day she might have had conferred upon her that somewhat questionable designation, "the toast of the town"; but to-day there are too many aspirants for this classification, too many cliques and violent schisms in the Lepidoptera of our café life, to permit of any one competitor being thus singled out. But, for all the darlings of both professional and lay press-agents, Margaret Odell was a character of unquestioned fame in her little world.

Her notoriety was due in part to certain legendary tales of her affairs with one or two obscure potentates in the backwashes of Europe. She had spent two years abroad after her first success in "The Bretonne Maid"—a popular musical comedy in which she had been mysteriously raised from obscurity to the rank of "star"—and, one may cynically imagine, her press-agent took full advantage of her absence to circulate vermilion tales of her conquests.

Her appearance went far toward sustaining her somewhat equivocal fame. There was no question that she was beautiful in a hard, slightly flamboyant way. I remember seeing her dancing one night at the Antlers Club—a famous rendezvous for post-midnight pleasure-seekers, run by the notorious Red Raegan.* She impressed me then as a girl of un-common loveliness, despite the calculating, preda-tory cast of her features. She was of medium height, slender, graceful in a leonine way, and, I thought, a trifle aloof and even haughty in manner—a result, perhaps, of her reputed association with European royalty. She had the traditional courtesan's full, red lips, and the wide, mongoose eyes of Rossetti's "Blessed Damozel." There was in her face that strange combination of sensual promise and spiri-tual renunciation with which the painters of all ages have sought to endow their conceptions of the Eter-nal Magdalene. Hers was the type of face, volup-tuous and with a hint of mystery, which rules man's emotions and, by subjugating his mind, drives him to desperate deeds.

Margaret Odell had received the sobriquet of Canary as a result of a part she had played in an elaborate ornithological ballet of the "Follies," in which each girl had been gowned to represent a va-riety of bird. To her had fallen the rôle of canary; and her costume of white-and-yellow satin, together with her mass of shining golden hair and pink-and-

---

* The Antlers Club has since been closed by the police; and Red Raegan is now serving a long term in Sing Sing for grand larceny.

white complexion, had distinguished her in the eyes
of the spectators as a creature of outstanding charm.
Before a fortnight had passed—so eulogistic were
her press notices, and so unerringly did the audience
single her out for applause—the "Bird Ballet" was
changed to the "Canary Ballet," and Miss Odell
was promoted to the rank of what might charitably
be called *première danseuse*, at the same time having a solo waltz and a song* interpolated for the
special display of her charms and talents.

She had quitted the "Follies" at the close of the
season, and during her subsequent spectacular career
in the haunts of Broadway's night life she had been
popularly and familiarly called the Canary. Thus
it happened that when her dead body was found,
brutally strangled, in her apartment, the crime immediately became known, and was always thereafter
referred to, as the Canary murder.

My own participation in the investigation of the
Canary murder case—or rather my rôle of Boswell-
ian spectator—constituted one of the most memora-
ble experiences of my life. At the time of Margaret
Odell's murder John F.-X. Markham was District
Attorney of New York, having taken office the preceding January. I need hardly remind you that
during the four years of his incumbency he distinguished himself by his almost uncanny success as a
criminal investigator. The praise which was constantly accorded him, however, was highly distasteful to him; for, being a man with a keen sense of
honor, he instinctively shrank from accepting credit
for achievements not wholly his own. The truth is

* Written especially for her by B. G. De Sylva.

that Markham played only a subsidiary part in the majority of his most famous criminal cases. The credit for their actual solution belonged to one of Markham's very close friends, who refused, at the time, to permit the facts to be made public.

This man was a young social aristocrat, whom, for purposes of anonymity, I have chosen to call Philo Vance.

Vance had many amazing gifts and capabilities. He was an art collector in a small way, a fine amateur pianist, and a profound student of æsthetics and psychology. Although an American, he had largely been educated in Europe, and still retained a slight English accent and intonation. He had a liberal independent income, and spent considerable time fulfilling the social obligations which devolved on him as a result of family connections; but he was neither an idler nor a dilettante. His manner was cynical and aloof; and those who met him only casually, set him down as a snob. But knowing Vance, as I did, intimately, I was able to glimpse the real man beneath the surface indications; and I knew that his cynicism and aloofness, far from being a pose, sprang instinctively from a nature which was at once sensitive and solitary.

Vance was not yet thirty-five, and, in a cold, sculptural fashion, was impressively good-looking. His face was slender and mobile; but there was a stern, sardonic expression to his features, which acted as a barrier between him and his fellows. He was not emotionless, but his emotions were, in the main, intellectual. He was often criticised for his asceticism, yet I have seen him exhibit rare bursts of en-

thusiasm over an æsthetic or psychological problem.
However, he gave the impression of remaining remote from all mundane matters; and, in truth, he
looked upon life like a dispassionate and impersonal
spectator at a play, secretly amused and debonairly
cynical at the meaningless futility of it all. Withal,
he had a mind avid for knowledge, and few details
of the human comedy that came within his sphere
of vision escaped him.

It was as a direct result of this intellectual inquisitiveness that he became actively, though un-
officially, interested in Markham's criminal investigations.

I kept a fairly complete record of the cases in
which Vance participated as a kind of *amicus curiæ*,
little thinking that I would ever be privileged to
make them public; but Markham, after being defeated, as you remember, on a hopelessly split ticket
at the next election, withdrew from politics; and last
year Vance went abroad to live, declaring he would
never return to America. As a result, I obtained
permission from both of them to publish my notes
in full. Vance stipulated only that I should not re-
veal his name; but otherwise no restrictions were
placed upon me.

I have related elsewhere* the peculiar circumstances which led to Vance's participation in criminal research, and how, in the face of almost in-
superable contradictory evidence, he solved the
mysterious shooting of Alvin Benson. The present
chronicle deals with his solution of Margaret Odell's
murder, which took place in the early fall of the

* "The Benson Murder Case" (Scribner's, 1926).

same year, and which, you will recall, created an even greater sensation than its predecessor.*

A curious set of circumstances was accountable for the way in which Vance was shouldered with this new investigation. Markham for weeks had been badgered by the anti-administration newspapers for the signal failures of his office in obtaining convictions against certain underworld offenders whom the police had turned over to him for prosecution. As a result of prohibition a new and dangerous, and wholly undesirable, kind of night life had sprung up in New York. A large number of well-financed cabarets, calling themselves night clubs, had made their appearance along Broadway and in its side streets; and already there had been an appalling number of serious crimes, both passional and monetary, which, it was said, had had their inception in these unsavory resorts.

At last, when a case of murder accompanying a hold-up and jewel robbery in one of the family hotels up-town was traced directly to plans and preparations made in one of the night clubs, and when two detectives of the Homicide Bureau investigating the case were found dead one morning in the neighborhood of the club, with bullet wounds in their backs, Markham decided to pigeonhole the other affairs of

* The Loeb-Leopold crime, the Dorothy King case, and the Hall-Mills murder came later; but the Canary murder proved fully as conspicuous a case as the Nan Patterson-"Cæsar" Young affair, Durant's murder of Blanche Lamont and Minnie Williams in San Francisco, the Molineux arsenic-poisoning case, and the Carlyle Harris morphine murder. To find a parallel in point of public interest one must recall the Borden double-murder in Fall River, the Thaw case, the shooting of Elwell, and the Rosenthal murder.

his office and take a hand personally in the intolerable criminal conditions that had arisen.*

* The case referred to here was that of Mrs. Elinor Quiggly, a wealthy
widow living at the Adlon Hotel in West 96th Street. She was found on
the morning of September 5 suffocated by a gag which had been placed
on her by robbers who had evidently followed her home from the Club
Turque—a small but luxurious all-night café at 89 West 48th Street.
The killing of the two detectives, McQuade and Cannison, was, the
police believe, due to the fact that they were in possession of incriminating evidence against the perpetrators of the crime. Jewellery amount-
ing to over $50,000 was stolen from the Quiggly apartment.

CHAPTER II

FOOTPRINTS IN THE SNOW

(*Sunday, September* 9)

On the day following his decision, Markham and Vance and I were sitting in a secluded corner of the lounge-room of the Stuyvesant Club. We often came together there, for we were all members of the club, and Markham frequently used it as a kind of unofficial up-town headquarters.*

"It's bad enough to have half the people in this city under the impression that the District Attorney's office is a kind of high-class collection agency," he remarked that night, "without being necessitated to turn detective because I'm not given sufficient evidence, or the right kind of evidence, with which to secure convictions."

Vance looked up with a slow smile, and regarded him quizzically.

"The difficulty would seem to be," he returned, with an indolent drawl, "that the police, being unversed in the exquisite abracadabra of legal procedure, labor under the notion that evidence which would convince a man of ordin'ry intelligence, would also convince a court of law. A silly notion, don't y' know. Lawyers don't really want evidence: they

* The Stuyvesant was a large club, somewhat in the nature of a glorified hotel; and its extensive membership was drawn largely from the political, legal, and financial ranks.

9

want erudite technicalities. And the average policeman's brain is too forthright to cope with the pedan-
tic demands of jurisprudence."

"It's not as bad as that," Markham retorted, with
an attempt at good nature, although the strain of
the past few weeks had tended to upset his habitual
equanimity. "If there weren't rules of evidence,
grave injustice would too often be done innocent
persons. And even a criminal is entitled to protection in our courts."

Vance yawned mildly.

"Markham, you should have been a pedagogue.
It's positively amazin' how you've mastered all the
standard oratorical replies to criticism. And yet,
I'm unconvinced. You remember the Wisconsin case
of the kidnapped man whom the courts declared
presumably dead. Even when he reappeared, hale
and hearty, among his former neighbors, his status
of being presumably dead was not legally altered.
The visible and demonstrable fact that he was actually alive was regarded by the court as an immaterial
and impertinent side-issue.* . . . Then there's the
touchin' situation—so prevalent in this fair country
—of a man being insane in one State and sane in
another. . . . Really, y' know, you can't expect a
mere lay intelligence, unskilled in the benign processes of legal logic, to perceive such subtle *nuances*.
Your layman, swaddled in the darkness of ordin'ry
common sense, would say that a person who is a
lunatic on one bank of a river would still be a lunatic if he was on the opposite bank. And he'd also

* The case to which Vance referred, I ascertained later, was Shatterham *v*. Shatterham, 417 Mich., 79—a testamentary case.

hold—erroneously, no doubt—that if a man was living, he would presumably be alive."

"Why this academic dissertation?" asked Markham, this time a bit irritably.

"It seems to touch rather vitally on the source of your present predicament," Vance explained equably. "The police, not being lawyers, have apparently got you into hot water, what? . . . Why not start an agitation to send all detectives to law school?"

"You're a great help," retorted Markham.

Vance raised his eyebrows slightly.

"Why disparage my suggestion? Surely you must perceive that it has merit. A man without legal training, when he knows a thing to be true, ignores all incompetent testimony to the contr'ry, and clings to the facts. A court of law listens solemnly to a mass of worthless testimony, and renders a decision not on the facts but according to a complicated set of rules. The result, d' ye see, is that a court often acquits a prisoner, realizing full well that he is guilty. Many a judge has said, in effect, to a culprit: 'I know, and the jury knows, that you committed the crime, but in view of the legally admissible evidence, I declare you innocent. Go and sin again.'"

Markham grunted. "I'd hardly endear myself to the people of this county if I answered the current strictures against me by recommending law courses for the Police Department."

"Permit me, then, to suggest the alternative of Shakespeare's butcher: 'Let's kill all the lawyers.'"

"Unfortunately, it's a situation, not a utopian theory, that has to be met."

"And just how," asked Vance lazily, "do you propose to reconcile the sensible conclusions of the police with what you touchingly call correctness of legal procedure?"

"To begin with," Markham informed him, "I've decided henceforth to do my own investigating of all important night-club criminal cases. I called a conference of the heads of my departments yesterday, and from now on there's going to be some real activity radiating direct from my office. I intend to produce the kind of evidence I need for convictions."

Vance slowly took a cigarette from his case and tapped it on the arm of his chair.

"Ah! So you are going to substitute the conviction of the innocent for the acquittal of the guilty?"

Markham was nettled; turning in his chair he frowned at Vance.

"I won't pretend not to understand your remark," he said acidulously. "You're back again on your favorite theme of the inadequacy of circumstantial evidence as compared with your psychological theories and æsthetic hypotheses."

"Quite so," agreed Vance carelessly. "Y' know, Markham, your sweet and charmin' faith in circumstantial evidence is positively disarming. Before it, the ordin'ry powers of ratiocination are benumbed. I tremble for the innocent victims you are about to gather into your legal net. You'll eventually make the mere attendance at any cabaret a frightful hazard."

Markham smoked a while in silence. Despite the seeming bitterness at times in the discussions of these two men, there was at bottom no animosity in their attitude toward each other. Their friendship was of long standing, and, despite the dissimilarity of their temperaments and the marked difference in their points of view, a profound mutual respect formed the basis of their intimate relationship.

At length Markham spoke.

"Why this sweeping deprecation of circumstantial evidence? I admit that at times it may be misleading; but it often forms powerful presumptive proof of guilt. Indeed, Vance, one of our greatest legal authorities has demonstrated that it is the most powerful actual evidence in existence. Direct evidence, in the very nature of crime, is almost always unavailable. If the courts had to depend on it, the great majority of criminals would still be at large."

"I was under the impression that this precious majority had always enjoyed its untrammelled freedom."

Markham ignored the interruption.

"Take this example: A dozen adults see an animal running across the snow, and testify that it was a chicken; whereas a child sees the same animal, and declares it was a duck. They thereupon examine the animal's footprints and find them to be the web-footed tracks made by a duck. Is it not conclusive, then, that the animal was a duck and not a chicken, despite the preponderance of direct evidence?"

"I'll grant you your duck," acceded Vance indifferently.

"And having gratefully accepted the gift," pursued Markham, "I propound a corollary: A dozen adults see a human figure crossing the snow, and

take oath it was a woman; whereas a child asserts
that the figure was a man. Now, will you not also
grant that the circumstantial evidence of a man's
footprints in the snow would supply incontrovertible proof that it was, in fact, a man, and not a
woman?"

"Not at all, my dear Justinian," replied Vance,
stretching his legs languidly in front of him; "unless, of course, you could show that a human being
possesses no higher order of brains than a duck."

"What have brains to do with it?" Markham
asked impatiently. "Brains don't affect one's footprints."

"Not those of a duck, certainly. But brains might
very well—and, no doubt, often do—affect the footprints of a human being."

"Am I having a lesson in anthropology, Dar-
winian adaptability, or merely metaphysical specu-
lation?"

"In none of those abstruse subjects," Vance assured him. "I'm merely stating a simple fact culled
from observation."

"Well, according to your highly and peculiarly
developed processes of reasoning, would the circumstantial evidence of those masculine footprints indicate a man or a woman?"

"Not necessarily either," Vance answered; "or,
rather, a possibility of each. Such evidence, when
applied to a human being—to a creature, that is,
with a reasoning mind—would merely mean to me
that the figure crossing the snow was either a man
in his own shoes, or a woman in man's shoes; or perhaps, even, a long-legged child. In short, it would

convey to my purely unlegal intelligence only that
the tracks were made by some descendant of the
Pithecanthropus erectus wearing men's shoes on his
nether limbs—sex and age unknown. A duck's
spoors, on the other hand, I might be tempted to
take at their face value."

"I'm delighted to observe," said Markham, "that,
at least, you repudiate the possibility of a duck
dressing itself up in the gardener's boots."

Vance was silent for a moment; then he said:

"The trouble with you modern Solons, d' ye see,
is that you attempt to reduce human nature to a
formula; whereas the truth is that man, like life, is
infinitely complex. He's shrewd and tricky—skilled
for centuries in all the most diabolical chicaneries.
He is a creature of low cunning, who, even in the
normal course of his vain and idiotic struggle for
existence, instinctively and deliberately tells ninety-
nine lies to one truth. A duck, not having had the
heaven-kissing advantages of human civilization, is
a straightforward and eminently honest bird."

"How," asked Markham, "since you jettison all
the ordinary means of arriving at a conclusion, would
you decide the sex or species of this person who left
the masculine footprints in the snow?"

Vance blew a spiral of smoke toward the ceiling.

"First, I'd repudiate all the evidence of the twelve
astigmatic adults and the one bright-eyed child.
Next, I'd ignore the footprints in the snow. Then,
with a mind unprejudiced by dubious testimony
and uncluttered with material clues, I'd determine
the exact nature of the crime which this fleeing person had committed. After having analyzed its vari-

ous factors, I could infallibly tell you not only whether the culprit was a man or a woman, but I could describe his habits, character, and personality. And I could do all this whether the fleeing figure left male or female or kangaroo tracks, or used stilts, or rode off on a velocipede, or levitated without leaving tracks at all."

Markham smiled broadly. "You'd be worse than the police in the matter of supplying me legal evidence, I fear."

"I, at least, wouldn't procure evidence against some unsuspecting person whose boots had been appropriated by the real culprit," retorted Vance. "And, y' know, Markham, as long as you pin your faith to footprints you'll inevitably arrest just those persons whom the actual criminals want you to— namely, persons who have had nothing to do with the criminal conditions you're about to investigate."

He became suddenly serious.

"See here, old man; there are some shrewd intelligences at present allied with what the theologians call the powers of darkness. The surface appearances of many of these crimes that are worrying you are palpably deceptive. Personally, I don't put much stock in the theory that a malevolent gang of cutthroats have organized an American camorra, and made the silly night clubs their headquarters. The idea is too melodramatic. It smacks too much of the gaudy journalistic imagination: it's too Eugène Sue-ish. Crime isn't a mass instinct except during war-time, and then it's merely an obscene sport. Crime, d' ye see, is a personal and individual business. One doesn't make up a *partie carrée* for a murder as one does for a bridge game. . . . Markham, old dear, don't let this romantic criminological idea lead you astray. And don't scrutinize the figurative footprints in the snow too closely. They'll confuse you most horribly—you're far too trustin' and literal for this wicked world. I warn you that no clever criminal is going to leave his own footprints for your tape-measure and calipers."

He sighed deeply, and gave Markham a look of bantering commiseration.

"And have you paused to consider that your first case may even be devoid of footprints? . . . Alas! What, then, will you do?"

"I could overcome that difficulty by taking you along with me," suggested Markham, with a touch of irony. "How would you like to accompany me on the next important case that breaks?"

"I am ravished by the idea," said Vance.

Two days later the front pages of our metropolitan press carried glaring headlines telling of the murder of Margaret Odell.

CHAPTER III

(Tuesday, September 11; 8.30 a. m.)

It was barely half past eight on that momentous morning of September the 11th when Markham brought word to us of the event.

I was living temporarily with Vance at his home in East 38th Street—a large remodelled apartment occupying the two top floors of a beautiful mansion. For several years I had been Vance's personal legal representative and adviser, having resigned from my father's law firm of Van Dine, Davis and Van Dine to devote myself to his needs and interests. His affairs were by no means voluminous, but his personal finances, together with his numerous purchases of paintings and *objets d'art*, occupied my full time without burdening me. This monetary and legal stewardship was eminently congenial to my tastes; and my friendship with Vance, which had dated from our undergraduate days at Harvard, supplied the social and human element in an arrangement which otherwise might easily have degenerated into one of mere drab routine.

On this particular morning I had risen early and was working in the library when Currie, Vance's valet and majordomo, announced Markham's presence in the living-room. I was considerably astonished at this early-morning visit, for Markham well knew that Vance, who rarely rose before noon, re-

18

sented any intrusion upon his matutinal slumbers. And in that moment I received the curious impression that something unusual and portentous was toward.

I found Markham pacing restlessly up and down, his hat and gloves thrown carelessly on the centre-table. As I entered he halted and looked at me with harassed eyes. He was a moderately tall man, clean-shaven, gray-haired, and firmly set up. His appearance was distinguished, and his manner courteous and kindly. But beneath his gracious exterior there was an aggressive sternness, an indomitable, grim strength, that gave one the sense of dogged efficiency and untiring capability.

"Good morning, Van," he greeted me, with impatient perfunctoriness. "There's been another half-world murder—the worst and ugliest thus far. . . ." He hesitated, and regarded me searchingly. "You recall my chat with Vance at the club the other night? There was something damned prophetic in his remarks. And you remember I half promised to take him along on the next important case. Well, the case has broken—with a vengeance. Margaret Odell, whom they called the Canary, has been strangled in her apartment; and from what I just got over the phone, it looks like another night-club affair. I'm headed for the Odell apartment now. . . . What about rousing out the sybarite?"

"By all means," I agreed, with an alacrity which, I fear, was in large measure prompted by purely selfish motives. The Canary! If one had sought the city over for a victim whose murder would stir up excitement, there could have been but few selections better calculated to produce this result.

Hastening to the door, I summoned Currie, and told him to call Vance at once.

"I'm afraid, sir——" began Currie, politely hesitant.

"Calm your fears," cut in Markham. "I'll take all responsibility for waking him at this indecent hour."

Currie sensed an emergency and departed.

A minute or two later Vance, in an elaborately embroidered silk kimono and sandals, appeared at the living-room door.

"My word!" he greeted us, in mild astonishment, glancing at the clock. "Haven't you chaps gone to bed yet?"

He strolled to the mantel, and selected a gold-tipped *Régie* cigarette from a small Florentine humidor.

Markham's eyes narrowed: he was in no mood for levity.

"The Canary has been murdered," I blurted out.

Vance held his wax vesta poised, and gave me a look of indolent inquisitiveness. "Whose canary?"

"Margaret Odell was found strangled this morning," amended Markham brusquely. "Even *you*, wrapped in your scented cotton-wool, have heard of her. And you can realize the significance of the crime. I'm personally going to look for those footprints in the snow; and if you want to come along, as you intimated the other night, you'll have to get a move on."

Vance crushed out his cigarette.

"Margaret Odell, eh?—Broadway's blonde Aspasia—or was it Phryne who had the *coiffure d'or?*

. . . Most distressin'!" Despite his offhand manner, I could see he was deeply interested. "The base
enemies of law and order are determined to chivvy
you most horribly, aren't they, old dear? Deuced
inconsiderate of 'em! . . . Excuse me while I seek
habiliments suitable to the occasion."

He disappeared into his bedroom, while Markham
took out a large cigar and resolutely prepared it for
smoking, and I returned to the library to put away
the papers on which I had been working.

In less than ten minutes Vance reappeared, dressed
for the street.

"*Bien, mon vieux,*" he announced gaily, as Currie
handed him his hat and gloves and a malacca cane.
"*Allons-y!*"

We rode up-town along Madison Avenue, turned
into Central Park, and came out by the West 72d
Street entrance. Margaret Odell's apartment was
at 184 West 71st Street, near Broadway; and as we
drew up to the curb, it was necessary for the patrolman on duty to make a passage for us through the
crowd that had already gathered as a result of the
arrival of the police.

Feathergill, an assistant District Attorney, was
waiting in the main hall for his Chief's arrival.

"It's too bad, sir," he lamented. "A rotten show
all round. And just at this time! . . ." He shrugged
his shoulders discouragingly.

"It may collapse quickly," said Markham, shaking the other's hand. "How are things going? Sergeant Heath phoned me right after you called, and
said that, at first glance, the case looked a bit stubborn."

"Stubborn?" repeated Feathergill lugubriously.
"It's downright impervious. Heath is spinning
round like a turbine. He was called off the Boyle
case, by the way, to devote his talents to this new
shocker Inspector Moran arrived ten minutes ago,
and gave him the official imprimatur."

"Well, Heath's a good man," declared Markham.
"We'll work it out. . . . Which is the apartment?"

Feathergill led the way to a door at the rear of
the main hall.

"Here you are, sir," he announced. "I'll be running along now. I need sleep. Good luck!" And
he was gone.

It will be necessary to give a brief description of
the house and its interior arrangement, for the somewhat peculiar structure of the building played a vital
part in the seemingly insoluble problem posed by the
murder.

The house, which was a four-story stone structure
originally built as a residence, had been remodelled,
both inside and outside, to meet the requirements of
an exclusive individual apartment dwelling. There
were, I believe, three or four separate suites on
each floor; but the quarters up-stairs need not concern us. The main floor was the scene of the crime,
and here there were three apartments and a dentist's
office.

The main entrance to the building was directly
on the street, and extending straight back from the
front door was a wide hallway. Directly at the rear
of this hallway, and facing the entrance, was the
door to the Odell apartment, which bore the nu-
meral "3." About half-way down the front hall,

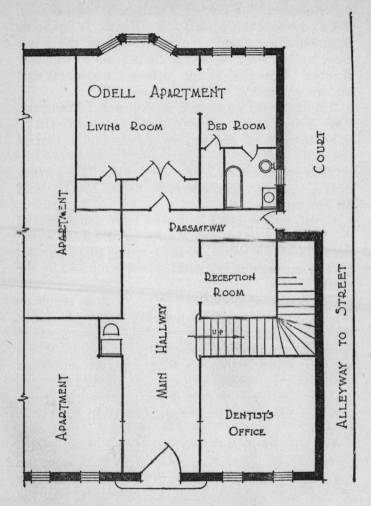

ODELL APARTMENT

LIVING ROOM   BED ROOM

APARTMENT

PASSAGEWAY

RECEPTION ROOM

APARTMENT

MAIN HALLWAY

UP

DENTIST'S OFFICE

COURT

ALLEYWAY TO STREET

WEST SEVENTY-FIRST STREET

on the right-hand side, was the stairway leading to the floors above; and directly beyond the stairway, also on the right, was a small reception-room with a wide archway instead of a door. Directly opposite to the stairway, in a small recess, stood the telephone switchboard. There was no elevator in the house.

Another important feature of this ground-floor plan was a small passageway at the rear of the main hall and at right angles to it,-which led past the front walls of the Odell apartment to a door opening on a court at the west side of the building. This court was connected with the street by an alley four feet wide.

In the accompanying diagram this arrangement of the ground floor can be easily visualized, and I suggest that the reader fix it in his mind; for I doubt if ever before so simple and obvious an architectural design played such an important part in a criminal mystery. By its very simplicity and almost conventional familiarity—indeed, by its total lack of any puzzling complications—it proved so baffling to the investigators that the case threatened, for many days, to remain forever insoluble.

As Markham entered the Odell apartment that morning Sergeant Ernest Heath came forward at once and extended his hand. A look of relief passed over his broad, pugnacious features; and it was obvious that the animosity and rivalry which always exist between the Detective Division and the District Attorney's office during the investigation of any criminal case had no place in his attitude on this occasion.

"I'm glad you've come, sir," he said; and meant it.

He then turned to Vance with a cordial smile, and held out his hand.*

"So the amachoor sleuth is with us again!" His tone held a friendly banter.

"Oh, quite," murmured Vance. "How's your induction coil working this beautiful September morning, Sergeant?"

"I'd hate to tell you!" Then Heath's face grew suddenly grave, and he turned to Markham. "It's a raw deal, sir. Why in hell couldn't they have picked some one besides the Canary for their dirty work? There's plenty of Janes on Broadway who coulda faded from the picture without causing a second alarm; but they gotta go and bump off the Queen of Sheba!"

As he spoke, William M. Moran, the commanding officer of the Detective Bureau, came into the little foyer and performed the usual hand-shaking ceremony. Though he had met Vance and me but once before, and then casually, he remembered us both and addressed us courteously by name.

"Your arrival," he said to Markham, in a well-bred, modulated voice, "is very welcome. Sergeant Heath will give you what preliminary information you want. I'm still pretty much in the dark myself —only just arrived."

"A lot of information *I've* got to give," grumbled Heath, as he led the way into the living-room.

Margaret Odell's apartment was a suite of two fairly large rooms connected by a wide archway draped with heavy damask portières. The entrance

* Heath had become acquainted with Vance during the investigation of the Benson murder case two months previously.

door from the main hall of the building led into a
small rectangular foyer about eight feet long and
four feet deep, with double Venetian-glass doors
opening into the main room beyond. There was no
other entrance to the apartment, and the bedroom
could be reached only through the archway from
the living-room.

There was a large davenport, covered with brocaded silk, in front of the fireplace in the left-hand
wall of the living-room, with a long narrow library-
table of inlaid rosewood extending along its back.
On the opposite wall, between the foyer and the
archway into the bedroom, hung a triplicate Marie
Antoinette mirror, beneath which stood a mahogany
gate-legged table. On the far side of the archway,
near the large oriel window, was a baby grand Stein-
way piano with a beautifully designed and decorated
case of Louis-Seize ornamentation. In the corner
to the right of the fireplace was a spindle-legged
escritoire and a square hand-painted waste-paper
basket of vellum. To the left of the fireplace stood
one of the loveliest Boule cabinets I have ever seen.
Several excellent reproductions of Boucher, Frago-
nard, and Watteau hung about the walls. The bedroom contained a chest of drawers, a dressing-table,
and several gold-leaf chairs. The whole apartment
seemed eminently in keeping with the Canary's
fragile and evanescent personality.

As we stepped from the little foyer into the living-
room and stood for a moment looking about, a scene
bordering on wreckage met our eyes. The rooms had
apparently been ransacked by some one in a frenzy
of haste, and the disorder of the place was appalling.

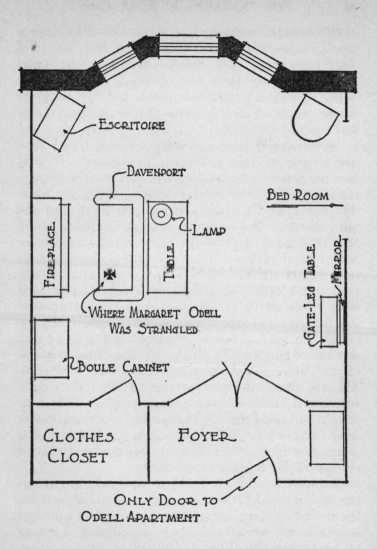

ESCRITOIRE

DAVENPORT

BED ROOM

LAMP

FIREPLACE

TABLE

GATE-LEG TABLE

MIRROR

WHERE MARGARET ODELL
WAS STRANGLED

BOULE CABINET

CLOTHES
CLOSET

FOYER

ONLY DOOR TO
ODELL APARTMENT

"They didn't exactly do the job in dainty fashion," remarked Inspector Moran.

"I suppose we oughta be grateful they didn't blow the joint up with dynamite," returned Heath acridly.

But it was not the general disorder that most attracted us. Our gaze was almost immediately drawn and held by the body of the dead girl, which rested in an unnatural, semi-recumbent attitude in the corner of the davenport nearest to where we stood. Her head was turned backward, as if by force, over the silken tufted upholstery; and her hair had come unfastened and lay beneath her head and over her bare shoulder like a frozen cataract of liquid gold. Her face, in violent death, was distorted and unlovely. Her skin was discolored; her eyes were staring; her mouth was open, and her lips were drawn back. Her neck, on either side of the thyroid cartilage, showed ugly dark bruises. She was dressed in a flimsy evening gown of black Chantilly lace over cream-colored chiffon, and across the arm of the davenport had been thrown an evening cape of cloth-of-gold trimmed with ermine.

There were evidences of her ineffectual struggle with the person who had strangled her. Besides the dishevelled condition of her hair, one of the shoulder-straps of her gown had been severed, and there was a long rent in the fine lace across her breast. A small corsage of artificial orchids had been torn from her bodice, and lay crumpled in her lap. One satin slipper had fallen off, and her right knee was twisted inward on the seat of the davenport, as if she had sought to lift herself out of the suffocating clutches of her antagonist. Her fingers were still flexed, no doubt as they had been at the moment of her capitulation to death, when she had relinquished her grip upon the murderer's wrists.

The spell of horror cast over us by the sight of the tortured body was broken by the matter-of-fact tones of Heath.

"You see, Mr. Markham, she was evidently sitting in the corner of this settee when she was grabbed suddenly from behind."

Markham nodded. "It must have taken a pretty strong man to strangle her so easily."

"I'll say!" agreed Heath. He bent over and pointed to the girl's fingers, on which showed several abrasions. "They stripped her rings off, too; and they didn't go about it gentle, either." Then he indicated a segment of fine platinum chain, set with tiny pearls, which hung over one of her shoulders. "And they grabbed whatever it was hanging round her neck, and broke the chain doing it. They weren't overlooking anything, or losing any time. . . . A swell, gentlemanly job. Nice and refined."

"Where's the Medical Examiner?" asked Markham.

"He's coming," Heath told him. "You can't get Doc Doremus to go anywheres without his breakfast."

"He may find something else—something that doesn't show."

"There's plenty showing for me," declared Heath. "Look at this apartment. It wouldn't be much worse if a Kansas cyclone had struck it."

We turned from the depressing spectacle of the dead girl and moved toward the centre of the room.

"Be careful not to touch anything, Mr. Markham," warned Heath. "I've sent for the finger-print experts—they'll be here any minute now."

Vance looked up in mock astonishment.

"Finger-prints? You don't say—really! How delightful!—Imagine a johnnie in this enlightened day leaving his finger-prints for you to find."

"All crooks aren't clever, Mr. Vance," declared Heath combatively.

"Oh, dear, no! They'd never be apprehended if they were. But, after all, Sergeant, even an authentic finger-print merely means that the person who made it was dallying around at some time or other. It doesn't indicate guilt."

"Maybe so," conceded Heath doggedly. "But I'm here to tell you that if I get any good honest-to-God finger-prints outa this devastated area, it's not going so easy with the bird that made 'em."

Vance appeared to be shocked. "You positively terrify me, Sergeant. Henceforth I shall adopt mittens as a permanent addition to my attire. I'm always handling the furniture and the teacups and the various knickknacks in the houses where I call, don't y' know."

Markham interposed himself at this point, and suggested they make a tour of inspection while waiting for the Medical Examiner.

"They didn't add anything much to the usual methods," Heath pointed out. "Killed the girl, and then ripped things wide open."

The two rooms had apparently been thoroughly ransacked. Clothes and various articles were strewn about the floor. The doors of both clothes-closets (there was one in each room) were open, and to judge from the chaos in the bedroom closet, it had been hurriedly searched; although the closet off of the living-room, which was given over to the storage of infrequently used items, appeared to have been ignored. The drawers of the dressing-table and chest had been partly emptied on to the floor, and the bedclothes had been snatched away and the mattress turned back. Two chairs and a small occasional table were upset; several vases were broken, as if they had been searched and then thrown down in the wrath of disappointment; and the Marie Antoinette mirror had been broken. The escritoire was open, and its pigeonholes had been emptied in a jumbled pile upon the blotter. The doors of the Boule cabinet swung wide, and inside there was the same confusion of contents that marked the interior of the escritoire. The bronze-and-porcelain lamp on the end of the library-table was lying on its side, its satin shade torn where it had struck the sharp corner of a silver *bonbonnière*.

Two objects in the general disarray particularly attracted my attention—a black metal document-box of the kind purchasable at any stationery store, and a large jewel-case of sheet steel with a circular inset lock. The latter of these objects was destined to play a curious and sinister part in the investigation to follow.

The document-box, which was now empty, had been placed on the library-table, next to the overturned lamp. Its lid was thrown back, and the key was still in the lock. In all the litter and disorganization of the room, this box seemed to be the one out-

standing indication of calm and orderly activity on
the part of the wrecker.

The jewel-case, on the other hand, had been violently wrenched open. It sat on the dressing-table
in the bedroom, dinted and twisted out of shape by
the terrific leverage that had been necessary to
force it, and beside it lay a brass-handled, cast-iron
poker which had evidently been brought from the
living-room and used as a makeshift chisel with
which to prize open the lock.

Vance had glanced but casually at the different
objects in the rooms as we made our rounds, but
when he came to the dressing-table, he paused
abruptly. Taking out his monocle, he adjusted it
carefully, and leaned over the broken jewel-case.

"Most extr'ordin'ry!" he murmured, tapping the
edge of the lid with his gold pencil. "What do you
make of that, Sergeant?"

Heath had been eyeing Vance with narrowed lids
as the latter bent over the dressing-table.

"What's in your mind, Mr. Vance?" he, in turn,
asked.

"Oh, more than you could ever guess," Vance answered lightly. "But just at the moment I was toy-
ing with the idea that this steel case was never torn
open by that wholly inadequate iron poker, what?"

Heath nodded his head approvingly. "So you,
too, noticed that, did you? . . . And you're dead
right. That poker might've twisted the box a little,
but it never snapped that lock."

He turned to Inspector Moran.

"That's the puzzler I've sent for 'Prof' Brenner
to clean up—*if* he can. The jimmying of that jewel-

case looks to me like a high-class professional job. No Sunday-school superintendent did it."

Vance continued for a while to study the box, but at length he turned away with a perplexed frown.

"I say!" he commented. "Something devilish queer took place here last night."

"Oh, not so queer," Heath amended. "It was a thorough job, all right, but there's nothing mysterious about it."

Vance polished his monocle and put it away.

"If you go to work on that basis, Sergeant," he returned carelessly, "I greatly fear you'll run aground on a reef. And may kind Heaven bring you safe to shore!"

CHAPTER IV

THE PRINT OF A HAND

(Tuesday, September 11; 9.30 a. m.)

A few minutes after we had returned to the living-room Doctor Doremus, the Chief Medical Examiner, arrived, jaunty and energetic. Immediately in his train came three other men, one of whom carried a bulky camera and a folded tripod. These were Captain Dubois and Detective Bellamy, finger-print experts, and Peter Quackenbush, the official photographer.

"Well, well, well!" exclaimed Doctor Doremus. "Quite a gathering of the clans. More trouble, eh? . . . I wish your friends, Inspector, would choose a more respectable hour for their little differences. This early rising upsets my liver."

He shook hands with everybody in a brisk, businesslike manner.

"Where's the body?" he demanded breezily, looking about the room. He caught sight of the girl on the davenport. "Ah! A lady."

Stepping quickly forward, he made a rapid examination of the dead girl, scrutinizing her neck and fingers, moving her arms and head to determine the condition of *rigor mortis*, and finally unflexing her stiffened limbs and laying her out straight on the long cushions, preparatory to a more detailed necropsy.

34

The rest of us moved toward the bedroom, and Heath motioned to the finger-print men to follow.

"Go over everything," he told them. "But take a special look at this jewel-case and the handle of this poker, and give that document-box in the other room a close up-and-down."

"Right," assented Captain Dubois. "We'll begin in here while the doc's busy in the other room." And he and Bellamy set to work.

Our interest naturally centred on the Captain's labors. For fully five minutes we watched him inspecting the twisted steel sides of the jewel-case and the smooth, polished handle of the poker. He held the objects gingerly by their edges, and, placing a jeweller's glass in his eye, flashed his pocket-light on every square inch of them. At length he put them down, scowling.

"No finger-prints here," he announced. "Wiped clean."

"I mignta known it," grumbled Heath. "It was a professional job, all right." He turned to the other expert. "Found anything, Bellamy?"

"Nothing to help," was the grumpy reply. "A few old smears with dust over 'em."

"Looks like a washout," Heath commented irritably; "though I'm hoping for something in the other room."

At this moment Doctor Doremus came into the bedroom and, taking a sheet from the bed, returned to the davenport and covered the body of the murdered girl. Then he snapped shut his case, and putting on his hat at a rakish angle, stepped forward with the air of a man in great haste to be on his way.

"Simple case of strangulation from behind," he said, his words running together. "Digital bruises about the front of the throat; thumb bruises in the sub-occipital region. Attack must have been unexpected. A quick, competent job though deceased evidently battled a little."

"How do you suppose her dress became torn, doctor?" asked Vance.

"Oh, that? Can't tell. She may have done it herself—instinctive motions of clutching for air."

"Not likely though, what?"

"Why not? The dress was torn and the bouquet was ripped off, and the fellow who was choking her had both hands on her throat. Who else could've done it?"

Vance shrugged his shoulders, and began lighting a cigarette.

Heath, annoyed by his apparently inconsequential interruption, put the next question.

"Don't those marks on the fingers mean that her rings were stripped off?"

"Possibly. They're fresh abrasions. Also, there's a couple of lacerations on the left wrist and slight contusions on the thenar eminence, indicating that a bracelet may have been forcibly pulled over her hand."

"That fits O. K.," pronounced Heath, with satisfaction. "And it looks like they snatched a pendant of some kind off her neck."

"Probably," indifferently agreed Doctor Doremus. "The piece of chain had cut into her flesh a little behind the right shoulder."

"And the time?"

"Nine or ten hours ago. Say, about eleven-thirty
—maybe a little before. Not after midnight, anyway." He had been teetering restlessly on his toes.
"Anything else?"

Heath pondered.

"I guess that's all, doc," he decided. "I'll get
the body to the mortuary right away. Let's have
the post-mortem as soon as you can."

"You'll get a report in the morning." And despite
his apparent eagerness to be off, Doctor Doremus
stepped into the bedroom, and shook hands with
Heath and Markham and Inspector Moran before
he hurried out.

Heath followed him to the door, and I heard him
direct the officer outside to telephone the Department of Public Welfare to send an ambulance at once
for the girl's body.

"I positively adore that official archiater of yours,"
Vance said to Markham. "Such detachment! Here
are you stewing most distressingly over the passing
of one damsel fair and frail, and that blithe *medicus*
is worrying only over a sluggish liver brought on by
early rising."

"What has he to be upset over?" complained
Markham. "The newspapers are not riding him
with spurs. . . . And by the way, what was the
point of your questions about the torn dress?"

Vance lazily inspected the tip of his cigarette.

"Consider," he said. "The lady was evidently
taken by surprise; for, had there been a struggle beforehand, she would not have been strangled from
behind while sitting down. Therefore, her gown and
corsage were undoubtedly intact at the time she

was seized. But—despite the conclusion of your dashing Paracelsus—the damage to her toilet was not of a nature that could have been self-inflicted in her struggle for air. If she had felt the constriction of the gown across her breast, she would have snatched the bodice itself by putting her fingers inside the band. But, if you noticed, her bodice was intact; the only thing that had been torn was the deep lace flounce on the outside; and it had been torn, or rather ripped, by a strong lateral pull; whereas, in the circumstances, any wrench on her part would have been downward or outward."

Inspector Moran was listening intently, but Heath seemed restless and impatient; apparently he regarded the torn gown as irrelevant to the simple main issue.

"Moreover," Vance went on, "there is the corsage. If she herself had torn it off while being strangled, it would doubtless have fallen to the floor; for, remember, she offered considerable resistance. Her body was twisted sidewise; her knee was drawn up, and one slipper had been kicked off. Now, no bunch of silken posies is going to remain in a lady's lap during such a commotion. Even when ladies sit still, their gloves and hand-bags and handkerchiefs and programmes and serviettes are forever sliding off of their laps on to the floor, don't y' know."

"But if your argument's correct," protested Markham, "then the tearing of the lace and the snatching off of the corsage could have been done only after she was dead. And I can't see any object in such senseless vandalism."

"Neither can I," sighed Vance. "It's all devilish queer."

Heath looked up at him sharply. "That's the second time you've said that. But there's nothing what you'd call queer about this mess. It is a straight-away case." He spoke with an overtone of insistence, like a man arguing against his own insecurity of opinion. "The dress might've been torn almost any time," he went on stubbornly. "And the flower might've got caught in the lace of her skirt so it couldn't roll off."

"And how would you explain the jewel-case, Sergeant?" asked Vance.

"Well, the fellow might've tried the poker, and then, finding it wouldn't work, used his jimmy."

"If he had the efficient jimmy," countered Vance, "why did he go to the trouble of bringing the silly poker from the living-room?"

The Sergeant shook his head perplexedly.

"You never can tell why some of these crooks act the way they do."

"Tut, tut!" Vance chided him. "There should be no such word as 'never' in the bright lexicon of detecting."

Heath regarded him sharply. "Was there anything else that struck you as queer?" His subtle doubts were welling up again.

"Well, there's the lamp on the table in the other room."

We were standing near the archway between the two rooms, and Heath turned quickly and looked blankly at the fallen lamp.

"I don't see anything queer about that."

"It has been upset—eh, what?" suggested Vance.

"What if it has?" Heath was frankly puzzled.

"Damn near everything in this apartment has been knocked crooked."

"Ah! But there's a reason for most of the other things having been disturbed—like the drawers and pigeonholes and closets and vases. They all indicate a search; they're consistent with a raid for loot. But that lamp, now, d' ye see, doesn't fit into the picture. It's a false note. It was standing on the opposite end of the table to where the murder was committed, at least five feet away; and it couldn't possibly have been knocked over in the struggle. . . . No, it won't do. It's got no business being upset, any more than that pretty mirror over the gate-legged table has any business being broken. That's why it's queer."

"What about those chairs and the little table?" asked Heath, pointing to two small gilded chairs which had been overturned, and a fragile tip-table that lay on its side near the piano.

"Oh, they fit into the ensemble," returned Vance. "They're all light pieces of furniture which could easily have been knocked over, or thrown aside, by the hasty gentleman who rifled these rooms."

"The lamp might've been knocked over in the same way," argued Heath.

Vance shook his head. "Not tenable, Sergeant. It has a solid bronze base, and isn't at all top-heavy; and being set well back on the table, it wasn't in any one's way. . . . That lamp was upset deliberately."

The Sergeant was silent for a while. Experience had taught him not to underestimate Vance's observations; and, I must confess, as I looked at the lamp lying on its side on the end of the library-table, well removed from any of the other disordered objects in the room, Vance's argument seemed to possess considerable force. I tried hard to fit it into a hasty reconstruction of the crime, but was utterly unable to do so.

"Anything else that don't seem to fit into the picture?" Heath at length asked.

Vance pointed with his cigarette toward the clothes-closet in the living-room. This closet was alongside of the foyer, in the corner near the Boule cabinet, directly opposite to the end of the davenport.

"You might let your mind dally a moment with the condition of that clothes-press," suggested Vance carelessly. "You will note that, though the door's ajar, the contents have not been touched. And it's about the only area in the apartment that hasn't been disturbed."

Heath walked over and looked into the closet.

"Well, anyway, I'll admit that's queer," he finally conceded.

Vance had followed him indolently, and stood gazing over his shoulder.

"And my word!" he exclaimed suddenly. "The key's on the inside of the lock. Fancy that, now! One can't lock a closet door with the key on the inside—can one, Sergeant?"

"The key may not mean anything," Heath observed hopefully. "Maybe the door was never locked. Anyhow, we'll find out about that pretty soon. I'm holding the maid outside, and I'm going to have her on the carpet as soon as the Captain finishes his job here."

He turned to Dubois, who, having completed his

search for finger-prints in the bedroom, was now in-specting the piano.

"Any luck yet?"

The Captain shook his head.

"Gloves," he answered succinctly.

"Same here," supplemented Bellamy gruffly, on his knees before the escritoire.

Vance, with a sardonic smile, turned and walked to the window, where he stood looking out and smoking placidly, as if his entire interest in the case had evaporated.

At this moment the door from the main hall opened, and a short thin little man, with gray hair and a scraggly gray beard, stepped inside and stood blinking against the vivid sunlight.

"Good morning, Professor," Heath greeted the newcomer. "Glad to see you. I've got something nifty, right in your line."

Deputy-Inspector Conrad Brenner was one of that small army of obscure, but highly capable, experts who are connected with the New York Police Department, and who are constantly being consulted on abstruse technical problems, but whose names and achievements rarely get into the public prints. His specialty was locks and burglars' tools; and I doubt if, even among those exhaustively pains-taking criminologists of the University of Lausanne, there was a more accurate reader of the evidential signs left by the implements of house-breakers. In appearance and bearing he was like a withered little college professor.* His black, unpressed suit was

---

* It is an interesting fact that for the nineteen years he had been con-nected with the New York Police Department, he had been referred to, by his superiors and subordinates alike, as "the Professor."

old-fashioned in cut; and he wore a very high stiff collar, like a *fin-de-siècle* clergyman, with a narrow black string tie. His gold-rimmed spectacles were so thick-lensed that the pupils of his eyes gave the impression of acute belladonna poisoning.

When Heath had spoken to him, he merely stood staring with a sort of detached expectancy; he seemed utterly unaware that there was any one else in the room. The Sergeant, evidently familiar with the little man's idiosyncrasies of manner, did not wait for a response, but started at once for the bedroom.

"This way, please, Professor," he directed cajolingly, going to the dressing-table and picking up the jewel-case. "Take a squint at this, and tell me what you see."

Inspector Brenner followed Heath, without looking to right or left, and, taking the jewel-case, went silently to the window and began to examine it. Vance, whose interest seemed suddenly to be re-awakened, came forward and stood watching him.

For fully five minutes the little expert inspected the case, holding it within a few inches of his myopic eyes. Then he lifted his glance to Heath and winked several times rapidly.

"Two instruments were used in opening this case." His voice was small and high-pitched, but there was in it an undeniable quality of authority. "One bent the lid and made several fractures on the baked enamel. The other was, I should say, a steel chisel of some kind, and was used to break the lock. The first instrument, which was blunt, was employed amateurishly, at the wrong angle of leverage; and the effort resulted only in twisting the overhang of the lid. But the steel chisel was inserted with a knowledge of the correct point of oscillation, where a minimum of leverage would produce the counteracting stress necessary to displace the lockbolts."

"A professional job?" suggested Heath.

"Highly so," answered the Inspector, again blinking. "That is to say, the forcing of the lock was professional. And I would even go so far as to advance the opinion that the instrument used was one especially constructed for such illegal purposes."

"Could this have done the job?" Heath held out the poker.

The other looked at it closely, and turned it over several times.

"It might have been the instrument that bent the cover, but it was not the one used for prying open the lock. This poker is cast iron and would have snapped under any great pressure; whereas this box is of cold rolled eighteen-gauge steel plate, with an inset cylinder pin-tumbler lock taking a paracentric key. The leverage force necessary to distort the flange sufficiently to lift the lid could have been made only by a steel chisel."

"Well, that's that." Heath seemed well satisfied with Inspector Brenner's conclusion. "I'll send the box down to you, Professor, and you can let me know what else you find out."

"I'll take it along, if you have no objection." And the little man tucked it under his arm and shuffled out without another word.

Heath grinned at Markham. "Queer bird. He ain't happy unless he's measuring jimmy marks on doors and windows and things. He couldn't wait till I sent him the box. He'll hold it lovingly on his lap all the way down in the subway, like a mother with a baby."

Vance was still standing near the dressing-table, gazing perplexedly into space.

"Markham," he said, "the condition of that jewel-case is positively astounding. It's unreasonable, illogical—insane. It complicates the situation most damnably. That steel box simply couldn't have been chiselled open by a professional burglar . . . and yet, don't y' know, it actually was."

Before Markham could reply, a satisfied grunt from Captain Dubois attracted our attention.

"I've got something for you, Sergeant," he announced.

We moved expectantly into the living-room. Dubois was bending over the end of the library-table almost directly behind the place where Margaret Odell's body had been found. He took out an insufflator, which was like a very small hand-bellows, and blew a fine light-yellow powder evenly over about a square foot of the polished rosewood surface of the table-top. Then he gently blew away the surplus powder, and there appeared the impression of a human hand distinctly registered in saffron. The bulb of the thumb and each fleshy hummock between the joints of the fingers and around the palm stood out like tiny circular islands. All the papillary ridges were clearly discernible. The photographer then hooked his camera to a peculiar adjustable tripod and, carefully focusing his lens, took two flash-light pictures of the hand-mark.

"This ought to do." Dubois was pleased with his find. "It's the right hand—a clear print—and the guy who made it was standing right behind the dame. . . . And it's the newest print in the place."

"What about this box?" Heath pointed to the black document-box on the table near the over-turned lamp.

"Not a mark—wiped clean."

Dubois began putting away his paraphernalia.

"I say, Captain Dubois," interposed Vance, "did you take a good look at the inside door-knob of that clothes-press?"

The man swung about abruptly, and gave Vance a glowering look.

"People ain't in the habit of handling the inside knobs of closet doors. They open and shut closets from the outside."

Vance raised his eyebrows in simulated astonishment.

"Do they, now, really?—Fancy that! . . . Still, don't y' know, if one were inside the closet, one couldn't reach the outside knob."

"The people *I* know don't shut themselves in clothes-closets." Dubois's tone was ponderously sarcastic.

"You positively amaze me!" declared Vance. "All the people I know are addicted to the habit—a sort of daily pastime, don't y' know."

Markham, always diplomatic, intervened.

"What idea have you about that closet, Vance?"

"Alas! I wish I had one," was the dolorous answer. "It's because I can't, for the life of me, make sense of its neat and orderly appearance that I'm so interested in it. Really, y' know, it should have been artistically looted."

Heath was not entirely free from the same vague misgivings that were disturbing Vance, for he turned to Dubois and said:

"You might go over the knob, Captain. As this gentleman says, there's something funny about the condition of that closet."

Dubois, silent and surly, went to the closet door and sprayed his yellow powder over the inside knob. When he had blown the loose particles away, he bent over it with his magnifying-glass. At length he straightened up, and gave Vance a look of ill-natured appraisal.

"There's fresh prints on it, all right," he grudgingly admitted; "and unless I'm mistaken they were made by the same hand as those on the table. Both thumb-marks are ulnar loops, and the index-fingers are both whorl patterns. . . . Here, Pete," he ordered the photographer, "make some shots of that knob."

When this had been done, Dubois, Bellamy, and the photographer left us.

A few moments later, after an interchange of pleasantries, Inspector Moran also departed. At the door he passed two men in the white uniform of internes, who had come to take away the girl's body.

CHAPTER V

THE BOLTED DOOR

(Tuesday, September 11; 10.30 a. m.)

Markham and Heath and Vance and I were now alone in the apartment. Dark, low-hanging clouds had drifted across the sun, and the gray spectral light intensified the tragic atmosphere of the rooms. Markham had lighted a cigar, and stood leaning against the piano, looking about him with a disconsolate but determined air. Vance had moved over to one of the pictures on the side wall of the living-room—Boucher's "La Bergère Endormie" I think it was—and stood looking at it with cynical contempt.

"Dimpled nudities, gambolling Cupids and woolly clouds for royal cocottes," he commented. His distaste for all the painting of the French decadence under Louis XV was profound. "One wonders what pictures courtesans hung in their boudoirs before the invention of these amorous eclogues, with their blue verdure and beribboned sheep."

"I'm more interested at present in what took place in this particular boudoir last night," retorted Markham impatiently.

"There's not much doubt about that, sir," said Heath encouragingly. "And I've an idea that when

Dubois checks up those finger-prints with our files, we'll about know who did it."

Vance turned toward him with a rueful smile.

"You're so trusting, Sergeant. I, in turn, have an idea that, long before this touchin' case is clarified, you'll wish the irascible Captain with the insect-powder had never found those finger-prints." He made a playful gesture of emphasis. "Permit me to whisper into your ear that the person who left his sign-manuals on yonder rosewood table and cut-glass door-knob had nothing whatever to do with the precipitate demise of the fair Mademoiselle Odell."

"What is it you suspect?" demanded Markham sharply.

"Not a thing, old dear," blandly declared Vance. "I'm wandering about in a mental murk as empty of sign-posts as interplanetary space. The jaws of darkness do devour me up; I'm in the dead vast and middle of the night. My mental darkness is Egyptian, Stygian, Cimmerian—I'm in a perfect Erebus of tenebrosity."

Markham's jaw tightened in exasperation; he was familiar with this evasive loquacity of Vance's. Dismissing the subject, he addressed himself to Heath.

"Have you done any questioning of the people in the house here?"

"I talked to Odell's maid and to the janitor and the switchboard operators, but I didn't go much into details—I was waiting for you. I'll say this, though: what they did tell me made my head swim. If they don't back down on some of their statements, we're up against it."

"Let's have them in now, then," suggested Markham; "the maid first." He sat down on the piano-bench with his back to the keyboard.

Heath rose, but instead of going to the door, walked to the oriel window.

"There's one thing I want to call your attention to, sir, before you interview these people, and that's the matter of entrances and exits in this apartment." He drew aside the gold-gauze curtain. "Look at that iron grating. All the windows in this place, including the ones in the bathroom, are equipped with iron bars just like these. It's only eight or ten feet to the ground here, and whoever built this house wasn't taking any chances of burglars getting in through the windows."

He released the curtain, and strode into the foyer.

"Now, there's only one entrance to this apartment, and that's this door here opening off the main hall. There isn't a transom or an air-shaft or a dumb-waiter in the place, and that means that the only way—*the only way*—that anybody can get in or out of this apartment is through this door. Just keep that fact in your mind, sir, while you're listening to the stories of these people. . . . Now, I'll have the maid brought in."

In response to Heath's order a detective led in a mulatto woman about thirty years old. She was neatly dressed, and gave one the impression of capability. When she spoke it was with a quiet, clear enunciation which attested to a greater degree of education than is ordinarily found in members of her class.

Her name, we learned, was Amy Gibson; and the

information elicited by Markham's preliminary questioning consisted of the following facts:

She had arrived at the apartment that morning a few minutes after seven, and, as was her custom, had let herself in with her own key, as her mistress generally slept till late.

Once or twice a week she came early to do sewing and mending for Miss Odell before the latter arose. On this particular morning she had come early to make an alteration in a gown.

As soon as she had opened the door she had been confronted by the disorder of the apartment, for the Venetian-glass doors of the foyer were wide open; and almost simultaneously she had noticed the body of her mistress on the davenport.

She had called at once to Jessup, the night telephone operator then on duty, who, after one glance into the living-room, had notified the police. She had then sat down in the public reception room and waited for the arrival of the officers.

Her testimony had been simple and direct and intelligently stated. If she was nervous or excited, she managed to keep her feelings well under control.

"Now," continued Markham, after a short pause, "let us go back to last night.—At what time did you leave Miss Odell?"

"A few minutes before seven, sir," the woman answered, in a colorless, even tone which seemed to be characteristic of her speech.

"Is that your usual hour for leaving?"

"No; I generally go about six. But last night Miss Odell wanted me to help her dress for dinner."

"Don't you always help her dress for dinner?"

"No, sir. But last night she was going with some gentleman to dinner and the theatre, and wanted to look specially nice."

"Ah!" Markham leaned forward. "And who was this gentleman?"

"I don't know, sir—Miss Odell didn't say."

"And you couldn't suggest who it might have been?"

"I couldn't say, sir."

"And when did Miss Odell tell you that she wanted you to come early this morning?"

"When I was leaving last night."

"So she evidently didn't anticipate any danger, or have any fear of her companion."

"It doesn't look that way." The woman paused, as if considering. "No, I know she didn't. She was in good spirits."

Markham turned to Heath.

"Any other questions you want to ask, Sergeant?"

Heath removed an unlighted cigar from his mouth, and bent forward, resting his hands on his knees.

"What jewellery did this Odell woman have on last night?" he demanded gruffly.

The maid's manner became cool and a bit haughty.

"Miss Odell"—she emphasized the "Miss," by way of reproaching him for the disrespect implied in his omission—"wore all her rings, five or six of them, and three bracelets—one of square diamonds, one of rubies, and one of diamonds and emeralds. She also had on a sunburst of pear-shaped diamonds on a chain round her neck, and she carried a platinum lorgnette set with diamonds and pearls."

"Did she own any other jewellery?"

"A few small pieces, maybe, but I'm not sure."

"And did she keep 'em in a steel jewel-case in the bedroom?"

"Yes—when she wasn't wearing them." There was more than a suggestion of sarcasm in the reply.

"Oh, I thought maybe she kept 'em locked up when she had 'em on." Heath's antagonism had been aroused by the maid's attitude; he could not have failed to note that she had consistently omitted the punctilious "sir" when answering him. He now stood up and pointed loweringly to the black document-box on the rosewood table.

"Ever see that before?"

The woman nodded indifferently. "Many times."

"Where was it generally kept?"

"In that thing." She indicated the Boule cabinet with a motion of the head.

"What was in the box?"

"How should I know?"

"You don't know—huh?" Heath thrust out his jaw, but his bullying attitude had no effect upon the impassive maid.

"I've got no idea," she replied calmly. "It was always kept locked, and I never saw Miss Odell open it."

The Sergeant walked over to the door of the living-room closet.

"See that key?" he asked angrily.

Again the woman nodded; but this time I detected a look of mild astonishment in her eyes.

"Was that key always kept on the inside of the door?"

"No; it was always on the outside."

Heath shot Vance a curious look. Then, after a moment's frowning contemplation of the knob, he waved his hand to the detective who had brought the maid in.

"Take her back to the reception-room, Snitkin,

and get a detailed description from her of all the Odell jewellery. . . . And keep her outside; I'll want her again."

When Snitkin and the maid had gone out, Vance lay back lazily on the davenport, where he had sat during the interview, and sent a spiral of cigarette smoke toward the ceiling.

"Rather illuminatin', what?" he remarked. "The dusky demoiselle got us considerably forrader. Now we know that the closet key is on the wrong side of the door, and that our *fille de joie* went to the theatre with one of her favorite *inamorati*, who presumably brought her home shortly before she took her departure from this wicked world."

"You think that's helpful, do you?" Heath's tone was contemptuously triumphant. "Wait till you hear the crazy story the telephone operator's got to tell."

"All right, Sergeant," put in Markham impatiently. "Suppose we get on with the ordeal."

"I'm going to suggest, Mr. Markham, that we question the janitor first. And I'll show you why." Heath went to the entrance door of the apartment, and opened it. "Look here for just a minute, sir."

He stepped out into the main hall, and pointed down the little passageway on the left. It was about ten feet in length, and ran between the Odell apartment and the blank rear wall of the reception-room. At the end of it was a solid oak door which gave on the court at the side of the house.

"That door," explained Heath, "is the only side or rear entrance to this building; and when that door is bolted nobody can get into the house except by the front entrance. You can't even get into the build-

ing through the other apartments, for every window
on this floor is barred. I checked up on that point
as soon as I got here."

He led the way back into the living-room.

"Now, after I'd looked over the situation this
morning," he went on, "I figured that our man had
entered through that side door at the end of the
passageway, and had slipped into this apartment
without the night operator seeing him. So I tried
the side door to see if it was open. But it was bolted
on the inside—not locked, mind you, but bolted.
And it wasn't a slip-bolt, either, that could have
been jimmied or worked open from the outside, but
a tough old-fashioned turn-bolt of solid brass. . . .
And now I want you to hear what the janitor's got
to say about it."

Markham nodded acquiescence, and Heath called
an order to one of the officers in the hall. A moment
later a stolid, middle-aged German, with sullen features and high cheek-bones, stood before us. His
jaw was clamped tight, and he shifted his eyes from
one to the other of us suspiciously.

Heath straightway assumed the rôle of inquisitor.

"What time do you leave here at night?" He
had, for some reason, assumed a belligerent manner.

"Six o'clock—sometimes earlier, sometimes later."
The man spoke in a surly monotone. He was obviously resentful at this unexpected intrusion upon
his orderly routine.

"And what time do you get here in the morning?"

"Eight o'clock, regular."

"What time did you go home last night?"

"About six—maybe quarter past."

Heath paused and finally lighted the cigar on which he had been chewing at intervals during the past hour.

"Now, tell me about that side door," he went on, with undiminished aggressiveness. "You told me you lock it every night before you leave—is that right?"

"*Ja*—that's right." The man nodded his head affirmatively several times. "Only I don't lock it—I bolt it."

"All right, you bolt it, then." As Heath talked his cigar bobbed up and down between his lips: smoke and words came simultaneously from his mouth. "And last night you bolted it as usual about six o'clock?"

"Maybe a quarter past," the janitor amended, with Germanic precision.

"You're sure you bolted it last night?" The question was almost ferocious.

"*Ja, ja.* Sure, I am. I do it every night. I never miss."

The man's earnestness left no doubt that the door in question had indeed been bolted on the inside at about six o'clock of the previous evening. Heath, however, belabored the point for several minutes, only to be reassured doggedly that the door had been bolted. At last the janitor was dismissed.

"Really, y' know, Sergeant," remarked Vance with an amused smile, "that honest Rheinlander bolted the door."

"Sure, he did," spluttered Heath; "and I found it still bolted this morning at quarter of eight. That's just what messes things up so nice and pretty.

If that door was bolted from six o'clock last evening until eight o'clock this morning, I'd appreciate having some one drive up in a hearse and tell me how the Canary's little playmate got in here last night. And I'd also like to know how he got out."

"Why not through the main entrance?" asked Markham. "It seems the only logical way left, according to your own findings."

"That's how I had it figured out, sir," returned Heath. "But wait till you hear what the phone operator has to say."

"And the phone operator's post," mused Vance, "is in the main hall half-way between the front door and this apartment. Therefore, the gentleman who caused all the disturbance hereabouts last night would have had to pass within a few feet of the operator both on arriving and departing—eh, what?"

"That's it!" snapped Heath. "And, according to the operator, no such person came or went."

Markham seemed to have absorbed some of Heath's irritability.

"Get the fellow in here, and let me question him," he ordered.

Heath obeyed with a kind of malicious alacrity.

CHAPTER VI

A CALL FOR HELP

(*Tuesday, September 11; 11 a. m.*)

Jessup made a good impression from the moment he entered the room. He was a serious, determined-looking man in his early thirties, rugged and well built; and there was a squareness to his shoulders that carried a suggestion of military training. He walked with a decided limp—his right foot dragged perceptibly—and I noted that his left arm had been stiffened into a permanent arc, as if by an unreduced fracture of the elbow. He was quiet and reserved, and his eyes were steady and intelligent. Markham at once motioned him to a wicker chair beside the closet door, but he declined it, and stood before the District Attorney in a soldierly attitude of respectful attention. Markham opened the interrogation with several personal questions. It transpired that Jessup had been a sergeant in the World War,* had twice been seriously wounded, and had been invalided home shortly before the Armistice. He had held his present post of telephone operator for over a year.

"Now, Jessup," continued Markham, "there are things connected with last night's tragedy that you can tell us."

"Yes, sir." There was no doubt that this ex-

* His full name was William Elmer Jessup, and he had been attached to the 308th Infantry of the 77th Division of the Overseas Forces.

soldier would tell us accurately anything he knew, and also that, if he had any doubt as to the correctness of his information, he would frankly say so. He possessed all the qualities of a careful and well-trained witness.

"First of all, what time did you come on duty last night?"

"At ten o'clock, sir." There was no qualification to this blunt statement; one felt that Jessup would arrive punctually at whatever hour he was due. "It was my short shift. The day man and myself alternate in long and short shifts."

"And did you see Miss Odell come in last night after the theatre?"

"Yes, sir. Every one who comes in has to pass the switchboard."

"What time did she arrive?"

"It couldn't have been more than a few minutes after eleven."

"Was she alone?"

"No, sir. There was a gentleman with her."

"Do you know who he was?"

"I don't know his name, sir. But I have seen him several times before when he has called on Miss Odell."

"You could describe him, I suppose."

"Yes, sir. He's tall and clean-shaven except for a very short gray moustache, and is about forty-five, I should say. He looks—if you understand me, sir—like a man of wealth and position."

Markham nodded. "And now, tell me: did he accompany Miss Odell into her apartment, or did he go immediately away?"

"He went in with Miss Odell, and stayed about half an hour."

Markham's eyes brightened, and there was a suppressed eagerness in his next words.

"Then he arrived about eleven, and was alone with Miss Odell in her apartment until about half past eleven. You're sure of these facts?"

"Yes, sir, that's correct," the man affirmed.

Markham paused and leaned forward.

"Now, Jessup, think carefully before answering: did any one else call on Miss Odell at any time last night?"

"No one, sir," was the unhesitating reply.

"How can you be so sure?"

"I would have seen them, sir. They would have had to pass the switchboard in order to reach this apartment."

"And don't you ever leave the switchboard?" asked Markham.

"No, sir," the man assured him vigorously, as if protesting against the implication that he would desert a post of duty. "When I want a drink of water, or go to the toilet, I use the little lavatory in the reception-room; but I always hold the door open and keep my eye on the switchboard in case the pilot-light should show up for a telephone call. Nobody could walk down the hall, even if I was in the lavatory, without my seeing them."

One could well believe that the conscientious Jessup kept his eye at all times on the switchboard lest a call should flash and go unanswered. The man's earnestness and reliability were obvious; and there was no doubt in any of our minds, I think, that if

Miss Odell had had another visitor that night, Jessup would have known of it.

But Heath, with the thoroughness of his nature, rose quickly and stepped out into the main hall. In a moment he returned, looking troubled but satisfied.

"Right!" he nodded to Markham. "The lavatory door's on a direct unobstructed line with the switchboard."

Jessup took no notice of this verification of his statement, and stood, his eyes attentively on the District Attorney, awaiting any further questions that might be asked him. There was something both admirable and confidence-inspiring in his unruffled demeanor.

"What about last night?" resumed Markham. "Did you leave the switchboard often, or for long?"

"Just once, sir; and then only to go to the lavatory for a minute or two. But I watched the board the whole time."

"And you'd be willing to state on oath that no one else called on Miss Odell from ten o'clock on, and that no one, except her escort, left her apartment after that hour?"

"Yes, sir, I would."

He was plainly telling the truth, and Markham pondered several moments before proceeding.

"What about the side door?"

"That's kept locked all night, sir. The janitor bolts it when he leaves, and unbolts it in the morning. I never touch it."

Markham leaned back and turned to Heath.

"The testimony of the janitor and Jessup here," he said, "seems to limit the situation pretty narrowly to Miss Odell's escort. If, as seems reasonable to assume, the side door was bolted all night, and if no other caller came or went through the front door, it looks as if the man we wanted to find was the one who brought her home."

Heath gave a short mirthless laugh.

"That would be fine, sir, if something else hadn't happened around here last night." Then, to Jessup: "Tell the District Attorney the rest of the story about this man."

Markham looked toward the operator with expectant interest; and Vance, lifting himself on one elbow, listened attentively.

Jessup spoke in a level voice, with the alert and careful manner of a soldier reporting to his superior officer.

"It was just this, sir. When the gentleman came out of Miss Odell's apartment at about half past eleven, he stopped at the switchboard and asked me to get him a Yellow Taxicab. I put the call through, and while he was waiting for the car, Miss Odell screamed and called for help. The gentleman turned and rushed to the apartment door, and I followed quickly behind him. He knocked; but at first there was no answer. Then he knocked again, and at the same time called out to Miss Odell and asked her what was the matter. This time she answered. She said everything was all right, and told him to go home and not to worry. Then he walked back with me to the switchboard, remarking that he guessed Miss Odell must have fallen asleep and had a nightmare. We talked for a few minutes about the war, and then the taxicab came. He said good night, and went out, and I heard the car drive away."

It was plain to see that this epilogue of the departure of Miss Odell's anonymous escort completely upset Markham's theory of the case. He looked down at the floor with a baffled expression, and smoked vigorously for several moments. At last he asked:

"How long was it after this man came out of the apartment that you heard Miss Odell scream?"

"About five minutes. I had put my connection through to the taxicab company, and it was a minute or so later that she screamed."

"Was the man near the switchboard?"

"Yes, sir. In fact, he had one arm resting on it."

"How many times did Miss Odell scream? And just what did she say when she called for help?"

"She screamed twice, and then cried 'Help! Help!'"

"And when the man knocked on the door the second time, what did he say?"

"As near as I can recollect, sir, he said: 'Open the door, Margaret! What's the trouble?'"

"And can you remember her exact words when she answered him?"

Jessup hesitated, and frowned reflectively.

"As I recall, she said: 'There's nothing the matter. I'm sorry I screamed. Everything's all right, so please go home, and don't worry.' . . . Of course, that may not be exactly what she said, but it was something very close to it."

"You could hear her plainly through the door, then?"

"Oh, yes. These doors are not very thick."

Markham rose, and began pacing meditatively. At length, halting in front of the operator, he asked another question:

"Did you hear any other suspicious sounds in this apartment after the man left?"

"Not a sound of any kind, sir," Jessup declared. "Some one from outside the building, however, telephoned Miss Odell about ten minutes later, and a man's voice answered from her apartment."

"What's this!" Markham spun round, and Heath sat up at attention, his eyes wide. "Tell me every detail of that call."

Jessup complied unemotionally.

"About twenty minutes to twelve a trunk-light flashed on the board, and when I answered it, a man asked for Miss Odell. I plugged the connection through, and after a short wait the receiver was lifted from her phone—you can tell when a receiver's taken off the hook, because the guide-light on the board goes out—and a man's voice answered 'Hello.' I pulled the listening-in key over, and, of course, didn't hear any more."

There was silence in the apartment for several minutes. Then Vance, who had been watching Jessup closely during the interview, spoke.

"By the bye, Mr. Jessup," he asked carelessly, "were you yourself, by any chance, a bit fascinated —let us say— by the charming Miss Odell?"

For the first time since entering the room the man appeared ill at ease. A dull flush overspread his cheeks.

"I thought she was a very beautiful lady," he answered resolutely.

Markham gave Vance a look of disapproval, and then addressed himself abruptly to the operator.

"That will be all for the moment, Jessup."

The man bowed stiffly and limped out.

"This case is becoming positively fascinatin'," murmured Vance, relaxing once more upon the davenport.

"It's comforting to know that some one's enjoying it." Markham's tone was irritable. "And what, may I ask, was the object of your question concerning Jessup's sentiments toward the dead woman?"

"Oh, just a vagrant notion struggling in my brain," returned Vance. "And then, y' know, a bit of *boudoir racontage* always enlivens a situation, what?"

Heath, rousing himself from gloomy abstraction, spoke up.

"We've still got the finger-prints, Mr. Markham. And I'm thinking that they're going to locate our man for us."

"But even if Dubois does identify those prints," said Markham, "we'll have to show how the owner of them got into this place last night. He'll claim, of course, they were made prior to the crime."

"Well, it's a sure thing," declared Heath stubbornly, "that there was some man in here last night when Odell got back from the theatre, and that he was still here until after the other man left at half past eleven. The woman's screams and the answering of that phone call at twenty minutes to twelve prove it. And since Doc Doremus said that the murder took place before midnight, there's no getting away from the fact that the guy who was hiding in here did the job."

"That appears incontrovertible," agreed Markham. "And I'm inclined to think it was some one she knew. She probably screamed when he first revealed himself, and then, recognizing him, calmed down and told the other man out in the hall that nothing was the matter. . . . Later on he strangled her."

"And, I might suggest," added Vance, "that his place of hiding was that clothes-press."

"Sure," the Sergeant concurred. "But what's bothering me is how he got in here. The day operator who was at the switchboard until ten last night old me that the man who called and took Odell out to dinner was the only visitor she had."

Markham gave a grunt of exasperation.

"Bring the day man in here," he ordered. "We've got to straighten this thing out. *Somebody* got in here last night, and before I leave I'm going to find out how it was done."

Vance gave him a look of patronizing amusement.

"Y' know, Markham," he said, "I'm not blessed with the gift of psychic inspiration, but I have one of those strange, indescribable feelings, as the minor poets say, that if you really contemplate remaining in this bestrewn boudoir till you've discovered how the mysterious visitor gained admittance here last night, you'd do jolly well to send for your toilet access'ries and several changes of fresh linen—not to mention your pyjamas. The chap who engineered this little *soirée* planned his entrance and exit most carefully and perspicaciously."

Markham regarded Vance dubiously, but made no reply.

CHAPTER VII

(Tuesday, September 11; 11.15 a. m.)

Heath had stepped out into the hall, and now returned with the day telephone operator, a sallow
thin young man who, we learned, was named Spively.
His almost black hair, which accentuated the pal-
lor of his face, was sleeked back from his forehead
with pomade; and he wore a very shallow moustache
which barely extended beyond the alæ of his nostrils.
He was dressed in an exaggeratedly dapper fashion,
in a dazzling chocolate colored suit cut very close
to his figure, a pair of cloth-topped buttoned shoes,
and a pink shirt with a stiff turn-over collar to match.
He appeared nervous, and immediately sat down in
the wicker chair by the door, fingering the sharp
creases of his trousers, and running the tip of his
tongue over his lips.

Markham went straight to the point.

"I understand you were at the switchboard yesterday afternoon and last night until ten o'clock.
Is that correct?"

Spively swallowed hard, and nodded his head.
"Yes, sir."

"What time did Miss Odell go out to dinner?"

"About seven o'clock. I'd just sent to the res-
taurant next door for some sandwiches——"

67

"Did she go alone?" Markham interrupted his explanation.

"No. A fella called for her."

"Did you know this 'fella'?"

"I'd seen him a couple of times calling on Miss Odell, but I didn't know who he was."

"What did he look like?" Markham's question was uttered with hurried impatience.

Spively's description of the girl's escort tallied with Jessup's description of the man who had accompanied her home, though Spively was more voluble and less precise than Jessup had been. Patently, Miss Odell had gone out at seven and returned at eleven with the same man.

"Now," resumed Markham, putting an added stress on his words, "I want to know who else called on Miss Odell between the time she went out to dinner and ten o'clock when you left the switchboard."

Spively was puzzled by the question, and his thin arched eyebrows lifted and contracted.

"I—don't understand," he stammered. "How could any one call on Miss Odell when she was out?"

"Some one evidently did," said Markham. "And he got into her apartment, and was there when she returned at eleven."

The youth's eyes opened wide, and his lips fell apart.

"My God, sir!" he exclaimed. "So that's how they murdered her!—laid in wait for her! . . ." He stopped abruptly, suddenly realizing his own proximity to the mysterious chain of events that had led up to the crime. "But nobody got into her apartment while I was on duty," he blurted, with frightened emphasis. "Nobody! I never left the board from the time she went out until quitting time."

"Couldn't any one have come in the side door?"

"What! Was it unlocked?" Spively's tone was startled. "It never is unlocked at night. The janitor bolts it when he leaves at six."

"And you didn't unbolt it last night for any purpose? Think!"

"No, sir, I didn't!" He shook his head earnestly.

"And you are positive that no one got into the apartment through the front door after Miss Odell left?"

"Positivo! I tell you I didn't leave the board the whole time, and nobody could've got by me without my knowing it. There was only one person that called and asked for her——"

"Oh! So some one did call!" snapped Markham. "When was it? And what happened?—Jog your memory before you answer."

"It wasn't anything important," the youth assured him, genuinely frightened. "Just a fella who came in and rang her bell and went right out again."

"Never mind whether it was important or not." Markham's tone was cold and peremptory. "What time did he call?"

"About half past nine."

"And who was he?"

"A young fella I've seen come here several times to see Miss Odell. I don't know his name."

"Tell me exactly what took place," pursued Markham.

Again Spively swallowed hard and wetted his lips.

"It was like this," he began, with effort. "The fella came in and started walking down the hall, and I said to him: 'Miss Odell isn't in.' But he kept on going, and said: 'Oh, well, I'll ring the bell anyway to make sure.' A telephone call came through just then, and I let him go on. He rang the bell and knocked on the door, but of course there wasn't any answer; and pretty soon he came on back and said: 'I guess you were right.' Then he tossed me half a dollar, and went out."

"You actually saw him go out?" There was a note of disappointment in Markham's voice.

"Sure, I saw him go out. He stopped just inside the front door and lit a cigarette. Then he opened the door and turned toward Broadway."

"'One by one the rosy petals fall,'" came Vance's indolent voice. "A most amusin' situation!"

Markham was loath to relinquish his hope in the criminal possibilities of this one caller who had come and gone at half past nine.

"What was this man like?" he asked. "Can you describe him?"

Spively sat up straight, and when he answered, it was with an enthusiasm that showed he had taken special note of the visitor.

"He was good-looking, not so old—maybe thirty. And he had on a full-dress suit and patent-leather pumps, and a pleated silk shirt——"

"What, what?" demanded Vance, in simulated unbelief, leaning over the back of the davenport. "A silk shirt with evening dress! Most extr'ordin'ry!"

"Oh, a lot of the best dressers are wearing them,"
Spively explained, with condescending pride. "It's
all the fashion for dancing."

"You don't say—really!" Vance appeared dumbfounded. "I must look into this. . . . And, by the
bye, when this Beau Brummel of the silk shirt paused
by the front door, did he take his cigarette from a
long flat silver case carried in his lower waistcoat
pocket?"

The youth looked at Vance in admiring astonishment.

"How did you know?" he exclaimed.

"Simple deduction," Vance explained, resuming
his recumbent posture. "Large metal cigarette-cases
carried in the waistcoat pocket somehow go with
silk shirts for evening wear."

Markham, clearly annoyed at the interruption,
out in sharply with a demand for the operator to
proceed with his description.

"He wore his hair smoothed down," Spively continued, "and you could see it was kind of long;
but it was cut in the latest style. And he had a
small waxed moustache; and there was a big carna-
tion in the lapel of his coat, and he had on chamois
gloves. . . ."

"My word!" murmured Vance. "A gigolo!"

Markham, with the incubus of the night clubs
riding him heavily, frowned and took a deep breath.
Vance's observation evidently had launched him
on an unpleasant train of thought.

"Was this man short or tall?" he asked next.

"He wasn't so tall—about my height," Spively
explained. "And he was sort of thin."

There was an easily recognizable undercurrent of admiration in his tone, and I felt that this youthful telephone operator had seen in Miss Odell's caller a certain physical and sartorial ideal. This palpable admiration, coupled with the somewhat *outré* clothes affected by the youth, permitted us to read between the lines of his remarks a fairly accurate description of the man who had unsuccessfully rung the dead girl's bell at half past nine the night before.

When Spively had been dismissed, Markham rose and strode about the room, his head enveloped in a cloud of cigar smoke, while Heath sat stolidly watching him, his brows knit.

Vance stood up and stretched himself.

"The absorbin' problem, it would seem, remains *in statu quo*," he remarked airily. "How, oh how, did the fair Margaret's executioner get in?"

"You know, Mr. Markham," rumbled Heath sententiously, "I've been thinking that the fellow may have come here earlier in the afternoon—say, before that side door was locked. Odell herself may have let him in and hidden him when the other man came to take her to dinner."

"It looks that way," Markham admitted. "Bring the maid in here again, and we'll see what we can find out."

When the woman had been brought in, Markham questioned her as to her actions during the afternoon, and learned that she had gone out at about four to do some shopping, and had returned about half past five.

"Did Miss Odell have any visitor with her when you got back?"

"No, sir," was the prompt answer. "She was alone."

"Did she mention that any one had called?"

"No, sir."

"Now," continued Markham, "could any one have been hidden in this apartment when you went home at seven?"

The maid was frankly astonished, and even a little horrified.

"Where could any one hide?" she asked, looking round the apartment.

"There are several possible places," Markham suggested: "in the bathroom, in one of the clothes-closets, under the bed, behind the window draperies. . . ."

The woman shook her head decisively. "No one could have been hidden," she declared. "I was in the bathroom half a dozen times, and I got Miss Odell's gown out of the clothes-closet in the bedroom. As soon as it began to get dark I drew all the window-shades myself. And as for the bed, it's built almost down to the floor; no one could squeeze under it." (I glanced closely at the bed, and realized that this statement was quite true.)

"What about the clothes-closet in this room?" Markham put the question hopefully, but again the maid shook her head.

"Nobody was in there. That's where I keep my own hat and coat, and I took them out myself when I was getting ready to go. I even put away one of Miss Odell's old dresses in that closet before I left."

"And you are absolutely certain," reiterated Markham, "that no one could have been hidden anywhere in these rooms at the time you went home?"

"Absolutely, sir."

"Do you happen to remember if the key of this clothes-closet was on the inside or the outside of the lock when you opened the door to get your hat?"

The woman paused, and looked thoughtfully at the closet door.

"It was on the outside, where it always was," she announced, after several moments' reflection. "I remember because it caught in the chiffon of the old dress I put away."

Markham frowned and then resumed his questioning.

"You say you don't know the name of Miss Odell's dinner companion last night. Can you tell us the names of any men she was in the habit of going out with?"

"Miss Odell never mentioned any names to me," the woman said. "She was very careful about it, too—secretive, you might say. You see, I'm only here in the daytime, and the gentlemen she knew generally came in the evening."

"And you never heard her speak of any one of whom she was frightened—any one she had reason to fear?"

"No, sir—although there was one man she was trying to get rid of. He was a bad character—I wouldn't have trusted him anywhere—and I told Miss Odell she'd better look out for him. But she'd known him a long time, I guess, and had been pretty soft on him once."

"How do you happen to know this?"

"One day, about a week ago," the maid explained, "I came in after lunch, and he was with her in the other room. They didn't hear me, because the portières were drawn. He was demanding money, and when she tried to put him off, he began threatening her. And she said something that showed she'd given him money before. I made a noise, and then they stopped arguing; and pretty soon he went out."

"What did this man look like?" Markham's interest was reviving.

"He was kind of thin—not very tall—and I'd say he was around thirty. He had a hard face—good-looking, some would say—and pale blue eyes that gave you the shivers. He always wore his hair greased back, and he had a little yellow moustache pointed at the ends."

"Ah!" said Vance. "Our gigolo!"

"Has this man been here since?" asked Markham.

"I don't know, sir—not when I was here."

"That will be all," said Markham; and the woman went out.

"She didn't help us much," complained Heath.

"What!" exclaimed Vance. "I think she did remarkably well. She cleared up several moot points."

"And just what portions of her information do you consider particularly illuminating?" asked Markham, with ill-concealed annoyance.

"We now know, do we not," rejoined Vance serenely, "that no one was lying *perdu* in here when the *bonne* departed yesterevening."

"Instead of that fact being helpful," retorted Markham, "I'd say it added materially to the complications of the situation."

"It would appear that way, wouldn't it, now? But, then—who knows?—it may prove to be your brightest and most comfortin' clue. . . . Furthermore, we learned that some one evidently locked himself in that clothes-press, as witness the shifting of the key, and that, moreover, this occultation did not occur until the abigail had gone, or, let us say, after seven o'clock."

"Sure," said Heath with sour facetiousness; "when the side door was bolted and an operator was sitting in the front hall, who swears nobody came in that way."

"It is a bit mystifyin'," Vance conceded sadly.

"Mystifying? It's impossible!" grumbled Markham.

Heath, who was now staring with meditative pugnacity into the closet, shook his head helplessly.

"What I don't understand," he ruminated, "is why, if the fellow was hiding in the closet, he didn't ransack it when he came out, like he did all the rest of the apartment."

"Sergeant," said Vance, "you've put your finger on the crux of the matter. . . . Y' know, the neat, undisturbed aspect of that closet rather suggests that the crude person who rifled these charming rooms omitted to give it his attention because it was locked on the inside and he couldn't open it."

"Come, come!" protested Markham. "That theory implies that there were two unknown persons in here last night."

Vance sighed. "Harrow and alas! I know it. And we can't introduce even one into this apartment logically. . . . Distressin', ain't it?"

Heath sought consolation in a new line of thought.

"Anyway," he submitted, "we know that the fancy fellow with the patent-leather pumps who called here last night at half past nine was probably Odell's lover, and was grafting on her."

"And in just what recondite way does that obvious fact help to roll the clouds away?" asked Vance. "Nearly every modern Delilah has an avaricious *amoroso*. It would be rather singular if there wasn't such a chap in the offing, what?"

"That's all right, too," returned Heath. "But I'll tell you something, Mr. Vance, that maybe you don't know. The men that these girls lose their heads over are generally crooks of some kind—professional criminals, you understand. That's why, knowing that this job was the work of a professional, it don't leave me cold, as you might say, to learn that this fellow who was threatening Odell and grafting on her was the same one who was prowling round here last night. . . . And I'll say this, too: the description of him sounds a whole lot like the kind of high-class burglars that hang out at these swell all-night cafés."

"You're convinced, then," asked Vance mildly, "that this job, as you call it, was done by a professional criminal?"

Heath was almost contemptuous in his reply. "Didn't the guy wear gloves, and use a jimmy? It was a yeggman's job, all right."

CHAPTER VIII

THE INVISIBLE MURDERER

(*Tuesday, September 11; 11.45 a. m.*)

Markham went to the window and stood, his hands behind him, looking down into the little paved rear yard. After several minutes he turned slowly.

"The situation, as I see it," he said, "boils down to this:—The Odell girl has an engagement for dinner and the theatre with a man of some distinction. He calls for her a little after seven, and they go out together. At eleven o'clock they return. He goes with her into her apartment and remains half an hour. He leaves at half past eleven and asks the phone operator to call him a taxi. While he is waiting the girl screams and calls for help, and, in response to his inquiries, she tells him nothing is wrong and bids him go away. The taxi arrives, and he departs in it. Ten minutes later some one telephones her, and a man answers from her apartment. This morning she is found murdered, and the apartment ransacked."

He took a long draw on his cigar.

"Now, it is obvious that when she and her escort returned last night, there was another man in this place somewhere; and it is also obvious that the

78

girl was alive after her escort had departed. Therefore, we must conclude that the man who was already in the apartment was the person who murdered her. This conclusion is further corroborated
by Doctor Doremus's report that the crime occurred
between eleven and twelve. But since her escort did
not leave till half past eleven, and spoke with her
after that time, we can put the actual hour of the
murder as between half past eleven and midnight.
. . . These are the inferable facts from the evidence
thus far adduced."

"There's not much getting away from 'em," agreed
Heath.

"At any rate, they're interestin'," murmured
Vance.

Markham, walking up and down earnestly, continued:

"The features of the situation revolving round
these inferable facts are as follows:—There was no
one hiding in the apartment at seven o'clock--the
hour the maid went home. Therefore, the murderer
entered the apartment later. First, then, let us consider the side door. At six o'clock—an hour before
the maid's departure—the janitor bolted it on the
inside, and both operators disavow emphatically that
they went near it. Moreover, you, Sergeant, found
it bolted this morning. Hence, we may assume that
the door was bolted on the inside all night, and that
nobody could have entered that way. Consequently,
we are driven to the inevitable alternative that the
murderer entered by the front door. Now, let us
consider this other means of entry. The phone operator who was on duty until ten o'clock last night

asserts positively that the only person who entered the front door and passed down the main hall to this apartment was a man who rang the bell and, getting no answer, immediately walked out again. The other operator, who was on duty from ten o'clock until this morning, asserts with equal positiveness that no one entered the front door and passed the switchboard coming to this apartment. Add to all this the fact that every window on this floor is barred, and that no one from up-stairs can descend into the main hall without coming face to face with the operator, and we are, for the moment, confronted with an impasse."

Heath scratched his head, and laughed mirthlessly.

"It don't make sense, does it, sir?"

"What about the next apartment?" asked Vance, "the one with the door facing the rear passageway —No. 2, I think?"

Heath turned to him patronizingly. "I looked into that the first thing this morning. Apartment No. 2 is occupied by a single woman; and I woke her up at eight o'clock and searched the place. Nothing there. Anyway, you have to walk past the switchboard to reach her apartment the same as you do to reach this one; and nobody called on her or left her apartment last night. What's more, Jessup, who's a shrewd sound lad, told me this woman is a quiet, ladylike sort, and that she and Odell didn't even know each other."

"You're so thorough, Sergeant!" murmured Vance.

"Of course," put in Markham, "it would have

been possible for some one from the other apartment to have slipped in here behind the operator's back between seven and eleven, and then to have slipped back after the murder. But as Sergeant Heath's search this morning failed to uncover any one, we can eliminate the possibility of our man having operated from that quarter."

"I dare say you're right," Vance indifferently admitted. "But it strikes me, Markham old dear, that your own affectin' recapitulation of the situation jolly well eliminates the possibility of your man's having operated from any quarter. . . . And yet he came in, garroted the unfortunate damsel, and departed—eh, what? . . . It's a charmin' little problem. I wouldn't have missed it for worlds."

"It's uncanny," pronounced Markham gloomily.

"It's positively spiritualistic," amended Vance. "It has the caressin' odor of a séance. Really, y' know, I'm beginning to suspect that some medium was hovering in the vicinage last night doing some rather tip-top materializations. . . . I say, Markham, could you get an indictment against an ecto-plasmic emanation?"

"It wasn't no spook that made those finger-prints," growled Heath, with surly truculence.

Markham halted his nervous pacing and regarded Vance irritably.

"Damn it! This is rank nonsense. The man got in some way, and he got out, too. There's something wrong somewhere. Either the maid is mistaken about some one being here when she left, or else one of those phone operators went to sleep and won't admit it."

"Or else one of 'em's lying," supplemented Heath.

Vance shook his head. "The dusky *fille de chambre*, I'd say, is eminently trustworthy. And if there was any doubt about any one's having come in the front door unnoticed, the lads on the switchboard would, in the present circumstances, be only too eager to admit it. . . . No, Markham, you'll simply have to approach this affair from the astral plane, so to speak."

Markham grunted his distaste of Vance's jocularity.

"That line of investigation I leave to you with your metaphysical theories and esoteric hypotheses."

"But, consider," protested Vance banteringly. "You've proved conclusively—or, rather, you've demonstrated legally—that no one could have entered or departed from this apartment last night; and, as you've often told me, a court of law must decide all matters, not in accord with the known or suspected facts, but according to the evidence; and the evidence in this case would prove a sound alibi for every corporeal being extant. And yet, it's not exactly tenable, d' ye see, that the lady strangled herself. If only it had been poison, what an exquisite and satisfyin' suicide case you'd have! . . . Most inconsiderate of her homicidal visitor not to have used arsenic instead of his hands!"

"Well, he strangled her," pronounced Heath. "Furthermore, I'll lay my money on the fellow who called here last night at half past nine and couldn't get in. He's the bird I want to talk to."

"Indeed?" Vance produced another cigarette.

"I shouldn't say, to judge from our description of him, that his conversation would prove particularly fascinatin'."

An ugly light came into Heath's eyes.

"We've got ways," he said through his teeth, "of getting damn interesting conversation outa people who haven't no great reputation for repartee."

Vance sighed. "How the Four Hundred needs you, my Sergeant!"

Markham looked at his watch.

"I've got pressing work at the office," he said, "and all this talk isn't getting us anywhere." He put his hand on Heath's shoulder. "I leave you to go ahead. This afternoon I'll have these people brought down to my office for another questioning —maybe I can jog their memories a bit. . . . You've got some line of investigation planned?"

"The usual routine," replied Heath drearily. "I'll go through Odell's papers, and I'll have three or four of my men check up on her."

"You'd better get after the Yellow Taxicab Company right away," Markham suggested. "Find out, if you can, who the man was who left here at half past eleven last night, and where he went."

"Do you imagine for one moment," asked Vance, "that if this man knew anything about the murder, he would have stopped in the hall and asked the operator to call a taxi for him?"

"Oh, I don't look for much in that direction." Markham's tone was almost listless. "But the girl may have said something to him that'll give us a lead."

Vance shook his head facetiously. "O welcome

pure-ey'd Faith, white-handed Hope, thou hovering
angel, girt with golden wings!"

Markham was in no mood for chaffing. He turned
to Heath, and spoke with forced cheeriness.

"Call me up later this afternoon. I may get some
new evidence out of the outfit we've just interviewed.
. . . And," he added, "be sure to put a man on
guard here. I want this apartment kept just as it
is until we see a little more light."

"I'll attend to that," Heath assured him.

Markham and Vance and I went out and entered
the car. A few minutes later we were winding rapidly across town through Central Park.

"Recall our recent *conversazione* about footprints
in the snow?" asked Vance, as we emerged into Fifth
Avenue and headed south.

Markham nodded abstractedly.

"As I remember," mused Vance, "in the hypothetical case you presented there were not only footprints but a dozen or more witnesses—including a
youthful prodigy—who saw a figure of some kind
cross the hibernal landscape. . . . *Grau, teurer
Freund, ist alle Theorie!* Here you are in a most
beastly pother because of the disheartenin' fact that
there are neither footprints in the snow nor witnesses
who saw a fleeing figure. In short, you are bereft of
both direct and circumstantial evidence. . . . Sad,
sad."

He wagged his head dolefully.

"Y' know, Markham, it appears to me that the
testimony in this case constitutes conclusive legal
proof that no one could have been with the deceased

at the hour of her passing, and that, *ergo*, she is presumably alive. The strangled body of the lady is, I take it, simply an irrelevant circumstance from the standpoint of legal procedure. I know that you learned lawyers won't admit a murder without a body; but how, in sweet Heaven's name, do you get around a *corpus delicti* without a murder?"

"You're talking nonsense" Markham rebuked him, with a show of anger.

"Oh, quite," agreed Vance. "And yet, it's a distressin' thing for a lawyer not to have footprints of some kind, isn't it, old dear? It leaves one so up in the air."

Suddenly Markham swung round. "*You*, of course, don't need footprints, or any other kind of material clues," he flung at Vance tauntingly. "*You* have powers of divination such as are denied ordinary mortals. If I remember correctly, you informed me, somewhat grandiloquently, that, knowing the nature and conditions of a crime, you could lead me infallibly to the culprit, whether he left footprints or not. You recall that boast? . . . Well, here's a crime, and the perpetrator left no footprints coming or going. Be so good as to end my suspense by confiding in me who killed the Odell girl."

Vance's serenity was not ruffled by Markham's ill-humored challenge. He sat smoking lazily for several minutes; then he leaned over and flicked his cigarette ash out of the window.

"'Pon my word, Markham," he rejoined evenly, "I'm half inclined to look into this silly murder. I think I'll wait, though, and see whom the nonplussed Heath turns up with his inquiries."

Markham grunted scoffingly, and sank back on the cushions.

"Your generosity wrings me," he said.

CHAPTER IX

(Tuesday, September 11; afternoon)

On our way down-town that morning we were delayed for a considerable time in the traffic congestion just north of Madison Square, and Markham anxiously looked at his watch.

"It's past noon," he said. "I think I'll stop at the club and have a bite of lunch. . . . I presume that eating at this early hour would be too plebeian for so exquisite a hothouse flower as you."

Vance considered the invitation.

"Since you deprived me of my breakfast," he decided, "I'll permit you to buy me some eggs *Bénédictine*."

A few minutes later we entered the almost empty grill of the Stuyvesant Club, and took a table near one of the windows looking southward over the tree-tops of Madison Square.

Shortly after we had given our order a uniformed attendant entered and, bowing deferentially at the District Attorney's elbow, held out an unaddressed communication sealed in one of the club's envelopes. Markham read it with an expression of growing curiosity, and as he studied the signature a look of mild surprise came into his eyes. At length he looked up and nodded to the waiting attendant. Then, excusing himself, he left us abruptly. It was fully twenty minutes before he returned.

"Funny thing," he said. "That note was from the man who took the Odell woman to dinner and the theatre last night. . . . A small world," he mused. "He's staying here at the club—he's a non-resident member and makes it his headquarters when he's in town."

"You know him?" Vance put the question disinterestedly.

"I've met him several times—chap named Spotswoode." Markham seemed perplexed. "He's a man of family, lives in a country house on Long Island, and is regarded generally as a highly respectable member of society—one of the last persons I'd suspect of being mixed up with the Odell girl. But, according to his own confession, he played around a good deal with her during his visits to New York— 'sowing a few belated wild oats,' as he expressed it— and last night took her to Francelle's for dinner and to the Winter Garden afterwards."

"Not my idea of an intellectual, or even edifyin', evening," commented Vance. "And he selected a deuced unlucky day for it. . . . I say, imagine opening the morning paper and learning that your *petite dame* of the preceding evening had been strangled! Disconcertin', what?"

"He's certainly disconcerted," said Markham. "The early afternoon papers were out about an hour ago, and he'd been phoning my office every ten minutes, when I suddenly walked in here. He's afraid his connection with the girl will leak out and disgrace him."

"And won't it?"

"I hardly see the necessity. No one knows who

her escort was last evening; and since he obviously had nothing to do with the crime, what's to be gained by dragging him into it? He told me the whole story, and offered to stay in the city as long as I wanted him to."

"I infer, from the cloud of disappointment that enveloped you when you returned just now, that his story held nothing hopeful for you in the way of clues."

"No," Markham admitted. "The girl apparently never spoke to him of her intimate affairs; and he couldn't give me a single helpful suggestion. His account of what happened last night agreed perfectly with Jessup's. He called for the girl at seven, brought her home at about eleven, stayed with her half an hour or so, and then left her. When he heard her call for help he was frightened, but on being assured by her there was nothing wrong, he concluded she had dozed off into a nightmare, and thought no more of it. He drove direct to the club here, arriving about ten minutes to twelve. Judge Redfern, who saw him descend from the taxi, insisted on his coming up-stairs and playing poker with some men who were waiting in the Judge's rooms for him. They played until three o'clock this morning."

"Your Long Island Don Juan has certainly not supplied you with any footprints in the snow."

"Anyway, his coming forward at this time closes one line of inquiry over which we might have wasted considerable time."

"If many more lines of inquiry are closed," remarked Vance dryly, "you'll be in a distressin' dilemma, don't y' know."

"There are enough still open to keep me busy," said Markham, pushing back his plate and calling for the check. He rose; then pausing, regarded Vance meditatingly. "Are you sufficiently interested to want to come along?"

"Eh, what? My word! . . . Charmed, I'm sure. But, I say, sit down just a moment—there's a good fellow!—till I finish my coffee."

I was considerably astonished at Vance's ready acceptance, careless and bantering though it was, for there was an exhibition of old Chinese prints at the Montross Galleries that afternoon, which he had planned to attend. A Riokai and a Moyeki, said to be very fine examples of Sung painting, were to be shown; and Vance was particularly eager to acquire them for his collection.

We rode with Markham to the Criminal Courts building and, entering by the Franklin Street door, took the private elevator to the District Attorney's spacious but dingy private office which overlooked the gray-stone ramparts of the Tombs. Vance seated himself in one of the heavy leather-upholstered chairs near the carved oak table on the right of the desk, and lighted a cigarette with an air of cynical amusement.

"I await with anticipat'ry delight the grinding of the wheels of justice," he confided, leaning back lazily.

"You are doomed not to hear the first turn of those wheels," retorted Markham. "The initial revolution will take place outside of this office." And he disappeared through a swinging door which led to the judges' chambers.

Five minutes later he returned, and sat down in the high-backed swivel chair at his desk, with his back to the four tall narrow windows in the south wall of the office.

"I just saw Judge Redfern," he explained—"it happened to be the midday recess—and he verified Spotswoode's statement in regard to the poker game. The Judge met him outside of the club at ten minutes before midnight, and was with him until three in the morning. He noted the time because he had promised his guests to be back at half past eleven, and was twenty minutes late."

"Why all this substantiation of an obviously unimportant fact?" asked Vance.

"A matter of routine," Markham told him, slightly impatient. "In a case of this kind every factor, however seemingly remote to the main issue, must be checked."

"Really, y' know, Markham"—Vance laid his head back on the chair and gazed dreamily at the ceiling—"one would think that this eternal routine, which you lawyer chaps worship so devoutly, actually got one somewhere occasionally; whereas it never gets one anywhere. Remember the Red Queen in 'Through the Looking-Glass——'"

"I'm too busy at present to debate the question of routine *versus* inspiration," Markham answered brusquely, pressing a button beneath the edge of his desk.

Swacker, his youthful and energetic secretary, appeared at the door which communicated with a narrow inner chamber between the District Attorney's office and the main waiting-room.

"Yes, Chief?" The secretary's eyes gleamed expectantly behind his enormous horn-rimmed glasses.

"Tell Ben to send me in a man at once." *

Swacker went out through the corridor door, and a minute or two later a suave, rotund man, dressed immaculately and wearing a *pince-nez*, entered, and stood before Markham with an ingratiating smile.

"Morning, Tracy." Markham's tone was pleasant but curt. "Here's a list of four witnesses in connection with the Odell case that I want brought down here at once—the two phone operators, the maid, and the janitor. You'll find them at 184 West 71st Street: Sergeant Heath is holding them there."

"Right, sir." Tracy took the memorandum, and with a priggish, but by no means inelegant, bow went out.

During the next hour Markham plunged into the general work that had accumulated during the forenoon, and I was amazed at the man's tremendous vitality and efficiency. He disposed of as many important matters as would have occupied the ordinary business man for an entire day. Swacker bobbed in and out with electric energy, and various clerks appeared at the touch of a buzzer, took their orders, and were gone with breathless rapidity. Vance, who had sought diversion in a tome of famous arson trials, looked up admiringly from time to time, and shook his head in mild reproach at such spirited activity.

It was just half past two when Swacker announced the return of Tracy with the four witnesses; and for two hours Markham questioned and cross-questioned

* "Ben" was Colonel Benjamin Hanlon, the commanding officer of the Detective Division attached to the District Attorney's office.

them with a thoroughness and an insight that even I, as a lawyer, had rarely seen equalled. His interrogation of the two phone operators was quite different from his casual questioning of them earlier in the day; and if there had been a single relevant omission in their former testimony, it would certainly have been caught now by Markham's gruelling catechism. But when, at last, they were told they could go, no new information had been brought to light. Their stories now stood firmly grounded: no one—with the exception of the girl herself and her escort, and the disappointed visitor at half past nine—had entered the front door and passed down the hall to the Odell apartment from seven o'clock on; and no one had passed out that way. The janitor reiterated stubbornly that he had bolted the side door a little after six, and no amount of wheedling or aggression could shake his dogged certainty on that point. Amy Gibson, the maid, could add nothing to her former testimony. Markham's intensive examination of her produced only repetitions of what she had already told him.

Not one new possibility—not one new suggestion—was brought out. In fact, the two hours' interlocutory proceedings resulted only in closing up every loophole in a seemingly incredible situation. When, at half past four, Markham sat back in his chair with a weary sigh, the chance of unearthing a promising means of approach to the astonishing problem seemed more remote than ever.

Vance closed his treatise on arson, and threw away his cigarette.

"I tell you, Markham old chap," he grinned, "this case requires umbilicular contemplation, not routine-

Why not call in an Egyptian seeress with a *flair* for crystal-gazing?"

"If this sort of thing goes on much longer," returned Markham dispiritedly, "I'll be tempted to take your advice."

Just then Swacker looked in through the door to say that Inspector Brenner was on the wire. Markham picked up the telephone receiver, and as he listened he jotted down some notes on a pad. When the call had ended, he turned to Vance.

"You seemed disturbed over the condition of the steel jewel-case we found in the bedroom. Well, the expert on burglar tools just called up; and he verifies his opinion of this morning. The case was pried open with a specially made cold chisel such as only a professional burglar would carry or would know how to use. It had an inch-and-three-eighths bevelled bit and a one-inch flat handle. It was an old instrument—there was a peculiar nick in the blade—and is the same one that was used in a successful house-break on upper Park Avenue early last summer. . . . Does that highly exciting information ameliorate your anxiety?"

"Can't say that it does." Vance had again become serious and perplexed. "In fact, it makes the situation still more fantastic. . . . I could see a glimmer of light—eerie and unearthly, perhaps, but still a perceptible illumination—in all this murkiness if it wasn't for that jewel-case and the steel chisel."

Markham was about to answer when Swacker again looked in and informed him that Sergeant Heath had arrived and wanted to see him.

Heath's manner was far less depressed than when we had taken leave of him that morning. He accepted the cigar Markham offered him, and seating himself at the conference table in front of the District Attorney's desk, drew out a battered note-book.

"We've had a little good luck," he began. "Burke and Emery—two of the men I put on the case—got a line on Odell at the first place they made inquiries. From what they learned, she didn't run around with many men—limited herself to a few live wires, and played the game with what you'd call *finesse*. . . . The principal one—the man who's been seen most with her—is Charles Cleaver."

Markham sat up.

"I know Cleaver—if it's the same one."

"It's him, all right," declared Heath. "Former Brooklyn Tax Commissioner; been interested in a pool-room for pony-betting over in Jersey City ever since. Hangs out at the Stuyvesant Club, where he can hobnob with his old Tammany Hall cronies."

"That's the one," nodded Markham. "He's a kind of professional gay-dog—known as Pop, I believe."

Vance gazed into space.

"Well, well," he murmured. "So old Pop Cleaver was also entangled with our subtle and sanguine Dolores. She certainly couldn't have loved him for his *beaux yeux*."

"I thought, sir," went on Heath, "that, seeing as how Cleaver is always in and out of the Stuyvesant Club, you might ask him some questions about Odell. He ought to know something."

"Glad to, Sergeant." Markham made a note on his pad. "I'll try to get in touch with him to-night. . . . Any one else on your list?"

"There's a fellow named Mannix—Louis Mannix —who met Odell when she was in the 'Follies'; but she chucked him over a year ago, and they haven't been seen together since. He's got another girl now. He's the head of the firm of Mannix and Levine, fur importers, and is one of your night-club rounders—a heavy spender. But I don't see much use of barking up that tree—his affair with Odell went cold too long ago."

"Yes," agreed Markham; "I think we can eliminate him."

"I say, if you keep up this elimination much longer," observed Vance, "you won't have anything left but the lady's corpse."

"And then, there's the man who took her out last night," pursued Heath. "Nobody seems to know his name—he must've been one of those discreet, careful old boys. I thought at first he might have been Cleaver, but the descriptions don't tally. . . . And by the way, sir, here's a funny thing: when he left Odell last night he took the taxi down to the Stuyvesant Club, and got out there."

Markham nodded. "I know all about that, Sergeant. And I know who the man was; and it wasn't Cleaver."

Vance was chuckling.

"The Stuyvesant Club seems to be well in the forefront of this case," he said. "I do hope it doesn't suffer the sad fate of the Knickerbocker Athletic." *

* Vance was here referring to the famous Molineux case, which, in 1898, sounded the death-knell of the old Knickerbocker Athletic Club at Madison Avenue and 45th Street. But it was commercialism that ended the Stuyvesant's career. This club, which stood on the north side of Madison Square, was razed a few years later to make room for a skyscraper.

Heath was intent on the main issue.

"Who was the man, Mr. Markham?"

Markham hesitated, as if pondering the advisability of taking the other into his confidence. Then he said: "I'll tell you his name, but in strict confidence. The man was Kenneth Spotswoode."

He then recounted the story of his being called away from lunch, and of his failure to elicit any helpful suggestions from Spotswoode. He also informed Heath of his verification of the man's statements regarding his movements after meeting Judge Redfern at the club.

"And," added Markham, "since he obviously left the girl before she was murdered, there's no necessity to bother him. In fact, I gave him my word I'd keep him out of it for his family's sake."

"If you're satisfied, sir, I am." Heath closed his note-book and put it away. "There's just one other little thing. Odell used to live on 110th Street, and Emery dug up her former landlady and learned that this fancy guy the maid told us about used to call on her regularly."

"That reminds me, Sergeant." Markham picked up the memorandum he had made during Inspector Brenner's phone call. "Here's some data the Professor gave me about the forcing of the jewel-case."

Heath studied the paper with considerable eagerness. "Just as I thought!" He nodded his head with satisfaction. "Clear-cut professional job, by somebody who's been in the line of work before."

Vance roused himself.

"Still, if such is the case," he said, "why did this experienced burglar first use the insufficient poker?

And why did he overlook the living-room clothes-press?"

"I'll find all that out, Mr. Vance, when I get my hands on him," asserted Heath, with a hard look in his eyes. "And the guy I want to have a nice quiet little chat with is the one with the pleated silk shirt and the chamois gloves."

"*Chacun à son goût*," sighed Vance. "For myself, I have no yearning whatever to hold converse with him. Somehow, I can't just picture a professional looter trying to rend a steel box with a cast-iron poker."

"Forget the poker," Heath advised gruffly. "He jimmied the box with a steel chisel; and that same chisel was used last summer in another burglary on Park Avenue. What about *that?*"

"Ah! That's what torments me, Sergeant. If it wasn't for that disturbin' fact, d' ye see, I'd be lightsome and *sans souci* this afternoon, inviting my soul over a dish of tea at Claremont."

Detective Bellamy was announced, and Heath sprang to his feet.

"That'll mean news about those finger-prints," he prophesied hopefully.

Bellamy entered unemotionally, and walked up to the District Attorney's desk.

"Cap'n Dubois sent me over," he said. "He thought you'd want the report on those Odell prints." He reached into his pocket and drew out a small flat folder which, at a sign from Markham, he handed to Heath. "We identified 'em. Both made by the same hand, like Cap'n Dubois said; and that hand belonged to Tony Skeel."

"'Dude' Skeel, eh?" The Sergeant's tone was vibrant with suppressed excitement. "Say, Mr. Markham, that gets us somewhere. Skeel's an ex-convict and an artist in his line."

He opened the folder and took out an oblong card and a sheet of blue paper containing eight or ten lines of typewriting. He studied the card, gave a satisfied grunt, and handed it to Markham. Vance and I stepped up and looked at it. At the top was the familiar rogues'-gallery photograph showing the full face and profile of a regular-featured youth with thick hair and a square chin. His eyes were wide-set and pale, and he wore a small, evenly trimmed moustache with waxed, needle-point ends. Below the double photograph was a brief tabulated description of its sitter, giving his name, aliases, residence, and Bertillon measurements, and designating the character of his illegal profession. Underneath were ten little squares arranged in two rows, each containing a finger-print impression made in black ink—the upper row being the impressions of the right hand, the lower row those of the left.

"So that's the *arbiter elegantiarum* who introduced the silk shirt for full-dress wear! My word!" Vance regarded the identification card satirically. "I wish he'd start a craze for gaiters with dinner-jackets—these New York theatres are frightfully drafty in winter."

Heath put the card back in the folder, and glanced over the typewritten paper that had accompanied it.

"He's our man, and no mistake, Mr. Markham. Listen to this: 'Tony (Dude) Skeel. Two years Elmira Reformatory, 1902 to 1904. One year in the

Baltimore County jail for petit larceny, 1906. Three
years in San Quentin for assault and robbery, 1908
to 1911. Arrested Chicago for house-breaking, 1912;
case dismissed. Arrested and tried for burglary in
Albany, 1913; no conviction. Served two years and
eight months in Sing Sing for house-breaking and
burglary, 1914 to 1916.'" He folded the paper and
put it, with the card, into his breast-pocket. "Sweet
little record."

"That dope what you wanted?" asked the imperturbable Bellamy.

"I'll say!" Heath was almost jovial.

Bellamy lingered expectantly with one eye on the
District Attorney; and Markham, as if suddenly
remembering something, took out a box of cigars
and held it out.

"Much obliged, sir," said Bellamy, helping himself to two *Mi Favoritas;* and putting them into his
waistcoat pocket with great care, he went out.

"I'll use your phone now, if you don't mind, Mr.
Markham," said Heath.

He called the Homicide Bureau.

"Look up Tony Skeel—Dude Skeel—*pronto*, and
bring him in as soon as you find him," were his
orders to Snitkin. "Get his address from the files,
and take Burke and Emery with you. If he's hopped
it, send out a general alarm and have him picked up—
some of the boys'll have a line on him. Lock him up
without booking him, see? . . . And, listen. Search
his room for burglar tools: he probably won't have
any laying around, but I specially want a one-and-
three-eighths-inch chisel with a nick in the blade. . . .
I'll be at Headquarters in half an hour."

He hung up the receiver and rubbed his hands together.

"Now we're sailing," he rejoiced.

Vance had gone to the window, and stood staring down on the "Bridge of Sighs," his hands thrust deep into his pockets. Slowly he turned, and fixed Heath with a contemplative eye.

"It simply won't do, don't y' know," he asserted. "Your friend, the Dude, may have ripped open that bally box, but his head isn't the right shape for the rest of last evening's performance."

Heath was contemptuous.

"Not being a phrenologist, I'm going by the shape of his finger-prints."

"A woeful error in the technic of criminal approach, *sergente mio*," replied Vance dulcetly. "The question of culpability in this case isn't so simple as you imagine. It's deuced complicated. And this glass of fashion and mould of form whose portrait you're carryin' next to your heart has merely added to its intricacy."

CHAPTER X

(Tuesday, September 11; 8 p. m.)

Markham dined at the Stuyvesant Club, as was his custom, and at his invitation Vance and I remained with him. He no doubt figured that our presence at the dinner-table would act as a bulwark against the intrusion of casual acquaintances; for he was in no mood for the pleasantries of the curious. Rain had begun to fall late in the afternoon, and when dinner was over it had turned into a steady downpour which threatened to last well into the night. Dinner over, the three of us sought a secluded corner of the lounge-room, and settled ourselves for a protracted smoke.

We had been there less than a quarter of an hour when a slightly rotund man, with a heavy, florid face and thin gray hair, strolled up to us with a stealthy, self-assured gait, and wished Markham a jovial good evening. Though I had not met the newcomer I knew him to be Charles Cleaver.

"Got your note at the desk saying you wanted to see me." He spoke with a voice curiously gentle for a man of his size; but, for all its gentleness, there was in it a timbre of calculation and coldness.

Markham rose and, after shaking hands, introduced him to Vance and me—though, it seemed, Vance had known him slightly for some time. He

102

took the chair Markham indicated, and, producing a *Corona Corona*, he carefully cut the end with a gold clipper attached to his heavy watch-chain, rolled the cigar between his lips to dampen it, and lighted it in closely cupped hands.

"I'm sorry to trouble you, Mr. Cleaver," began Markham, "but, as you probably have read, a young woman by the name of Margaret Odell was murdered last night in her apartment in 71st Street. . . ."

He paused. He seemed to be considering just how he could best broach a subject so obviously delicate; and perhaps he hoped that Cleaver would volunteer the fact of his acquaintance with the girl. But not a muscle of the man's face moved; and, after a moment, Markham continued.

"In making inquiries into the young woman's life I learned that you, among others, were fairly well acquainted with her."

Again he paused. Cleaver lifted his eyebrows almost imperceptibly, but said nothing.

"The fact is," went on Markham, a trifle annoyed by the other's deliberately circumspect attitude, "my report states that you were seen with her on many occasions during a period of nearly two years. Indeed, the only inference to be drawn from what I've learned is that you were more than casually interested in Miss Odell."

"Yes?" The query was as non-committal as it was gentle.

"Yes," repeated Markham. "And I may add, Mr. Cleaver, that this is not the time for pretenses or suppressions. I am talking to you to-night, in large measure *ex officio*, because it occurred to me that you could give me some assistance in clearing the matter up. I think it only fair to say that a certain man is now under grave suspicion, and we hope to arrest him very soon. But, in any event, we will need help, and that is why I requested this little chat with you at the club."

"And how can I assist you?" Cleaver's face remained blank; only his lips moved as he put the question.

"Knowing this young woman as well as you did," explained Markham patiently, "you are no doubt in possession of some information—certain facts or confidences, let us say—which would throw light on her brutal, and apparently unexpected, murder."

Cleaver was silent for some time. His eyes had shifted to the wall before him, but otherwise his features remained set.

"I'm afraid I can't accommodate you," he said at length.

"Your attitude is not quite what might be expected in one whose conscience is entirely clear," returned Markham, with a show of resentment.

The man turned a mildly inquisitive gaze upon the District Attorney.

"What has my knowing the girl to do with her being murdered? She didn't confide in me who her murderer was to be. She didn't even tell me that she knew any one who intended to strangle her. If she'd known, she most likely could have avoided being murdered."

Vance was sitting close to me, a little removed from the others, and, leaning over, murmured in my ear *sotto voce*:

"Markham's up against another lawyer—poor dear! . . . A crumplin' situation."

But however inauspiciously this interlocutory skirmish may have begun, it soon developed into a grim combat which ended in Cleaver's complete surrender. Markham, despite his suavity and graciousness, was an unrelenting and resourceful antagonist; and it was not long before he had forced from Cleaver some highly significant information.

In response to the man's ironically evasive rejoinder, he turned quickly and leaned forward.

"You're not on the witness-stand in your own defense, Mr. Cleaver," he said sharply, "however much you appear to regard yourself as eligible for that position."

Cleaver glared back fixedly without replying; and Markham, his eyelids level, studied the man opposite, determined to decipher all he could from the other's phlegmatic countenance. But Cleaver was apparently just as determined that his *vis-à-vis* should decipher absolutely nothing; and the features that met Markham's scrutiny were as arid as a desert. At length Markham sank back in his chair.

"It doesn't matter particularly," he remarked indifferently, "whether you discuss the matter or not here in the club to-night. If you prefer to be brought to my office in the morning by a sheriff with a subpœna, I'll be only too glad to accommodate you."

"That's up to you," Cleaver told him hostilely.

"And what's printed in the newspapers about it will be up to the reporters," rejoined Markham. "I'll explain the situation to them and give them a verbatim report of the interview."

"But I've nothing to tell you." The other's tone was suddenly conciliatory; the idea of publicity was evidently highly distasteful to him.

"So you informed me before," said Markham coldly. "Therefore I wish you good evening."

He turned to Vance and me with the air of a man who had terminated an unpleasant episode.

Cleaver, however, made no move to go. He smoked thoughtfully for a minute or two; then he gave a short, hard laugh which did not even disturb the contours of his face.

"Oh, hell!" he grumbled, with forced good nature. "As you said, I'm not on the witness-stand. . . . What do you want to know?"

"I've told you the situation." Markham's voice betrayed a curious irritation. "You know the sort of thing I want. How did this Odell girl live? Who were her intimates? Who would have been likely to want her out of the way? What enemies had she?— Anything that might lead us to an explanation of her death. . . . And incidentally," he added with tartness, "anything that'll eliminate yourself from any suspected participation, direct or indirect, in the affair."

Cleaver stiffened at these last words, and started to protest indignantly. But immediately he changed his tactics. Smiling contemptuously, he took out a leather pocket-case and, extracting a small folded paper, handed it to Markham.

"I can eliminate myself easily enough," he proclaimed, with easy confidence. "There's a speeding summons from Boonton, New Jersey. Note the date and the time: September the 10th—last night—at half past eleven. Was driving down to Hopatcong, and was ticketed by a motorcycle cop just as I had passed Boonton and was heading for Mountain Lakes. Got to appear in court there to-morrow morning. Damn nuisance, these country constables." He gave Markham a long, calculating look. "You couldn't square it for me, could you? It's a rotten ride to Jersey, and I've got a lot to do to-morrow."

Markham, who had inspected the summons casually, put it in his pocket.

"I'll attend to it for you," he promised, smiling amiably. "Now tell me what you know."

Cleaver puffed meditatively on his cigar. Then, leaning back and crossing his knees, he spoke with apparent candor.

"I doubt if I know much that'll help you. . . . I liked the Canary, as she was called—in fact, was pretty much attached to her at one time. Did a number of foolish things; wrote her a lot of damn-fool letters when I went to Cuba last year. Even had my picture taken with her down at Atlantic City." He made a self-condemnatory grimace. "Then she began to get cool and distant; broke several appointments with me. I raised the devil with her, but the only answer I got was a demand for money. . . ."

He stopped and looked down at his cigar ash. A venomous hatred gleamed from his narrowed eyes, and the muscles of his jowls hardened.

"No use lying about it. She had those letters and things, and she touched me for a neat little sum before I got 'em back. . . ."

"When was this?"

There was a momentary hesitation. "Last June," Cleaver replied. Then he hurried on: "Mr. Markham"—his voice was bitter—"I don't want to throw mud on a dead person; but that woman was the shrewdest, coldest-blooded blackmailer it's ever been my misfortune to meet. And I'll say this, too: I wasn't the only easy mark she squeezed. She had others on her string. . . . I happen to know she once dug into old Louey Mannix for a plenty—he told me about it."

"Could you give me the names of any of these other men?" asked Markham, attempting to dissemble his eagerness. "I've already heard of the Mannix episode."

"No, I couldn't." Cleaver spoke regretfully. "I've seen the Canary here and there with different men; and there's one in particular I've noticed lately. But they were all strangers to me."

"I suppose the Mannix affair is dead and buried by this time?"

"Yes—ancient history. You won't get any line on the situation from that angle. But there are others—more recent than Mannix—who might bear looking into, if you could find them. I'm easy-going myself; take things as they come. But there's a lot of men who'd go red-headed if she did the things to them that she did to me."

Cleaver, despite his confession, did not strike me as easy-going, but rather as a cold, self-contained, nerveless person whose immobility was at all times dictated by policy and expediency.

Markham studied him closely.

"You think, then, her death may have been due

to vengeance on the part of some disillusioned admirer?"

Cleaver carefully considered his answer.

"Seems reasonable," he said finally. "She was riding for a fall."

There was a short silence; then Markham asked:

"Do you happen to know of a young man she was interested in—good-looking, small, blond moustache, light blue eyes—named Skeel?"

Cleaver snorted derisively.

"That wasn't the Canary's specialty—she let the young ones alone, as far as I know."

At this moment a page-boy approached Cleaver, and bowed.

"Sorry to disturb you, sir, but there's a phone call for your brother. Party said it was important and, as your brother isn't in the club now, the operator thought you might know where he'd gone."

"How would I know?" fumed Cleaver. "Don't ever bother me with his calls."

"Your brother in the city?" asked Markham casually. "I met him years ago. He's a San Franciscan, isn't he?"

"Yes—rabid Californian. He's visiting New York for a couple of weeks so he'll appreciate Frisco more when he gets back."

It seemed to me that this information was given reluctantly; and I got the impression that Cleaver, for some reason, was annoyed. But Markham, apparently, was too absorbed in the problem before him to take notice of the other's disgruntled air, for he reverted at once to the subject of the murder.

"I happen to know one man who has been inter-

ested in the Odell woman recently; he may be the
same one you've seen her with—tall, about forty-
five, and wears a gray, close-cropped moustache."
(He was, I knew, describing Spotswoode.)

"That's the man," averred Cleaver. "Saw them
together only last week at Mouquin's."

Markham was disappointed.

"Unfortunately, he's checked off the list. . . .
But there must be somebody who was in the girl's
confidence. You're sure you couldn't cudgel your
brains to any advantage?"

Cleaver appeared to think.

"If it's merely a question of some one who had
her confidence," he said, "I might suggest Doctor
Lindquist—first name's Ambroise, I think; and he
lives somewhere in the Forties near Lexington
Avenue. But I don't know that he'd be of any value
to you. Still, he was pretty close to her at one time."

"You mean that this Doctor Lindquist might have
been interested in her otherwise than professionally?"

"I wouldn't like to say." Cleaver smoked for a
while as if inwardly debating the situation. "Anyway, here are the facts: Lindquist is one of these exclusive society specialists—a neurologist he calls
himself—and I believe he's the head of a private
sanitarium of some kind for nervous women. He
must have money, and, of course, his social standing
is a vital asset to him—just the sort of man the
Canary might have selected as a source of income.
And I know this: he came to see her a good deal
oftener than a doctor of his type would be apt to.
I ran into him one night at her apartment, and when
she introduced us, he wasn't even civil."

"It will at least bear looking into," replied Markham unenthusiastically. "You've no one else in mind who might know something helpful?"

Cleaver shook his head.

"No—no one."

"And she never mentioned anything to you that indicated she was in fear of any one, or anticipated trouble?"

"Not a word. Fact is, I was bowled over by the news. I never read any paper but the morning *Herald*—except, of course, *The Daily Racing Form* at night. And as there was no account of the murder in this morning's paper, I didn't hear about it until just before dinner. The boys in the billiard-room were talking about it, and I went out and looked at an afternoon paper. If it hadn't been for that, I might not have known of it till to-morrow morning."

Markham discussed the case with him until half past eight, but could elicit no further suggestions. Finally Cleaver rose to go.

"Sorry I couldn't give you more help," he said. His rubicund face was beaming now, and he shook hands with Markham in the friendliest fashion.

"You wangled that viscid old sport rather cleverly, don't y' know," remarked Vance, when Cleaver had gone. "But there's something deuced queer about him. The transition from his gambler's glassy stare to his garrulous confidences was too sudden—suspiciously sudden, in fact. I may be evil-minded, but he didn't impress me as a luminous pillar of truth. Maybe it's because I don't like those cold, boiled eyes of his—somehow they didn't harmonize with his gushing imitation of open-hearted frankness."

"We can allow him something for his embarrassing position," suggested Markham charitably. "It isn't exactly pleasant to admit having been taken in and blackmailed by a charmer."

"Still, if he got his letters back in June, why did he continue paying court to the lady? Heath reported he was active in that sector right up to the end."

"He may be the complete amorist," smiled Markham.

"Some like Abra, what?——

> 'Abra was ready ere I call'd her name;
> And, though I call'd another, Abra came.'

Maybe—yes. He might qualify as a modern Cayley Drummle."

"At any rate, he gave us, in Doctor Lindquist, a possible source of information."

"Quite so," agreed Vance. "And that's about the only point of his whole passionate unfoldment that I particularly put any stock in, because it was the only point he indicated with any decent reticence. . . . My advice is that you interview this Æsculapius of the fair sex without further delay."

"I'm dog-tired," objected Markham. "Let it wait till to-morrow."

Vance glanced at the great clock over the stone mantel.

"It's latish, I'll admit, but why not, as Pittacus advised, seize time by the forelock?

> 'Who lets slip fortune, her shall never find:
> Occasion once past by, is bald behind.'

A Paramount Picture.   REPORTERS SWARMED TO THE SCENE OF THE MURDER.   The Canary Murder Case.

But the elder Cato anticipated Cowley. In his 'Disticha de Moribus' he wrote: *Fronte capillata*——"

"Come!" pleaded Markham, rising. "Anything to dam this flow of erudition."

CHAPTER XI

(Tuesday, September 11; 9 p. m.)

Ten minutes later we were ringing the bell of a stately old brownstone house in East 44th Street.

A resplendently caparisoned butler opened the door, and Markham presented his card.

"Take this to the doctor at once, and say that it's urgent."

"The doctor is just finishing dinner," the stately seneschal informed him; and conducted us into a richly furnished reception-room, with deep comfortable chairs, silken draperies, and subdued lights.

"A typical gynecologist's seraglio," observed Vance, looking around. "I'm sure the pasha himself is a majestic and elegant personage."

The prediction proved true. Doctor Lindquist entered the room a moment later inspecting the District Attorney's card as if it had been a cuneiform inscription whose import he could not quite decipher. He was a tall man in his late forties, with bushy hair and eyebrows, and a complexion abnormally pale. His face was long, and, despite the asymmetry of his features, he might easily have been called handsome. He was in dinner clothes, and he carried himself with the self-conscious precision of a man unduly impressed with his own importance. He seated him-

114

self at a kidney-shaped desk of carved mahogany, and lifted his eyes with polite inquiry to Markham.

"To what am I indebted for the honor of this call?" he asked in a studiously melodious voice, lingering over each word caressingly. "You are most fortunate to have found me in," he added, before Markham could speak. "I confer with patients only by appointment." One felt that he experienced a certain humiliation at having received us without elaborate ceremonial preliminaries.

Markham, whose nature was opposed to all circumlocution and pretense, came direct to the point.

"This isn't a professional consultation, doctor; but it happens that I want to speak to you about one of your former patients—a Miss Margaret Odell."

Doctor Lindquist regarded the gold paper weight before him with vacantly reminiscent eyes.

"Ah, yes. Miss Odell. I was just reading of her violent end. A most unfortunate and tragic affair. . . . In just what way can I be of service to you? You understand, of course, that the relationship between a physician and his patient is one of sacred confidence——"

"I understand that thoroughly," Markham assured him abruptly. "On the other hand, it is the sacred duty of every citizen to assist the authorities in bringing a murderer to justice. And if there is anything you can tell me which will help toward that end, I shall certainly expect you to tell me."

The doctor raised his hand slightly in polite protestation.

"I shall, of course, do all I can to assist you, if you will but indicate your desires."

"There's no need to beat about the bush, doctor," said Markham. "I know that Miss Odell was a patient of yours for a long time; and I realize that it is highly possible, not to say probable, that she told you certain personal things which may have direct bearing on her death."

"But, my dear Mr. —"—Doctor Lindquist glanced ostentatiously at the card—"ah—Markham, my relations with Miss Odell were of a purely professional character."

"I had understood, however," ventured Markham, "that, while what you say may be technically true, nevertheless there was an informality, let me say, in that relationship. Perhaps I may state it better by saying that your professional attitude transcended a merely scientific interest in her case."

I heard Vance chuckle softly; and I myself could hardly suppress a smile at Markham's verbose and orbicular accusation. But Doctor Lindquist, it seemed, was in no wise disconcerted. Assuming an air of beguiling pensiveness, he said:

"I will confess, in the interests of strict accuracy, that during my somewhat protracted treatment of her case, I came to regard the young woman with a certain—shall I say, fatherly liking? But I doubt if she was even aware of this mild sentiment on my part."

The corners of Vance's mouth twitched slightly. He was sitting with drowsy eyes, watching the doctor with a look of studious amusement.

"And she never at any time told you of any private or personal affairs that were causing her anxiety?" persisted Markham.

Doctor Lindquist pyramided his fingers, and appeared to give the question his undivided thought. "No, I can't recall a single statement of that nature." His words were measured and urbane. "I know, naturally, in a general way, her manner of living; but the details, you will readily perceive, were wholly outside my province as a medical consultant. The disorganization of her nerves was due— so my diagnosis led me to conclude—to late hours, excitement, irregular and rich eating—what, I believe, is referred to vulgarly as going the pace. The modern woman, in this febrile age, sir——"

"When did you see her last, may I ask?" Markham interrupted impatiently.

The doctor made a pantomime of eloquent surprise.

"When did I see her last? . . . Let me see." He could, apparently, recall the occasion only with considerable difficulty. "A fortnight ago, perhaps— though it may have been longer. I really can't recall. . . . Shall I refer to my files?"

"That won't be necessary," said Markham. He paused, and regarded the doctor with a look of disarming affability. "And was this last visit a paternal or merely a professional one?"

"Professional, of course." Doctor Lindquist's eyes were impassive and only mildly interested; but his face, I felt, was by no means the unedited reflection of his thoughts.

"Did the meeting take place here or at her apartment?"

"I believe I called on her at her home."

"You called on her a great deal, doctor—so I am informed—and at rather unconventional hours. . . .

Is this entirely in accord with your practice of seeing
patients only by appointment?"

Markham's tone was pleasant, but from the nature
of his question I knew that he was decidedly irritated
by the man's bland hypocrisy, and felt that he was
deliberatly withholding relevant information.

Before Doctor Lindquist could reply, however, the
butler appeared at the door, and silently indicated
an extension telephone on a taboret beside the desk.
With an unctuously murmured apology, the doctor
turned and lifted the receiver.

Vance took advantage of this opportunity to
scribble something on a piece of paper and pass it
surreptitiously to Markham.

His call completed, Doctor Lindquist drew himself
up haughtily, and faced Markham with chilling scorn.

"Is it the function of the District Attorney," he
asked distantly, "to harass respectable physicians
with insulting questions? I did not know that it was
illegal—or even original, for that matter—for a doctor
to visit his patients."

"I am not discussing *now*"—Markham emphasized
the adverb—"your infractions of the law; but since
you suggest a possibility which, I assure you, was
not in my mind, would you be good enough to tell
me—merely as a matter of form—where you were
last night between eleven and twelve?"

The question produced a startling effect. Doctor
Lindquist became suddenly like a tautly drawn rope,
and, rising slowly and stiffly, he glared, with cold in-
tense venom, at the District Attorney. His velvety
mask had fallen off; and I detected another emotion
beneath his repressed anger: his expression cloaked

a fear, and his wrath but partly veiled a passionate uncertainty.

"My whereabouts last night is no concern of yours." He spoke with great effort, his breath coming and going noisily.

Markham waited, apparently unmoved, his eyes riveted on the trembling man before him. This calm scrutiny completely broken down the other's self-control.

"What do you mean by forcing yourself in here with your contemptible insinuations?" he shouted. His face, now livid and mottled, was hideously contorted; his hands made spasmodic movements; and his whole body shook as with a tremor. "Get out of here—you and your two myrmidons! Get out, before I have you thrown out!"

Markham, himself enraged now, was about to reply, when Vance took him by the arm.

"The doctor is gently hinting that we go," he said. And with amazing swiftness he spun Markham round, and led him firmly out of the room.

When we were again in the taxicab on our way back to the club, Vance sniggered gaily.

"A sweet specimen, that! Paranoia. Or, more likely, manic-depressive insanity—the *folie circulaire* type: recurring periods of maniacal excitement alternating with periods of the clearest sanity, don't y' know. Anyway, the doctor's disorder belongs in the category of psychoses—associated with the maturation or waning of the sexual instinct. He's just the right age, too. Neurotic degenerate—that's what this oily Hippocrates is. In another minute he would have attacked you. . . . My word! It's a good thing I came to the rescue. Such chaps are about as safe as rattlesnakes."

He shook his head in a mock discouragement.

"Really, y' know, Markham, old thing," he added, "you should study the cranial indications of your fellow man more carefully—*vultus est index animi.* Did you, by any chance, note the gentleman's wide rectangular forehead, his irregular eyebrows, and pale luminous eyes, and his outstanding ears with their thin upper rims, their pointed tragi and split lobes? . . . A clever devil, this Ambroise—but a moral imbecile. Beware of those pseudo-pyriform faces, Markham; leave their Apollonian Greek suggestiveness to misunderstood women."

"I wonder what he really knows?" grumbled Markham irritably.

"Oh, he knows something—rest assured of that! And if only we knew it, too, we'd be considerably further along in the investigation. Furthermore, the information he is hiding is somewhat unpleasantly connected with himself. His euphoria is a bit shaken. He frightfully overdid the grand manner; his valedict'ry fulmination was the true expression of his feeling toward us."

"Yes," agreed Markham. "That question about last night acted like a petard. What prompted you to suggest my asking it?"

"A number of things—his gratuitous and obviously mendacious statement that he had just read of the murder; his wholly insincere homily on the sacredness of professional confidences; the cautious and Pecksniffian confession of his fatherly regard for the girl; his elaborate struggle to remember when he had last seen her—this particularly, I think, made me suspicious; and then, the psychopathic indicants of his physiognomy."

"Well," admitted Markham, "the question had its effect. . . . I feel that I shall see this fashionable M.D. again."

"You will," iterated Vance. "We took him unawares. But when he has had time to ponder the matter and concoct an appealin' tale, he'll become downright garrulous. . . . Anyhow, the evening is over, and you can meditate on buttercups till the morrow."

But the evening was not quite over as far as the Odell case was concerned. We had been back in the lounge-room of the club but a short time when a man walked by the corner in which we sat, and bowed with formal courtesy to Markham. Markham, to my surprise, rose and greeted him, at the same time indicating a chair.

"There's something further I wanted to ask you, Mr. Spotswoode," he said, "if you can spare a moment."

At the mention of the name I regarded the man closely, for, I confess, I was not a little curious about the anonymous escort who had taken the girl to dinner and the theatre the night before. Spotswoode was a typical New England aristocrat, inflexible, slow in his movements, reserved, and quietly but modishly dressed. His hair and moustache were slightly gray—which, no doubt, enhanced the pinkness of his complexion. He was just under six feet tall, and well proportioned, but a trifle angular.

Markham introduced him to Vance and me, and briefly explained that we were working with him on

the case, and that he had thought it best to take us
fully into his confidence.

Spotswoode gave him a dubious look, but immediately bowed his acceptance of the decision.

"I'm in your hands, Mr. Markham," he replied,
in a well-bred but somewhat high-pitched voice,
"and I concur, of course, with whatever you think
advisable." He turned to Vance with an apologetic
smile. "I'm in a rather unpleasant position, and
naturally feel a little sensitive about it."

"I'm something of an antinomian," Vance pleasantly informed him. "At any rate, I'm not a moralist; so my attitude in the matter is quite academic."

Spotswoode laughed softly.

"I wish my family held a similar point of view;
but I'm afraid they would not be so tolerant of my
foibles."

"It's only fair to tell you, Mr. Spotswoode," interposed Markham, "that there is a bare possibility I
may have to call you as a witness."

The man looked up quickly, his face clouding
over, but he made no comment.

"The fact is," continued Markham, "we are about
to make an arrest, and your testimony may be
needed to establish the time of Miss Odell's return to
her apartment, and also to substantiate the fact
that there was presumably some one in her rooms
after you had left. Her screams and calls for help,
which you heard, may prove vital evidence in obtaining a conviction."

Spotswoode seemed rather appalled at the thought
of his relations with the girl becoming public, and
for several minutes he sat with averted eyes.

"I see your point," he acknowledged at length. "But it would be a terrible thing for me if the fact of my delinquencies became known."

"That contingency may be entirely avoided," Markham encouraged him. "I promise you that you will not be called upon unless it is absolutely necessary. . . . And now, what I especially wanted to ask you is this: do you happen to know a Doctor Lindquist who, I understand, was Miss Odell's personal physician?"

Spotswoode was frankly puzzled. "I never heard the name," he answered. "In fact, Miss Odell never mentioned any doctor to me."

"And did you ever hear her mention the name of Skeel . . . or refer to any one as Tony?"

"Never." His answer was emphatic.

Markham lapsed into a disappointed silence. Spotswoode, too, was silent: he sat as if in a revery.

"You know, Mr. Markham," he said, after several minutes, "I ought to be ashamed to admit it, but the truth is I cared a good deal for the girl. I suppose you've kept her apartment intact. . . ." He hesitated, and a look almost of appeal came into his eyes. "I'd like to see it again if I could."

Markham regarded him sympathetically, but finally shook his head.

"It wouldn't do. You'd be sure to be recognized by the operator—or there might be a reporter about—and then I'd be unable to keep you out of the case."

The man appeared disappointed, but did not protest; and for several minutes no one spoke. Then Vance raised himself slightly in his chair.

"I say, Mr. Spotswoode, do you happen to remember anything unusual occurring last night during the half-hour you remained with Miss Odell after the theatre?"

"Unusual?" The man's manner was eloquent of his astonishment. "To the contrary. We chatted a while, and then, as she seemed tired, I said good night and came away, making a luncheon appointment with her for to-day."

"And yet, it now seems fairly certain that some other man was hiding in the apartment when you were there."

"There's little doubt on that point," agreed Spotswoode, with the suggestion of a shudder. "And her screams would seem to indicate that he came forth from hiding a few minutes after I went."

"And you had no suspicion of the fact when you heard her call for help?"

"I did at first—naturally. But when she assured me that nothing was the matter, and told me to go home, I attributed her screams to a nightmare. I knew she had been tired, and I had left her in the wicker chair near the door, from where her screams seemed to come; so I naturally concluded she had dozed off and called out in her sleep. . . . If only I hadn't taken so much for granted!"

"It's a harrowin' situation." Vance was silent for a while; then he asked: "Did you, by any chance, notice the door of the living-room closet? Was it open or closed?"

Spotswoode frowned, as if attempting to visualize the picture; but the result was a failure.

"I suppose it was closed. I probably would have noticed it if it had been open."

"Then you couldn't say if the key was in the lock or not?"

"Good Lord, no! I don't even know if it ever had a key."

The case was discussed for another half-hour; then Spotswoode excused himself and left us.

"Funny thing," ruminated Markham, "how a man of his upbringing could be so attracted by the empty-headed, butterfly type."

"I'd say it was quite natural," returned Vance. . . . "You're such an incorrigible moralist, Markham."

CHAPTER XII

CIRCUMSTANTIAL EVIDENCE

(*Wednesday, September 12; 9 a. m.*)

The following day, which was Wednesday, not only brought forth an important and, as it appeared, conclusive development in the Odell case, but marked the beginning of Vance's active co-operation in the proceedings. The psychological elements in the case had appealed to him irresistibly, and he felt, even at this stage of the investigation, that a final answer could never be obtained along the usual police lines. At his request Markham had called for him at a little before nine o'clock, and we had driven direct to the District Attorney's office.

Heath was waiting impatiently when we arrived. His eager and covertly triumphant expression plainly indicated good news.

"Things are breaking find and dandy," he announced, when we had sat down. He himself was too elated to relax, and stood before Markham's desk rolling a large black cigar between his fingers. "We got the Dude—six o'clock yesterday evening—and we got him right. One of the C. O. boys, named Riley, who was patrolling Sixth Avenue in the Thirties, saw him swing off a surface car and head for McAnerny's Pawn-Shop. Right away Riley wigwags the traffic officer on the corner, and follows the Dude into McAnerny's. Pretty soon the traffic officer comes in with a patrolman, who he's picked up; and the three of 'em nab our stylish friend in the act of pawning this ring."

He tossed a square solitaire diamond in a filigreed platinum setting on the District Attorney's desk.

"I was at the office when they brought him in, and I sent Snitkin with the ring up to Harlem to see what the maid had to say about it, and she identified it as belonging to Odell."

"But, I say, it wasn't a part of the *bijouterie* the lady was wearing that night, was it, Sergeant?" Vance put the question casually.

Heath jerked about and eyed him with sullen calculation.

"What if it wasn't? It came out of that jimmied jewel-case—or I'm Ben Hur."

"Of course it did," murmured Vance, lapsing into lethargy.

"And that's where we're in luck," declared Heath, turning back to Markham. "It connects Skeel directly with the murder and the robbery."

"What has Skeel to say about it?" Markham was leaning forward intently. "I suppose you questioned him."

"I'll say we did," replied the Sergeant; but his tone was troubled. "We had him up all night giving him the works. And the story he tells is this: he says the girl gave him the ring a week ago, and that he didn't see her again until the afternoon of day before yesterday. He came to her apartment between four and five—you remember the maid said she was out then—and entered and left the house by the side door, which was unlocked at that time. He admits he called again at half past nine that night, but he says that when he found she was out, he went straight home and stayed there. His alibi is that he sat up with his landlady till after midnight playing Khun Khan and drinking beer. I hopped up to his place this morning, and the old girl verified it. But that don't mean anything. The house he lives in is a pretty tough hang-out, and this landlady, besides being a heavy boozer, has been up the river a coupla times for shoplifting."

"What does Skeel say about the finger-prints?"

"He says, of course, he made 'em when he was there in the afternoon."

"And the one on the closet door-knob?"

Heath gave a derisive grunt.

"He's got an answer for that, too—says he thought he heard some one coming in, and locked himself in the clothes-closet. Didn't want to be seen and spoil any game Odell mighta been playing."

"Most considerate of him to keep out of the way of the *belles poires*," drawled Vance. "Touchin' loyalty, what?"

"You don't believe the rat, do you, Mr. Vance?" asked Heath, with indignant surprise.

"Can't say that I do. But our Antonio at least spins a consistent yarn."

"Too damn consistent to suit me," growled the Sergeant.

"That's all you could get out of him?" It was plain that Markham was not pleased with the results of Heath's third degree of Skeel.

"That's about all, sir. He stuck to his story like a leech."

"You found no chisel in his room?"

Heath admitted that he hadn't.

"But you couldn't expect him to keep it around," he added.

Markham pondered the facts for several minutes.

"I can't see that we've got a very good case, however much we may be convinced of Skeel's guilt. His alibi may be thin, but taken in connection with the phone operator's testimony, I'm inclined to think it would hold tight in court."

"What about the ring, sir?" Heath was desperately disappointed. "And what about his threats, and his finger-prints, and his record of similar burglaries?"

"Contributory factors only," Markham explained. "What we need for a murder is more than a *prima facie* case. A good criminal lawyer could have him discharged in twenty minutes, even if I could secure an indictment. It's not impossible, you know, that the woman gave him the ring a week ago—you recall that the maid said he was demanding money from her about that time. And there's nothing to show that the finger-prints were not actually made late Monday afternoon. Moreover, we can't connect him in any way with the chisel, for we don't know who did the Park Avenue job last summer. His whole story fits the facts perfectly; and we haven't anything contradictory to offer."

Heath shrugged helplessly: all the wind had been taken out of his sails.

"What do you want done with him?" he asked desolately.

Markham considered—he, too, was discomfited.

"Before I answer I think I'll have a go at him myself."

He pressed a buzzer, and ordered a clerk to fill out the necessary requisition. When it had been signed in duplicate, he sent Swacker with it to Ben Hanlon.

"Do ask him about those silk shirts," suggested Vance. "And find out, if you can, if he considers a white waistcoat *de rigueur* with a dinner-jacket."

"This office isn't a male millinery shop," snapped Markham.

"But, Markham dear, you won't learn anything else from this Petronius "

Ten minutes later a Deputy Sheriff from the Tombs entered with his handcuffed prisoner.

Skeel's appearance that morning belied his sobriquet of Dude. He was haggard and pale: his ordeal of the previous night had left its imprint upon him. He was unshaven; his hair was uncombed; the ends of his moustache drooped; and his cravat was awry. But despite his bedraggled condition, his manner was jaunty and contemptuous. He gave Heath a defiant leer, and faced the District Attorney with swaggering indifference.

To Markham's questions he doggedly repeated the same story he had told Heath. He clung tenaciously to every detail of it with the ready accuracy of a man who had painstakingly memorized a lesson and was thoroughly familiar with it. Markham coaxed, threatened, bullied. All hint of his usual affability was gone: he was like an inexorable dynamic machine. But Skeel, whose nerves seemed to be made of iron, withstood the vicious fire of his cross-questioning without wincing; and, I confess, his resistance somewhat aroused my admiration despite my revulsion toward him and all he stood for.

After half an hour Markham gave up, completely baffled in his efforts to elicit any damaging admissions from the man. He was about to dismiss him when Vance rose languidly and strolled to the District Attorney's desk. Seating himself on the edge of it, he regarded Skeel with impersonal curiosity.

"So you're a devotee of Khun Khan, eh?" he remarked indifferently. "Silly game, what? More interestin' than Conquain or Rum, though. Used to be played in the London clubs. Of East Indian origin, I believe. . . . You still play it with two decks, I suppose, and permit round-the-corner mating?"

An involuntary frown gathered on Skeel's forehead. He was used to violent district attorneys, and familiar with the bludgeoning methods of the police, but here was a type of inquisitor entirely new to him; and it was plain that he was both puzzled and apprehensive. He decided to meet this novel antagonist with a smirk of arrogant amusement.

"By the bye," continued Vance, with no change in tone, "can any one hidden in the clothes-press of the Odell living-room see the davenport through the key-hole?"

Suddenly all trace of a smile was erased from the man's features.

"And I say," Vance hurried on, his eyes fixed steadily on the other, "why didn't you give the alarm?"

I was watching Skeel closely, and, though his set expression did not alter, I saw the pupils of his eyes

dilate. Markham, also, I think, noted this phe-
nomenon.

"Don't bother to answer," pursued Vance, as
the man opened his lips to speak. "But tell me:
didn't the sight shake you up a bit?"

"I don't know what you're talking about,"
Skeel retorted with sullen impertinence. But,
for all his sang-froid, one sensed an uneasiness in
his manner. There was an overtone of effort in
his desire to appear indifferent, which robbed his
words of complete conviction.

"Not a pleasant situation, that." Vance ignored his retort. "How did you feel, crouching
there in the dark, when the closet door-knob was
turned and some one tried to get in?" His eyes
were boring into the man.

The muscles of Skeel's face tightened, but he
did not speak.

"Lucky thing you took the precaution of lock-
ing yourself in—eh, what?" Vance went on.
"Suppose he'd got the door open—my word!
Then what? . . ."

He paused and smiled with a kind of silky
sweetness more impressive than glowering.

"I say, did you have your steel chisel ready for
him? Maybe he'd have been too quick and strong
for you—maybe there would have been thumbs
pressing against your larynx too before you could
have struck him—eh? . . . Did you think of that,
there in the dark? . . . No, not precisely a pleasant situation. A bit gruesome, in fact."

"What are you raving about?" Skeel spat out
insolently. "You're balmy." But his swagger had

been forgotten, and a look akin of horror had passed across his face. This slackening of pose was momentary, however; almost at once his smirk returned, and his head swayed in contempt.

Vance sauntered back to his chair and stretched himself in it listlessly, as if all his interest in the case had again evaporated.

Markham had watched the little drama attentively, but Heath had sat smoking with ill-concealed annoyance. The silence that followed was broken by Skeel.

"Well, I suppose I'm to be railroaded. Got it all planned, have you? . . . Try and railroad me!" He laughed harshly. "My lawyer's Abe Rubin, and you might phone him that I'd like to see him."*

Markham, with a gesture of annoyance, waved the Deputy Sheriff to take Skeel to the Tombs.

"What were you trying to get at?" he asked Vance, when the man was gone.

"Just an elusive notion in the depths of my being struggling for the light." Vance smoked placidly a moment. "I thought Mr. Skeel might be persuaded to pour out his heart to us. So I wooed him with words."

"That's bully," gibed Heath. "I was expecting you any minute to ask if he played mumbly-peg or if his grandmother was a hoot-owl."

"Sergeant, dear Sergeant," pleaded Vance, "don't be unkind. I simply couldn't endure it. . . . And really, now, didn't my chat with Mr. Skeel suggest a possibility to you?"

* Abe Rubin was at that time the most resourceful and unscrupulous criminal lawyer in New York. Since his disbarment two years ago, little has been heard from him.

"Sure," said Heath, "—that he was hiding in the closet when Odell was killed. But where does that get us? It lets Skeel out, although the job was a professional one, and he was caught red-handed with some of the swag."

He turned disgustedly to the District Attorney.

"And now what, sir?"

"I don't like the look of things," Markham complained. "If Skeel has Abe Rubin to defend him, we won't stand a chance with the case we've got. I feel convinced he was mixed up in it; but no judge will accept my personal feelings as evidence."

"We could turn the Dude loose, and have him tailed," suggested Heath grudgingly. "We might catch him doing something that'll give the game away."

Markham considered.

"That might be a good plan," he acceded. "We'll certainly get no more evidence on him as long as he's locked up."

"It looks like our only chance, sir."

"Very well," agreed Markham. "Let him think we're through with him: he may get careless. I'll leave the whole thing to you, Sergeant. Keep a couple of good men on him day and night. Something may happen."

Heath rose, an unhappy man.

"Right, sir. I'll attend to it."

"And I'd like to have more data on Charles Cleaver," added Markham. "Find out what you can of his relations with the Odell girl.—Also, get me a line on Doctor Ambroise Lindquist. What's his history?—what are his habits?—you know the kind of thing. He treated the girl for some mysterious or imaginary ailment; and I think he has something up his sleeve. But don't go near him personally—yet."

Heath jotted the name down in his note-book, without enthusiasm.

"And before you set your stylish captive free," put in Vance, yawning, "you might, don't y' know, see if he carries a key that fits the Odell apartment."

Heath jerked up short, and grinned.

"Now, that idea's got some sense to it. . . . Funny I didn't think of it myself." And shaking hands with all of us, he went out.

CHAPTER XIII

(Wednesday, September 12; 10.30 a. m.)

Swacker was evidently waiting for an opportunity
to interrupt, for, when Sergeant Heath had passed
through the door, he at once stepped into the room.
"The reporters are here, sir," he announced, with
a wry face. "You said you'd see them at ten-thirty."

In response to a nod from his Chief, he held open
the door, and a dozen or more newspaper men came
trooping in.

"No questions, please, this morning," Markham
begged pleasantly. "It's too early in the game. But
I'll tell you all I know. . . . I agree with Sergeant
Heath that the Odell murder was the work of a professional criminal—the same who broke into Arn-
heim's house on Park Avenue last summer."

Briefly he told of Inspector Brenner's findings in
connection with the chisel.

"We've made no arrests, but one may be expected
in the very near future. In fact, the police have the
case well in hand, but are going carefully in order to
avoid any chance of an acquittal. We've already
recovered some of the missing jewellery. . . ."

He talked to the reporters for five minutes or so,
but he made no mention of the testimony of the maid
or the phone operators, and carefully avoided the
mention of any names.

When we were again alone, Vance chuckled admiringly.

"A masterly evasion, my dear Markham! Legal training has its advantages—decidedly it has its advantages. . . . 'We've recovered some of the missing jewellery!' Sweet wingèd words! Not an untruth—oh, no!—but how deceivin'! Really, y' know, I must devote more time to the caressin' art of *suggestio falsi* and *suppressio veri*. You should be crowned with an anadem of myrtle."

"Leaving all that to one side," Markham rejoined impatiently, "suppose you tell me, now that Heath's gone, what was in your mind when you applied your verbal voodooism to Skeel. What was all the conjurer-talk about dark closets, and alarums, and pressing thumbs, and peering through keyholes?"

"Well, now, I didn't think my little chit-chat was so cryptic," answered Vance. "The *recherché* Tony was undoubtedly ambuscaded *à la sourdine* in the clothes-press at some time during the fatal evening; and I was merely striving, in my amateurish way, to ascertain the exact hour of his concealment."

"And did you?"

"Not conclusively." Vance shook his head sadly. "Y' know, Markham, I'm the proud possessor of a theory—it's vague and obscure and unsubstantial; and it's downright unintelligible. And even if it were verified, I can't see how it would help us any, for it would leave the situation even more incomprehensible than it already is. . . . I almost wish I hadn't questioned Heath's Beau Nash. He upset my ideas frightfully."

"From what I could gather, you seem to think it

possible that Skeel witnessed the murder. That couldn't, by any stretch of the imagination, be your precious theory?"

"That's part of it, anyway."

"My dear Vance, you do astonish me!" Markham laughed outright. "Skeel, then, according to you, is innocent; but he keeps his knowledge to himself, invents an alibi, and doesn't even tattle when he's arrested. . . . It won't hold water."

"I know," sighed Vance. "It's a veritable sieve. And yet, the notion haunts me—it rides me like a hag—it eats into my vitals."

"Do you realize that this mad theory of yours presupposes that, when Spotswoode and Miss Odell returned from the theatre, there were *two* men hidden in the apartment—two men *unknown to each other*—namely Skeel and your hypothetical murderer?"

"Of course I realize it; and the thought of it is breaking down my reason."

"Furthermore, they must have entered the apartment separately, and hidden separately. . . . How, may I ask, did they get in? And how did they get out? And which one caused the girl to scream after Spotswoode had left? And what was the other one doing in the meantime? And if Skeel was a passive spectator, horrified and mute, how do you account for his breaking open the jewel-case and securing the ring——?"

"Stop! Stop! Don't torture me so," Vance pleaded. "I know I'm insane. Been given to hallucinations since birth; but—Merciful Heaven!—I've never before had one as crazy as this."

"On that point at least, my dear Vance, we are

in complete and harmonious agreement," smiled Markham.

Just then Swacker came in and handed Markham a letter.

"Brougnt by messenger, and marked 'immediate,'" he explained.

The letter, written on heavy engraved stationery, was from Doctor Lindquist, and explained that between the hours of 11 P. M. and 1 A. M. on Monday night he had been in attendance on a patient at his sanitarium. It also apologized for his actions when asked regarding his whereabouts, and offered a wordy, but not particularly convincing, explanation of his conduct. He had had an unusually trying day, it scemed—neurotic cases were trying, at best—and the suddenness of our visit, together with the apparently hostile nature of Markham's questions, had completely upset him. He was more than sorry for his outburst, he said, and stood ready to assist in any way he could. It was unfortunate for all concerned, he added, that he had lost his temper, for it would have been a simple matter for him to explain about Monday night.

"He has thought the situation over calmly," said Vance, "and hereby offers you a neat little alibi which, I think, you will have difficulty in shaking. . . . An artful beggar—like all these unbalanced pseudo-psychiatrists. Observe: he was with a patient. To be sure! What patient? Why, one too ill to be questioned. . . . There you are. A *cul-de-sac* masquerading as an alibi. Not bad, what?"

"It doesn't interest me overmuch." Markham put the letter away. "That pompous professional ass could never have got into the Odell apartment without having been seen; and I can't picture him sneaking in by devious means." He reached for some papers. . . . "And now, if you don't object, I'll make an effort to earn my $15,000 salary."

But Vance, instead of making a move to go, sauntered to the table and opened a telephone directory.

"Permit me a suggestion, Markham," he said, after a moment's search. "Put off your daily grind for a bit, and let's hold polite converse with Mr. Louis Mannix. Y' know, he's the only presumptive swain of the inconstant Margaret, so far mentioned, who hasn't been given an audience. I hanker to gaze upon him and hearken to his rune. He'd make the family circle complete, so to speak. . . . He still holds forth in Maiden Lane, I see; and it wouldn't take long to fetch him here."

Markham had swung half round in his chair at the mention of Mannix's name. He started to protest, but he knew from experience that Vance's suggestions were not the results of idle whims; and he was silent for several moments weighing the matter. With practically every other avenue of inquiry closed for the moment, I think the idea of questioning Mannix rather appealed to him.

"All right," he consented, ringing for Swacker; "though I don't see how he can help. According to Heath, the Odell girl gave him his *congé* a year ago."

"He may still have hay on his horns, or, like Hotspur, be drunk with choler. You can't tell." Vance resumed his chair. "With such a name, he'd bear investigation *ipso facto*."

Markham sent Swacker for Tracy; and when the

latter arrived, suave and beaming, he was given
instructions to take the District Attorney's car
and bring Mannix to the office.

"Get a subpœna," said Markham; "and use it
if necessary."

Half an hour or so later Tracy returned.

"Mr. Mannix made no difficulty about coming," he reported. "Was quite agreeable, in fact.
He's in the waiting-room now."

Tracy was dismissed, and Mannix ushered in.

He was a large man, and walked with the
forced elasticity of gait which epitomizes the silent struggle of incipiently corpulent middle age
to deny the on-rush of the years and cling to the
semblance of youth. He carried a slender wang-
hee cane; and his checkered suit, brocaded waistcoat, pearl-gray gaiters, and beribboned Hom-
burg hat gave him an almost foppish appearance. But these various indications of sportive-
ness were forgotten when one inspected his
features. His small eyes were bright and
crafty; his nose bibative, and appeared dispro-
portionately small above his sensual lips and
prognathous jaw. There was an oiliness in his
manner which was repulsive and arresting.

At a gesture from Markham he sat down on
the edge of a chair, placing a podgy hand on each
knee. His attitude was one of alert suspicion.

"Mr. Mannix," said Markham, an engaging note
of apology in his voice, "I am sorry to have discom-
moded you; but the matter in hand is both serious
and urgent. . . . A Miss Margaret Odell was
murdered night before last, and in the course of our

inquiries we learned that you had at one time known her quite well. It occurred to me that you might be in possession of some facts about her that would assist us in our investigation."

A saponaceous smile, meant to be genial, parted the man's heavy lips.

"Sure, I knew the Canary—a long time ago, y' understand." He permitted himself a sigh. "A fine, high-class girl, if I do say so. A good looker and a good dresser. Too damn bad she didn't go on with the show business. But"—he made a repudiative motion with his hand—"I haven't seen the lady, y' understand, for over a year—not to speak to, if you know what I mean."

Mannix clearly was on his guard, and his beady little eyes did not once leave the District Attorney's face.

"You had a quarrel with her perhaps?" Markham asked the question incuriously.

"Well, now, I wouldn't go so far as to say we quarrelled. No." Mannix paused, seeking the correct word. "You might say we disagreed—got tired of the arrangement and decided to separate; kind of drifted apart. Last thing I told her was, if she ever needed a friend she'd know where to find me."

"Very generous of you," murmured Markham. "And you never renewed your little affair?"

"Never—never. Don't remember ever speaking to her from that day to this."

"In view of certain things I've learned, Mr. Mannix"—Markham's tone was regretful—"I must ask you a somewhat personal question. Did she ever make an attempt to blackmail you?"

Mannix hesitated, and his eyes seemed to grow even smaller, like those of a man thinking rapidly.

"Certainly not!" he replied, with belated emphasis. "Not at all. Nothing of the kind." He raised both hands in protest against the thought. Then he asked furtively: "What gave you such an idea?"

"I have been told," explained Markham, "that she had extorted money from one or two of her admirers."

Mannix made a wholly unconvincing grimace of astonishment.

"Well, well! You don't tell me! Can it be possible?" He peered shrewdly at the District Attorney. "Maybe it was Charlie Cleaver she blackmailed—yes?"

Markham picked him up quickly.

"Why do you say Cleaver?"

Again Mannix waved his thick hand, this time deprecatingly.

"No special reason, y' understand. Just thought it might be him. . . . No special reason."

"Did Cleaver ever tell you he'd been blackmailed?"

"Cleaver tell me? . . . Now, I ask you, Mr. Markham: why should Cleaver tell me such a story—why should he?"

"And you never told Cleaver that the Odell girl had blackmailed you?"

"Positively not!" Mannix gave a scornful laugh which was far too theatrical to have been genuine. "Me tell Cleaver I'd been blackmailed? Now, that's funny, that is."

"Then why did you mention Cleaver a moment ago?"

"No reason at all—like I told you. . . . He knew the Canary; but that ain't no secret."

Markham dropped the subject.

"What do you know about Miss Odell's rela-tions with a Doctor Ambroise Lindquist?"

Mannix was now obviously perplexed.

"Never heard of him—no, never. She didn't know him when I was taking her around."

"Whom else besides Cleaver did she know well?"

Mannix shook his head ponderously.

"Now, that I couldn't say—positively I couldn't say. Seen her with this man and that, same as everybody saw her; but who they were I don't know—absolutely."

"Ever hear of Tony Skeel?" Markham quickly leaned over and met the other's gaze inquiringly.

Once more Mannix hesitated, and his eyes glit-tered calculatingly.

"Well, now that you ask me, I believe I did hear of the fellow. But I couldn't swear to it, y' understand. . . . What makes you think I heard of this Skeel fellow?"

"Can you think of no one who might have borne Miss Odell a grudge, or had cause to fear her?"

Mannix was volubly emphatic on the subject of his complete ignorance of any such person; and after a few more questions, which elicited only denials, Markham let him go.

"Not bad at all, Markham old thing—eh, what?" Vance seemed pleased with the conference. "Won-der why he's so coy? Not a nice person, this Man-nix. And he's so fearful lest he be informative. Again, I wonder why. He was so careful.

"He was sufficiently careful, at any rate, not to tell us anything," declared Markham gloomily.

"I shouldn't say that, don't y' know." Vance lay back and smoked placidly. "A ray of light filtered through here and there. Our fur-importing philogynist denied he'd been blackmailed—which was obviously untrue—and tried to make us believe that he and the lovely Margaret cooed like turtle-doves at parting.—Tosh! . . . And then, the mention of Cleaver. That wasn't spontaneous—dear me, no. Brother Mannix and spontaneity are as the poles apart. He had a reason for bringing Cleaver in; and I fancy that if you knew what that reason was, you'd feel like flinging roses riotously, and that sort of thing. Why Cleaver? That *secret-de-Polichinelle* explanation was a bit weak. The orbits of these two paramours cross somewhere. On that point, at least, Mannix inadvertently enlightened us. . . . Moreover, it's plain that he doesn't know our fashionable healer with the satyr ears. But, on the other hand, he's aware of the existence of Mr. Skeel, and would rather like to deny the acquaintance. . . . So—*violà l'affaire*. Plenty of information; but—my word!—what to do with it?"

"I give it up," acknowledged Markham hopelessly.

"I know: it's a sad, sad world," Vance commiserated him. "But you must face the olla podrida with a bright eye. It's time for lunch, and a fillet of sole *Marguéry* will cheer you no end."

Markham glanced at the clock, and permitted himself to be led to the Lawyers Club.

CHAPTER XIV

(Wednesday, September 12; evening)

Vance and I did not return to the District Attorney's office after lunch, for Markham had a busy afternoon before him, and nothing further was likely to transpire in connection with the Odell case until Sergeant Heath had completed his investigations of Cleaver and Doctor Lindquist. Vance had seats for Giordano's "Madame Sans-Gêne," and two o'clock found us at the Metropolitan. Though the performance was excellent, Vance was too *distrait* to enjoy it; and it was significant that, after the opera, he directed the chauffeur to the Stuyvesant Club. I knew he had a tea appointment, and that he had planned to motor to Longue Vue for dinner; and the fact that he should have dismissed these social engagements from his mind in order to be with Markham showed how intensely the problem of the murder had absorbed his interest.

It was after six o'clock when Markham came in, looking harassed and tired. No mention of the case was made during dinner, with the exception of Markham's casual remark that Heath had turned in his reports on Cleaver and Doctor Lindquist and Mannix. (It seemed that, immediately after lunch, he had telephoned to the Sergeant to add Mannix's name to the two others as a subject for inquiry.) It

146

was not until we had retired to our favorite corner of the lounge-room that the topic of the murder was brought up for discussion.

And that discussion, brief and one-sided, was the beginning of an entirely new line of investigation—a line which, in the end, led to the guilty person

Markham sank wearily into his chair. He had begun to show the strain of the last two days of fruitless worry. His eyes were a trifle heavy, and there was a grim tenacity in the lines of his mouth. Slowly and deliberately he lighted a cigar, and took several deep inhalations.

"Damn the newspapers!" he grumbled. "Why can't they let the District Attorney's office handle its business in its own way? . . . Have you seen the afternoon papers? They're all clamoring for the murderer. You'd think I had him up my sleeve."

"You forget, my dear chap," grinned Vance, "that we are living under the benign and upliftin' reign of Democritus, which confers upon every ignoramus the privilege of promiscuously criticising his betters."

Markham snorted.

"I don't complain about criticism: it's the lurid imagination of these bright young reporters that galls me. They're trying to turn this sordid crime into a spectacular Borgia melodrama, with passion running rampant, and mysterious influences at work, and all the pomp and trappings of a mediæval romance. . . . You'd think even a schoolboy could see that it was only an ordinary robbery and murder of the kind that's taking place regularly throughout the country."

Vance paused in the act of lighting a cigarette,

and his eyebrows lifted. Turning, he regarded Markham with a look of mild incredulity.

"I say! Do you really mean to tell me that your statement for the press was given out in good faith?"

Markham looked up in surprise.

"Certainly it was. . . . What do you mean by 'good faith'?"

Vance smiled indolently.

"I rather thought, don't y' know, that your oration to the reporters was a bit of strategy to lull the real culprit into a state of false security, and to give you a clear field for investigation."

Markham contemplated him a moment.

"See here, Vance," he demanded irritably, "what are you driving at?"

"Nothing at all—really, old fellow," the other assured him affably. "I knew that Heath was deadly sincere about his belief in Skeel's guilt, but it never occurred to me, d' ye see, that you yourself actually regarded the crime as one committed by a professional burglar. I foolishly thought that you let Skeel go this morning in the hope that he would lead you somehow to the guilty person. I rather imagined you were spoofing the trusting Sergeant by pretending to fall in with his silly notion."

"Ah, I see! Still clinging to your weird theory that a brace of villains were present, hiding in separate clothes-closets, or something of the kind." Markham made no attempt to temper his sarcasm. "A sapient idea—so much more intelligent than Heath's!"

"I know it's weird. But it happens not to be any weirder than your theory of a lone yeggman."

"And for what reason, pray," persisted Markham,

with considerable warmth, "do you consider the
yeggman theory weird?"

"For the simple reason that it was not the crime
of a professional thief at all, but the wilfully deceptive
act of a particularly clever man who doubtless spent
weeks in its preparation."

Markham sank back in his chair and laughed
heartily.

"Vance, you have contributed the one ray of sunshine to an otherwise gloomy and depressing case."

Vance bowed with mock humility.

"It gives me great pleasure," was his dulcet rejoinder, "to be able to bring even a wisp of light into
so clouded a mental atmosphere."

A brief silence followed. Then Markham asked:

"Is this fascinating and picturesque conclusion of
yours regarding the highly intellectual character of
the Odell woman's murderer based on your new and
original psychological methods of [deduction?"
There was no mistaking the ridicule in his voice.

"I arrived at it," explained Vance sweetly, "by
the same processes of logic I used in determining the
guilt of Alvin Benson's murderer."

Markham smiled.

"*Touché!* . . . Don't think I'm so ungrateful as
to belittle the work you did in that case. But this
time, I fear, you've permitted your theories to lead
you hopelessly astray. The present case is what the
police call an open-and-shut affair."

"Particularly shut," amended Vance dryly. "And
both you and the police are in the distressin' situation
of waiting inactively for your suspected victim to give
the game away."

"I'll admit the situation is not all one could desire." Markham spoke morosely. "But even so, I can't see that there's any opportunity in this affair for your recondite psychological methods. The thing's too obvious—that's the trouble. What we need now is evidence, not theories. If it wasn't for the spacious and romantic imaginings of the newspaper men, public interest in the case would already have died out."

"Markham," said Vance quietly, but with unwonted seriousness, "if that's what you really believe, then you may as well drop the case now; for you're foredoomed to failure. You think it's an obvious crime. But let me tell you, it's a subtle crime, if ever there was one. And it's as clever as it is subtle. No common criminal committed it—believe me. It was done by a man of very superior intellect and astoundin' ingenuity."

Vance's assured, matter-of-fact tone had a curiously convincing quality; and Markham, restraining his impulse to scoff, assumed an air of indulgent irony.

"Tell me," he said, "by what cryptic mental process you arrived at so fantastic a conclusion."

"With pleasure." Vance took a few puffs on his cigarette, and lazily watched the smoke curl upward.*

"Y' know, Markham," he began, in his emotionless drawl, "every genuine work of art has a quality which the critics call *élan*—namely, enthusiasm and spontaneity. A copy, or imitation, lacks that dis-

---

* I sent a proof of the following paragraphs to Vance, and he edited and corrected them; so that, as they now stand, they represent his theories in practically his own words.

tinguishing characteristic; it's too perfect, too carefully done, too exact. Even enlightened scions of the law, I fancy, are aware that there is bad drawing in Botticelli and disproportions in Rubens, what? In an original, d' ye see, such flaws don't matter. But an imitator never puts 'em in: he doesn't dare—he's too intent on getting all the details correct. The imitator works with a self-consciousness and a meticulous care which the artist, in the throes of creative labor, never exhibits. And here's the point: there's no way of imitating that enthusiasm and spontaneity —that *élan*—which an original painting possesses. However closely a copy may resemble an original, there's a vast psychological difference between them. The copy breathes an air of insincerity, of ultra-perfection, of conscious effort. . . . You follow me, eh?"

"Most instructive, my dear Ruskin."

Vance meekly bowed his appreciation, and proceeded pleasantly.

"Now, let us consider the Odell murder. You and Heath are agreed that it is a commonplace, brutal, sordid, unimaginative crime. But, unlike you two bloodhounds on the trail, I have ignored its mere appearances, and have analyzed its various factors— I have looked at it psychologically, so to speak. And I have discovered that it is not a genuine and sincere crime—that is to say, an original—but only a sophisticated, self-conscious and clever imitation, done by a skilful copyist. I grant you it is correct and typical in every detail. But just there is where it fails, don't y' know. Its technic is too good, its craftsmanship too perfect. The *ensemble*, as it were, is not convincing—it lacks *élan*. Æsthetically speaking, it has all the earmarks of a *tour de force*. Vulgarly speaking, it's a fake." He paused and gave Markham an engaging smile. "I trust this somewhat oracular peroration has not bored you."

"Pray continue," urged Markham, with exaggerated politeness. His manner was jocular, but something in his tone led me to believe that he was seriously interested.

"What is true of art is true of life," Vance resumed placidly. "Every human action, d' ye see, conveys unconsciously an impression either of genuineness or of spuriousness—of sincerity or calculation. For example, two men at table eat in a similar way, handle their knives and forks in the same fashion, and apparently do the identical things. Although the sensitive spectator cannot put his finger on the points of difference, he none the less senses at once which man's breeding is genuine and instinctive and which man's is imitative and self-conscious."

He blew a wreath of smoke toward the ceiling, and settled more deeply into his chair.

"Now, Markham, just what are the universally recognized features of a sordid crime of robbery and murder? . . . Brutality, disorder, haste, ransacked drawers, cluttered desks, broken jewel-cases, rings stripped from the victim's fingers, severed pendant chains, torn clothing, tipped-over chairs, upset lamps, broken vases, twisted draperies, strewn floors, and so forth. Such are the accepted immemorial indications —eh, what? But—consider a moment, old chap. Outside of fiction and the drama, in how many crimes

do they *all* appear—all in perfect ordination, and
without a single element to contradict the general
effect? That is to say, how many actual crimes are
technically perfect in their settings? . . . None!
And why? Simply because nothing actual in this
life—nothing that is spontaneous and genuine—runs
to accepted form in every detail. The law of chance
and fallibility invariably steps in."

He made a slight indicative gesture.

"But regard this particular crime: look at it
closely. What do you find? You will perceive that
its *mise-en-scène* has been staged, and its drama enacted, down to every minute detail—like a Zola
novel. It is almost mathematically perfect. And
therein, d' ye see, lies the irresistible inference of its
having been carefully premeditated and planned. To
use an art term, it is a tickled-up crime. Therefore,
its conception was not spontaneous. . . . And yet,
don't y' know, I can't point out any specific flaw;
for its great flaw lies in its being flawless. And nothing flawless, my dear fellow, is natural or genuine."

Markham was silent for a while.

"You deny even the remote possibility of a common
thief having murdered the girl?" he asked at length;
and now there was no hint of sarcasm in his voice.

"If a common thief did it," contended Vance,
"then there's no science of psychology, there are no
philosophic truths, and there are no laws of art. If
it was a genuine crime of robbery, then, by the same
token, there is no difference whatever between an old
master and a clever technician's copy."

"You'd entirely eliminate robbery as the motive, I
take it."

"The robbery," Vance affirmed, "was only a manu-factured detail. The fact that the crime was com-mitted by a highly astute person indicates unques-tionably that there was a far more potent motive behind it. Any man capable of so ingenious and clever a piece of deception is obviously a person of education and imagination; and he most certainly would not have run the stupendous risk of killing a woman unless he had feared some overwhelming dis-aster—unless, indeed, her continuing to live would have caused him greater mental anguish, and would have put him in greater jeopardy, even than the crime itself. Between two colossal dangers, he chose the murder as the lesser."

Markham did not speak at once: he seemed lost in reflection. But presently he turned and, fixing Vance with a dubious stare, said:

"What about that chiselled jewel-box? A pro-fessional burglar's jimmy wielded by an experienced hand doesn't fit into your æsthetic hypothesis—it is, in fact, diametrically opposed to such a theory."

"I know it only too well." Vance nodded slowly. "And I've been harried and hectored by that steel chisel ever since I beheld the evidence of its work that first morning. . . . Markham, that chisel is the one genuine note in an otherwise spurious per-formance. It's as if the real artist had come along at the moment the copyist had finished his faked picture, and painted in a single small object with the hand of a master."

"But doesn't that bring us back inevitably to Skeel?"

"Skeel—ah, yes. That's the explanation, no

doubt; but not the way you conceive it. Skeel ripped the box open—I don't question that; but—deuce take it!—it's the only thing he did do: it's the only thing that was left for him to do. That's why he got only a ring which La Belle Marguerite was not wearing that night. All her other baubles—to wit, those that adorned her—had been stripped from her and were gone."

"Why are you so positive on this point?"

"The poker, man—the poker! . . . Don't you see? That amateurish assault upon the jewel-case with a cast-iron coal-prodder couldn't have been made *after* the case had been prized open—it would have had to be made *before*. And that seemingly insane attempt to break steel with cast iron was part of the stage-setting. The real culprit didn't care if he got the case open or not. He merely wanted it to look as if he had *tried* to get it open; so he used the poker and then left it lying beside the dinted box."

"I see what you mean." This point, I think, impressed Markham more strongly than any other Vance had raised; for the presence of the poker on the dressing-table had not been explained away either by Heath or Inspector Brenner. . . . "Is that the reason you questioned Skeel as if he might have been present when your other visitor was there?"

"Exactly. By the evidence of the jewel-case I knew he either was in the apartment when the bogus crime of robbery was being staged, or else had come upon the scene when it was over and the stage-director had cleared out. . . . From his reactions to my questions I rather fancy he was present."

"Hiding in the closet?"

"Yes. That would account for the closet not having been disturbed. As I see it, it wasn't ransacked, for the simple and rather grotesque reason that the elegant Skeel was locked within. How else could that one clothes-press have escaped the rifling activities of the pseudo-burglar? He wouldn't have omitted it deliberately, and he was far too thorough-going to have overlooked it accidentally.—Then there are the finger-prints on the knob. . . ."

Vance lightly tapped on the arm of his chair.

"I tell you, Markham old dear, you simply must build your conception of the crime on this hypothesis, and proceed accordingly. If you don't, each edifice you rear will come toppling about your ears."

CHAPTER XV

(Wednesday, September 12; evening)

When Vance finished speaking, there was a long silence. Markham, impressed by the other's earnestness, sat in a brown study. His ideas had been shaken. The theory of Skeel's guilt, to which he had clung from the moment of the identification of the finger-prints, had, it must be admitted, not entirely satisfied him, although he had been able to suggest no alternative. Now Vance had categorically repudiated this theory and at the same time had advanced another which, despite its indefiniteness, had nevertheless taken into account all the physical points of the case; and Markham, at first antagonistic, had found himself, almost against his will, becoming more and more sympathetic to this new point of view.

"Damn it, Vance!" he said. "I'm not in the least convinced by your theatrical theory. And yet, I feel a curious undercurrent of plausibility in your analyses. . . . I wonder——"

He turned sharply, and scrutinized the other steadfastly for a moment.

"Look here! Have you any one in mind as the protagonist of the drama you've outlined?"

"'Pon my word, I haven't the slightest notion as

to who killed the lady," Vance assured him. "But if you are ever to find the murderer, you must look for a shrewd, superior man with nerves of iron, who was in imminent danger of being irremediably ruined by the girl—a man of inherent cruelty and vindictiveness; a supreme egoist; a fatalist more or less; and—I'm inclined to believe—something of a madman."

"Mad!"

"Oh, not a lunatic—just a madman, a perfectly normal, logical, calculating madman—same as you and I and Van here. Only, our hobbies are harmless, d' ye see. This chap's mania is outside your preposterously revered law. That's why you're after him. If his aberration were stamp-collecting, or golf, you wouldn't give him a second thought. But his perfectly rational *penchant* for eliminating *déclassées* ladies who bothered him, fills you with horror: it's not *your* hobby. Consequently, you have a hot yearning to flay him alive."

"I'll admit," said Markham coolly, "that a homicidal mania is my idea of madness."

"But he didn't have a homicidal mania, Markham old thing. You miss all the fine distinctions in psychology. This man was annoyed by a certain person, and set to work, masterfully and reasonably, to do away with the source of his annoyance. And he did it with surpassin' cleverness. To be sure, his act was a bit grisly. But when, if ever, you get your hands on him, you'll be amazed to find how normal he is. And able, too—oh, able no end."

Again Markham lapsed into a long thoughtful silence. At last he spoke.

"The only trouble with your ingenious deductions is that they don't accord with the known circumstances of the case. And facts, my dear Vance, are still regarded by a few of us old-fashioned lawyers as more or less conclusive."

"Why this needless confession of your shortcomings?" inquired Vance whimsically. Then, after a moment: "Let me have the facts which appear to you antagonistic to my deductions."

"Well, there are only four men of the type you describe who could have had any remote reason for murdering the Odell woman. Heath's scouts went into her history pretty thoroughly, and for over two years—that is, since her appearance in the 'Follies' —the only *personæ gratæ* at her apartment have been Mannix, Doctor Lindquist, Pop Cleaver, and, of course, Spotswoode. The Canary was a bit exclusive, it seems; and no other man got near enough to her even to be considered as a possible murderer."

"It appears, then, that you have a complete quartet to draw on." Vance's tone was apathetic. "What do you crave—a regiment?"

"No," answered Markham patiently. "I crave only one logical possibility. But Mannix was through with the girl over a year ago; Cleaver and Spotswoode both have water-tight alibis; and that leaves only Doctor Lindquist, whom I can't exactly picture as a strangler and meretricious burglar, despite his irascibility. Moreover, he, too, has an alibi; and it may be a genuine one."

Vance wagged his head.

"There's something positively pathetic about the childlike faith of the legal mind."

"It does cling to rationality at times, doesn't it?" observed Markham.

"My dear fellow!" Vance rebuked him. "The presumption implied in that remark is most immodest. If you could distinguish between rationality and irrationality you wouldn't be a lawyer— you'd be a god. . . . No; you're going at this thing the wrong way. The real factors in the case are not what you call the known circumstances, but the unknown quantities—the human x's, so to speak— the personalities, or natures, of your quartet."

He lit a fresh cigarette, and lay back, closing his eyes.

"Tell me what you know of these four *cavalieri serventi*—you say Heath has turned in his report. Who were their mamas? What do they eat for breakfast? Are they susceptible to poison-ivy? . . . Let's have Spotswoode's *dossier* first. Do you know anything about him?"

"In a general way," returned Markham. "Old Puritan stock, I believe—governors, burgomasters, a few successful traders. All Yankee forebears—no intermixture. As a matter of fact, Spotswoode represents the oldest and hardiest of the New England aristocracy—although I imagine the so-called wine of the Puritans has become pretty well diluted by now. His affair with the Odell girl is hardly consonant with the older Puritans' mortification of the flesh."

"It's wholly consonant, though, with the psychological reactions which are apt to follow the inhibitions produced by such mortification," submitted Vance. "But what does he do? Whence cometh his lucre?"

"His father manufactured automobile accessories, made a fortune at it, and left the business to him. He tinkers at it, but not seriously, though I believe he has designed a few appurtenances."

"I do hope the hideous cut-glass olla for holding paper bouquets is not one of them. The man who invented that tonneau decoration is capable of any fiendish crime."

"It couldn't have been Spotswoode then," said Markham tolerantly, "for he certainly can't qualify as your potential strangler. We know the girl was alive after he left her, and that, during the time she was murdered, he was with Judge Redfern. . . . Even you, friend Vance, couldn't manipulate those facts to the gentleman's disadvantage."

"On that, at least, we agree," conceded Vance. "And that's all you know of the gentleman?"

"I think that's all, except that he married a well-to-do woman—a daughter of a Southern senator, I believe."

"Doesn't help any. . . . And now, let's have Mannix's history."

Markham referred to a typewritten sheet of paper.

"Both parents immigrants—came over in the steerage. Original name Mannikiewicz, or something like that. Born on the East Side; learned the fur business in his father's retail shop in Hester Street; worked for the Sanfrasco Cloak Company, and got to be factory foreman. Saved his money, and sweetened the pot by manipulating real estate; then went into the fur business for himself, and steadily worked up to his present opulent state. Public school, and night commercial college. Married in 1900 and divorced a year later. Lives a gay life—helps support the night clubs, but never gets drunk. I suppose he comes under the head of a spender and wine-opener. Has invested some money in musical comedies, and always has a stage beauty in tow. Runs to blondes."

"Not very revealin'," sighed Vance. "The city is full of Mannixes. . . . What did you garner in connection with our *bon-ton* medico?"

"The city has its quota of Doctor Lindquists, too, I fear. He was brought up in a small Middle-West bailiwick—French and Magyar extraction; took his M.D. from the Ohio State Medical, practised in Chicago—some shady business there, but never convicted; came to Albany and got in on the X-ray-machine craze; invented a breast-pump and formed a stock company—made a small fortune out of it; went to Vienna for two years——"

"Ah, the Freudian motif!"

"—returned to New York, and opened a private sanitarium; charged outrageous prices, and thereby endeared himself to the *nouveau riche*. Has been at the endearing process ever since. Was defendant in a breach-of-promise suit some years ago, but the case was settled out of court. He's not married."

"He wouldn't be," commented Vance. "Such gentry never are. . . . Interestin' summary, though —yes, decidedly interestin'. I'm tempted to develop a psychoneurosis and let Ambroise treat me. I do so want to know him better. And where—oh, where— was this egregious healer at the moment of our erring sister's demise? Ah, who can tell, my Markham: who knows—who knows?"

"In any event, I don't think he was murdering any one."

"You're so prejudicial!" said Vance. "But let us move reluctantly on.—What's your *portrait parlé* of Cleaver? The fact that he's familiarly called Pop is helpful as a starter. You simply couldn't imagine Beethoven being called Shorty, or Bismarck being referred to as Snookums."

"Cleaver has been a politician most of his life—a Tammany Hall 'regular.' Was a ward-boss at twenty-five; ran a Democratic club of some kind in Brooklyn for a time; was an alderman for two terms, and practised general law. Was appointed Tax Commissioner; left politics, and raised a small racing-stable. Later secured an illegal gambling concession at Saratoga; and now operates a pool-room in Jersey City. He's what you might call a professional sport. Loves his liquor."

"No marriages?"

"None on the records.—But see here: Cleaver's out of it. He was ticketed in Boonton that night at half past eleven."

"Is that, by any chance, the water-tight alibi you mentioned a moment ago?"

"In my primitive legal way I considered it as such." Markham resented Vance's question. "The summons was handed him at half past eleven: it's so marked and dated. And Boonton is fifty miles from here—a good two hours' motor ride. Therefore, Cleaver unquestionably left New York about half past nine; and even if he'd driven directly back, he couldn't have reached here until long after the time the Medical Examiner declared the girl was dead. As a matter of routine, I investigated the summons, and even spoke by phone to the officer who issued it.

It was genuine enough—I ought to know: I had it quashed."

"Did this Boonton Dogberry know Cleaver by sight?"

"No, but he gave me an accurate description of him. And naturally he took the car's number."

Vance looked at Markham with open-eyed sorrow.

"My dear Markham—my very dear Markham— can't you see that all you've actually proved is that a bucolic traffic Nemesis handed a speed-violation summons to a smooth-faced, middle-aged, stout man who was driving Cleaver's car near Boonton at half past eleven on the night of the murder? . . . And, my word! Isn't that exactly the sort of alibi the old boy would arrange if he intended taking the lady's life at midnight or thereabouts?"

"Come, come!" laughed Markham. "That's a bit too far-fetched. You'd give every law-breaker credit for concocting schemes of the most diabolical cunning."

"So I would," admitted Vance apathetically. "And—d'ye know?—I rather fancy that's just the kind of schemes a law-breaker would concoct, if he was planning a murder, and his own life was at stake. What really amazes me is the naïve assumption of you investigators that a murderer gives no intelligent thought whatever to his future safety. It's rather touchin', y' know."

Markham grunted.

"Well, you can take it from me, it was Cleaver himself who got that summons."

"I dare say you're right," Vance conceded. "I merely suggested the possibility of deception, don't y' know. The only point I really insist on is that the fascinatin' Miss Odell was killed by a man of subtle and superior mentality."

"And I, in turn," irritably rejoined Markham, "insist that the only men of that type who touched her life intimately enough to have had any reason to do it are Mannix, Cleaver, Lindquist, and Spotswoode. And I further insist that not one of them can be regarded as a promising possibility."

"I fear I must contradict you, old dear," said Vance serenely. "They're all possibilities—and one of them is guilty."

Markham glared at him derisively.

"Well, well! So the case is settled! Now, if you'll but indicate which is the guilty one, I'll arrest him at once, and return to my other duties."

"You're always in such haste," Vance lamented. "Why leap and run? The wisdom of the world's philosophers is against it. *Festina lente*, says Cæsar; or, as Rufus has it, *Festinatio tarda est*. And the Koran says quite frankly that haste is of the Devil. Shakespeare was constantly belittling speed:

'He tires betimes that spurs too fast betimes';

and

'Wisely, and slow; they stumble that run fast.'

Then there was Molière—remember 'Sganarelle'?—: '*Le trop de promptitude à l'erreur nous expose.*' Chaucer also held similar views. 'He hasteth wel,' said he, 'that wysely can abyde.' Even God's common people have embalmed the idea in numberless proverbs: 'Good and quickly seldom meet'; and 'Hasty men never want woe——'"

Markham rose with a gesture of impatience.

"Hell! I'm going home before you start a bedtime story," he growled.

The ironical aftermath of this remark was that Vance did tell a "bedtime story" that night; but he told it to me in the seclusion of his own library; and the gist of it was this:

"Heath is committed, body and soul, to a belief in Skeel's guilt; and Markham is as effectively strangled with legal red tape as the poor Canary was strangled with powerful hands. *Eheu*, Van! There's nothing left for me but to set forth to-morrow *a cappella*, like Gaboriau's Monsieur Lecoq, and see what can be done in the noble cause of justice. I shall ignore both Heath and Markham, and become as a pelican of the wilderness, an owl of the desert, a sparrow alone upon the housetop. . . . Really, y' know, I'm no avenger of society, but I do detest an unsolved problem."

CHAPTER XVI

SIGNIFICANT DISCLOSURES

(Thursday, September 13; forenoon)

Greatly to Currie's astonishment Vance gave instructions to be called at nine o'clock the following morning; and at ten o'clock we were sitting on his little roof-garden having breakfast in the mellow mid-September sunshine.

"Van," he said to me, when Currie had brought us our second cup of coffee, "however secretive a woman may be, there's always some one to whom she unburdens her soul. A confidant is an essential to the feminine temperament. It may be a mother, or a lover, or a priest, or a doctor, or, more generally, a girl chum. In the Canary's case we haven't a mother or a priest. Her lover—the elegant Skeel— was a potential enemy; and we're pretty safe in ruling out her doctor—she was too shrewd to confide in such a creature as Lindquist. The girl chum, then, remains. And to-day we seek her." He lit a cigarette and rose. "But, first, we must visit Mr. Benjamin Browne of Seventh Avenue."

Benjamin Browne was a well-known photographer of stage celebrities, with galleries in the heart of the city's theatrical district; and as we entered the reception-room of his luxurious studio later that morning my curiosity as to the object of our visit was at the breaking-point. Vance went straight to the desk,

167

behind which sat a young woman with flaming red
hair and mascaro-shaded eyes, and bowed in his
most dignified manner. Then, taking a small un-
mounted photograph from his pocket, he laid it before her.

"I am producing a musical comedy, *mademoiselle*,"
he said, "and I wish to communicate with the young
lady who left this picture of herself with me. Unfortunately I've misplaced her card; but as her
photograph bore the imprint of Browne's, I thought
you might be good enough to look in your files and
tell me who she is and where I may find her."

He slipped a five-dollar bill under the edge of the
blotter, and waited with an air of innocent expectancy.

The young woman looked at him quizzically, and
I thought I detected the hint of a smile at the corners of her artfully rouged lips. But after a moment
she took the photograph without a word and disappeared through a rear door. Ten minutes later
she returned and handed Vance the picture. On the
back of it she had written a name and address.

"The young lady is Miss Alys La Fosse, and she
lives at the Belafield Hotel." There was now no
doubt as to her smile. "You really shouldn't be so
careless with the addresses of your applicants—some
poor girl might lose an engagement." And her smile
suddenly turned into soft laughter.

"*Mademoiselle*," replied Vance, with mock seriousness, "in the future I shall be guided by your
warning." And with another dignified bow, he went
out.

"Good Lord!" he said, as we emerged into

Seventh Avenue. "Really, y' know, I should have disguised myself as an impresario, with a gold-headed cane, a derby, and a purple shirt. That young woman is thoroughly convinced that I'm contemplating an intrigue. . . . A jolly smart *tête-rouge*, that."

He turned into a florist's shop at the corner, and selecting a dozen American Beauties, addressed them to "Benjamin Browne's Receptionist."

"And now," he said, "let us stroll to the Belafield, and seek an audience with Alys."

As we walked across town Vance explained.

"That first morning, when we were inspecting the Canary's rooms, I was convinced that the murder would never be solved by the usual elephantine police methods. It was a subtle and well-planned crime, despite its obvious appearances. No routine investigation would suffice. Intimate information was needed. Therefore, when I saw this photograph of the xanthous Alys half hidden under the litter of papers on the escritoire, I reflected: 'Ah! A girl friend of the departed Margaret's. She may know just the things that are needed.' So, when the Sergeant's broad back was turned, I put the picture in my pocket. There was no other photograph about the place, and this one bore the usual sentimental inscription, 'Ever thine,' and was signed 'Alys.' I concluded, therefore, that Alys had played Anactoria to the Canary's Sappho. Of course I erased the inscription before presenting the picture to the penetrating sibyl at Browne's. . . . And here we are at the Belafield, hopin' for a bit of enlightenment."

The Belafield was a small, expensive apartment-hotel in the East Thirties, which, to judge from the guests to be seen in the Americanized Queen Anne lobby, catered to the well-off sporting set. Vance sent his card up to Miss La Fosse, and received the message that she would see him in a few minutes. The few minutes, however, developed into three-quarters of an hour, and it was nearly noon when a resplendent bell-boy came to escort us to the lady's apartment.

Nature had endowed Miss La Fosse with many of its arts, and those that Nature had omitted, Miss La Fosse herself had supplied. She was slender and blonde. Her large blue eyes were heavily lashed, but though she looked at one with a wide-eyed stare, she was unable to disguise their sophistication. Her toilet had been made with elaborate care; and as I looked at her, I could not help thinking what an excellent model she would have been for Chéret's pastel posters.

"So you are Mr. Vance," she cooed. "I've often seen your name in *Town Topics*."

Vance gave a shudder.

"And this is Mr. Van Dine," he said sweetly, "—a mere attorney, who, thus far, has been denied the pages of that fashionable weekly."

"Won't you sit down?" (I am sure Miss La Fosse had spoken the line in a play: she made of the invitation an impressive ceremonial.) "I really don't know why I should have received you. But I suppose you called on business. Perhaps you wish me to appear at a society bazaar, or something of the kind. But I'm so busy, Mr. Vance. You simply can't imagine how occupied I am with my work. . . . I just love my work," she added, with an ecstatic sigh.

"And I'm sure there are many thousands of others who love it, too," returned Vance, in his best drawing-room manner. "But unfortunately I have no bazaar to be graced by your charming presence. I have come on a much more serious matter. . . . You were a very close friend of Miss Margaret Odell's——"

The mention of the Canary's name brought Miss La Fosse suddenly to her feet. Her ingratiating air of affected elegance had quickly disappeared. Her eyes flashed, and their lids drooped harshly. A sneer distorted the lines of her cupid's-bow mouth, and she tossed her head angrily.

"Say, listen! Who do you think you are? I don't know nothing, and I got nothing to say. So run along—you and your lawyer."

But Vance made no move to obey. He took out his cigarette-case and carefully selected a *Régie*.

"Do you mind if I smoke?—And won't you have one? I import them direct from my agent in Constantinople. They're exquisitely blended."

The girl snorted, and gave him a look of cold disdain. The doll-baby had become a virago.

"Get yourself outa my apartment, or I'll call the house detective." She turned to the telephone on the wall at her side.

Vance waited until she had lifted the receiver.

"If you do that, Miss La Fosse, I'll order you taken to the District Attorney's office for questioning," he told her indifferently, lighting his cigarette and leaning back in his chair.

Slowly she replaced the receiver and turned.

"What's your game, anyway? . . . Suppose I

did know Margy—then what? And where do you
fit into the picture?"

"Alas! I don't fit in at all." Vance smiled
pleasantly. "But, for that matter, nobody seems to
fit in. The truth is, they're about to arrest a poor
blighter for killing your friend, who wasn't in the
tableau, either. I happen to be a friend of the District Attorney's; and I know exactly what's being
done. The police are scouting round in a perfect
frenzy of activity, and it's hard to say what trail
they'll strike next. I thought, don't y' know, I
might save you a lot of unpleasantness by a friendly
little chat. . . . Of course," he added, "if you prefer
to have me give your name to the police, I'll do so,
and let them hold the audition in their own inimitable
but crude fashion. I might say, however, that, as yet,
they are blissfully unaware of your relationship
with Miss Odell, and that, if you are reasonable, I
see no reason why they should be informed of it."

The girl had stood, one hand on the telephone,
studying Vance intently. He had spoken carelessly
and with a genial inflection; and she at length resumed her seat.

"Now, won't you have one of my cigarettes?" he
asked, in a tone of gracious reconciliation.

Mechanically she accepted his offer, keeping her
eyes on him all the time, as if attempting to determine
how far he was to be trusted.

"Who are they thinking of arresting?" She asked
the question with scarcely a movement of her features.

"A johnny named Skeel.—Silly idea, isn't it?"

"Him!" Her tone was one of mingled contempt

and disgust. "That cheap crook? He hasn't got nerve enough to strangle a cat."

"Precisely. But that's no reason for sending him to the electric chair, what?" Vance leaned forward and smiled engagingly. "Miss La Fosse, if you will talk to me for five minutes, and forget I'm a stranger, I'll give you my word of honor not to let the police or the District Attorney know anything about you. I'm not connected with the authorities, but somehow I dislike the idea of seeing the wrong man punished. And I'll promise to forget the source of any information you will be kind enough to give me. If you will trust me, it will be infinitely easier for you in the end."

The girl made no answer for several minutes. She was, I could see, trying to estimate Vance; and evidently she decided that, in any case, she had nothing to lose—now that her friendship with the Canary had been discovered—by talking to this man who had promised her immunity from further annoyance.

"I guess you're all right," she said, with a reservation of dubiety; "but I don't know why I should think so." She paused. "But, look here: I was told to keep out of this. And if I don't keep out of it, I'm apt to be back hoofing it in the chorus again. And that's no life for a sweet young thing like me with extravagant tastes—believe me, my friend!"

"That calamity will never befall you through any lack of discretion on my part," Vance assured her, with good-natured earnestness. . . . "Who told you to keep out of it?"

"My—fiancé." She spoke somewhat coquettishly. "He's very well known, and he's afraid there might

be scandal if I got mixed up in the case as a witness,
or anything like that."

"I can readily understand his feelings." Vance
nodded sympathetically. "And who, by the bye, is
this luckiest of men?"

"Say! You're good." She complimented him
with a coy *moue*. "But I'm not announcing my engagement yet."

"Don't be horrid," begged Vance. "You know
perfectly well that I could find out his name by
making a few inquiries. And if you drove me to
learn the facts elsewhere, then my promise to keep
your name a secret would no longer bind me."

Miss La Fosse considered this point.

"I guess you could find out, all right . . . so I
might as well tell you—only I'm trusting to your
word to protect me." She opened her eyes wide and
gave Vance a melting look. "I know you wouldn't
let me down."

"My dear Miss La Fosse!" His tone was one of
pained surprise.

"Well, my fiancé is Mr. Mannix, and he's the
head of a big fur-importing house. . . . You see"
—she became clingingly confidential—"Louey—that
is, Mr. Mannix—used to go round with Margy.
That's why he didn't want me to get mixed up in
the affair. He said the police might bother him with
questions, and his name might get into the papers.
And that would hurt his commercial standing."

"I quite understand," murmured Vance. "And
do you happen to know where Mr. Mannix was
Monday night?"

The girl looked startled.

"Of course I know. He was right here with me from half past ten until two in the morning. We were discussing a new musical show he was interested in; and he wanted me to take the leading rôle."

"I'm sure it will be a success." Vance spoke with disarming friendliness. "Were you home alone all Monday evening?"

"Hardly." The idea seemed to amuse her. "I went to the 'Scandals'—but I came home early. I knew Louey—Mr. Mannix—was coming."

"I trust he appreciated your sacrifice." Vance, I believe, was disappointed by this unexpected alibi of Mannix's. It was, indeed, so final that further interrogation concerning it seemed futile. After a momentary pause, he changed the subject.

"Tell me; what do you know about a Mr. Charles Cleaver? He was a friend of Miss Odell's."

"Oh, Pop's all right." The girl was plainly relieved by this turn in the conversation. "A good scout. He was certainly gone on Margy. Even after she threw him over for Mr. Spotswoode, he was faithful, as you might say—always running after her, sending her flowers and presents. Some men are like that. Poor old Pop! He even phoned me Monday night to call up Margy for him and try to arrange a party.—Maybe if I'd done it, she wouldn't be dead now. . . . It's a funny world, isn't it?"

"Oh, no end funny." Vance smoked calmly for a minute; I could not help admiring his self-control. "What time did Mr. Cleaver phone you Monday night—do you recall?" From his voice one would have thought the question of no importance.

"Let me see. . . ." She pursed her lips prettily. "It was just ten minutes to twelve. I remember that the little chime clock on the mantel over there was striking midnight, and at first I couldn't hear Pop very well. You see, I always keep my clock ten minutes fast so I'll never be late for an appointment."

Vance compared the clock with his watch.

"Yes, it's ten minutes fast.—And what about the party?"

"Oh, I was too busy talking about the new show, and I had to refuse. Anyway, Mr. Mannix didn't want to have a party that night. . . . It wasn't my fault, was it?"

"Not a bit of it," Vance assured her. "Work comes before pleasure—especially work as important as yours. . . . And now, there is one other man I want to ask you about, and then I won't bother you any more.—What was the situation between Miss Odell and Doctor Lindquist?"

Miss La Fosse became genuinely perturbed.

"I was afraid you were going to ask me about him." There was apprehension in her eyes. "I don't know just what to say. He was wildly in love with Margy; and she led him on, too. But she was sorry for it afterward, because he got jealous—like a crazy person. He used to pester the life out of her. And once—do you know!—he threatened to shoot her and then shoot himself. I told Margy to look out for him. But she didn't seem to be afraid. Anyway, I think she was taking awful chances. . . . Oh! Do you think it could have been—do you really think——?"

"And wasn't there any one else," Vance interrupted, "who might have felt the same way?—any one Miss Odell had reason to fear?"

"No." Miss La Fosse shook her head. "Margy didn't know many men intimately. She didn't change often, if you know what I mean. There wasn't anybody else outside of those you've mentioned, except, of course, Mr. Spotswoode. He cut Pop out—several months ago. She went to dinner with him Monday night, too. I wanted her to go to the 'Scandals' with me—that's how I know."

Vance rose and held out his hand.

"You've been very kind. And you have nothing whatever to fear. No one shall ever know of our little visit this morning."

"Who do you think killed Margy?" There was genuine emotion in the girl's voice. "Louey says it was probably some burglar who wanted her jewels."

"I'm too wise to sow discord in this happy ménage by even questioning Mr. Mannix's opinion," said Vance half banteringly. "No one *knows* who's guilty; but the police agree with Mr. Mannix."

For a moment the girl's doubts returned, and she gave Vance a searching look.

"Why are you so interested? You didn't know Margy, did you? She never mentioned you."

Vance laughed.

"My dear child! I only wish I knew why I am so deuced concerned in this affair. 'Pon my word, I can't give you even the sketchiest explanation. . . . No, I never met Miss Odell. But it would offend my sense of proportion if Mr. Skeel were punished and the real culprit went free. Maybe I'm getting sentimental. A sad fate, what?"

"I guess I'm getting soft, too." She nodded her head, still looking Vance squarely in the eyes. "I risked my happy home to tell you what I did, because somehow I believed you. . . . Say, you weren't stringing me, by any chance?"

Vance put his hand on his heart, and became serious.

"My dear Miss La Fosse, when I leave here it will be as though I had never entered. Dismiss me and Mr. Van Dine here from your mind."

Something in his manner banished her misgivings, and she bade us a kittenish farewell.

CHAPTER XVII

CHECKING AN ALIBI

(*Thursday, September 13; afternoon*)

"My sleuthing goes better," exulted Vance, when we were again in the street. "Fair Alys was a veritable mine of information—eh, what? Only, you should have controlled yourself better when she mentioned her beloved's name—really, you should, Van old thing. I saw you jump and heard you heave. Such emotion is most unbecoming in a lawyer."

From a booth in a drug-store near the hotel he telephoned Markham: "I am taking you to lunch. I have numerous confidences I would pour into your ear." A debate ensued, but in the end Vance emerged triumphant; and a moment later a taxicab was driving us down-town.

"Alys is clever—there are brains in that fluffy head," he ruminated. "She's much smarter than Heath; she knew at once that Skeel wasn't guilty. Her characterization of the immaculate Tony was inelegant but how accurate—oh, how accurate! And you noticed, of course, how she trusted me. Touchin', wasn't it? . . . It's a knotty problem, Van. Something's amiss somewhere."

He was silent, smoking, for several blocks.

"Mannix. . . . Curious he should crop up again. And he issued orders to Alys to keep mum. Now,

why? Maybe the reason he gave her was the real
one. Who knows?—On the other hand, was he with
his *chère amie* from half past ten till early morning?
Well, well. Again, who knows? Something queer
about that business discussion. . . . Then Cleaver.
He called up just ten minutes before midnight—oh,
yes, he called up. That wasn't a fairy-tale. But how
could he telephone from a speeding car? He couldn't.
Maybe he really wanted to have a party with his
recalcitrant Canary, don't y' know. But then, why
the brummagem alibi? Funk? Maybe. But why
the circuitousness?—why didn't he call his lost love
direct? Ah, perhaps he did! Some one certainly
called her by phone at twenty minutes to twelve.
We must look into that, Van. . . . Yes, he may
have called her, and then when a man answered—
who the deuce was that man, anyway?—he may have
appealed to Alys. Quite natural, y' know. Anyway,
he wasn't in Boonton.—Poor Markham! How upset
he'll be when he finds out! . . . But what really
worries me is that story of the doctor. Jealous
mania: it squares with Ambroise's character perfectly. He's the kind that does go off his head. I
knew his confession of paternalism was a red herring.
My word! So the doctor was making threats and
flourishing pistols, eh? Bad, bad. I don't like it.
With those ears of his, he wouldn't hesitate to pull
the trigger. Paranoia—that's it. Delusions of perse-
cution. Probably thought the girl and Pop—or maybe the girl and Spotswoode—were plotting his misery
and laughing at him. You can't tell about those
chaps. They're deep—and they're dangerous. The
canny Alys had him sized up—warned the Canary

against him. . . . Taken by and large, it's a devilish
tangle. Anyway, I feel rather bucked. We're moving
—oh, undoubtedly we're moving—though in what
direction I can't even guess. It's beastly annoyin'."

Markham was waiting for us at the Bankers' Club.
He greeted Vance irritably.

"What have you got to tell me that's so damned
important?"

"Now, don't get ratty." Vance was beaming.
"How's your lode-star, Skeel, behaving?"

"So far he's done everything that's pure and refined except join the Christian Endeavor Society."

"Sunday's coming. Give him time. . . . So you're
not happy, Markham dear?"

"Was I dragged away from another engagement
to report on my state of mind?"

"No need. Your state of mind's execrable. . . .
Cheerio! I've brought you something to think
about."

"Damn it! I've got too much to think about now."

"Here, have some brioche." Vance gave the
order for lunch without consulting either of us.
"And now for my revelations. *Imprimis:* Pop
Cleaver wasn't in Boonton last Monday night. He
was very much in the midst of our modern Gomorrah,
trying to arrange a midnight party."

"Wonderful!" snorted Markham. "I lave in the
font of your wisdom. His *alter ego*, I take it, was on
the road to Hopatcong. The supernatural leaves me
cold."

"You may be as pancosmic as you choose. Cleaver
was in New York at midnight Monday, craving
excitement."

"What about the summons for speeding?"

"That's for you to explain. But if you'll take my advice you'll send for this Boonton catchpole, and let him have a look at Pop. If he says Cleaver is the man he ticketed, I'll humbly do away with myself."

"Well! That makes it worth trying. I'll have the officer at the Stuyvesant Club this afternoon, and I'll point out Cleaver to him. . . . What other staggering revelations have you in store?"

"Mannix will bear looking into."

Markham put down his knife and fork and leaned back.

"I'm overcome! Such Himalayan sagacity! With that evidence against him, he should be arrested at once. . . . Vance, my dear old friend, are you feeling quite normal? No dizzy spells lately? No shooting pains in the head? Knee-jerks all right?"

"Furthermore, Doctor Lindquist was wildly infatuated with the Canary, and insanely jealous. Recently threatened to take a pistol and hold a little pogrom of his own."

"That's better." Markham sat up. "Where did you get this information?"

"Ah! That's my secret."

Markham was annoyed.

"Why so mysterious?"

"Needs must, old chap. Gave my word, and all that sort of thing. And I'm a bit quixotic, don't y' know—too much Cervantes in my youth." He spoke lightly, but Markham knew him too well to push the question.

In less than five minutes after we had returned to the District Attorney's office Heath came in.

"I got something else on Mannix, sir; thought you might want to add it to the report I turned in yesterday. Burke secured a picture of him, and showed it to the phone operators at Odell's house. Both of 'em recognized it. He's been there several times, but it wasn't the Canary he called on. It was the woman in Apartment 2. She's named Frisbee, and used to be one of Mannix's fur models. He's been to see her several times during the past six months, and has taken her out once or twice; but he hasn't called on her for a month or more. . . . Any good?"

"Can't tell." Markham shot Vance an inquisitive look. "But thanks for the information, Sergeant."

"By the bye," said Vance dulcetly, when Heath had left us, "I'm feeling tophole. No pains in the head; no dizzy spells. Knee-jerks perfect."

"Delighted. Still, I can't charge a man with murder because he calls on his fur model."

"You're so hasty! Why should you charge him with murder?" Vance rose and yawned. "Come, Van. I'd rather like to gaze on Perneb's tomb at the Metropolitan this afternoon. Could you bear it?" At the door he paused. "I say, Markham, what about the Boonton bailiff?"

Markham rang for Swacker.

"I'll see to it at once. Drop in at the club around five, if you feel like it. I'll have the officer there then, as Cleaver is sure to come in before dinner."

When Vance and I returned to the club late that afternoon, Markham was stationed in the lounge-room facing the main door of the rotunda; and beside him sat a tall, heavy-set, bronzed man of about forty, alert but ill at ease.

"Traffic Officer Phipps arrived from Boonton a little while ago," said Markham, by way of introduction. "Cleaver is expected at any moment now. He has an appointment here at half past five."

Vance drew up a chair.

"I do hope he's a punctual beggar."

"So do I," returned Markham viciously. "I'm looking forward to your *felo-de-se*."

" 'Our hap is loss, our hope but sad despair,' " murmured Vance.

Less than ten minutes later Cleaver entered the rotunda from the street, paused at the desk, and sauntered into the lounge-room. There was no escaping the observation point Markham had chosen; and as he walked by us he paused and exchanged greetings. Markham detained him a moment with a few casual questions; and then Cleaver passed on.

"That the man you ticketed, officer?" asked Markham, turning to Phipps.

Phipps was scowling perplexedly.

"It looks something like him, sir; there's a kind of resemblance. But it ain't him." He shook his head. "No, sir; it ain't him. The fellow I hung a summons on was stouter than this gent, and wasn't as tall."

"You're positive?"

"Yes, sir—no mistake. The guy I tagged tried to argue with me, and then he tried to slip me a fiver to forget it. I had my headlight on him full."

Phipps was dismissed with a substantial *pourboire*.

"*Væ misero mihi!*" sighed Vance. "My worthless existence is to be prolonged. Sad. But you must try to bear it. . . . I say, Markham, what does Pop Cleaver's brother look like?"

"That's it," nodded Markham. "I've met his brother; he's shorter and stouter. . . . This thing is getting beyond me. I think I'll have it out with Cleaver now."

He started to rise, but Vance forced him back into his seat.

"Don't be impetuous. Cultivate patience. Cleaver's not going to do a bunk; and there are one or two prelimin'ry steps strongly indicated. Mannix and Lindquist still seduce my curiosity."

Markham clung to his point.

"Neither Mannix nor Lindquist is here now, and Cleaver is. And I want to know why he lied to me about that summons."

"I can tell you that," said Vance. "He wanted you to think he was in the wilds of New Jersey at midnight Monday.—Simple, what?"

"The inference is a credit to your intelligence! But I hope you don't seriously think that Cleaver is guilty. It's possible he knows something; but I certainly cannot picture him as a strangler."

"And why?"

"He's not the type. It's inconceivable—even if there were evidence against him."

"Ah! The psychological judgment! You eliminate Cleaver because you don't think his nature harmonizes with the situation. I say, doesn't that come perilously near being an esoteric hypothesis? —or a metaphysical deduction? . . . However, I don't entirely agree with you in your application of the theory to Cleaver. That fish-eyed gambler has unsuspected potentialities for evil. But with the theory itself I am wholly in accord. And behold, my dear Markham: you yourself apply psychology in its abecedarian implications, yet ridicule my application of it in its higher developments. Consistency may be the hobgoblin of little minds, y' know, but it's none the less a priceless jewel. . . . How about a cup of tea?"

We sought the Palm Room, and sat down at a table near the entrance. Vance ordered oolong tea, but Markham and I took black coffee. A very capable four-piece orchestra was playing Tchaikovsky's *Casse-Noisette* Suite, and we sat restfully in the comfortable chairs without speaking. Markham was tired and dispirited, and Vance was busy with the problem that had absorbed him continuously since Tuesday morning. Never before had I seen him so preoccupied.

We had been there perhaps half an hour when Spotswoode strolled in. He stopped and spoke, and Markham asked him to join us. He, too, appeared depressed, and his eyes showed signs of worry.

"I hardly dare ask you, Mr. Markham," he said diffidently, after he had ordered a ginger ale, "but how do my chances stand now of being called as a witness?"

"That fate is certainly no nearer than when I last saw you," Markham replied. "In fact, nothing has happened to change the situation materially."

"And the man you had under suspicion?"

"He's still under suspicion, but no arrest has been made. We're hoping, however, that something will break before long."

"And I suppose you still want me to remain in the city?"

"If you can arrange it—yes."

Spotswoode was silent for a time; then he said:

"I don't want to appear to shirk any responsibility—and perhaps it may seem wholly selfish for me even to suggest it—but, in any event, wouldn't the testimony of the telephone operator as to the hour of Miss Odell's return and her calls for help be sufficient to establish the facts, without my corroboration?"

"I have thought of that, of course; and if it is at all possible to prepare the case for the prosecution without summoning you to appear, I assure you it will be done. At the moment, I can see no necessity of your being called as a witness. But one never knows what may turn up. If the defense hinges on a question of exact time, and the operator's testimony is questioned or disqualified for any reason, you may be required to come forward. Otherwise not."

Spotswoode sipped his ginger ale. A little of his depression seemed to have departed.

"You're very generous, Mr. Markham. I wish there was some adequate way of thanking you." He looked up hesitantly. "I presume you are still opposed to my visiting the apartment. . . . I know you think me unreasonable and perhaps sentimental; but the girl represented something in my life that I find very difficult to tear out. I don't expect you to understand it—I hardly understand it myself."

"I think it's easily understandable, don't y' know," remarked Vance, with a sympathy I had rarely seen him manifest. "Your attitude needs no apology. History and fable are filled with the same situation, and the protagonists have always exhibited sentiments similar to yours. Your most famous prototype, of course, was Odysseus on the citron-scented isle of Ogygia with the fascinatin' Calypso. The soft arms of sirens have gone snaking round men's necks ever since the red-haired Lilith worked her devastatin' wiles on the impressionable Adam. We're all sons of that racy old boy."

Spotswoode smiled.

"You at least give me an historic background," he said. Then he turned to Markham. "What will become of Miss Odell's possessions—her furniture and so forth?"

"Sergeant Heath heard from an aunt of hers in Seattle," Markham told him. "She's on her way to New York, I believe, to take over what there is of the estate."

"And everything will be kept intact until then?"

"Probably longer, unless something unexpected happens. Anyway, until then."

"There are one or two little trinkets I'd like to keep," Spotswoode confessed, a bit shamefacedly, I thought.

After a few more minutes of desultory talk he rose, and, pleading an engagement, bade us good afternoon.

"I hope I can keep his name clear of the case," said Markham, when he had gone.

"Yes; his situation is not an enviable one," concurred Vance. "It's always sad to be found out. The moralist would set it down to retribution."

"In this instance chance was certainly on the side of righteousness. If he hadn't chosen Monday night for the Winter Garden, he might now be in the bosom of his family, with nothing more troublesome to bother him than a guilty conscience."

"It certainly looks that way." Vance glanced at his watch. "And your mention of the Winter Garden reminds me. Do you mind if we dine early? Frivolity beckons me to-night. I'm going to the 'Scandals.'"

We both looked at him as though he had taken leave of his senses.

"Don't be so horrified, my Markham. Why should I not indulge an impulse? . . . And, incidentally, I hope to have glad tidings for you by lunch-time to-morrow."

CHAPTER XVIII

(Friday, September 14; noon)

Vance slept late the following day. I had accompanied him to the "Scandals" the night before, utterly at a loss to understand his strange desire to attend a type of entertainment which I knew he detested. At noon he ordered his car, and instructed the chauffeur to drive to the Belafield Hotel.

"We are about to call again on the allurin' Alys," he said. "I'd bring posies to lay at her shrine, but I fear dear Mannix might question her unduly about them.

Miss La Fosse received us with an air of crestfallen resentment.

"I might've known it!" She nodded her head with sneering perception. "I suppose you've come to tell me the cops found out about me without the slightest assistance from you." Her disdain was almost magnificent. "Did you bring 'em with you? . . . A swell guy *you* are!—But it's my own fault for being a damn fool."

Vance waited unmoved until she had finished her contemptuous tirade. Then he bowed pleasantly.

"Really, y' know, I merely dropped in to pay my respects, and to tell you that the police have turned in their report of Miss Odell's acquaintances, and that your name was not mentioned in it. You seemed a little worried yesterday on that score, and it occurred to me I could set your mind wholly at ease."

The vigilance of her attitude relaxed.

"Is that straight? . . . My God! I don't know what would happen if Louey'd find out I'd been blabbing."

"I'm sure he won't find out, unless you choose to tell him. . . . Won't you be generous and ask me to sit down a moment?"

"Of course—I'm so sorry. I'm just having my coffee. Please join me." She rang for two extra services.

Vance had drunk two cups of coffee less than half an hour before, and I marvelled at his enthusiasm for this atrocious hotel beverage.

"I was a belated spectator of the 'Scandals' last night," he remarked in a negligent, conversational tone. "I missed the *revue* earlier in the season.— How is it you yourself were so late in seeing it?"

"I've been so busy," she confided. "I was rehearsing for 'A Pair of Queens'; but the production's been postponed. Louey couldn't get the theatre he wanted."

"Do you like *revues?*" asked Vance. "I should think they'd be more difficult for the principals than the ordin'ry musical comedy."

"They are." Miss La Fosse adopted a professional air. "And they're unsatisfactory. The individual is lost in them. There's no real scope for one's talent. They're breathless, if you know what I mean."

"I should imagine so." Vance bravely sipped his

coffee. "And yet, there were several numbers in the 'Scandals' that you could have done charmingly; they seemed particularly designed for you. I thought of you doing them, and—d' ye know?—the thought rather spoiled my enjoyment of the young lady who appeared in them."

"You flatter me, Mr. Vance. But, really, I have a good voice. I've studied very hard. And I learned dancing with Professor Markoff."

"Indeed!" (I'm sure Vance had never heard the name before, but his exclamation seemed to imply that he regarded Professor Markoff as one of the world's most renowned ballet-masters.) "Then you certainly should have been starred in the 'Scandals.' The young lady I have in mind sang rather indifferently, and her dancing was most inadequate. Moreover, she was many degrees your inferior in personality and attractiveness. . . . Confess: didn't you have just a little desire last Monday night to be singing the 'Chinese Lullaby' song?"

"Oh, I don't know." Miss La Fosse carefully considered the suggestion. "They kept the lights awfully low; and I don't look so well in cerise. But the costumes were adorable, weren't they?"

"On you they certainly would have been adorable. . . . What color are you partial to?"

"I love the orchid shades," she told him enthusiastically; "though I don't look at all bad in turquoise blue. But an artist once told me I should always wear white. He wanted to paint my portrait, but the gentleman I was engaged to then didn't like him."

Vance regarded her appraisingly.

"I think your artist friend was right. And, y' know, the St. Moritz scene in the 'Scandals' would have suited you perfectly. The little brunette who sang the snow song, all in white, was delightful; but really, now, she should have had golden hair. Dusky beauties belong to the southern climes. And she impressed me as lacking the sparkle and vitality of a Swiss resort in midwinter. You could have supplied those qualities admirably."

"Yes; I'd have liked that better than the Chinese number, I think. White fox is my favorite fur, too. But, even so, in a *revue* you're on in one number and off in another. When it's all over, you're forgotten." She sighed unhappily.

Vance set down his cup, and looked at her with whimsically reproachful eyes. After a moment he said:

"My dear, why did you fib to me about the time Mr. Mannix returned to you last Monday night? It wasn't a bit nice of you."

"What do you mean!" Miss La Fosse exclaimed in frightened indignation, drawing herself up into an attitude of withering hauteur.

"You see," explained Vance, "the St. Moritz scene of the 'Scandals' doesn't go on until nearly eleven, and it closes the bill. So you couldn't possibly have seen it and also received Mr. Mannix here at half past ten.—Come. What time did he arrive here Monday night?"

The girl flushed angrily.

"You're pretty slick, aren't you? You shoulda been a cop. . . . Well, what if I didn't get home till after the show? Any crime in that?"

"None whatever," answered Vance mildly. "Only a little breach of good faith in telling me you came home early." He bent forward earnestly. "I'm not here to make you trouble. On the contr'ry, I'd like to protect you from any distress or bother. You see, if the police go nosing round, they may run on to you. But if I'm able to give the District Attorney accurate information about certain things connected with Monday night, there'll be no danger of the police being sent to look for you."

Miss La Fosse's eyes grew suddenly hard and her brow crinkled with determination.

"Listen! I haven't got anything to hide, and neither has Louey. But if Louey asks me to say he's somewhere at half past ten, I'm going to say it—see? That's my idea of friendship. Louey had some good reason to ask it, too, or he wouldn't have done it. However, since you're so smart, and have accused me of playing unfair, I'm going to tell you that he didn't get in till after midnight. But if anybody else asks me about it, I'll see 'em in hell before I tell 'em anything but the half-past-ten story. Get that?"

Vance bowed.

"I get it; and I like you for it."

"But don't go away with the wrong idea," she hurried on, her eyes sparkling with fervor. "Louey may not have got here till after midnight, but if you think he knows anything about Margy's death, you're crazy. He was through with Margy a year ago. Why, he hardly knew she was on earth. And if any fool cop gets the notion in his head that Louey was mixed up in the affair, I'll alibi him—so help me God!—if it's the last thing I do in this world."

"I like you more and more," said Vance; and when she gave him her hand at parting he lifted it to his lips.

As we rode down-town Vance was thoughtful. We were nearly to the Criminal Courts Building before he spoke.

"The primitive Alys rather appeals to me," he said. "She's much too good for the oleaginous Mannix. . . . Women are so shrewd—and so gullible. A woman can read a man with almost magical insight; but, on the other hand, she is inexpressibly blind when it comes to *her* man. Witness sweet Alys's faith in Mannix. He probably told her he was slaving at the office Monday night. Naturally, she doesn't believe it; but she knows—*knows*, mind you—that her Louey just couldn't have been concerned in the Canary's death. Ah, well, let us hope she's right and that Mannix is not apprehended—at least not until her new show is financed. . . . My word! If this being a detective involves many more *revues*, I shall have to resign. Thank Heaven, though, the lady didn't attend the cinema Monday night!"

When we arrived at the District Attorney's office we found Heath and Markham in consultation. Markham had a pad before him, several pages of which were covered with tabulated and annotated entries. A cloud of cigar-smoke enveloped him. Heath sat facing him, his elbows on the table, his chin resting in his hands. He looked pugnacious but disconsolate.

"I'm going over the case with the Sergeant," Markham explained, with a brief glance in our direction. "We're trying to get all the salient points down in some kind of order, to see if there are any connecting links we've overlooked. I've told the Sergeant about the doctor's infatuation and his threats, and of the failure of Traffic Officer Phipps to identify Cleaver. But the more we learn, the worse, apparently, the jumble grows."

He picked up the sheets of paper and fastened them together with a clip.

"The truth is, we haven't any real evidence against anybody. There are suspicious circumstances connected with Skeel and Doctor Lindquist and Cleaver; and our interview with Mannix didn't precisely allay suspicions in his direction, either. But when we come right down to it, what's the situation?—We've got some finger-prints of Skeel, which might have been made late Monday afternoon.—Doctor Lindquist goes berserk when we ask him where he was Monday night, and then offers us a weak alibi. He admits a fatherly interest in the girl, whereas he's really in love with her—a perfectly natural bit of mendacity. —Cleaver lent his car to his brother and lied about it, so that I'd think he was in Boonton Monday at midnight.—And Mannix gives us a number of shifty answers to our questions concerning his relations with the girl. . . . Not an embarrassment of riches."

"I wouldn't say your information was exactly negligent," observed Vance, taking a chair beside the Sergeant. "It may all prove devilish valuable if only it could be put together properly. The difficulty, it appears to me, is that certain parts of the puzzle are missing. Find 'em, and I'll warrant everything will fit beautifully—like a mosaic."

"Easy enough to say 'find 'em,'" grumbled Markham. "The trouble is to know where to look."

Heath relighted his dead cigar and made an impatient gesture.

"You can't get away from Skeel. He's the boy that did it, and, if it wasn't for Abe Rubin, I'd sweat the truth outa him.—And by the way, Mr. Vance, he had his own private key to the Odell apartment, all right." He glanced at Markham hesitantly. "I don't want to look as if I was criticising, sir, but I got a feeling we're wasting time chasing after these gentlemen friends of Odell—Cleaver and Mannix and this here doctor."

"You may be right." Markham seemed inclined to agree with him. "However, I'd like to know why Lindquist acted the way he did."

"Well, that might help some," Heath compromised. "If the doc was so far gone on Odell as to threaten to shoot her, and if he went off his head when you asked him to alibi himself, maybe he could tell us something. Why not throw a little scare into him? His record ain't any too good, anyway."

"An excellent idea," chimed in Vance.

Markham looked up sharply. Then he consulted his appointment book.

"I'm fairly free this afternoon, so suppose you bring him down here, Sergeant. Get a subpœna if you have to—only see that he comes. And make it as soon after lunch as you can." He tapped on the desk irritably. "If I don't do anything else, I'm going to eliminate some of this human flotsam that's cluttering up the case. And Lindquist is as good as any to start with. I'll either develop these various suspicious circumstances into something workable, or I'll root them up. Then we'll see where we stand."

Heath shook hands pessimistically and went out.

"Poor hapless man!" sighed Vance, looking after him. "He giveth way to all the pangs and fury of despair."

"And so would you," snapped Markham, "if the newspapers were butchering you for a political holiday.—By the way, weren't you to be a harbinger of glad tidings this noon, or something of the sort?"

"I believe I did hold out some such hope." Vance sat looking meditatively out of the window for several minutes. "Markham, this fellow Mannix lures me like a magnet. He irks and whirrets me. He infests my slumbers. He's the raven on my bust of Pallas. He plagues me like a banshee."

"Does this jeremiad come under the head of tidings?"

"I sha'n't rest peacefully," pursued Vance, "until I know where Louey the furrier was between eleven o'clock and midnight Monday. He was somewhere he shouldn't have been. And you, Markham, must find out. Please make Mannix the second offensive in your assault upon the flotsam. He'll parley, with the right amount of pressure. Be brutal, old dear; let him think you suspect him of the throttling. Ask him about the fur model—what's her name?—Frisbee——" He stopped short and knit his brows. "My eye—oh, my eye! I wonder. . . . Yes, yes, Markham; you must question him about the fur model. Ask him when he saw her last; and try to look wise and mysterious when you're doing it."

"See here, Vance"—Markham was exasperated—"you've been harping on Mannix for three days. What's keeping your nose to that scent?"

"Intuition—sheer intuition. My psychic temperament, don't y' know."

"I'd believe that if I hadn't known you for fifteen years." Markham inspected him shrewdly; then shrugged his shoulders. "I'll have Mannix on the tapis when I'm through with Lindquist."

CHAPTER XIX

THE DOCTOR EXPLAINS

(*Friday, September 14; 2 p. m.*)

We lunched in the District Attorney's private
sanctum; and at two o'clock Doctor Lindquist was
announced. Heath accompanied him, and, from the
expression on the Sergeant's face, it was plain he did
not at all like his companion.

The doctor, at Markham's request, seated himself
facing the District Attorney's desk.

"What is the meaning of this new outrage?" he
demanded coldly. "Is it your prerogative to force a
citizen to leave his private affairs in order to be bullied?"

"It's my duty to bring murderers to justice," replied Markham, with equal coldness. "And if any
citizen considers that giving aid to the authorities is
an outrage, that's *his* prerogative. If you have anything to fear by answering my questions, doctor, you
are entitled to have your attorney present. Would
you care to phone him to come here now and give
you legal protection?"

Doctor Lindquist hesitated. "I need no legal protection, sir. Will you be good enough to tell me at
once why I was brought here?"

"Certainly; to explain a few points which have
been discovered regarding your relationship with
Miss Odell, and to elucidate—if you care to—your

reasons for deceiving me, at our last conference, in regard to that relationship."

"You have, I infer, been prying unwarrantably into my private affairs. I had heard that such practices were once common in Russia. . . ."

"If the prying was unwarranted, you can, Doctor Lindquist, easily convince me on that point; and whatever we may have learned concerning you will be instantly forgotten.—It is true, is it not, that your interest in Miss Odell went somewhat beyond mere paternal affection?"

"Are not even a man's sacred sentiments respected by the police of this country?" There was insolent scorn in the doctor's tone.

"Under some conditions, yes; under others, no." Markham controlled his fury admirably. "You need not answer me, of course; but, if you choose to be frank, you may possibly save yourself the humiliation of being questioned publicly by the People's attorney in a court of law."

Doctor Lindquist winced and considered the matter at some length.

"And if I admit that my affection for Miss Odell was other than paternal—what then?"

Markham accepted the question as an affirmation.

"You were intensely jealous of her, were you not, doctor?"

"Jealousy," Doctor Lindquist remarked, with an air of ironic professionalism, "is not an unusual accompaniment to an infatuation. Authorities such as Krafft-Ebing, Moll, Freud, Ferenczi, and Adler, I believe, regard it as an intimate psychological corollary of amatory attraction."

"Most instructive," Markham nodded his head appreciatively. "I am to assume, then, that you were infatuated with—or, let us say, amatorily attracted by—Miss Odell, and that on occasions you exhibited the intimate psychological corollary of jealousy?"

"You may assume what you please. But I fail to understand why my emotions are any of your affair."

"Had your emotions not led you to highly questionable and suspicious acts, I would not be interested in them. But I have it on unimpeachable authority that your emotions so reacted on your better judgment that you threatened to take Miss Odell's life and also your own. And, in view of the fact that the young woman has since been murdered, the law naturally—and reasonably—is curious."

The doctor's normally pale face seemed to turn yellow, and his long splay fingers tightened over the arms of his chair; but otherwise he sat immobile and rigidly dignified, his eyes fixed intently on the District Attorney.

"I trust," added Markham, "you will not augment my suspicions by any attempt at denial."

Vance was watching the man closely. Presently he leaned forward.

"I say, doctor, what method of extermination did you threaten Miss Odell with?"

Doctor Lindquist jerked round, thrusting his head toward Vance. He drew in a long rasping breath, and his whole frame became tense. Blood suffused his cheeks; and there was a twitching of the muscles about his mouth and throat. For a moment I was afraid he was going to lose his self-control. But after a moment's effort he steadied himself.

"You think perhaps I threatened to strangle her?" His words were vibrant with the intensity of his passionate anger. "And you would like to turn my threat into a noose to hang me?—Paugh!" He paused, and when he spoke again his voice had become calmer. "It is quite true I once inadvisedly attempted to frighten Miss Odell with a threat to kill her and to commit suicide. But if your information is as accurate as you would have me believe, you are aware that I threatened her with a revolver. It is the weapon, I believe, that is conventionally mentioned when making empty threats. I certainly would not have threatened her with thuggee, even had I contemplated so abominable an act."

"True," nodded Vance. "And it's a rather good point, don't y' know."

The doctor was evidently encouraged by Vance's attitude. He again faced Markham and elaborated his confession.

"A threat, I presume you know, is rarely the forerunner of a violent deed. Even a brief study of the human mind would teach you that a threat is *prima facie* evidence of one's innocence. A threat, generally, is made in anger, and acts as its own safety-valve." He shifted his eyes. "I am not a married man; my emotional life has not been stabilized, as it were; and I am constantly coming in close contact with hypersensitive and overwrought people. During a period of abnormal susceptibility I conceived an infatuation for the young woman, an infatuation which she did not reciprocate—certainly not with an

ardor commensurate with my own. I suffered deeply;
and she made no effort to mitigate my sufferings.
Indeed, I suspected her, more than once, of deliberately and perversely torturing me with other men.
At any rate, she took no pains to hide her infideli-
ties from me. I confess that once or twice I was
almost distracted. And it was in the hope of fright-
ening her into a more amenable and considerate attitude that I threatened her.—I trust that you are a
sufficiently discerning judge of human nature to believe me."

"Leaving that point for a moment," answered
Markham non-committally, "will you give me more
specific information as to your whereabouts Monday
night?"

Again I noted a yellow tinge creep over the man's
features, and his body stiffened perceptibly. But
when he spoke it was with his habitual suavity.

"I considered that my note to you covered that
question satisfactorily. What did I omit?"

"What was the name of the patient on whom you
were calling that night?"

"Mrs. Anna Breedon. She is the widow of the late
Amos H. Breedon of the Breedon National Bank of
Long Branch."

"And you were with her, I believe you stated,
from eleven until one?"

"That is correct."

"And was Mrs. Breedon the only witness to your
presence at the sanitarium between those hours?"

"I am afraid that is so. You see, after ten o'clock
at night I never ring the bell. I let myself in with
my own key."

"And I suppose that I may be permitted to question Mrs. Breedon?"

Doctor Lindquist was profoundly regretful.

"Mrs. Breedon is a very ill woman. She suffered a tremendous shock at the time of her husband's death last summer, and has been practically in a semiconscious condition ever since. There are times when I even fear for her reason. The slightest disturbance or excitement might produce very serious results."

He took a newspaper cutting from a gold-edged letter-case and handed it to Markham.

"You will observe that this obituary notice mentions her prostration and confinement in a private sanitarium. I have been her physician for years."

Markham, after glancing at the cutting, handed it back. There was a short silence broken by a question from Vance.

"By the bye, doctor, what is the name of the night nurse at your sanitarium?"

Doctor Lindquist looked up quickly.

"My night nurse? Why—what has she to do with it? She was very busy Monday night. I can't understand. . . . Well, if you want her name I have no objection. It's Finckle—Miss Amelia Finckle."

Vance wrote down the name and, rising, carried the slip of paper to Heath.

"Sergeant, bring Miss Finckle here to-morrow morning at eleven," he said, with a slight lowering of one eyelid.

"I sure will, sir. Good idea." His manner boded no good for Miss Finckle.

A cloud of apprehension spread over Doctor Lindquist's face.

"Forgive me if I say that I am insensible to the sanity of your cavalier methods." His tone betrayed only contempt. "May I hope that for the present your inquisition is ended?"

"I think that will be all, doctor," returned Markham politely. "May I have a taxicab called for you?"

"Your consideration overwhelms me. But my car is below." And Doctor Lindquist haughtily withdrew.

Markham immediately summoned Swacker and sent him for Tracy. The detective came at once, polishing his *pince-nez* and bowing affably. One would have taken him for an actor rather than a detective, but his ability in matters requiring delicate handling was a byword in the department.

"I want you to fetch Mr. Louis Mannix again," Markham told him. "Bring him here at once; I'm waiting to see him."

Tracy bowed genially and, adjusting his glasses, departed on his errand.

"And now," said Markham, fixing Vance with a reproachful look, "I want to know what your idea was in putting Lindquist on his guard about the night nurse. Your brain isn't at par this afternoon. Do you think I didn't have the nurse in mind? And now you've warned him. He'll have until eleven to-morrow morning to coach her in her answers. Really, Vance, I can't conceive of anything better calculated to defeat us in our attempt to substantiate the man's alibi."

"I did put a little fright into him, didn't I?" Vance grinned complacently. "Whenever your antagonist begins talking exaggeratedly about the insanity of your notions, he's already deuced hot under the collar. But, Markham old thing, don't burst into tears over my mental shortcomings. If you and I both thought of the nurse, don't you suppose the wily doctor also thought of her? If this Miss Finckle were the type that could be suborned, he would have enlisted her perjurious services two days ago, and she would have been mentioned, along with the comatose Mrs. Breedon, as a witness to his presence at the sanitarium Monday night. The fact that he avoided all reference to the nurse shows that she's not to be wheedled into swearing falsely. . . . No, Markham. I deliberately put him on his guard. Now he'll have to do something before we question Miss Finckle. And I'm vain enough to think I know what it'll be."

"Let me get this right," put in Heath. "Am I, or am I not, to round up the Finckle woman to-morrow morning?"

"There'll be no need," said Vance. "We are doomed, I fear, not to gaze upon this Florence Nightingale. A meeting between us is about the last thing the doctor would desire."

"That may be true," admitted Markham. "But don't forget that he may have been up to something Monday night wholly unconnected with the murder, that he simply doesn't want known."

"Quite—quite. And yet, nearly every one who knew the Canary seems to have selected Monday night for the indulgence of *sub-rosa* peccadilloes. It's a bit thick, what? Skeel tries to make us believe he was immersed in Khun Khan. Cleaver was—if you take his word for it—touring the countryside in Jersey's lake district. Lindquist wants us to picture him as comforting the afflicted. And Mannix, I happen to know, has gone to some trouble to build up an alibi in case we get nosey. All of 'em, in fact, were doing something they don't want us to know about. Now, what was it? And why did they, of one accord, select the night of the murder for mysterious affairs which they don't dare mention, even to clear themselves of suspicion? Was there an invasion of efreets in the city that night? Was there a curse on the world, driving men to dark bawdy deeds? Was there Black Magic abroad? I think not."

"I'm laying my money on Skeel," declared Heath stubbornly. "I know a professional job when I see it. And you can't get away from those finger-prints and the Professor's report on the chisel."

Markham was sorely perplexed. His belief in Skeel's guilt had, I knew, been undermined in some measure by Vance's theory that the crime was the carefully premeditated act of a shrewd and educated man. But now he seemed to swing irresolutely back to Heath's point of view.

"I'll admit," he said, "that Lindquist and Cleaver and Mannix don't inspire one with a belief in their innocence. But since they're all tarred with the same stick, the force of suspicion against them is somewhat dispersed. After all, Skeel is the only logical aspirant for the rôle of strangler. He's the only one with a visible motive; and he's the only one against whom there's any evidence."

Vance sighed wearily.

"Yes, yes. Finger-prints—chisel marks. You're

A Paramount Picture.   The Canary Murder Case.

DR. LINDQUIST WAS AT ONCE SUSPECTED OF THE MURDER.

such a trustin' soul, Markham. Skeel's finger-prints
are found in the apartment; therefore, Skeel strangled
the lady. So beastly simple. Why bother further?
A *chose jugée*—an adjudicated case. Send Skeel to
the chair, and that's that! . . . It's effective, y'
know, but is it art?"

"In your critical enthusiasm you understate our
case against Skeel," Markham reminded him testily.

"Oh, I'll grant that your case against him is
ingenious. It's so deuced ingenious I just haven't
the heart to reject it. But most popular truth is
mere ingenuity—that's why it's so wrong-headed.
Your theory would appeal strongly to the popular
mind. And yet, y' know, Markham, it isn't true."

The practical Heath was unmoved. He sat stolidly, scowling at the table. I doubt if he had even
heard the exchange of opinions between Markham
and Vance.

"You know, Mr. Markham," he said, like one
unconsciously voicing an obscure line of thought,
"if we could show how Skeel got in and out of Odell's
apartment we'd have a better case against him. I
can't figure it out—it's got me stopped. So, I've
been thinking we oughta get an architect to go over
those rooms. The house is an old-timer—God knows
when it was originally built—and there may be some
way of getting into it that we haven't discovered
yet."

"'Pon my soul!" Vance stared at him in satirical
wonderment. "You're becoming downright romantic! Secret passageways—hidden doors—stairways
between the walls. So that's it, is it? Oh, my word!
. . . Sergeant, beware of the cinema. It has ruined

many a good man. Try grand opera for a while—
it's more borin' but less corruptin'."

"That's all right, Mr. Vance." Apparently Heath
himself did not relish the architectural idea particularly. "But as long as we don't know how Skeel
got in, it's just as well to make sure of a few ways
he didn't get in."

"I agree with you, Sergeant," said Markham.
"I'll get an architect on the job at once." He rang
for Swacker, and gave the necessary instructions.

Vance extended his legs and yawned.

"All we need now is a Favorite of the Harem, a
few blackamoors with palm-leaf fans, and some
pizzicato music."

"You will joke, Mr. Vance." Heath lit a fresh
cigar. "But even if the architect don't find anything
wrong with the apartment, Skeel's liable to give his
hand away 'most any time."

"I'm pinnin' my childish faith on Mannix," said
Vance. "I don't know why I should; but he's not
a nice man, and he's suppressing something.—Markham, don't you dare let him go until he tells you
where he was Monday night. And don't forget to
hint mysteriously about the fur model."

CHAPTER XX

(Friday, September 14; 3.30 p. m.)

In less than half an hour Mannix arrived. Heath relinquished his seat to the newcomer, and moved to a large chair beneath the windows. Vance had taken a place at the small table on Markham's right where he was able to face Mannix obliquely.

It was patent that Mannix did not relish the idea of another interview. His little eyes shifted quickly about the office, lingered suspiciously for a moment on Heath, and at last came to rest on the District Attorney. He was more vigilant even than during his first visit; and his greeting to Markham, while fulsome, had in it a note of trepidation. Nor was Markham's air calculated to put him at ease. It was an ominous, indomitable Public Prosecutor who motioned him to be seated. Mannix laid his hat and cane on the table, and sat down on the edge of his chair, his back as perpendicular as a flag-pole.

"I'm not at all satisfied with what you told me Wednesday, Mr. Mannix," Markham began, "and I trust you won't necessitate me to take drastic steps to find out what you know about Miss Odell's death."

"What I know!" Mannix forced a smile intended to be disarming. "Mr. Markham—Mr. Markham!"

He seemed oilier than usual as he spread his hands in hopeless appeal. "If I knew anything, believe me, I would tell you—positively I would tell you."

"I'm delighted to hear it. Your willingness makes my task easier. First, then, please tell me where you were at midnight Monday."

Mannix's eyes slowly contracted until they looked like two tiny shining disks, but otherwise the man did not move. After what seemed an interminable pause, he spoke.

"I should tell you where I was Monday? Why should I have to do that? . . . Maybe I'm suspected of the murder—yes?"

"You're not suspected now. But your apparent unwillingness to answer my question is certainly suspicious. Why don't you care to have me know where you were?"

"I got no reason to keep it from you, y' understand." Mannix shrugged. "I got nothing to be ashamed of—absolutely! . . . I had a lot of accounts to go over at the office—winter-season stocks. I was down at the office until ten o'clock—maybe later. Then at half past ten——"

"That'll do!" Vance's voice cut in tartly. "No need to drag any one else into this thing."

He spoke with a curious significance of emphasis, and Mannix studied him craftily, trying to read what knowledge, if any, lay behind his words. But he received no enlightenment from Vance's features. The warning, however, had been enough to halt him.

"You don't want to know where I was at half past ten?"

"Not particularly," said Vance. "We want to

know where you were at midnight. And it won't be
necess'ry to mention any one who saw you at that
time. When you tell us the truth, we'll know it."
He himself had assumed the air of wisdom and mystery that he had deputed to Markham earlier in the
afternoon. Without breaking faith with Alys La
Fosse, he had sowed the seeds of doubt in Mannix's
mind.

Before the man could frame an answer, Vance
stood up and leaned impressively over the District
Attorney's desk.

"You know a Miss Frisbee. Lives in 71st Street;
accurately speaking—at number 184; to be more
exact—in the house where Miss Odell lived; to put
it precisely—in Apartment Number 2. Miss Frisbee
was a former model of yours. Sociable girl: still
charitable to the advances of her erstwhile employer
—meanin' yourself.—When did you see her last,
Mr. Mannix? . . . Take your time about answering. You may want to think it over."

Mannix took his time. It was a full minute before
he spoke, and then it was to put another question.

"Haven't I got a right to call on a lady—haven't
I?"

"Certainly. Therefore, why should a question
about so obviously correct and irreproachable an
episode make you uneasy?"

"Me uneasy?" Mannix, with considerable effort, produced a grin. "I'm just wondering what
you got in your mind, asking me about my private
affairs."

"I'll tell you. Miss Odell was murdered at about
midnight Monday. No one came or went through

the front door of the house, and the side door was locked. The only way any one could have entered her apartment was by way of Apartment 2; and nobody who knew Miss Odell ever visited Apartment 2 except yourself."

At these words Mannix leaned over the table, grasping the edge of it with both hands for support. His eyes were wide and his sensual lips hung open. But it was not fear that one read in his attitude; it was sheer amazement. He sat for a moment staring at Vance, stunned and incredulous.

"That's what you think, is it? No one could've got in or out except by Apartment 2, because the side door was locked?" He gave a short vicious laugh. "If that side door didn't happen to be locked Monday night, where'd I stand then—huh? Where'd I stand?"

"I rather think you'd stand with us—with the District Attorney." Vance was watching him like a cat.

"Sure I would!" spat Mannix. "And let me tell you something, my friend: that's just where I stand—absolutely!" He swung heavily about and faced Markham. "I'm a good fellow, y' understand, but I've kept my mouth shut long enough. . . . *That side door wasn't locked Monday night. And I know who sneaked out of it at five minutes to twelve!*"

"*Ça marche!*" murmured Vance, reseating himself and calmly lighting a cigarette.

Markham was too astonished to speak at once; and Heath sat stock-still, his cigar half-way to his mouth.

At length Markham leaned back and folded his arms.

"I think you'd better tell us the whole story, Mr. Mannix." His voice held a quality which made the request an imperative.

Mannix, too, settled back in his chair.

"Oh, I'm going to tell it—believe me, I'm going to tell it.—You had the right idea. I spent the evening with Miss Frisbee. No harm in that, though."

"What time did you go there?"

"After office hours—half past five, quarter to six. Came up in the subway, got off at 72d, and walked over."

"And you entered the house through the front door?"

"No. I walked down the alleyway and went in the side door—like I generally do. It's nobody's business who I call on, and what the telephone operator in the front hall don't know don't hurt him."

"That's all right so far," observed Heath. "The janitor didn't bolt the side door until after six."

"And did you stay the entire evening, Mr. Mannix?" asked Markham.

"Sure—till just before midnight. Miss Frisbee cooked the dinner, and I'd brought along a bottle of wine. Social little party—just the two of us. And I didn't go outside the apartment, understand, until five minutes to twelve. You can get the lady down here and ask her. I'll call her up now and tell her to explain the exact situation about Monday night. I'm not asking you to take my word for it—positively not."

Markham made a gesture dismissing the suggestion.

"What took place at five minutes to twelve?"

Mannix hesitated, as if loath to come to the point. "I'm a good fellow, y' understand. And a friend's a friend. But—I ask you—is that any reason why I should get in wrong for something I didn't have absolutely nothing to do with?"

He waited for an answer, but receiving none, continued.

"Sure, I'm right.—Anyway, here's what happened. As I said, I was calling on the lady. But I had another date for later that night; so a few minutes before midnight I said good-bye and started to go. Just as I opened the door I saw some one sneaking away from the Canary's apartment down the little back hall to the side door. There was a light in the hall, and the door of Apartment 2 faces that side door. I saw the fellow as plain as I see you—positively as plain."

"Who was it?"

"Well, if you got to know, it was Pop Cleaver."

Markham's head jerked slightly.

"What did you do then?"

"Nothing, Mr. Markham—nothing at all. I didn't think much about it, y' understand. I knew Pop was chasing after the Canary, and I just supposed he'd been calling on her. But I didn't want Pop to see me—none of his business where I spend my time. So I waited quietly till he went out——"

"By the side door?"

"Sure.—Then I went out the same way. I was going to leave by the front door, because I knew the side door was always locked at night. But when I saw Pop go out that way, I said to myself I'd do the same. No sense giving your business away to a tele-

phone operator if you haven't got to—no sense at all.
So I went out the same way I came in. Picked up a
taxi on Broadway, and went——"

"That's enough!" Again Vance's command cut
him short.

"Oh, all right—all right." Mannix seemed content to end his statement at this point. "Only, y'
understand, I don't want you to think——"

"We don't."

Markham was puzzled at these interruptions, but
made no comment.

"When you read of Miss Odell's death," he said,
"why didn't you come to the police with this highly
important information?"

"I should get mixed up in it!" exclaimed Mannix
in surprise. "I got enough trouble without looking
for it—plenty."

"An exigent course," commented Markham with
open disgust. "But you nevertheless suggested to
me, after you knew of the murder, that Cleaver was
being blackmailed by Miss Odell."

"Sure I did. Don't that go to show I wanted to
do the right thing by you—giving you a valuable
tip?"

"Did you see any one else that night in the halls
or alleyway?"

"Nobody—absolutely nobody."

"Did you hear any one in the Odell apartment—
any one speaking or moving about, perhaps?"

"Didn't hear a thing." Mannix shook his head
emphatically.

"And you're certain of the time you saw Cleaver
go out—five minutes to twelve?"

"Positively. I looked at my watch, and I said to the lady: 'I'm leaving the same day I came; it won't be to-morrow for five minutes yet.'"

Markham went over his story point by point, attempting by various means to make him admit more than he had already told. But Mannix neither added to his statement nor modified it in any detail; and after half an hour's cross-examination he was permitted to go.

"We've found one missing piece of the puzzle, at any rate," commented Vance. "I don't see now just how it fits into the complete pattern, but it's helpful and suggestive. And, I say, how beautifully my intuition about Mannix was verified, don't y' know!"

"Yes, of course—your precious intuition." Markham looked at him sceptically. "Why did you shut him up twice when he was trying to tell me something?"

"*O, tu ne sauras jamais*," recited Vance. "I simply can't tell you, old dear. Awfully sorry, and all that."

His manner was whimsical, but Markham knew that at such times Vance was at heart most serious, and he did not press the question. I could not help wondering if Miss La Fosse realized just how secure she had been in putting her faith in Vance's integrity.

Heath had been considerably shaken by Mannix's story.

"I don't savvy that side door being unlocked," he complained. "How the hell did it get bolted again on the inside after Mannix went out? And who unbolted it after six o'clock?"

"In God's good time, my Sergeant, all things will be revealed," said Vance.

"Maybe—and maybe not. But if we do find out, you can take it from me that the answer'll be Skeel. He's the bird we gotta get the goods on. Cleaver is no expert jimmy artist; and neither is Mannix."

"Just the same, there was a very capable technician on hand that night, and it wasn't your friend the Dude—though he was probably the Donatello who sculptured open the jewel-case."

"A pair of 'em, was there? That's your theory, is it, Mr. Vance? You said that once before; and I'm not saying you're wrong. But if we can hang any part of it on Skeel, we'll make him come across as to who his pal was."

"It wasn't a pal, Sergeant. It was more likely a stranger."

Markham sat glowering into space.

"I don't at all like the Cleaver end of this affair," he said. "There's been something damned wrong about him ever since Monday."

"And I say," put in Vance, "doesn't the gentleman's false alibi take on a certain shady significance now, what? You apprehend, I trust, why I restrained you from questioning him about it at the club yesterday. I rather fancied that if you could get Mannix to pour out his heart to you, you'd be in a stronger position to draw a few admissions from Cleaver. And behold! Again the triumph of intuition! With what you now know about him, you can chivvy him most unconscionably—eh, what?"

"And that's precisely what I'm going to do." Markham rang for Swacker. "Get hold of Charles Cleaver," he ordered irritably. "Phone him at the Stuyvesant Club and also his home—he lives round

the corner from the club in West 27th Street. And
tell him I want him to be here in half an hour, or I'll
send a couple of detectives to bring him in handcuffs."

For five minutes Markham stood before the window, smoking agitatedly, while Vance, with a smile
of amusement, busied himself with *The Wall Street
Journal.* Heath got himself a drink of water, and
took a turn up and down the room. Presently Swacker re-entered.

"Sorry, Chief, but there's nothing doing. Cleaver's gone into the country somewhere. Won't be
back till late to-night."

"Hell! . . . All right—that'll do." Markham
turned to Heath. "You have Cleaver rounded up
to-night, Sergeant, and bring him in here to-morrow
morning at nine."

"He'll be here, sir!" Heath paused in his pacing
and faced Markham. "I've been thinking, sir; and
there's one thing that keeps coming up in my mind,
so to speak. You remember that black document-
box that was setting on the living-room table? It
was empty; and what a woman generally keeps in
that kind of a box is letters and things like that.
Well, now, here's what's been bothering me: that
box wasn't jimmied open—it was unlocked with a
key. And, anyway, a professional crook don't take
letters and documents. . . . You see what I mean,
sir?"

"Sergeant of mine!" exclaimed Vance. "I abase
myself before you! I sit at your feet! . . . The
document-box—the tidily opened, empty document-
box! Of course! Skeel didn't open it—never in this
world! That was the other chap's handiwork."

"What was in your mind about that box, Sergeant?" asked Markham.

"Just this, sir. As Mr. Vance has insisted right along, there mighta been some one besides Skeel in that apartment during the night. And you told me that Cleaver admitted to you he'd paid Odell a lot of money last June to get back his letters. But suppose he never paid that money; suppose he went there Monday night and took those letters. Wouldn't he have told you just the story he did about buying 'em back? Maybe that's how Mannix happened to see him there."

"That's not unreasonable," Markham acknowledged. "But where does it lead us?"

"Well, sir, if Cleaver did take 'em Monday night, he mighta held on to 'em. And if any of those letters were dated later than last June, when he says he bought 'em back, then we'd have the goods on him."

"Well?"

"As I say, sir, I've been thinking. . . . Now, Cleaver is outa town to-day; and if we could get hold of those letters. . . ."

"It might prove helpful, of course," said Markham coolly, looking the Sergeant straight in the eye. "But such a thing is quite out of the question."

"Still and all," mumbled Heath, "Cleaver's been pulling a lot of raw stuff on you, sir."

CHAPTER XXI

(Saturday, September 15; 9 a. m.)

The next morning Markham and Vance and I breakfasted together at the Prince George, and arrived at the District Attorney's office a few minutes past nine. Heath, with Cleaver in tow, was waiting in the reception-room.

To judge by Cleaver's manner as he entered, the Sergeant had been none too considerate of him. He strode belligerently to the District Attorney's desk and fixed a cold, resentful eye on Markham.

"Am I, by any chance, under arrest?" he demanded softly, but it was the rasping, suppressed softness of wrathful indignation.

"Not yet," said Markham curtly. "But if you were, you'd have only yourself to blame.—Sit down."

Cleaver hesitated, and took the nearest chair.

"Why was I routed out of bed at seven-thirty by this detective of yours"—he jerked his thumb toward Heath—"and threatened with patrol-wagons and warrants because I objected to such high-handed and illegal methods?"

"You were merely threatened with legal procedure if you refused to accept my invitation voluntarily. This is my short day at the office; and there was some explaining I wanted from you without delay."

"I'm damned if I'll explain anything to you under these conditions!" For all his nerveless poise, Cleaver was finding it difficult to control himself. "I'm no pickpocket that you can drag in here when it suits your convenience and put through a third degree."

"That's eminently satisfactory to me." Markham spoke ominously. "But since you refuse to do your explaining as a free citizen, I have no other course than to alter your present status." He turned to Heath. "Sergeant, go across the hall and have Ben swear out a warrant for Charles Cleaver. Then lock this gentleman up."

Cleaver gave a start, and caught his breath sibilantly.

"On what charge?" he demanded.

"The murder of Margaret Odell."

The man sprang to his feet. The color had gone from his face, and the muscles of his jowls worked spasmodically.

"Wait! You're giving me a raw deal. And you'll lose out, too. You couldn't make that charge stick in a thousand years."

"Maybe not. But if you don't want to talk here, I'll make you talk in court."

"I'll talk here." Cleaver sat down again. "What do you want to know?"

Markham took out a cigar and lit it with deliberation.

"First: why did you tell me you were in Boonton Monday night?"

Cleaver apparently had expected the question.

"When I read of the Canary's death I wanted an

alibi; and my brother had just given me the summons he'd been handed in Boonton. It was a ready-made alibi right in my hand. So I used it."

"Why did you need an alibi?"

"I didn't need it; but I thought it might save me trouble. People knew I'd been running round with the Odell girl; and some of them knew she'd been blackmailing me—I'd told 'em, like a damn fool. I told Mannix, for instance. We'd both been stung."

"Is that your only reason for concocting this alibi?" Markham was watching him sharply.

"Wasn't it reason enough? Blackmail would have constituted a motive, wouldn't it?"

"It takes more than a motive to arouse unpleasant suspicion."

"Maybe so. Only I didn't want to be drawn into it.—You can't blame me for trying to keep clear of it."

Markham leaned over with a threatening smile.

"The fact that Miss Odell had blackmailed you wasn't your only reason for lying about the summons. It wasn't even your main reason."

Cleaver's eyes narrowed, but otherwise he was like a graven image.

"You evidently know more about it than I do." He managed to make his words sound casual.

"Not more, Mr. Cleaver," Markham corrected him, "but nearly as much.—Where were you between eleven o'clock and midnight Monday?"

"Perhaps that's one of the things you know."

"You're right.—You were in Miss Odell's apartment."

Cleaver sneered, but he did not succeed in disguising the shock that Markham's accusation caused him.

"If that's what you think, then it happens you don't know, after all. I haven't put foot in her apartment for two weeks."

"I have the testimony of reliable witnesses to the contrary. '

"Witnesses!" The word seemed to force itself from Cleaver's compressed lips.

Markham nodded. "You were seen coming out of Miss Odell's apartment and leaving the house by the side door at five minutes to twelve on Monday night."

Cleaver's jaw sagged slightly, and his labored breathing was quite audible.

"And between half past eleven and twelve o'clock," pursued Markham's relentless voice, "Miss Odell was strangled and robbed.—What do you say to that?"

For a long time there was tense silence. Then Cleaver spoke.

"I've got to think this thing out."

Markham waited patiently. After several minutes Cleaver drew himself together and squared his shoulders.

"I'm going to tell you what I did that night, and you can take it or leave it." Again he was the cold, self-contained gambler. "I don't care how many witnesses you've got; it's the only story you'll ever get out of me. I should have told you in the first place, but I didn't see any sense of stepping into hot water if I wasn't pushed in. You might have believed me last Tuesday, but now you've got something in your head, and you want to make an arrest to shut up the newspapers———"

"Tell your story," ordered Markham. "If it's straight, you needn't worry about the newspapers."

Cleaver knew in his heart that this was true. No one—not even his bitterest political enemies—had ever accused Markham of buying *kudos* with any act of injustice, however small.

"There's not much to tell, as a matter of fact," the man began. "I went to Miss Odell's house a little before midnight, but I didn't enter her apartment; I didn't even ring her bell."

"Is that your customary way of paying visits?"

"Sounds fishy, doesn't it? But it's the truth, nevertheless. I intended to see her—that is, I wanted to—but when I reached her door, something made me change my mind——"

"Just a moment.—How did you enter the house?"

"By the side door—the one off the alleyway. I always used it when it was open. Miss Odell requested me to, so that the telephone operator wouldn't see me coming in so often."

"And the door was unlocked at that time Monday night?"

"How else could I have got in by it? A key wouldn't have done me any good, even if I'd had one, for the door locks by a bolt on the inside. I'll say this, though: that's the first time I ever remember finding the door unlocked at night."

"All right. You went in the side entrance. Then what?"

"I walked down the rear hall and listened at the door of Miss Odell's apartment for a minute. I thought there might be some one else with her, and I didn't want to ring unless she was alone. . . ."

"Pardon my interrupting, Mr. Cleaver," interposed Vance. "But what made you think some one else was there?"

The man hesitated.

"Was it," prompted Vance, "because you had telephoned to Miss Odell a little while before, and had been answered by a man's voice?"

Cleaver nodded slowly. "I can't see any particular point in denying it. . . . Yes, that's the reason."

"What did this man say to you?"

"Damn little. He said 'Hello,' and when I asked to speak to Miss Odell, he informed me she wasn't in, and hung up."

Vance addressed himself to Markham.

"That, I think, explains Jessup's report of the brief phone call to the Odell apartment at twenty minutes to twelve."

"Probably." Markham spoke without interest. He was intent on Cleaver's account of what happened later, and he took up the interrogation at the point where Vance had interrupted.

"You say you listened at the apartment door. What caused you to refrain from ringing?"

"I heard a man's voice inside."

Markham straightened up.

"A man's voice? You're sure?"

"That's what I said." Cleaver was matter of fact about it. "A man's voice. Otherwise I'd have rung the bell."

"Could you identify the voice?"

"Hardly. It was very indistinct; and it sounded a little hoarse. It wasn't any one's voice I was familiar with; but I'd be inclined to say it was the same one that answered me over the phone."

"Could you make out anything that was said?"

Cleaver frowned and looked past Markham through the open window.

"I know what the words sounded like," he said slowly. "I didn't think anything of them at the time. But after reading the papers the next day, those words came back to me——"

"What were the words?" Markham cut in impatiently.

"Well, as near as I could make out, they were: 'Oh, my God! Oh, my God!'—repeated two or three times."

This statement seemed to bring a sense of horror into the dreary old office—a horror all the more potent because of the casual, phlegmatic way in which Cleaver repeated that cry of anguish. After a brief pause Markham asked:

"When you heard this man's voice, what did you do?"

"I walked softly back down the rear hall and went out again through the side door. Then I went home."

A short silence ensued. Cleaver's testimony had been in the nature of a surprise; but it fitted perfectly with Mannix's statement.

Presently Vance lifted himself out of the depths of his chair.

"I say, Mr. Cleaver, what were you doing between twenty minutes to twelve—when you phoned Miss Odell—and five minutes to twelve—when you entered the side door of her apartment-house?"

"I was riding up-town in the Subway from 23d Street," came the answer after a short pause.

"Strange—very strange." Vance inspected the

tip of his cigarette. "You couldn't possibly have phoned any one during that fifteen minutes?"

I suddenly remembered Alys La Fosse's statement that Cleaver had telephoned to her on Monday night at ten minutes to twelve. Vance, by his question, had, without revealing his own knowledge, created a state of uncertainty in the other's mind. Afraid to commit himself too emphatically, Cleaver resorted to an evasion.

"It's possible, is it not, that I could have phoned some one after leaving the Subway at 72d Street and before I walked the block to Miss Odell's house?"

"Oh, quite," murmured Vance. "Still, looking at it mathematically, if you phoned Miss Odell at twenty minutes to twelve, and then entered the Subway, rode to 72d Street, walked a block to 71st, went into the building, listened at her door, and departed at five minutes to twelve—making the total time consumed only fifteen minutes— you'd scarcely have sufficient leeway to stop en route and phone to any one. However, I sha'n't press the point. But I'd really like to know what you did between eleven o'clock and twenty minutes to twelve, when you phoned to Miss Odell."

"To tell you the truth, I was upset that night. I knew Miss Odell was out with another man— she'd broken an appointment with me—and I walked the streets for an hour or more, fuming and fretting."

"Walked the streets?" Vance frowned.

"So I said." Cleaver spoke with animus.

Then, turning, he gave Markham a long calculating look. "You remember I once suggested to you that you might learn something from a Doctor Lindquist. . . . Did you ever get after him?"

Before Markham could answer, Vance broke in.

"Ah! That's it!—Doctor Lindquist! Well, well—of course! . . . So, Mr. Cleaver, you were walking the streets? The *streets*, mind you! Precisely!—You state the fact, and I echo the word 'streets.' And you—apparently out of a clear sky—ask about Doctor Lindquist. Why Doctor Lindquist? No one has mentioned him. But that word 'streets'—that's the connection. The streets and Doctor Lindquist are one—same as Paris and springtime are one. Neat, very neat. . . . And now I've got another piece to the puzzle."

Markham and Heath looked at him as if he had suddenly gone mad. He calmly selected a *Régie* from his case and proceeded to light it. Then he smiled beguilingly at Cleaver.

"The time has come, my dear sir, for you to tell us when and where you met Doctor Lindquist while roaming the streets Monday night. If you don't, 'pon my word, I'll come pretty close to doing it for you."

A full minute passed before Cleaver spoke; and during that time his cold staring eyes never moved from the District Attorney's face.

"I've already told most of the story; so here's the rest." He gave a soft mirthless laugh. "I went to Miss Odell's house a little before half past eleven—thought she might be home by that time. There I ran into Doctor Lindquist standing in the entrance to the alleyway. He spoke to me, and told me some one was with Miss Odell in her apartment. Then I walked round the corner to the Ansonia Hotel. After ten minutes or so I telephoned Miss Odell, and, as I said, a man answered. I waited another ten minutes and phoned a friend of Miss Odell's, hoping to arrange a party; but failing, I walked back to the house. The doctor had disappeared, and I went down the alleyway and in the side door. After listening a minute, as I told you, and hearing a man's voice, I came away and went home. . . . That's everything."

At that moment Swacker came in and whispered something to Heath. The Sergeant rose with alacrity and followed the secretary out of the room. Almost at once he returned, bearing a bulging Manila folder. Handing it to Markham, he said something in a low voice inaudible to the rest of us. Markham appeared both astonished and displeased. Waving the Sergeant back to his seat, he turned to Cleaver.

"I'll have to ask you to wait in the reception-room for a few minutes. Another urgent matter has just arisen."

Cleaver went out without a word, and Markham opened the folder.

"I don't like this sort of thing, Sergeant. I told you so yesterday when you suggested it."

"I understand, sir." Heath, I felt, was not as contrite as his tone indicated. "But if those letters and things are all right, and Cleaver hasn't been lying to us about 'em, I'll have my man put 'em back so's no one'll ever know they were taken. And if they do make Cleaver out a liar, then we've got a good excuse for grabbing 'em."

Markham did not argue the point. With a gesture of distaste he began running through the letters, looking particularly at the dates. Two photographs he put back after a cursory glance; and one piece of paper, which appeared to contain a pen-and-ink sketch of some kind, he tore up with disgust and threw into the waste-basket. Three letters, I noticed, he placed to one side. After five minutes' inspection of the others, he returned them to the folder. Then he nodded to Heath.

"Bring Cleaver back." He rose and, turning, gazed out of the window.

As soon as Cleaver was again seated before the desk Markham said, without looking round:

"You told me it was last June that you bought your letters back from Miss Odell. Do you recall the date?"

"Not exactly," said Cleaver easily. "It was early in the month, though—during the first week, I think."

Markham now spun about and pointed to the three letters he had segregated.

"How, then, do you happen to have in your possession compromising letters which you wrote to Miss Odell from the Adirondacks late in July?"

Cleaver's self-control was perfect. After a moment's stoical silence, he merely said in a mild, quiet voice:

"You of course came by those letters legally."

Markham was stung, but he was also exasperated by the other's persistent deceptions.

"I regret to confess," he said, "that they were taken from your apartment—though, I assure you, it was against my instructions. But since they have come unexpectedly into my possession, the wisest thing you can do is to explain them. There was an empty document-box in Miss Odell's apartment the morning her body was found, and, from all appearances, it had been opened Monday night."

"I see." Cleaver laughed harshly. "Very well. The fact is—though I frankly don't expect you to believe me—I didn't pay my blackmail to Miss Odell until the middle of August, about three weeks ago. That's when all my letters were returned. I told you it was June in order to set back the date as far as possible. The older the affair was, I figured, the less likelihood there'd be of your suspecting me."

Markham stood fingering the letters undecidedly. It was Vance who put an end to his irresolution.

"I rather think, don't y' know," he said, "that you'd be safe in accepting Mr. Cleaver's explanation and returning his *billets-doux*."

Markham, after a momentary hesitation, picked up the Manila folder and, replacing the three letters, handed it to Cleaver.

"I wish you to understand that I did not sanction the appropriating of this correspondence. You'd better take it home and destroy it.—I won't detain you any longer now. But please arrange to remain where I can reach you if necessary."

"I'm not going to run away," said Cleaver; and Heath directed him to the elevator.

CHAPTER XXII

A TELEPHONE CALL

(Saturday, September 15; 10 a. m.)

Heath returned to the office, shaking his head hopelessly.

"There musta been a regular wake at Odell's Monday night."

"Quite," agreed Vance. "A midnight conclave of the lady's admirers. Mannix was there, unquestionably; and he saw Cleaver; and Cleaver saw Lindquist; and Lindquist saw Spotswoode——"

"Humph! But nobody saw Skeel."

"The trouble is," said Markham, "we don't know how much of Cleaver's story is true.—And, by the way, Vance, do you believe he really bought his letters back in August?"

"If only we knew! Dashed confusin', ain't it?"

"Anyway," argued Heath, "Cleaver's statement about phoning Odell at twenty minutes to twelve, and a man answering, is verified by Jessup's testimony. And I guess Cleaver saw Lindquist all right that night, for it was him who first tipped us off about the doc. He took a chance doing it, because the doc was liable to tell us he saw Cleaver."

"But if Cleaver had an allurin' alibi," said Vance, "he could simply have said the doctor was lying. However, whether you accept Cleaver's absorbin'

234

legend or not, you can take my word for it there was a visitor, other than Skeel, in the Odell apartment that night."

"That's all right, too," conceded Heath reluctantly. "But, even so, this other fellow is only valuable to us as a possible source of evidence against Skeel."

"That may be true, Sergeant." Markham frowned perplexedly. "Only, I'd like to know how that side door was unbolted and then rebolted on the inside. We know now that it was open around midnight, and that Mannix and Cleaver both used it."

"You worry so over trifles," said Vance negligently. "The door problem will solve itself once we discover who was keeping company with Skeel in the Canary's gilded cage."

"I should say it boils down to Mannix, Cleaver, and Lindquist. They were the only three at all likely to be present; and if we accept Cleaver's story in its essentials, each of them had an opportunity of getting into the apartment between half past eleven and midnight."

"True. But you have only Cleaver's word that Lindquist was in the neighborhood. And that evidence, uncorroborated, can't be accepted as the lily-white truth."

Heath stirred suddenly and looked at the clock.

"Say, what about that nurse you wanted at eleven o'clock?"

"I've been worrying horribly about her for an hour." Vance appeared actually troubled. "Really, y' know, I haven't the slightest desire to meet the lady. I'm hoping for a revelation, don't y' know.

Let's wait for the doctor until half past ten, Sergeant."

He had scarcely finished speaking when Swacker informed Markham that Doctor Lindquist had arrived on a mission of great urgency. It was an amusing situation. Markham laughed outright, while Heath stared at Vance with uncomprehending astonishment.

"It's not necromancy, Sergeant," smiled Vance. "The doctor realized yesterday that we were about to catch him in a falsehood; so he decided to forestall us by explaining personally. Simple, what?"

"Sure." Heath's look of wonderment disappeared.

As Doctor Lindquist entered the room I noted that his habitual urbanity had deserted him. His air was at once apologetic and apprehensive. That he was laboring under some great strain was evident.

"I've come, sir," he announced, taking the chair Markham indicated, "to tell you the truth about Monday night."

"The truth is always welcome, doctor," said Markham encouragingly.

Doctor Lindquist bowed agreement.

"I deeply regret that I did not follow that course at our first interview. But at that time I had not weighed the matter sufficiently; and, having once committed myself to a false statement, I felt I had no option but to abide by it. However, after more mature consideration, I have come to the conclusion that frankness is the wiser course.—The fact is, sir, I was not with Mrs. Breedon Monday night between the hours I mentioned. I remained at home until about half past ten. Then I went to Miss

Odell's house, arriving a little before eleven. I stood outside in the street until half past eleven; then I returned home."

"Such a bare statement needs considerable amplification."

"I realize it, sir; and I am prepared to amplify it." Doctor Lindquist hesitated, and a strained look came into his white face. His hands were tightly clinched. "I had learned that Miss Odell was going to dinner and the theatre with a man named Spotswoode; and the thought of it began to prey on my mind. It was Spotswoode to whom I owed the alienation of Miss Odell's affections; and it was his interference that had driven me to my threat against the young woman. As I sat at home that night, letting my mind dwell morbidly on the situation, I was seized by the impulse to carry out that threat. Why not, I asked myself, end the intolerable situation at once? And why not include Spotswoode in the débâcle? . . ."

As he talked he became more and more agitated. The nerves about his eyes had begun to twitch, and his shoulders jerked like those of a man attempting vainly to control a chill.

"Remember, sir, I was suffering agonies, and my hatred of Spotswoode seemed to cloud my reason. Scarcely realizing what I was doing, and yet operating under an irresistible determination, I put my automatic in my pocket and hurried out of the house. I thought Miss Odell and Spotswoode would be returning from the theatre soon, and I intended to force my way into the apartment and perform the act I had planned. . . . From across the street I saw them enter the house—it was about eleven then

—but, when I came face to face with the actuality, I hesitated. I delayed my revenge; I—I played with the idea, getting a kind of insane satisfaction out of it—knowing they were now at my mercy. . . ."

His hands were shaking as with a coarse tremor; and the twitching about his eyes had increased.

"For half an hour I waited, gloating. Then, as I was about to go in and have it over with, a man named Cleaver came along and saw me. He stopped and spoke. I thought he might be going to call on Miss Odell, so I told him she already had a visitor. He then went on toward Broadway, and while I was waiting for him to turn the corner, Spotswoode came out of the house and jumped into a taxicab that had just driven up. . . . My plan had been thwarted—I had waited too long. Suddenly I seemed to awake as from some terrible nightmare. I was almost in a state of collapse, but I managed to get home. . . . That's what happened—so help me God!"

He sank back weakly in his chair. The suppressed nervous excitement that had fired him while he spoke had died out, and he appeared listless and indifferent. He sat several minutes breathing stertorously, and twice he passed his hand vaguely across his forehead. He was in no condition to be questioned, and finally Markham sent for Tracy and gave orders that he was to be taken to his home.

"Temporary exhaustion from hysteria," commented Vance indifferently. "All these paranoia lads are hyperneurasthenic. He'll be in a psychopathic ward in another year."

"That's as may be, Mr. Vance," said Heath, with an impatience that repudiated all enthusiasm for the subject of abnormal psychology. "What interests me just now is the way all these fellows' stories hang together."

"Yes," nodded Markham. "There is undeniably a groundwork of truth in their statements."

"But please observe," Vance pointed out, "that their stories do not eliminate any one of them as a possible culprit. Their tales, as you say, synchronize perfectly; and yet, despite all that neat co-ordination, any one of the three could have got into the Odell apartment that night. For instance: Mannix could have entered from Apartment 2 before Cleaver came along and listened; and he could have seen Cleaver going away when he himself was leaving the Odell apartment.—Cleaver could have spoken to the doctor at half past eleven, walked to the Ansonia, returned a little before twelve, gone into the lady's apartment, and come out just as Mannix opened Miss Frisbee's door.—Again, the excitable doctor may have gone in after Spotswoode came out at half past eleven, stayed twenty minutes or so, and departed before Cleaver returned from the Ansonia. . . . No; the fact that their stories dovetail doesn't in the least tend to exculpate any one of them."

"And," supplemented Markham, "that cry of 'Oh, my God!' might have been made by either Mannix or Lindquist—provided Cleaver really heard it."

"He heard it unquestionably," said Vance. "Some one in the apartment was invoking the Deity around midnight. Cleaver hasn't sufficient sense of the dramatic to fabricate such a thrillin' *bonne-bouche*."

"But if Cleaver actually heard that voice," pro-

tested Markham, "then he is automatically eliminated as a suspect."

"Not at all, old dear. He may have heard it after
he had come out of the apartment, and realized then,
for the first time, that some one had been hidden in
the place during his visit."

"Your man in the clothes-closet, I presume you
mean."

"Yes—of course. . . . You know, Markham, it
might have been the horrified Skeel, emerging from
his hiding-place upon a scene of tragic wreckage, who
let out that evangelical invocation."

"Except," commented Markham, with sarcasm,
"Skeel doesn't impress me as particularly religious."

"Oh, that?" Vance shrugged. "A point in substantiation. Irreligious persons call on God much
more than Christians. The only true and consistent
theologians, don't y' know, are the atheists."

Heath, who had been sitting in gloomy meditation,
took his cigar from his mouth and heaved a heavy
sigh.

"Yes," he rumbled, "I'm willing to admit somebody besides Skeel got into Odell's apartment, and
that the Dude hid in the clothes-closet. But, if that's
so, then this other fellow didn't see Skeel; and it's
not going to do us a whole lot of good even if we
identify him."

"Don't fret on that point, Sergeant," Vance
counselled him cheerfully. "When you've identified
this other mysterious visitor you'll be positively
amazed how black care will desert you. You'll rubri-
cate the hour you find him. You'll leap gladsomely
in the air. You'll sing a roundelay."

"The hell I will!" said Heath.

Swacker came in with a typewritten memorandum, and put it on the District Attorney's desk.

"The architect just phoned in this report."

Markham glanced it over: it was very brief.

"No help here," he said. "Walls solid. No waste space. No hidden entrances."

"Too bad, Sergeant," sighed Vance. "You'll have to drop the cinema idea. . . . Sad."

Heath grunted and looked disconsolate.

"Even without no other way of getting in or out except that side door," he said to Markham, "couldn't we get an indictment against Skeel, now that we know the door was unlocked Monday night?"

"We might, Sergeant. But our chief snag would be to show how it was originally unlocked and then rebolted after Skeel left. And Abe Rubin would concentrate on that point.—No, we'd better wait a while and see what develops."

Something "developed" at once. Swacker entered and informed the Sergeant that Snitkin wanted to see him immediately.

Snitkin came in, visibly agitated, accompanied by a wizened, shabbily dressed little man of about sixty, who appeared awed and terrified. In the detective's hand was a small parcel wrapped in newspaper, which he laid on the District Attorney's desk with an air of triumph.

"The Canary's jewellery," he announced. "I've checked it up from the list the maid gave me, and it's all there."

Heath sprang forward, but Markham was already

untying the package with nervous fingers. When the paper had been opened, there lay before us a small heap of dazzling trinkets—several rings of exquisite workmanship, three magnificent bracelets, a sparkling sunburst, and a delicately wrought lorgnette. The stones were all large and of unconventional cut.

Markham looked up from them inquisitively, and Snitkin, not waiting for the inevitable question, explained.

"This man Potts found 'em. He's a street-cleaner, and he says they were in one of the D. S. C. cans at 23d Street near the Flatiron Building. He found 'em yesterday afternoon, so he says, and took 'em home. Then he got scared and brought 'em to Police Headquarters this morning."

Mr. Potts, the "white-wing," was trembling visibly.

"Thass right, sir—thass right," he assured Markham, with frightened eagerness. "I allus look into any bundles I find. I didn't mean no harm takin' 'em home, sir. I wasn't gonna keep 'em. I laid awake worryin' all night, an' this mornin', as soon as I got a chance, I took 'em to the p'lice." He shook so violently I was afraid he was going to break down completely.

"That's all right, Potts," Markham told him in a kindly voice. Then to Snitkin: "Let the man go—only get his full name and address."

Vance had been studying the newspaper in which the jewels had been wrapped.

"I say, my man," he asked, "is this the original paper you found them in?"

"Yes, sir—the same. I ain't touched nothin'."

"Right-o."

Mr. Potts, greatly relieved, shambled out, followed by Snitkin.

"The Flatiron Building is directly across Madison Square from the Stuyvesant Club," observed Markham, frowning.

"So it is." Vance then pointed to the left-hand margin of the newspaper that held the jewels. "And you'll notice that this *Herald* of yesterday has three punctures evidently made by the pins of a wooden holder such as is generally used in a club's reading-room."

"You got a good cyc, Mr. Vance," nodded Heath, inspecting the newspaper.

"I'll see about this." Markham viciously pressed a button. "They keep their papers on file for a week at the Stuyvesant Club."

When Swacker appeared, he asked that the club's steward be got immediately on the telephone. After a short delay, the connection was made. At the end of five minutes' conversation Markham hung up the receiver and gave Heath a baffled look.

"The club takes two *Heralds*. Both of yesterday's copies are there, on the rack."

"Didn't Cleaver once tell us he read nothing but *The Herald*—that and some racing-sheet at night?" Vance put the question offhandedly.

"I believe he did." Markham considered the suggestion. "Still, both the club *Heralds* are accounted for." He turned to Heath. "When you were checking up on Mannix, did you find out what clubs he belonged to?"

"Sure." The Sergeant took out his note-book and riffled the pages for a minute or two. "He's a member of the Furriers' and the Cosmopolis."

Markham pushed the telephone toward him.
"See what you can find out."

Heath was fifteen minutes at the task.

"A blank," he announced finally. "The Furriers'
don't use holders, and the Cosmopolis don't keep
any back numbers."

"What about Mr. Skeel's clubs, Sergeant?" asked
Vance, smiling.

"Oh, I know the finding of that jewellery gums up
my theory about Skeel," said Heath, with surly ill
nature. "But what's the good of rubbing it in? Still,
if you think I'm going to give that bird a clean bill
of health just because the Odell swag was found in a
trash-can, you're mighty mistaken. Don't forget
we're watching the Dude pretty close. He may have
got leery, and tipped off some pal he'd cached the
jewels with."

"I rather fancy the experienced Skeel would have
turned his booty over to a professional receiver. But
even had he passed it on to a friend, would this friend
have been likely to throw it away because Skeel was
worried?"

"Maybe not. But there's some explanation for
those jewels being found, and when we get hold of it,
it won't eliminate Skeel."

"No; the explanation won't eliminate Skeel," said
Vance; "but—my word!—how it'll change his *locus
standi.*"

Heath contemplated him with shrewdly appraising
eyes. Something in Vance's tone had apparently
piqued his curiosity and set him to wondering.
Vance had too often been right in his diagnoses of
persons and things for the Sergeant to ignore his
opinions wholly.

But before he could answer, Swacker stepped alertly into the room, his eyes animated.

"Tony Skeel's on the wire, Chief, and wants to speak to you."

Markham, despite his habitual reserve, gave a start.

"Here, Sergeant," he said quickly. "Take that extension phone on the table and listen in." He nodded curtly to Swacker, who disappeared to make the connection. Then he took up the receiver of his own telephone and spoke to Skeel.

For a minute or so he listened. Then, after a brief argument, he concurred with some suggestion that had evidently been made; and the conversation ended.

"Skeel craves an audience, I gather," said Vance. "I've rather been expecting it, y' know."

"Yes. He's coming here to-morrow at ten."

"And he hinted that he knew who slew the Canary—eh, what?"

"That's just what he did say. He promised to tell me the whole story to-morrow morning."

"He's the lad that's in a position to do it," murmured Vance.

"But, Mr. Markham," said Heath, who still sat with his hand on the telephone, gazing at the instrument with dazed incredulity, "I don't see why you don't have him brought here to-day."

"As you heard, Sergeant, Skeel insisted on to-morrow, and threatened to say nothing if I forced the issue. It's just as well not to antagonize him. We might spoil a good chance of getting some light on this case if I ordered him brought here and used pressure. And to-morrow suits me. It'll be quiet around here then. Moreover, your man's watching Skeel, and he won't get away."

"I guess you're right, sir. The Dude's touchy, and he can give a swell imitation of an oyster when he feels like it." The Sergeant spoke with feeling.

"I'll have Swacker here to-morrow to take down his statement," Markham went on; "and you'd better put one of your men on the elevator,—the regular operator is off Sundays. Also, plant a man in the hall outside, and put another one in Swacker's office."

Vance stretched himself luxuriously and rose.

"Most considerate of the gentleman to call up at this time, don't y' know. I had a longing to see the Monets at Durand-Ruel's this afternoon, and I was afraid I wasn't going to be able to drag myself away from this fascinatin' case. Now that the apocalypse has been definitely scheduled for to-morrow, I'll indulge my taste for Impressionism. . . . *À demain*, Markham. By-bye, Sergeant."

CHAPTER XXIII

THE TEN O'CLOCK APPOINTMENT

(Sunday, September 16; 10 a. m.)

A fine drizzle was falling the next morning when we rose; and a chill—the first forerunner of winter—was in the air. We had breakfast in the library at half past eight, and at nine o'clock Vance's car—which had been ordered the night before—called for us. We rode down Fifth Avenue, now almost deserted in its thick blanket of yellow fog, and called for Markham at his apartment in West 12th Street. He was waiting for us in front of the house, and stepped quickly into the car with scarcely a word of greeting. From his anxious, preoccupied look I knew that he was depending a good deal on what Skeel had to tell him.

We had turned into West Broadway beneath the Elevated tracks before any of us spoke. Then Markham voiced a doubt which was plainly an articulation of his troubled ruminations.

"I'm wondering if, after all, this fellow Skeel can have any important information to give us. His phone call was very strange. Yet he spoke confidently enough regarding his knowledge. No dramatics, no request for immunity—just a plain, assured statement that he knew who murdered the Odell girl, and had decided to come clean."

"It's certain he himself didn't strangle the lady,"

247

pronounced Vance. "My theory, as you know, is that he was hiding in the clothes-press when the shady business was being enacted; and all along I've clung lovingly to the idea that he was *au secret* to the entire proceedings. The keyhole of that closet door is on a direct line with the end of the davenport where the lady was strangled; and if a rival was operating at the time of his concealment, it's not unreasonable to assume that he peered forth—eh, what? I questioned him on this point, you remember; and he didn't like it a bit."

"But, in that case——"

"Oh, I know. There are all kinds of erudite objections to my wild dream.—Why didn't he give the alarm? Why didn't he tell us about it before? Why this? and why that? . . . I make no claim to omniscience, y'·know; I don't even pretend to have a logical explanation for the various *traits d'union* of my vagary. My theory is only sketched in, as it were. But I'm convinced, nevertheless, that the modish Tony knows who killed his *bona roba* and looted her apartment."

"But of the three persons who possibly could have got into the Odell apartment that night—namely, Mannix, Cleaver, and Lindquist—Skeel evidently knows only one—Mannix."

"Yes—to be sure. And Mannix, it would seem, is the only one of the trio who knows Skeel. . . . An interestin' point."

Heath met us at the Franklin Street entrance to the Criminal Courts Building. He, too, was anxious and subdued, and he shook hands with us in a detached manner devoid of his usual heartiness.

"I've got Snitkin running the elevator," he said, after the briefest of salutations. "Burke's in the hall up-stairs, and Emery is with him, waiting to be let into Swacker's office."

We entered the deserted and almost silent building and rode up to the fourth floor. Markham unlocked his office door and we passed in.

"Guilfoyle, the man who's tailing Skeel," Heath explained, when we were seated, "is to report by phone to the Homicide Bureau as soon as the Dude leaves his rooms."

It was now twenty minutes to ten. Five minutes later Swacker arrived. Taking his stenographic note-book, he stationed himself just inside of the swinging door of Markham's private sanctum, where he could hear all that was said without being seen. Markham lit a cigar, and Heath followed suit. Vance was already smoking placidly. He was the calmest person in the room, and lay back languorously in one of the great leather chairs as though immune to all cares and vicissitudes. But I could tell by the over-deliberate way he flicked his ashes into the receiver that he, too, was uneasy.

Five or six minutes passed in complete silence. Then the Sergeant gave a grunt of annoyance.

"No, sir," he said, as if completing some unspoken thought, "I can't get a slant on this business. The finding of that jewellery, now, all nicely wrapped up . . . and then the Dude offering to squeal. . . . There's no sense to it."

"It's tryin', I know, Sergeant; but it's not altogether senseless." Vance was gazing lazily at the ceiling. "The chap who confiscated those baubles didn't have any use for them. He didn't want them, in fact—they worried him abominably."

The point was too complex for Heath. The previous day's developments had shaken the foundation of all his arguments; and he lapsed again into brooding silence.

At ten o'clock he rose impatiently and, going to the hall door, looked out. Returning, he compared his watch with the office clock and began pacing restlessly. Markham was attempting to sort some papers on his desk, but presently he pushed them aside with an impatient gesture.

"He ought to be coming along now," he remarked, with an effort at cheerfulness.

"He'll come," growled Heath, "or he'll get a free ride." And he continued his pacing.

A few minutes later he turned abruptly and went out into the hall. We could hear him calling to Snitkin down the elevator shaft, but when he came back into the office his expression told us that as yet there was no news of Skeel.

"I'll call up the Bureau," he decided, "and see what Guilfoyle had to report. At least we'll know then when the Dude left his house."

But when the Sergeant had been connected with Police Headquarters he was informed that Guilfoyle had as yet made no report.

"That's damn funny," he commented, hanging up the receiver.

It was now twenty minutes past ten. Markham was growing restive. The tenacity with which the Canary murder case had resisted all his efforts toward a solution had filled him with discouragement; and he had hoped, almost desperately, that this morning's interview with Skeel would clear up the mystery, or at least supply him with information on which definite action could be taken. Now, with Skeel late for this all-important appointment, the strain was becoming tense.

He pushed back his chair nervously and, going to the window, gazed out into the dark haze of fine rain. When he returned to his desk his face was set.

"I'll give our friend until half past ten," he said grimly. "If he isn't here then, Sergeant, you'd better call up the local station-house and have them send a patrol-wagon for him."

There was another few minutes of silence. Vance lolled in his chair with half-closed eyes, but I noticed that, though he still held his cigarette, he was not smoking. His forehead was puckered by a frown, and he was very quiet. I knew that some unusual problem was occupying him. His lethargy had in it a quality of intentness and concentration.

As I watched him he suddenly sat up straight, his eyes open and alert. He tossed his dead cigarette into the receiver with a jerky movement that attested to some inner excitement.

"Oh, my word!" he exclaimed. "It really can't be, y' know! And yet"—his face darkened—"and yet, by Jove, that's it! . . . What an ass I've been— what an unutterable ass! . . . Oh!"

He sprang to his feet; then stood looking down at the floor like a man dazed, afraid of his own thoughts.

"Markham, I don't like it—I don't like it at all." He spoke almost as if he were frightened. "I tell you, there's something terrible going on—something

uncanny. The thought of it makes my flesh creep.
. . . I must be getting old and sentimental," he
added, with an effort at lightness; but the look in his
eyes belied his tone. "Why didn't I see this thing
yesterday? . . . But I let it go on. . . ."

We were all staring at him in amazement. I had
never seen him affected in this way before, and the
fact that he was habitually so cynical and aloof, so
adamant to emotion and impervious to outside influences, gave his words and actions an impelling
and impressive quality.

After a moment he shook himself slightly, as if to
throw off the pall of horror that had descended upon
him, and, stepping to Markham's desk, he leaned
over, resting on both hands.

"Don't you see?" he asked. "Skeel's not coming.
No use to wait—no use of our having come here in
the first place. We have to go to him. He's waiting
for us. . . . Come! Get your hat."

Markham had risen, and Vance took him firmly by
the arm.

"You needn't argue," he persisted. "You'll have
to go to him sooner or later. You might as well go
now, don't y' know.—My word! What a situation!"

He had led Markham, astonished and but mildly
protesting, into the middle of the room, and he now
beckoned to Heath with his free hand.

"You, too, Sergeant. Sorry you had all this
trouble. My fault. I should have foreseen this thing.
A devilish shame; but my mind was on Monets all
yesterday afternoon. . . . You know where Skeel
lives?"

Heath nodded mechanically. He had fallen under

the spell of Vance's strange and dynamic impor-
tunities.

"Then don't wait.—And, Sergeant! You'd better
bring Burke or Snitkin along. They won't be needed
here—nobody'll be needed here any more to-day."

Heath looked inquiringly to Markham for counsel;
his bewilderment had thrown him into a state of
mute indecision. Markham nodded his approval of
Vance's suggestions, and, without a word, slipped
into his raincoat. A few minutes later the four of us,
accompanied by Snitkin, had entered Vance's car
and were lurching up-town. Swacker had been sent
home; the office had been locked up; and Burke and
Emery had departed for the Homicide Bureau to
await further instructions.

Skeel lived in 35th Street, near the East River, in
a dingy, but once pretentious, house which formerly
had been the residence of some old family of the
better class. It now had an air of dilapidation and
decay; there was rubbish in the areaway; and a large
sign announcing rooms for rent was posted in one of
the ground-floor windows.

As we drew up before it Heath sprang to the street
and looked sharply about him. Presently he espied
an unkempt man slouching in the doorway of a
grocery-store diagonally opposite, and beckoned to
him. The man shambled over furtively.

"It's all right, Guilfoyle," the Sergeant told him.
"We're paying the Dude a social visit.—What's the
trouble? Why didn't you report?"

Guilfoyle looked surprised.

"I was told to phone in when he left the house,
sir. But he ain't left yet. Mallory tailed him home

last night round ten o'clock, and I relieved Mallory at nine this morning. The Dude's still inside."

"Of course he's still inside, Sergeant," said Vance, a bit impatiently.

"Where's his room situated, Guilfoyle?" asked Heath.

"Second floor, at the back."

"Right. We're going in.—Stand by."

"Look out for him," admonished Guilfoyle. "He's got a gat."

Heath took the lead up the worn steps which led from the pavement to the little vestibule. Without ringing, he roughly grasped the door-knob and shook it. The door was unlocked, and we stepped into the stuffy lower hallway.

A bedraggled woman of about forty, in a disreputable dressing-gown, and with hair hanging in strings over her shoulders, emerged suddenly from a rear door and came toward us unsteadily, her bleary eyes focused on us with menacing resentment.

"Say!" she burst out, in a rasping voice. "What do youse mean by bustin' in like this on a respectable lady?" And she launched forth upon a stream of profane epithets.

Heath, who was nearest her, placed his large hand over her face, and gave her a gentle but firm shove backward.

"You keep outa this, Cleopatra!" he advised her, and began to ascend the stairs.

The second-floor hallway was dimly lighted by a small flickering gas-jet, and at the rear we could distinguish the outlines of a single door set in the middle of the wall.

"That'll be Mr. Skeel's abode," observed Heath.

He walked up to it and, dropping one hand in his right coat-pocket, turned the knob. But the door was locked. He then knocked violently upon it, and placing his ear to the jamb, listened. Snitkin stood directly behind him, his hand also in his pocket. The rest of us remained a little in the rear.

Heath had knocked a second time when Vance's voice spoke up from the semidarkness.

"I say, Sergeant, you're wasting time with all that formality."

"I guess you're right," came the answer after a moment of what seemed unbearable silence.

Heath bent down and looked at the lock. Then he took some instrument from his pocket and inserted it into the keyhole.

"You're right," he repeated. "The key's gone."

He stepped back and, balancing on his toes like a sprinter, sent his shoulders crashing against the panel directly over the knob. But the lock held.

"Come on, Snitkin," he ordered.

The two detectives hurled themselves against the door. At the third onslaught there was a splintering of wood and a tearing of the lock's bolt through the moulding. The door swung drunkenly inward.

The room was in almost complete darkness. We all hesitated on the threshold, while Snitkin crossed warily to one of the windows and sent the shade clattering up. The yellow-gray light filtered in, and the objects of the room at once took definable form. A large, old-fashioned bed projected from the wall on the right.

"Look!" cried Snitkin, pointing; and something in his voice sent a shiver over me.

We pressed forward. On the foot of the bed, at the side toward the door, sprawled the crumpled body of Skeel. Like the Canary, he had been strangled. His head hung back over the foot-board, his face a hideous distortion. His arms were outstretched and one leg trailed over the edge of the mattress, resting on the floor.

"Thuggee," murmured Vance. "Lindquist mentioned it.—Curious!"

Heath stood staring fixedly at the body, his shoulders hunched. His normal ruddiness of complexion was gone, and he seemed like a man hypnotized.

"Mother o' God!" he breathed, awe-stricken. And, with an involuntary motion, he crossed himself.

Markham was shaken also. He set his jaw rigidly.

"You're right, Vance." His voice was strained and unnatural. "Something sinister and terrible has been going on here. . . . There's a fiend loose in this town—a werewolf."

"I wouldn't say that, old man." Vance regarded the murdered Skeel critically. "No, I wouldn't say that. Not a werewolf. Just a desperate human being. A man of extremes, perhaps—but quite rational, and logical—oh, how deuced logical!"

CHAPTER XXIV

AN ARREST

(Sunday, p. m., Monday, a. m.; September 16–17)

The investigation into Skeel's death was pushed with great vigor by the authorities. Doctor Doremus, the Medical Examiner, arrived promptly and declared that the crime had taken place between ten o'clock and midnight. Immediately Vance insisted that all the men who were known to have been intimately acquainted with the Odell girl—Mannix, Lindquist, Cleaver, and Spotswoode—be interviewed at once and made to explain where they were during these two hours. Markham agreed without hesitation, and gave the order to Heath, who at once put four of his men on the task.

Mallory, the detective who had shadowed Skeel the previous night, was questioned regarding possible visitors; but inasmuch as the house where Skeel lived accommodated over twenty roomers, who were constantly coming and going at all hours, no information could be gained through that channel. All that Mallory could say definitely was that Skeel had returned home at about ten o'clock, and had not come out again. The landlady, sobered and subdued by the tragedy, repudiated all knowledge of the affair. She explained that she had been "ill" in her room from dinner-time until we had disturbed her recuperation the next morning. The front door, it seemed,

was never locked, since her tenants objected to such
an unnecessary inconvenience. The tenants themselves were questioned, but without result: they were
not of a class likely to give information to the police,
even had they possessed any.

The finger-print experts made a careful examination of the room, but failed to find any marks except
Skeel's own. A thorough search through the murdered man's effects occupied several hours; but
nothing was discovered that gave any hint of the
murderer's identity. A .38 Colt automatic, fully
loaded, was found under one of the pillows on the
bed; and eleven hundred dollars, in bills of large de-
nomination, was taken from a hollow brass curtain-
rod. Also, under a loose board in the hall, the missing steel chisel, with the fissure in the blade, was
found. But these items were of no value in solving
the mystery of Skeel's death; and at four o'clock in
the afternoon the room was closed with an emergency padlock and put under guard.

Markham and Vance and I had remained several
hours after our discovery of the body. Markham had
taken immediate charge of the case, and had conducted the interrogation of the tenants. Vance had
watched the routine activities of the police with unwonted intentness, and had even taken part in the
search. He had seemed particularly interested in
Skeel's evening clothes, and had examined them garment by garment. Heath had looked at him from
time to time, but there had been neither contempt
nor amusement in the Sergeant's glances.

At half past two Markham departed, after in-
forming Heath that he would be at the Stuyvesant

Club during the remainder of the day; and Vance and I went with him. We had a belated luncheon in the empty grill.

"This Skeel episode rather knocks the foundation from under everything," Markham said dispiritedly, as our coffee was served.

"Oh, no—not that," Vance answered. "Rather, let us say that it has added a new column to the edifice of my giddy theory."

"Your theory—yes. It's about all that's left to go on." Markham sighed. "It has certainly received substantiation this morning. . . . Remarkable how you called the turn when Skeel failed to show up."

Again Vance contradicted him.

"You overestimate my little flutter in forensics, Markham dear. You see, I assumed that the lady's strangler knew of Skeel's offer to you. That offer was probably a threat of some kind on Skeel's part; otherwise he wouldn't have set the appointment a day ahead. He no doubt hoped the victim of his threat would become amenable in the meantime. And that money hidden in the curtain-rod leads me to think he was blackmailing the Canary's murderer, and had been refused a further donation just before he phoned you yesterday. That would account, too, for his having kept his guilty knowledge to himself all this time."

"You may be right. But now we're worse off than ever, for we haven't even Skeel to guide us."

"At least we've forced our elusive culprit to commit a second crime to cover up his first, don't y' know. And when we have learned what the Canary's various amorists were doing last night between ten

and twelve, we may have something suggestive on
which to work.—By the bye, when may we expect
this thrillin' information?"

"It depends upon what luck Heath's men have.
To-night some time, if everything goes well."

It was, in fact, about half past eight when Heath
telephoned the reports. But here again Markham
seemed to have drawn a blank. A less satisfactory
account could scarcely be imagined. Doctor Lindquist had suffered a "nervous stroke" the preceding
afternoon, and had been taken to the Episcopal Hospital. He was still there under the care of two eminent physicians whose word it was impossible to
doubt; and it would be a week at least before he
would be able to resume his work. This report was
the only definite one of the four, and it completely
exonerated the doctor from any participation in the
previous night's crime.

By a curious coincidence neither Mannix, nor
Cleaver, nor Spotswoode could furnish a satisfactory
alibi. All three of them, according to their statements, had remained at home the night before. The
weather had been inclement; and though Mannix
and Spotswoode admitted to having been out earlier
in the evening, they stated that they had returned
home before ten o'clock. Mannix lived in an apartment-hotel, and, as it was Saturday night, the lobby
was crowded, so that no one would have been likely
to see him come in. Cleaver lived in a small private
apartment-house without a door-man or hallboys to
observe his movements. Spotswoode was staying at
the Stuyvesant Club, and since his rooms were on
the third floor, he rarely used the elevator. More-

over, there had been a political reception and dance at the club the previous night, and he might have walked in and out at random a dozen times without being noticed.

"Not what you'd call illuminatin'," said Vance, when Markham had given him this information.

"It eliminates Lindquist, at any rate."

"Quite. And, automatically, it eliminates him as an object of suspicion in the Canary's death also; for these two crimes are part of a whole—integers of the same problem. They complement each other. The latter was conceived in relation to the first—was, in fact, a logical outgrowth of it."

Markham nodded.

"That's reasonable enough. Anyway, I've passed the combative stage. I think I'll drift for a while on the stream of your theory and see what happens."

"What irks me is the disquietin' feeling that positively nothing will happen unless we force the issue. The lad who manœuvred those two obits had real bean in him."

As he spoke Spotswoode entered the room and looked about as if searching for some one. Catching sight of Markham, he came briskly forward, with a look of inquisitive perplexity.

"Forgive me for intruding, sir," he apologized, nodding pleasantly to Vance and me, "but a police officer was here this afternoon inquiring as to my whereabouts last night. It struck me as strange, but I thought little of it until I happened to see the name of Tony Skeel in the headlines of a 'special' to-night and read he had been strangled. I remember you asked me regarding such a man in connection with Miss Odell, and I wondered if, by any chance, there could be any connection between the two murders, and if I was, after all, to be drawn into the affair."

"No, I think not," said Markham. "There seemed a possibility that the two crimes were related; and, as a matter of routine, the police questioned all the close friends of Miss Odell in the hope of turning up something suggestive. You may dismiss the matter from your mind. I trust," he added, "the officer was not unpleasantly importunate."

"Not at all." Spotswoode's look of anxiety disappeared. "He was extremely courteous but a bit mysterious.—Who was this man Skeel?"

"A half-world character and ex-burglar. He had some hold on Miss Odell, and, I believe, extorted money from her."

A cloud of angry disgust passed over Spotswoode's face.

"A creature like that deserves the fate that overtook him."

We chatted on various matters until ten o'clock, when Vance rose and gave Markham a reproachful look.

"I'm going to try to recover some lost sleep. I'm temperamentally unfitted for a policeman's life."

Despite this complaint, however, nine o'clock the next morning found him at the District Attorney's office. He had brought several newspapers with him, and was reading, with much amusement, the first complete accounts of Skeel's murder. Monday was generally a busy day for Markham, and he had arrived at the office before half past eight in an effort to clean up some pressing routine matters before proceeding with his investigation of the Odell case. Heath, I knew, was to come for a conference at ten o'clock. In the meantime there was nothing for Vance to do but read the newspapers; and I occupied myself in like manner.

Punctually at ten Heath arrived, and from his manner it was plain that something had happened to cheer him immeasurably. He was almost jaunty, and his formal, self-satisfied salutation to Vance was like that of a conqueror to a vanquished adversary. He shook hands with Markham with more than his customary punctility.

"Our troubles are over, sir," he said, and paused to light his cigar. "I've arrested Jessup."

It was Vance who broke the dramatic silence following this astounding announcement.

"In the name of Heaven—what for?"

Heath turned deliberately, in no wise abashed by the other's tone.

"For the murder of Margaret Odell and Tony Skeel."

"Oh, my aunt! Oh, my precious aunt!" Vance sat up and stared at him in amazement. "Sweet angels of heaven, come down and solace me!"

Heath's complacency was unshaken.

"You won't need no angels, or aunts either, when you hear what I've found out about this fellow. I've got him tied up in a sack, ready to hand to the jury."

The first wave of Markham's astonishment had subsided.

"Let's have the story, Sergeant."

Heath settled himself in a chair. He took a few moments to arrange his thoughts.

"It's like this, sir. Yesterday afternoon I got to thinking. Here was Skeel murdered, same like Odell, after he'd promised to squeal; and it certainly looked as though the same guy had strangled both of 'em. Therefore, I concluded that there musta been two guys in the apartment Monday night—the Dude and the murderer—just like Mr. Vance has been saying all along. Then I figured that they knew each other pretty well, because not only did the other fellow know where the Dude lived, but he musta been wise to the fact that the Dude was going to squeal yesterday. It looked to me, sir, like they had pulled the Odell job together—which is why the Dude didn't squeal in the first place. But after the other fellow lost his nerve and threw the jewellery away, Skeel thought he'd play safe by turning state's evidence, so he phoned you."

The Sergeant smoked a moment.

"I never put much stock in Mannix and Cleaver and the doc. They weren't the kind to do a job like that, and they certainly weren't the kind that would be mixed up with a jailbird like Skeel. So I stood all three of 'em to one side, and began looking round for a bad egg—somebody who'd have been likely to be Skeel's accomplice. But first I tried to figure out what you might call the physical obstacles in the case—that is, the snags we were up against in our reconstruction of the crime."

Again he paused.

"Now, the thing that's been bothering us most is that side door. How did it get unbolted after six o'clock? And who bolted it again after the crime? Skeel musta come in by it before eleven, because he was in the apartment when Spotswoode and Odell returned from the theatre; and he probably went out by it after Cleaver had come to the apartment at about midnight. But that wasn't explaining how it got bolted again on the inside. Well, sir, I studied over this for a long time yesterday, and then I went up to the house and took another look at the door. Young Spively was running the switchboard, and I asked him where Jessup was, for I wanted to ask him some questions. And Spively told me he'd quit his job the day before—Saturday afternoon!"

Heath waited to let this fact sink in.

"I was on my way down-town before the idea came to me. Then it hit me sudden-like; and the whole case broke wide open.—Mr. Markham, nobody but Jessup coulda opened that side door and locked it again—nobody. Figure it out for yourself, sir— though I guess you've pretty well done it already. Skeel couldn't've done it. And there wasn't nobody else to do it."

Markham had become interested, and leaned forward.

"After this idea had hit me," Heath continued, "I decided to take a chance; so I got outa the Subway at the Penn Station, and phoned Spively for Jessup's address. Then I got my first good news: Jessup lived on Second Avenue, right around the corner from Skeel! I picked up a coupla men from the local station, and went to his house. We found him packing up his things, getting ready to go to Detroit. We locked him up, and I took his finger-prints and sent 'em to Dubois. I thought I might get a line on him that way, because crooks don't generally begin with a job as big as the Canary prowl."

Heath permitted himself a grin of satisfaction.

"Well, sir, Dubois nailed him up! His name ain't Jessup at all. The William part is all right, but his real moniker is Benton. He was convicted of assault and battery in Oakland in 1909, and served a year in San Quentin when Skeel was a prisoner there. He was also grabbed as a lookout in a bank robbery in Brooklyn in 1914, but didn't come to trial—that's how we happen to have his finger-prints at Head-quarters. When we put him on the grill last night, he said he changed his name after the Brooklyn racket, and enlisted in the army. That's all we could get outa him; but we didn't need any more.—Now, here are the facts: Jessup has served time for assault and battery. He was mixed up in a bank robbery. Skeel was a fellow prisoner of his. He's got no alibi for Saturday night when Skeel was killed, and he lives round the corner. He quit his job suddenly Saturday afternoon. He's husky and strong and could easily have done the business. He was planning his getaway when we nabbed him. *And*—he's the only person who could've unbolted and rebolted that side door Monday night. . . . Is that a case, or ain't it, Mr. Markham?"

Markham sat several minutes in thought.

"It's a good case as far as it goes," he said slowly. "But what was his motive in strangling the girl?"

"That's easy. Mr. Vance here suggested it the first day. You remember he asked Jessup about his feelings for Odell; and Jessup turned red and got nervous."

"Oh, Lord!" exclaimed Vance. "Am I to be made responsible for any part of this priceless lunacy? . . . True, I pried into the chap's emotions toward the lady; but that was before anything had come to light. I was bein' careful—tryin' to test each possibility as it arose."

"Well, that was a lucky question of yours, just the same." Heath turned back to Markham. "As I see it: Jessup was stuck on Odell, and she told him to trot along and sell his papers. He got all worked up over it, sitting there night after night, seeing these other guys calling on her. Then Skeel comes along, and, recognizing him, suggests burglarizing Odell's apartment. Skeel can't do the job without help, for he has to pass the phone operator coming and going; and as he's been there before, he'd be recognized. Jessup sees a chance of getting even with Odell and putting the blame on some one else; so the two of 'em cook up the job for Monday night. When Odell goes out Jessup unlocks the side door, and the Dude lets himself into the apartment with his own key. Then Odell and Spotswoode arrive unexpectedly. Skeel hides in the closet, and after Spotswoode has gone, he accidentally makes a noise, and Odell screams. He steps out, and when she sees who he is, she tells Spotswoode it's a mistake. Jessup now knows Skeel has been discovered, and decides to make use of the fact. Soon after Spotswoode has gone, he enters the apartment with a pass-key. Skeel, thinking it's somebody else, hides again in the closet; and then Jessup grabs the girl and strangles her, intending to let Skeel get the credit for it. But Skeel comes out of hiding and they talk it over. Finally they come to an agreement, and proceed with their original plan to loot the place. Jessup tries to open the jewel-case with the poker, and Skeel finishes the job with his chisel. They then go out. Skeel leaves by the side door, and Jessup rebolts it. The next day Skeel hands the swag to Jessup to keep till things blow over; and Jessup gets scared and throws it away. Then they have a row. Skeel decides to tell everything, so he can get cut from under; and Jessup, suspecting he's going to do it, goes round to his house Saturday night and strangles him like he did Odell."

Heath made a gesture of finality and sank back in his chair.

"Clever—deuced clever," murmured Vance. "Sergeant, I apologize for my little outburst a moment ago. Your logic is irreproachable. You've reconstructed the crime beautifully. You've solved the case. . . . It's wonderful—simply wonderful. But it's wrong."

"It's right enough to send Mr. Jessup to the chair."

"That's the terrible thing about logic," said Vance. "It so often leads one irresistibly to a false conclusion."

He stood up and walked across the room and back, his hands in his coat-pockets. When he came abreast of Heath he halted.

"I say, Sergeant; if somebody else could have unlocked that side door, and then rebolted it again after the crime, you'd be willing to admit that it would weaken your case against Jessup—eh, what?"

Heath was in a generous mood.

"Sure. Show me some one else who coulda done that, and I'll admit that maybe I'm wrong."

"Skeel could have done it, Sergeant. And he did do it—without any one knowing it."

"Skeel!—This ain't the age of miracles, Mr. Vance."

Vance swung about and faced Markham.

"Listen! I'm telling you Jessup's innocent." He spoke with a fervor that amazed me. "And I'm going to prove it to you—some way. My theory is pretty complete; it's deficient only in one or two small points; and, I'll confess, I haven't yet been able to put a name to the culprit. But it's the right theory, Markham, and it's diametrically opposed to the Sergeant's. Therefore, you've got to give me an opportunity to demonstrate it before you proceed against Jessup. Now, I can't demonstrate it here; so you and Heath must come with me to the Odell house. It won't take over an hour. But if it took a week, you'd have to come just the same."

He stepped nearer to the desk.

"I know that it was Skeel, and not Jessup, who unbolted that door before the crime, and rebolted it afterward."

Markham was impressed.

"You know this—you know it for a fact?"

"Yes! And I know how he did it!"

CHAPTER XXV

(*Monday, September 17; 11.30 a. m.*)

Half an hour later we entered the little apartment-house in 71st Street. Despite the plausibility of Heath's case against Jessup, Markham was not entirely satisfied with the arrest; and Vance's attitude had sown further seeds of doubt in his mind. The strongest point against Jessup was that relating to the bolting and unbolting of the side door; and when Vance had asserted that he was able to demonstrate how Skeel could have manipulated his own entrance and exit, Markham, though only partly convinced, had agreed to accompany him. Heath, too, was interested, and, though supercilious, had expressed a willingness to go along.

Spively, scintillant in his chocolate-colored suit, was at the switchboard, and stared at us apprehensively. But when Vance suggested pleasantly that he take a ten-minute walk round the block, he appeared greatly relieved, and lost no time in complying.

The officer on guard outside of the Odell apartment came forward and saluted.

"How goes it?" asked Heath. "Any visitors?"

"Only one—a toff who said he'd known the Canary and wanted to see the apartment. I told him to get an order from you or the District Attorney."

"That was correct, officer," said Markham; then, turning to Vance: "Probably Spotswoode—poor devil."

"Quite," murmured Vance. "So persistent! Rosemary and all that. . . . Touchin'."

Heath told the officer to go for a half-hour's stroll; and we were left alone.

"And now, Sergeant," said Vance cheerfully, "I'm sure you know how to operate a switchboard. Be so kind as to act as Spively's understudy for a few minutes—there's a good fellow. . . . But, first, please bolt the side door—and be sure that you bolt it securely, just as it was on the fatal night."

Heath grinned good-naturedly.

"Sure thing." He put his forefinger to his lips mysteriously, and, crouching, tiptoed down the hall like a burlesque detective in a farce. After a few moments he came tiptoeing back to the switchboard, his finger still on his lips. Then, glancing surreptitiously about him with globular eyes, he put his mouth to Vance's ear.

"His-s-s-t!" he whispered. "The door's bolted. G-r-r-r. . . ." He sat down at the switchboard. "When does the curtain go up, Mr. Vance?"

"It's up, Sergeant." Vance fell in with Heath's jocular mood. "Behold! The hour is half past nine on Monday night. You are Spively—not nearly so elegant; and you forgot the moustache—but still Spively. And I am the bedizened Skeel. For the sake of realism, please try to imagine me in chamois gloves and a pleated silk shirt. Mr. Markham and Mr. Van Dine here represent 'the many-headed monster of the pit.'—And, by the bye, Sergeant, let

me have the key to the Odell apartment: Skeel had
one, don't y' know."

Heath produced the key and handed it over, still
grinning.

"A word of stage-direction," Vance continued.
"When I have departed by the front door, you are
to wait exactly three minutes, and then knock at
the late Canary's apartment.

He sauntered to the front door and, turning,
walked back toward the switchboard. Markham
and I stood behind Heath in the little alcove, facing
the front of the building.

"Enter Mr. Skeel!" announced Vance. "Remember, it's half past nine." Then, as he came abreast
of the switchboard: "Dash it all! You forgot your
lines, Sergeant. You should have told me that Miss
Odell was out. But it doesn't matter. . . . Mr.
Skeel continues to the lady's door . . . thus."

He walked past us, and we heard him ring the
apartment bell. After a brief pause, he knocked on
the door. Then he came back down the hall.

"I guess you were right," he said, quoting the
words of Skeel as reported by Spively; and went on
to the front door. Stepping out into the street, he
turned toward Broadway.

For exactly three minutes we waited. None of
us spoke. Heath had become serious, and his ac-
celerated puffing on his cigar bore evidence of his
state of expectancy. Markham was frowning stoi-
cally. At the end of the three minutes Heath rose
and hurried up the hall, with Markham and me at
his heels. In answer to his knock, the apartment
door was opened from the inside. Vance was standing in the little foyer.

"The end of the first act," he greeted us airily. "Thus did Mr. Skeel enter the lady's boudoir Monday night after the side door had been bolted, without the operator's seeing him."

Heath narrowed his eyes, but said nothing. Then he suddenly swung round and looked down the rear passageway to the oak door at the end. The handle of the bolt was in a vertical position, showing that the catch had been turned and that the door was unbolted. Heath regarded it for several moments; then he turned his eyes toward the switchboard. Presently he let out a gleeful whoop.

"Very good, Mr. Vance—very good!" he proclaimed, nodding his head knowingly. "That was easy, though. And it don't take psychology to explain it.—After you rang the apartment bell, you ran down this rear hallway and unbolted the door. Then you ran back and knocked. After that you went out the front entrance, turned toward Broadway, swung round across the street, came in the alley, walked in the side door, and quietly let yourself into the apartment behind our backs."

"Simple, wasn't it?" agreed Vance.

"Sure." The Sergeant was almost contemptuous. "But that don't get you nowhere. Anybody coulda figured it out if that had been the only problem connected with Monday night's operations. But it's the rebolting of that side door, after Skeel had gone, that's been occupying my mind. Skeel might've—*might*'ve, mind you—got in the way you did. But he couldn't have got out that way, because the door was bolted the next morning. And if there was some one here to bolt the door after him, then that same person could've unbolted the door for him earlier, without his doing the ten-foot dash down the rear hall to unbolt the door himself at half past nine. So I don't see that your interesting little drama helps Jessup out any."

"Oh, but the drama isn't over," Vance replied. "The curtain is about to go up on the next act."

Heath lifted his eyes sharply.

"Yeah?" His tone was one of almost jeering incredulity, but his expression was searching and dubious. "And you're going to show us how Skeel got out and bolted the door on the inside without Jessup's help?"

"That is precisely what I intend to do, my Sergeant."

Heath opened his mouth to speak, but thought better of it. Instead, he merely shrugged his shoulders and gave Markham a sly look.

"Let us repair to the public atrium," proceeded Vance; and he led us into the little reception-room diagonally opposite to the switchboard. This room, as I have explained, was just beyond the staircase, and along its rear wall ran the little passageway to the side door. (A glance at the accompanying diagram will clarify the arrangement.)

Vance shepherded us ceremoniously to chairs, and cocked his eye at the Sergeant.

"You will be so good as to rest here until you hear me knock at the side door. Then come and open it for me." He went toward the archway. "Once more I personate the departed Mr. Skeel; so picture me again *en grande tenue*—sartorially radiant. . . . The curtain ascends."

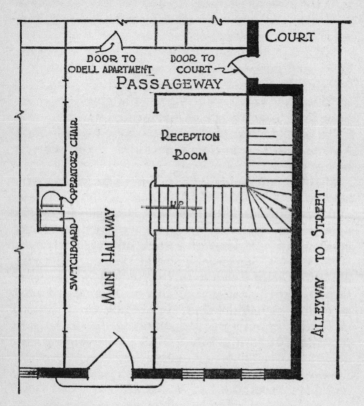

COURT

DOOR TO
ODELL APARTMENT

DOOR TO
COURT

PASSAGEWAY

RECEPTION
ROOM

OPERATOR'S CHAIR

SWITCHBOARD

MAIN HALLWAY

UP

ALLEYWAY TO STREET

WEST SEVENTY-FIRST STREET

He bowed and, stepping from the reception-room into the main hall, disappeared round the corner into the rear passageway.

Heath shifted his position restlessly and gave Markham a questioning, troubled look.

"Will he pull it off, sir, do you think?" All jocularity had gone out of his tone.

"I can't see how." Markham was scowling. "If he does, though, it will knock the chief underpinning from your theory of Jessup's guilt."

"I'm not worrying," declared Heath. "Mr. Vance knows a lot; he's got ideas. But how in hell——?"

He was interrupted by a loud knocking on the side door. The three of us sprang up simultaneously and hurried round the corner of the main hall. The rear passageway was empty. There was no door or aperture of any kind on either side of it. It consisted of two blank walls; and at the end, occupying almost its entire width, was the oak door which led to the court. Vance could have disappeared only through that oak door. And the thing we all noticed at once—for our eyes had immediately sought it—was the horizontal position of the bolt-handle. This meant that the door was bolted.

Heath was not merely astonished—he was dumbfounded. Markham had halted abruptly, and stood staring down the empty passageway as if he saw a ghost. After a momentary hesitation Heath walked rapidly to the door. But he did not open it at once. He went down on his knees before the lock and scrutinized the bolt carefully. Then he took out his pocket-knife and inserted the blade into the crack between the door and the casing. The point halted against the inner moulding, and the edge of the blade scraped upon the circular bolt. There was no question that the heavy oak casings and mouldings of the door were solid and well fitted, and that the bolt had been securely thrown from the inside. Heath, however, was still suspicious, and, grasping the door-knob, he tugged at it violently. But the door held firmly. At length he threw the bolt-handle to a vertical position and opened the door. Vance was standing in the court, placidly smoking and inspecting the brickwork of the alley wall.

"I say, Markham," he remarked, "here's a curious thing. This wall, d' ye know, must be very old. It wasn't built in these latter days of breathless efficiency. The beauty-loving mason who erected it laid the bricks in Flemish bond instead of the Running—or Stretcher—bond of our own restless age. And up there a bit"—he pointed toward the rear yard—"is a Rowlock and Checkerboard pattern. Very neat and very pretty—more pleasing even than the popular English Cross bond. And the mortar joints are all V-tooled. . . . Fancy!"

Markham was fuming.

"Damn it, Vance! I'm not building brick walls. What I want to know is how you got out here and left the door bolted on the inside."

"Oh, that!" Vance crushed out his cigarette and re-entered the building. "I merely made use of a bit of clever criminal mechanism. It's very simple, like all truly effective appliances—oh, simple beyond words. I blush at its simplicity. . . . Observe!"

He took from his pocket a tiny pair of tweezers

to the end of which was tied a piece of purple twine about four feet long. Placing the tweezers over the vertical bolt-handle, he turned them at a very slight angle to the left and then ran the twine under the door so that about a foot of it projected over the sill. Stepping into the court, he closed the door.

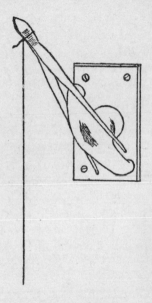

The tweezers still held the bolt-handle as in a vise, and the string extended straight to the floor and disappeared under the door into the court. The three of us stood watching the bolt with fascinated attention. Slowly the string became taut, as Vance gently pulled upon the loose end outside, and then the downward tug began slowly but surely to turn the bolt-handle. When the bolt had been thrown and the handle was in a horizontal position, there came a slight jerk on the string. The tweezers were disengaged from the bolt-handle, and fell noiselessly to the carpeted floor. Then as the string was pulled from without, the tweezers disappeared under the crack between the bottom of the door and the sill.

"Childish, what?" commented Vance, when Heath had let him in. "Silly, too, isn't it? And yet, Sergeant dear, that's how the deceased Tony left these premises last Monday night. . . . But let's go into the lady's apartment, and I'll tell you a story. I see that Mr. Spively has returned from his promenade; so he can resume his telephonic duties and leave us free for a *causerie.*"

"When did you think up that hocus-pocus with the tweezers and string?" demanded Markham irritably, when we were seated in the Odell living-room.

"I didn't think it up at all, don't y' know," Vance told him carelessly, selecting a cigarette with annoying deliberation. "It was Mr. Skeel's idea. Ingenious lad—eh, what?"

"Come, come!" Markham's equanimity was at last shaken. "How can you possibly know that Skeel used this means of locking himself out?"

"I found the little apparatus in his evening clothes yesterday morning."

"What!" cried Heath belligerently. "You took that outa Skeel's room yesterday during the search, without saying anything about it?"

"Oh, only after your ferrets had passed it by. In fact, I didn't even look at the gentleman's clothes until your experienced searchers had inspected them and relocked the wardrobe door. Y' see, Sergeant,

this little thingumbob was stuffed away in one of
the pockets of Skeel's dress waistcoat, under the
silver cigarette-case. I'll admit I went over his evening suit rather lovin'ly. He wore it, y' know, on
the night the lady departed this life, and I hoped to
find some slight indication of his collaboration in
the event. When I found this little eyebrow-plucker,
I hadn't the slightest inkling of its significance. And
the purple twine attached to it bothered me frightfully, don't y' know. I could see that Mr. Skeel
didn't pluck his eyebrows; and even if he had been
addicted to the practice, why the twine? The
tweezers are a delicate little gold affair—just what
the ravishin' Margaret might have used; and last
Tuesday morning I noticed a small lacquer tray containing similar toilet accessories on her dressing-
table near the jewel-case.—But that wasn't all."

He pointed to the little vellum waste-basket beside
the escritoire, in which lay a large crumpled mass of
heavy paper.

"I also noticed that piece of discarded wrapping-
paper stamped with the name of a well-known Fifth
Avenue novelty shop; and this morning, on my way
down-town, I dropped in at the shop and learned
that they make a practice of tying up their bundles
with purple twine. Therefore, I concluded that
Skeel had taken the tweezers and the twine from
this apartment during his visit here that eventful
night. . . . Now, the question was: Why should he
have spent his time tying strings to eyebrow-pluckers? I confess, with maidenly modesty, that I
couldn't find an answer. But this morning when you
told of arresting Jessup, and emphasized the rebolt-

ing of the side door after Skeel's departure, the fog lifted, the sun shone, the birds began to sing. I became suddenly mediumistic: I had a psychic seizure. The whole *modus operandi* came to me—as they say —in a flash. . . . I told you, Markham old thing, it would take spiritualism to solve this case."

CHAPTER XXVI

RECONSTRUCTING THE CRIME

(Monday, September 17; noon)

When Vance finished speaking, there was several minutes' silence. Markham sat deep in his chair glaring into space. Heath, however, was watching Vance with a kind of grudging admiration. The corner-stone in the foundation of his case against Jessup had been knocked out, and the structure he had built was tottering precariously. Markham realized this, and the fact played havoc with his hopes.

"I wish your inspirations were more helpful," he grumbled, turning his gaze upon Vance. "This latest revelation of yours puts us back almost to where we started from."

"Oh, don't be pessimistic. Let us face the future with a bright eye. . . . Want to hear my theory? —it's fairly bulging with possibilities." He arranged himself comfortably in his chair. "Skeel needed money—no doubt his silk shirts were running low— and after his unsuccessful attempt to extort it from the lady a week before her demise, he came here last Monday night. He had learned she would be out, and he intended to wait for her; for she had probably refused to receive him in the custom'ry social way. He knew the side door was bolted at night, and, as he

282

didn't want to be seen entering the apartment, he devised the little scheme of unbolting the door for himself under cover of a futile call at half past nine. The unbolting accomplished, he returned *via* the alleyway, and let himself into the apartment at some time before eleven. When the lady returned with an escort, he quickly hid in the clothes-closet, and remained there until the escort had departed. Then he came forth, and the lady, startled by his sudden appearance, screamed. But, on recognizing him, she told Spotswoode, who was now hammering at the door, that it was all a mistake. So Spotswoode ran along and played poker. A financial discussion between Skeel and the lady—probably a highly acrimonious tiff—ensued. In the midst of it the telephone rang, and Skeel snatched off the receiver and said the Canary was out. The tiff was resumed; but presently another suitor appeared on the scene. Whether he rang the bell or let himself in with a key I can't say—probably the latter, for the phone operator was unaware of his visit. Skeel hid himself a second time in the closet, and luckily took the precaution of locking himself in. Also, he quite naturally put his eye to the keyhole to see who the second intruder was."

Vance pointed to the closet door.

"The keyhole, you will observe, is on a line with the davenport; and as Skeel peered out into the room he saw a sight that froze his blood. The new arrival —in the midst, perhaps, of some endearing sentence —seized the lady by the throat and proceeded to throttle her. . . . Imagine Skeel's emotions, my dear Markham. There he was, crouching in a dark

closet, and a few feet from him stood a murderer in
the act of strangling a lady! *Pauvre Antoine!* I
don't wonder he was petrified and speechless. He
saw what he imagined to be maniacal fury in the
strangler's eyes; and the strangler must have been
a fairly powerful creature, whereas Skeel was slender
and almost undersized. . . . No, *merci*. Skeel
wasn't having any. He lay doggo. And I can't
say that I blame the beggar, what?"

He made a gesture of interrogation.

"What did the strangler do next? Well, well;
we'll probably never know, now that Skeel, the horrified witness, has gone to his Maker. But I rather
imagine he got out that black document-box, opened
it with a key he had taken from the lady's hand-bag,
and extracted a goodly number of incriminating
documents. Then, I fancy, the fireworks began.
The gentleman proceeded to wreck the apartment in
order to give the effect of a professional burglary.
He tore the lace on the lady's gown and severed
the shoulder-strap; snatched her orchid corsage and
threw it in her lap; stripped off her rings and bracelets; and tore the pendant from its chain. After that
he upset the lamp, rifled the escritoire, ransacked the
Boule cabinet, broke the mirror, overturned the
chairs, tore the draperies. . . . And all the time
Skeel kept his eye glued to the keyhole with fascinated horror, afraid to move, terrified lest he be discovered and sent to join his erstwhile *inamorata*,
for by now he was no doubt thoroughly convinced
that the man outside was a raving lunatic.—I can't
say that I envy Skeel his predicament: it was tick-
lish, y' know. Rather!—And the devastation went

on. He could hear it even when the operations had passed from out his radius of vision. And he himself was caught like a rat in a trap, with no means of escape. A harrowin' situation—my word!"

Vance smoked a moment, and then shifted his position slightly.

"Y' know, Markham, I imagine that the worst moment in the whole of Skeel's checkered career came when that mysterious wrecker tried to open the closet door behind which he was crouching. Fancy! There he was cornered, and not two inches from him stood, apparently, a homicidal maniac trying to get to him, rattling that thin barricade of white pine. . . . Can you picture the blighter's relief when the murderer finally released the knob and turned away? It's a wonder he didn't collapse from the reaction. But he didn't. He listened and watched in a sort of hypnotic panic, until he heard the invader leave the apartment. Then, weak-kneed and in a cold sweat, he came forth and surveyed the battle-field."

Vance glanced about him.

"Not a pretty sight—eh, what? And there on the davenport reclined the lady's strangled body. That corpse was Skeel's dominant horror. He staggered to the table to look at it, and steadied himself with his right hand—that's how you got your finger-prints, Sergeant. Then the realization of his own position suddenly smote him. Here he was alone with a murdered person. He was known to have been intimate with the lady; and he was a burglar with a record. Who would believe that he was inno-cent? And though he had probably recognized the man who had negotiated the business, he was in no position to tell his story. Everything was against him—his sneaking in, his presence in the house at half past nine, his relations with the girl, his profession, his reputation. He hadn't a chance in the world. . . . I say, Markham, would *you* have credited his tale?"

"Never mind that," retorted Markham. "Go on with your theory." He and Heath had been listening with rapt interest.

"My theory from this point on," resumed Vance, "is what you might term self-developing. It proceeds on its own inertia, so to speak.—Skeel was confronted by the urgent problem of getting away and covering up his tracks. His mind in this emergency became keen and highly active: his life was forfeit if he didn't succeed. He began to think furiously. He could have left by the side door at once without being seen; but then, the door would have been found unbolted. And this fact, taken in connection with his earlier visit that night, would have suggested his manner of unbolting the door. . . . No, that method of escape wouldn't do—decidedly it wouldn't do. He knew he was likely, in any event, to be suspected of the murder, in view of his shady association with the lady and his general character. Motive, place, opportunity, time, means, conduct, and his own record—all were against him. Either he must cover up his tracks, don't y' know, or else his career as a Lothario was at an end. A sweet dilemma! He realized, of course, that if he could get out and leave that side door bolted on the inside, he'd be comparatively safe. No one could then explain how he

had come in or gone out. It would establish his only
possible alibi—a negative one, to be sure; but, with
a good lawyer, he could probably make it hold.
Doubtless he searched for other means of escape, but
found himself confronted with obstacles on every
hand. The side door was his only hope. How could
it be worked?"

Vance rose and yawned.

"That's my caressin' theory. Skeel was caught
in a trap, and with his shrewd, tricky brain he figured
his way out. He may have roamed up and down
these two rooms for hours before he hit on his plan;
and it's not unlikely that he appealed to the Deity
with an occasional 'Oh, my God!' As for his using
the tweezers, I'm inclined to think the mechanism of
the idea came to him almost immediately.—Y' know,
Sergeant, this locking of a door on the inside is an
old trick. There are any number of recorded cases of
it in the criminal literature of Europe. Indeed, in
Professor Hans Gross's handbook of criminology
there's a whole chapter on the devices used by burglars for illegal entries and exits.* But all such devices have had to do with the locking—not the bolting—of doors. The principle, of course, is the same,
but the technic is different. To lock a door on the
inside, a needle, or strong slender pin, is inserted
through the bow of the key, and pulled downward
with a string. But on the side door of this house
there is no lock and key; nor is there a bow in the
bolt-handle.—Now, the resourceful Skeel, while pacing nervously about, looking for something that

* The treatise referred to by Vance was *Handbuch für Untersuchungs-
richter als System der Kriminalistik.*

might offer a suggestion, probably espied the tweezers on the lady's dressing-table—no lady nowadays is without these little eyebrow-pluckers, don't y' know —and immediately his problem was solved. It remained only to test the device. Before departing, however, he chiselled open the jewel-case which the other chap had merely dinted, and found the solitaire diamond ring that he later attempted to pawn. Then he erased, as he thought, all his finger-prints, forgetting to wipe off the inside door-knob of the closet, and overlooking the hand-mark on the table. After that, he let himself out quietly, and rebolted the side door the same as I did, stuffing the tweezers in his waistcoat pocket and forgetting them."

Heath nodded his head oracularly.

"A crook, no matter how clever he is, always overlooks something."

"Why single out crooks for your criticism, Sergeant?" asked Vance lazily. "Do you know of anybody in this imperfect world who doesn't always overlook something?" He gave Heath a benignant smile. "Even the police, don't y' know, overlooked the tweezers."

Heath grunted. His cigar had gone out, and he relighted it slowly and thoroughly.

"What do you think, Mr. Markham?"

"The situation doesn't become much clearer," was Markham's gloomy comment.

"My theory isn't exactly a blindin' illumination," said Vance. "Yet I wouldn't say that it left things in pristine darkness. There are certain inferences to be drawn from my vagaries. To wit: Skeel either knew or recognized the murderer; and once he had

made good his escape from the apartment and had regained a modicum of self-confidence, he undoubtedly
blackmailed his homicidal confrère. His death was
merely another manifestation of our *inconnu's* bent
for ridding himself of persons who annoyed him.
Furthermore, my theory accounts for the chiselled
jewel-case, the finger-prints, the unmolested closet,
the finding of the gems in the refuse-tin—the person
who took them really didn't want them, y' know—
and Skeel's silence. It also explains the unbolting
and bolting of the side door."

"Yes," sighed Markham. "It seems to clarify
everything but the one all-important point—the
identity of the murderer."

"Exactly," said Vance. "Let's go to lunch."

Heath, morose and confused, departed for Police
Headquarters; and Markham, Vance, and I rode to
Delmonico's, where we chose the main dining-room
in preference to the grill.

"The case now would seem to centre in Cleaver and
Mannix," said Markham, when we had finished our
luncheon. "If your theory that the same man killed
both Skeel and the Canary is correct, then Lindquist
is out of it, for he certainly was in the Episcopal
Hospital Saturday night."

"Quite," agreed Vance. "The doctor is unquestionably eliminated. . . . Yes; Cleaver and Mannix
—they're the allurin' twins. Don't see any way to go
beyond them." He frowned and sipped his coffee.
"My original quartet is dwindling, and I don't like it.
It narrows the thing down too much—there's no
scope for the mind, as it were, in only two choices.
What if we should succeed in eliminating Cleaver

and Mannix? Where would we be—eh, what? Nowhere—simply nowhere. And yet, one of the quartet is guilty; let's cling to that consolin' fact. It can't be Spotswoode and it can't be Lindquist. Cleaver and Mannix remain: two from four leaves two. Simple arithmetic, what? The only trouble is, this case isn't simple. Lord, no!—I say, how would the equation work out if we used algebra, or spherical trigonometry, or differential calculus? Let's cast it in the fourth dimension—or the fifth, or the sixth. . . ." He held his temples in both hands. "Oh, promise, Markham—promise me that you'll hire a kind, gentle keeper for me."

"I know how you feel. I've been in the same mental state for a week."

"It's the quartet idea that's driving me mad," moaned Vance. "It wrings me to have my tetrad lopped off in such brutal fashion. I'd set my young trustin' heart on that quartet, and now it's only a pair. My sense of order and proportion has been outraged. . . . I want my quartet."

"I'm afraid you'll have to be satisfied with two of them," Markham returned wearily. "One of them can't qualify, and one is in bed. You might send some flowers to the hospital, if it would cheer you any."

"One is in bed—one is in bed," repeated Vance. "Well, well—to be sure! And one from four leaves three. More arithmetic. Three! . . . On the other hand, there is no such thing as a straight line. All lines are curved; they transcribe circles in space. They look straight, but they're not. Appearances, y' know—so deceptive! . . . Let's enter the silence, and substitute mentation for sight."

He gazed up out of the great windows into Fifth Avenue. For several moments he sat smoking thoughtfully. When he spoke again, it was in an even, deliberate voice.

"Markham, would it be difficult for you to invite Mannix and Cleaver and Spotswoode to spend an evening—this evening, let us say—in your apartment?"

Markham set down his cup with a clatter, and regarded Vance narrowly.

"What new harlequinade is this?"

"Fie on you! Answer my question."

"Well—of course—I might arrange it," replied Markham hesitantly. "They're all more or less under my jurisdiction at present."

"So that such an invitation would be rather in line with the situation—eh, what? And they wouldn't be likely to refuse you, old dear—would they?"

"No; I hardly think so. . . ."

"And if, when they had assembled in your quarters, you should propose a few hands of poker, they'd probably accept, without thinking the suggestion strange?"

"Probably," said Markham, nonplussed at Vance's amazing request. "Cleaver and Spotswoode both play, I know; and Mannix doubtless knows the game. But why poker? Are you serious, or has your threatened dementia already overtaken you?"

"Oh, I'm deuced serious." Vance's tone left no doubt as to the fact. "The game of poker, d' ye see, is the crux of the matter. I knew Cleaver was an old hand at the game; and Spotswoode, of course, played

with Judge Redfern last Monday night. So that gave
me a basis for my plan. Mannix, we'll assume, also
plays."

He leaned forward, speaking earnestly.

"Nine-tenths of poker, Markham, is psychology;
and if one understands the game, one can learn more
of a man's inner nature at a poker table in an hour
than during a year's casual association with him.
You rallied me once when I said I could lead you to
the perpetrator of any crime by examining the factors
of the crime itself. But naturally I must know the
man to whom I am to lead you; otherwise I cannot
relate the psychological indications of the crime to
the culprit's nature. In the present case, I know the
kind of man who committed the crime; but I am
not sufficiently acquainted with the suspects to point
out the guilty one. However, after our game of
poker, I hope to be able to tell you who planned and
carried out the Canary's murder." *

Markham gazed at him in blank astonishment.
He knew that Vance played poker with amazing
skill, and that he possessed an uncanny knowledge of
the psychological elements involved in the game; but

* Recently I ran across an article by Doctor George A. Dorsey, professor of anthropology at the University of Chicago, and author of "Why
We Behave Like Human Beings," which bore intimate testimony to the
scientific accuracy of Vance's theory. In it Doctor Dorsey said: "Poker
is a cross-section of life. The way a man behaves in a poker game is the
way he behaves in life. . . . His success or failure lies in the way his
physical organism responds to the stimuli supplied by the game. . . .
I have studied humanity all my life from the anthropologic and psychological view-point. And I have yet to find a better laboratory ex-
ercise than to observe the manners of men as they see my raise and
come back at me. . . . The psychologist's verbalized, visceral, and
manual behaviors are functioning at their highest in a poker game. . . .
I can truthfully say that I learned about men from poker."

he was unprepared for the latter's statement that he might be able to solve the Odell murder by means of it. Yet Vance had spoken with such undoubted earnestness that Markham was impressed. I knew what was passing in his mind almost as well as if he had voiced his thoughts. He was recalling the way in which Vance had, in a former murder case, put his finger unerringly on the guilty man by a similar process of psychological deduction. And he was also telling himself that, however incomprehensible and seemingly extravagant Vance's requests were, there was always a fundamentally sound reason behind them.

"Damn it!" he muttered at last. "The whole scheme seems idiotic. . . . And yet, if you really want a game of poker with these men, I've no special objection. It'll get you nowhere—I'll tell you that beforehand. It's stark nonsense to suppose that you can find the guilty man by such fantastic means."

"Ah, well," sighed Vance, "a little futile recreation will do us no harm."

"But why do you include Spotswoode?"

"Really, y' know, I haven't the slightest notion —except, of course, that he's one of my quartet. And we'll need an extra hand."

"Well, don't tell me afterwards that I'm to lock him up for murder. I'd have to draw the line. Strange as it may seem to your layman's mind, I wouldn't care to prosecute a man, knowing that it was physically impossible for him to have committed the crime."

"As to that," drawled Vance, "the only obstacles that stand in the way of physical impossibilities are material facts. And material facts are notoriously deceivin'. Really, y' know, you lawyers would do better if you ignored them entirely."

Markham did not deign to answer such heresy, but the look he gave Vance was most expressive.

CHAPTER XXVII

A GAME OF POKER

(Monday, September 17; 9 p. m.)

Vance and I went home after lunch, and at about four o'clock Markham telephoned to say that he had made the necessary arrangements for the evening with Spotswoode, Mannix, and Cleaver. Immediately following this confirmation Vance left the house, and did not return until nearly eight o'clock. Though I was filled with curiosity at so unusual a proceeding, he refused to enlighten me. But when, at a quarter to nine, we went down-stairs to the waiting car, there was a man I did not know in the tonneau; and I at once connected him with Vance's mysterious absence.

"I've asked Mr. Allen to join us to-night," Vance vouchsafed, when he had introduced us. "You don't play poker, and we really need another hand to make the game interestin', y' know. Mr. Allen, by the bye, is an old antagonist of mine."

The fact that Vance would, apparently without permission, bring an uninvited guest to Markham's apartment amazed me but little more than the appearance of the man himself. He was rather short, with sharp, shrewd features; and what I saw of his hair beneath his jauntily tipped hat was black and sleek, like the painted hair on Japanese dolls. I noted, too, that his evening tie was enlivened by a

design of tiny white forget-me-nots, and that his
shirt-front was adorned with diamond studs.

The contrast between him and the immaculately
stylish and meticulously correct Vance was aggres-
sively evident. I wondered what could be the relationship between them. Obviously it was neither
social nor intellectual.

Cleaver and Mannix were already on hand when
we were ushered into Markham's drawing-room,
and a few minutes later Spotswoode arrived. The
amenities of introduction over, we were soon seated
comfortably about the open log fire, smoking, and
sipping very excellent Scotch high-balls. Markham
had, of course, accepted the unexpected Mr. Allen
cordially, but his occasional glances in the latter's
direction told me he was having some difficulty in
reconciling the man's appearance with Vance's spon-
sorship.

A tense atmosphere lay beneath the spurious and
affected affability of the little gathering. Indeed,
the situation was scarcely conducive to spontaneity.
Here were three men each of whom was known to
the others to have been interested in the same
woman; and the reason for their having been brought
together was the fact that this woman had been
murdered. Markham, however, handled the situation with such tact that he largely succeeded in giving each one the feeling of being a disinterested spectator summoned to discuss an abstract problem.
He explained at the outset that the "conference"
had been actuated by his failure to find any approach to the problem of the murder. He hoped,
he said, by a purely informal discussion, divested

of all officialism and coercion, to turn up some suggestion that might lead to a fruitful line of inquiry. His manner was one of friendly appeal, and when he finished speaking the general tension had been noticeably relaxed.

During the discussion that followed I was interested in the various attitudes of the men concerned. Cleaver spoke bitterly of his part in the affair, and was more self-condemnatory than suggestive. Mannix was voluble and pretentiously candid, but beneath his comments ran a strain of apologetic wariness. Spotswoode, unlike Mannix, seemed loath to discuss the matter, and maintained a consistently reticent attitude. He responded politely to Markham's questions, but he did not succeed entirely in hiding his resentment at thus being dragged into a general discussion. Vance had little to say, limiting himself to occasional remarks directed always to Markham. Allen did not once speak, but sat contemplating the others with a sort of canny amusement.

The entire conversation struck me as utterly futile. Had Markham really hoped to garner information from it, he would have been woefully disappointed. I realized, though, that he was merely endeavoring to justify himself for having taken so unusual a step, and to pave the way for the game of poker which Vance had requested. When the time came to broach the subject, however, there was no difficulty about it.

It was exactly eleven o'clock when he made the suggestion. His tone was gracious and unassuming; but by couching his invitation in terms of a

personal request, he practically precluded declina-
tion. But his verbal strategy, I felt, was unnecessary. Both Cleaver and Spotswoode seemed genuinely to welcome the opportunity of dropping a
distasteful discussion in favor of playing cards; and
Vance and Allen, of course, concurred instantly.
Mannix alone declined. He explained that he knew
the game only slightly, and disliked it; though he
expressed an enthusiastic desire to watch the others.
Vance urged him to reconsider, but without success;
and Markham finally ordered his man to arrange
the table for five.

I noticed that Vance waited until Allen had taken
his place, and then dropped into the chair at his
right. Cleaver took the seat at Allen's left. Spotswoode sat at Vance's right; and then came Markham. Mannix drew up his chair midway behind
Markham and Cleaver. Thus:

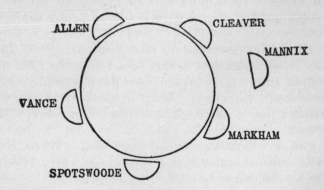

Cleaver first named a rather moderate limit, but
Spotswoode at once suggested much larger stakes.

Then Vance went still higher, and as both Markham and Allen signified their agreement, his figure
was accepted. The prices placed on the chips somewhat took my breath away, and even Mannix whis-
tled softly.

That all five men at the table were excellent players
became obvious before the game had progressed ten
minutes. For the first time that night Vance's friend
Allen seemed to have found his *milieu* and to be
wholly at ease.

Allen won the first two hands, and Vance the
third and fourth. Spotswoode then had a short run
of good luck, and a little later Markham took a large
jack-pot which put him slightly in the lead. Cleaver
was the only loser thus far; but in another half-hour
he had succeeded in recovering a large portion of
his losses. After that Vance forged steadily ahead,
only to relinquish his winning streak to Allen. Then
for a while the fortunes of the game were rather
evenly distributed. But later on both Cleaver and
Spotswoode began to lose heavily. By half past
twelve a grim atmosphere had settled over the party;
for so high were the stakes, and so rapidly did the
betting pyramid, that even for men of means—such
as all these players undoubtedly were—the amounts
which continually changed hands represented very
considerable items.

Just before one o'clock, when the fever of the
game had reached a high point, I saw Vance glance
quickly at Allen and pass his handkerchief across
his forehead. To a stranger the gesture would have
appeared perfectly natural; but, so familiar was I
with Vance's mannerisms, I immediately recognized

its artificiality. And simultaneously I noticed that
it was Allen who was shuffling the cards preparatory
to dealing. Some smoke from his cigar evidently
went into his eye at this moment, for he blinked,
and one of the cards fell to the floor. Quickly retrieving it, he reshuffled the deck and placed it before Vance to cut.

The hand was a jack-pot, and there was a small
fortune in chips already on the table. Cleaver,
Markham, and Spotswoode passed. The decision
thus reached Vance, and he opened for an unusually
large amount. Allen at once laid down his hand, but
Cleaver stayed. Then Markham and Spotswoode
both dropped out, leaving the entire play between
Vance and Cleaver. Cleaver drew one card, and
Vance, who had opened, drew two. Vance made a
nominal wager, and Cleaver raised it substantially.
Vance in turn raised Cleaver, but only for a small
amount; and Cleaver again raised Vance—this time
for an even larger sum than before. Vance hesitated,
and called him. Cleaver exposed his hand trium-
phantly.

"Straight flush—jack high," he announced. "Can
you beat that?"

"Not on a two-card draw," said Vance ruefully.
He put his cards down to show his openers. He had
four kings.

About half an hour later Vance again took out
his handkerchief and passed it across his forehead.
As before, I noted that it was Allen's deal, and also
that the hand was a jack-pot which had been twice
sweetened. Allen paused to take a drink of his high-
ball and to light his cigar. Then, after Vance had
cut the cards, he dealt them.

Cleaver, Markham, and Spotswoode passed, and again Vance opened, for the full amount of the pot. No one stayed except Spotswoode; and this time it was a struggle solely between him and Vance. Spotswoode asked for one card; and Vance stood pat. Then there followed a moment of almost breathless silence. The atmosphere seemed to me to be electrically charged, and I think the others sensed it too, for they were watching the play with a curiously strained intentness. Vance and Spotswoode, however, appeared frozen in attitudes of superlative calm. I watched them closely, but neither revealed the slightest indication of any emotion.

It was Vance's first bet. Without speaking he moved a stack of yellow chips to the centre of the table—it was by far the largest wager that had been made during the game. But immediately Spotswoode measured another stack alongside of it. Then he coolly and deftly counted the remainder of his chips, and pushed them all forward with the palm of his hand, saying quietly:

"The limit."

Vance shrugged almost imperceptibly.

"The pot, sir, is yours." He smiled pleasantly at Spotswoode, and put down his hand face up, to establish his openers. He had held four aces!

"Gad! That's poker!" exclaimed Allen, chuckling.

"Poker?" echoed Markham. "To lay down four aces with all that money at stake?"

Cleaver also grunted his astonishment, and Mannix pursed his lips disgustedly.

"I don't mean any offense, y' understand, Mr. Vance," he said. "But looking at that play from a strictly business standpoint, I'd say you quit too soon."

Spotswoode glanced up.

"You gentlemen wrong Mr. Vance," he said. "He played his hand perfectly. His withdrawal, even with four aces, was scientifically correct."

"Sure it was," agreed Allen. "Oh, boy! What a battle that was!"

Spotswoode nodded and, turning to Vance, said:

"Since the exact situation is never likely to occur again, the least I can do, by way of showing my appreciation of your remarkable perception, is to gratify your curiosity.—I held nothing."

Spotswoode put down his hand and extended his fingers gracefully toward the upturned cards. There were revealed a five, six, seven, and eight of clubs, and a knave of hearts.

"I can't say that I follow your reasoning, Mr. Spotswoode," Markham confessed. "Mr. Vance had you beaten—and he quit."

"Consider the situation," Spotswoode replied, in a suave, even voice. "I most certainly would have opened so rich a pot, had I been able to, after Mr. Cleaver and you had passed. But since I nevertheless stayed after Mr. Vance had opened for so large an amount, it goes without saying that I must have had either a four-straight, a four-flush, or a four-straight-flush. I believe I may state without immodesty that I am too good a player to have stayed otherwise. . . ."

"And I assure you, Markham," interrupted Vance, "that Mr. Spotswoode is too good a player to have stayed unless he had actually had a four-

straight-flush. That is the only hand he would have
been justified in backing at the betting odds of two
to one.—You see, I had opened for the amount in
the pot, and Mr. Spotswoode had to put up half the
amount of the money on the table in order to stay
—making it a two-to-one bet.—Now, these odds are
not high, and any non-opening hand smaller than a
four-straight-flush would not have warranted the
risk. As it was, he had, with a one-card draw, two
chances in forty-seven of making a straight-flush,
nine chances in forty-seven of making a flush, and
eight chances in forty-seven of making a straight; so
that he had nineteen chances in forty-seven—or more
than one chance in three—of strengthening his hand
into either a straight-flush, a flush, or a straight."

"Exactly," assented Spotswoode. "However, after
I had drawn my one card, the only possible question
in Mr. Vance's mind was whether or not I had made
my straight-flush. If I had not made it—or had
merely drawn a straight or a flush—Mr. Vance figured, and figured rightly, that I would not have seen
his large bet and also have raised it the limit. To
have done so, in those circumstances, would have
been irrational poker. Not one player in a thousand would have taken such a risk on a mere bluff.
Therefore, had Mr. Vance not laid down his four
aces when I raised him, he would have been fool-
hardy in the extreme. It turned out, of course, that
I was actually bluffing; but that does not alter the
fact that the correct and logical thing was for Mr.
Vance to quit."

"Quite true," Vance agreed. "As Mr. Spotswoode
says, not one player in a thousand would have

wagered the limit without having filled his straight-flush, knowing I had a pat hand. Indeed, one might almost say that Mr. Spotswoode, by doing so, has added another decimal point to the psychological subtleties of the game; for, as you see, he analyzed my reasoning, and carried his own reasoning a step further."

Spotswoode acknowledged the compliment with a slight bow; and Cleaver reached for the cards and began to shuffle them. But the tension had been broken, and the game was not resumed.

Something, however, seemed to have gone wrong with Vance. For a long while he sat frowning at his cigarette and sipping his high-ball in troubled abstraction. At last he rose and walked to the mantel, where he stood studying a Cézanne water-color he had given Markham years before. His action was a typical indication of his inner puzzlement.

Presently, when there came a lull in the conversation, he turned sharply and looked at Mannix.

"I say, Mr. Mannix"—he spoke with only casual curiosity—"how does it happen you've never acquired a taste for poker? All good business men are gamblers at heart."

"Sure they are," Mannix replied, with pensive deliberation. "But poker, now, isn't my idea of gambling—positively not. It's got too much science. And it ain't quick enough for me—it hasn't got the kick in it, if you know what I mean. Roulette's my speed. When I was in Monte Carlo last summer I dropped more money in ten minutes than you gentlemen lost here this whole evening. But I got action for my money."

A Paramount Picture.

The Canary Murder Case.

"THE CANARY'S DEATH HAS UNNERVED ME—I LOVED HER VERY MUCH."

"I take it, then, you don't care for cards at all."

"Not to play games with." Mannix had become expansive. "I don't mind betting money on the draw of a card, for instance. But no two out of three, y' understand. I want my pleasures to come rapid." And he snapped his thick fingers several times in quick succession to demonstrate the rapidity with which he desired to have his pleasures come.

Vance sauntered to the table and carelessly picked up a deck of cards.

"What do you say to cutting once for a thousand dollars?"

Mannix rose instantly.

"You're on!"

Vance handed the cards over, and Mannix shuffled them. Then he put them down and cut. He turned up a ten. Vance cut, and showed a king.

"A thousand I owe you," said Mannix, with no more concern than if it had been ten cents.

Vance waited without speaking, and Mannix eyed him craftily.

"I'll cut with you again—two thousand this time. Yes?"

Vance raised his eyebrows. "Double? . . . By all means." He shuffled the cards, and cut a seven.

Mannix's hand swooped down and turned a five.

"Well, that's three thousand I owe you," he said. His little eyes had now narrowed into slits, and he held his cigar clamped tightly between his teeth.

"Like to double it again—eh, what?" Vance asked. "Four thousand this time?"

Markham looked at Vance in amazement, and over Allen's face there came an expression of almost ludicrous consternation. Every one present, I believe, was astonished at the offer, for obviously Vance knew that he was giving Mannix tremendous odds by permitting successive doubling. In the end he was sure to lose. I believe Markham would have protested if at that moment Mannix had not snatched the cards from the table and begun to shuffle them.

"Four thousand it is!" he announced, putting down the deck and cutting. He turned up the queen of diamonds. "You can't beat that lady—positively not!" He was suddenly jovial.

"I fancy you're right," murmured Vance; and he cut a trey.

"Want some more?" asked Mannix, with good-natured aggressiveness.

"That's enough." Vance seemed bored. "Far too excitin'. I haven't your rugged constitution, don't y' know."

He went to the desk and made out a check to Mannix for a thousand dollars. Then he turned to Markham and held out his hand.

"Had a jolly evening and all that sort of thing. . . . And, don't forget: we lunch together to-morrow. One o'clock at the club, what?"

Markham hesitated. "If nothing interferes."

"But really, y' know, it mustn't," insisted Vance. "You've no idea how eager you are to see me."

He was unusually silent and thoughtful during the ride home. Not one explanatory word could I get out of him. But when he bade me good night he said:

"There's a vital part of the puzzle still missing, and until it's found none of it has any meaning."

CHAPTER XXVIII

(Tuesday, September 18; 1 p. m.)

Vance slept late the following morning, and spent the hour or so before lunch checking a catalogue of ceramics which were to be auctioned next day at the Anderson Galleries. At one o'clock we entered the Stuyvesant Club and joined Markham in the grill.

"The lunch is on you, old thing," said Vance. "But I'll make it easy. All I want is a rasher of English bacon, a cup of coffee, and a *croissant*."

Markham gave him a mocking smile.

"I don't wonder you're economizing after your bad luck of last night."

Vance's eyebrows went up.

"I rather fancied my luck was most extr'ordin'ry."

"You held four of a kind twice, and lost both hands."

"But, y' see," blandly confessed Vance, "I happened to know both times exactly what cards my opponents held."

Markham stared at him in amazement.

"Quite so," Vance assured him. "I had arranged before the game, d' ye see, to have those particular hands dealt." He smiled benignly. "I can't tell you, old chap, how I admire your delicacy in not referring to my rather unique guest, Mr. Allen, whom I had

307

the bad taste to introduce so unceremoniously into
your party. I owe you an explanation and an
apology. Mr. Allen is not what one would call a
charming companion. He is deficient in the patrician
elegancies, and his display of jewellery was a bit
vulgar—though I infinitely preferred his diamond
studs to his piebald tie. But Mr. Allen has his points
—decidedly he has his points. He ranks with Andy
Blakely, Canfield, and Honest John Kelly as an in-
door soldier of fortune. In fact, our Mr. Allen is
none other than Doc Wiley Allen, of fragrant
memory."

"Doc Allen! Not the notorious old crook who ran
the Eldorado Club?"

"The same. And, incidentally, one of the cleverest
card manipulators in a once lucrative but shady
profession."

"You mean this fellow Allen stacked the cards last
night?" Markham was indignant.

"Only for the two hands you mentioned. Allen,
if you happen to remember, was the dealer both
times. I, who purposely sat on his right, was careful
to cut the cards in accordance with his instructions.
And you really must admit that no stricture can
possibly attach to my deception, inasmuch as the
only beneficiaries of Allen's manipulations were
Cleaver and Spotswoode. Although Allen did deal
me four of a kind on each occasion, I lost heavily
both times."

Markham regarded Vance for a moment in puzzled
silence, and then laughed good-naturedly.

"You appear to have been in a philanthropic mood
last night. You practically gave Mannix a thousand

dollars by permitting him to double the stakes on each draw. A rather quixotic procedure, I should say."

"It all depends on one's point of view, don't y' know. Despite my financial losses—which, by the bye, I have every intention of charging up to your office budget—the game was most successful. . . . Y' see, I attained the main object of my evening's entertainment."

"Oh, I remember!" said Markham vaguely, as if the matter, being of slight importance, had for the moment eluded his memory. "I believe you were going to ascertain who murdered the Odell girl."

"Amazin' memory! . . . Yes, I let fall the hint that I might be able to clarify the situation to-day."

"And whom am I to arrest?"

Vance took a drink of coffee and slowly lit a cigarette.

"I'm quite convinced, y' know, that you won't believe me," he returned, in an even, matter-of-fact voice. "But it was Spotswoode who killed the girl."

"You don't tell me!" Markham spoke with undisguised irony. "So it was Spotswoode! My dear Vance, you positively bowl me over. I would telephone Heath at once to polish up his handcuffs, but, unfortunately, miracles—such as strangling persons from across town—are not recognized possibilities in this day and age. . . . Do let me order you another *croissant*."

Vance extended his hands in a theatrical gesture of exasperated despair.

"For an educated, civilized man, Markham, there's something downright primitive about the way you cling to optical illusions. I say, y' know, you're exactly like an infant who really believes that the magician generates a rabbit in a silk hat, simply because he sees it done."

"Now you're becoming insulting."

"Rather!" Vance pleasantly agreed. "But something drastic must be done to disentangle you from the Lorelei of legal facts. You're so deficient in imagination, old thing."

"I take it that you would have me close my eyes and picture Spotswoode sitting up-stairs here in the Stuyvesant Club and extending his arms to 71st Street. But I simply couldn't do it. I'm a commonplace chap. Such a vision would strike me as ludicrous; it would smack of a hasheesh dream. . . . You yourself don't use *Cannabis indica*, do you?"

"Put that way, the idea does sound a bit supernatural. And yet: *Certum est quia impossibile est.* I rather like that maxim, don't y' know; for, in the present case, the impossible is true. Oh, Spotswoode's guilty—no doubt about it. And I'm going to cling tenaciously to that apparent hallucination. Moreover, I'm going to try to lure you into its toils; for your own—as we absurdly say—good name is at stake. As it happens, Markham, you are at this moment shielding the real murderer from publicity."

Vance had spoken with the easy assurance that precludes argument; and from the altered expression on Markham's face I could see he was moved.

"Tell me," he said, "how you arrived at your fantastic belief in Spotswoode's guilt."

Vance crushed out his cigarette and folded his arms on the table.

"We begin with my quartet of possibilities— Mannix, Cleaver, Lindquist, and Spotswoode. Realizing, as I did, that the crime was carefully planned with the sole object of murder, I knew that only some one hopelessly ensnared in the lady's net could have done it. And no suitor outside of my quartet could have been thus enmeshed, or we would have learned of him. Therefore, one of the four was guilty. Now, Lindquist was eliminated when we found out that he was bedridden in a hospital at the time of Skeel's murder; for obviously the same person committed both crimes——"

"But," interrupted Markham, "Spotswoode had an equally good alibi for the night of the Canary's murder. Why eliminate one and not the other?"

"Sorry, but I can't agree with you. Being prostrated at a known place surrounded by incorruptible and disinterested witnesses, both preceding and during an event, is one thing; but being actually on the ground, as Spotswoode was that fatal evening, within a few minutes of the time the lady was murdered, and then being alone in a taxicab for fifteen minutes or so following the event—that is another thing. No one, as far as we know, actually saw the lady alive after Spotswoode took his departure."

"But the proof of her having been alive and spoken to him is incontestable."

"Granted. I admit that a dead woman doesn't scream and call for help, and then converse with her murderer."

"I see." Markham spoke with sarcasm. "You think it was Skeel, disguising his voice."

"Lord no! What a priceless notion! Skeel didn't

want any one to know he was there. Why should he have staged such a masterpiece of idiocy? That certainly isn't the explanation. When we find the answer it will be reasonable and simple."

"That's encouraging," smiled Markham. "But proceed with your reasons for Spotswoode's guilt."

"Three of my quartet, then, were potential murderers," Vance resumed. "Accordingly, I requested an evening of social relaxation, that I might put them under the psychological microscope, as it were. Although Spotswoode's ancestry was wholly consistent with his having been the guilty one, nevertheless I confess I thought that Cleaver or Mannix had committed the crime; for, by their own statements, either of them could have done it without contradicting any of the known circumstances of the situation. Therefore, when Mannix declined your invitation to play poker last night, I put Cleaver to the first test. I wig-wagged to Mr. Allen, and he straightway proceeded to perform his first feat of prestidigitation."

Vance paused and looked up.

"You perhaps recall the circumstances? It was a jack-pot. Allen dealt Cleaver a four-straight-flush and gave me three kings. The other hands were so poor that every one else was compelled to drop out. I opened; and Cleaver stayed. On the draw, Allen gave me another king, and gave Cleaver the card he needed to complete his straight-flush. Twice I bet a small amount, and each time Cleaver raised me. Finally I called him, and, of course, he won. He couldn't help but win, d' ye see. He was betting on a sure-thing. Since I opened the pot and drew two cards, the highest hand I could possibly have held would have been four of a kind. Cleaver knew this, and having a straight-flush, he also knew, before he raised my bet, that he had me beaten. At once I realized that he was not the man I was after."

"By what reasoning?"

"A poker-player, Markham, who would bet on a sure-thing is one who lacks the egotistical self-confidence of the highly subtle and supremely capable gambler. He is not a man who will take hazardous chances and tremendous risks, for he possesses, to some degree, what the psychoanalysts call an inferiority complex, and instinctively he grasps at every possible opportunity of protecting and bettering himself. In short, he is not the ultimate, unadulterated gambler. And the man who killed the Odell girl was a supreme gambler who would stake everything on a single turn of the wheel, for, in killing her, that is exactly what he did. And only a gambler whose paramount self-confidence would make him scorn, through sheer egotism, to bet on a sure-thing, could have committed such a crime.—Therefore, Cleaver was eliminated as a suspect."

Markham was now listening intently.

"The test to which I put Spotswoode a little later," Vance went on, "had originally been intended for Mannix, but he was out of the game. That didn't matter, however, for, had I been able to eliminate both Cleaver and Spotswoode, then Mannix would undoubtedly have been the guilty man. Of course I would have planned something else to substantiate the fact; but, as it was, that wasn't necess'ry. . . . The test I applied to Spotswoode was pretty well explained by the gentleman himself. As he said, not one player in a thousand would have wagered the limit against a pat hand, when he himself held nothing. It was tremendous —superb! It was probably the most remarkable bluff ever made in a game of poker. I couldn't help admiring him when he calmly shoved forward all his chips, knowing, as I did, that he held nothing. He staked everything, d' ye see, wholly on his conviction that he could follow my reasoning step by step and, in the last analysis, outwit me. It took courage and daring to do that. And it also took a degree of self-confidence which would never have permitted him to bet on a sure-thing. The psychological principles involved in that hand were identical with those of the Odell crime. I threatened Spotswoode with a powerful hand—a pat hand —just as the girl, no doubt, threatened him; and instead of compromising—instead of calling me or laying down—he outreached me; he resorted to one supreme *coup*, though it meant risking everything. . . . My word, Markham! Can't you see how the man's character, as revealed in that amazing gesture, dovetails with the psychology of the crime?"

Markham was silent for a while; he appeared to be pondering the matter.

"But you yourself, Vance, were not satisfied at the time," he submitted at length. "In fact, you looked doubtful and worried."

"True, old dear. I was no end worried. The psychological proof of Spotswoode's guilt came so dashed unexpectedly—I wasn't looking for it, don't y' know. After eliminating Cleaver I had a *parti pris*, so to speak, in regard to Mannix; for all the material evidence in favor of Spotswoode's innocence —that is, the seeming physical impossibility of his having strangled the lady—had, I admit, impressed me. I'm not perfect, don't y' know. Being unfortunately human, I'm still susceptible to the malicious animal magnetism about facts and appearances, which you lawyer chaps are continuously exuding over the earth like some vast asphyxiating effluvium. And even when I found that Spotswoode's psychological nature fitted perfectly with all the factors of the crime, I still harbored a doubt in regard to Mannix. It was barely possible that he would have played the hand just as Spotswoode played it. That is why, after the game was over, I tackled him on the subject of gambling. I wanted to check his psychological reactions."

"Still, he staked everything on one turn of the wheel, as you put it."

"Ah! But not in the same sense that Spotswoode did. Mannix is a cautious and timid gambler as compared with Spotswoode. To begin with, he had an equal chance and an even bet, whereas Spotswoode had no chance at all—his hand was worthless. And yet Spotswoode wagered the limit on a pure bit of mental calculation. That was gambling in the higher ether. On the other hand, Mannix was merely tossing a coin, with an even chance of winning. Furthermore, no calculation of any kind entered into it; there was no planning, no figuring, no daring. And, as I have told you from the start, the Odell murder was premeditated and carefully worked out with shrewd calculation and supreme daring. . . . And what true gambler would ask an adversary to double a bet on the second flip of the coin, and then accept an offer to redouble on the third flip? I purposely tested Mannix in that way, so as to preclude any possibility of error. Thus I not only eliminated him—I expunged him, eradicated him, wiped him out utterly. It cost me a thousand dollars, but it purged my mind of any lingering doubt. I then knew, despite all the contr'ry material indications, that Spotswoode had done away with the lady."

"You make your case theoretically plausible. But, practically, I'm afraid I can't accept it." Markham was more impressed, I felt, than he cared to admit. "Damn it, man!" he exploded after a moment. "Your conclusion demolishes all the established landmarks of rationality and sane credibility. —Just consider the facts." He had now reached the argumentative stage of his doubt. "You say Spotswoode is guilty. Yet we know, on irrefutable evidence, that five minutes after he came out of the apartment the girl screamed and called for help. He was standing by the switchboard, and, accompanied by Jessup, he went to the door and carried on a brief conversation with her. She was certainly alive then. Then he went out the front door, entered a taxicab, and drove away. Fifteen minutes later he was joined by Judge Redfern as he alighted from the taxicab in front of the club here—nearly forty blocks away from the apartment-house! It would have been impossible for him to have made the trip in less time; and, moreover, we have the chauffeur's record. Spotswoode simply did not have either the opportunity or the time to commit the murder between half past eleven and ten minutes of twelve when Judge Redfern met him. And, remember, he played poker in the club here until three in the morning—hours after the murder took place."

Markham shook his head with emphasis.

"Vance, there's no human way to get round those facts. They're firmly established; and they preclude Spotswoode's guilt as effectively and finally as though he had been at the North Pole that night."

Vance was unmoved.

"I admit everything you say," he rejoined. "But as I have stated before, when material facts and psychological facts conflict, the material facts are wrong. In this case, they may not actually be wrong, but they're deceptive."

"Very well, *magnus Apollo!*" The situation was too much for Markham's exacerbated nerves. "Show me how Spotswoode could have strangled the girl and ransacked the apartment, and I'll order Heath to arrest him."

"'Pon my word, I can't do it," expostulated Vance. "Omniscience was denied me. But—deuce take it!—I think I've done rather well in pointing out the culprit. I never agreed to expound his technic, don't y' know."

"So! Your vaunted penetration amounts only to that, does it? Well, well! Here and now I become a professor of the higher mental sciences, and I pronounce solemnly that Doctor Crippen murdered the Odell girl. To be sure, Crippen's dead; but that fact doesn't interfere with my newly adopted psychological means of deduction. Crippen's nature, you see, fits perfectly with all the esoteric and recondite indications of the crime. To-morrow I'll apply for an order of exhumation."

Vance looked at him with waggish reproachfulness, and sighed.

"Recognition of my transcendent genius, I see, is destined to be posthumous. *Omnia post obitum fingit majora vetustas.* In the meantime I bear the taunts and jeers of the multitude with a stout heart. My head is bloody, but unbowed."

He looked at his watch, and then seemed to become absorbed with some line of thought.

"Markham," he said, after several minutes, "I've a concert at three o'clock, but there's an hour to spare. I want to take another look at that apartment and its various approaches. Spotswoode's trick—and I'm convinced it was nothing more than a trick—was enacted there; and if we are ever to find the explanation, we shall have to look for it on the scene."

I had got the impression that Markham, despite his emphatic denial of the possibility of Spotswoode's guilt, was not entirely unconvinced. Therefore, I was not surprised when, with only a half-hearted protest, he assented to Vance's proposal to revisit the Odell apartment.

CHAPTER XXIX

BEETHOVEN'S "ANDANTE"

(Tuesday, September 18; 2 p. m.)

Less than half an hour later we again entered the main hall of the little apartment building in 71st Street. Spively, as usual, was on duty at the switchboard. Just inside the public reception-room the officer on guard reclined in an easy chair, a cigar in his mouth. On seeing the District Attorney, he rose with forced alacrity.

"When you going to open things up, Mr. Markham?" he asked. "This rest-cure is ruinin' my health."

"Very soon, I hope, officer," Markham told him. "Any more visitors?"

"Nobody, sir." The man stifled a yawn.

"Let's have your key to the apartment.—Have you been inside?"

"No, sir. Orders were to stay out here."

We passed into the dead girl's living-room. The shades were still up, and the sunlight of midday was pouring in. Nothing apparently had been touched: not even the overturned chairs had been righted. Markham went to the window and stood, his hands behind him, surveying the scene despondently. He was laboring under a growing uncertainty, and he watched Vance with a cynical amusement which was far from spontaneous.

Vance, after lighting a cigarette, proceeded to inspect the two rooms, letting his eyes rest searchingly on the various disordered objects. Presently he went into the bathroom and remained several minutes. When he came out he carried a towel with several dark smudges on it.

"This is what Skeel used to erase his finger-prints," he said, tossing the towel on the bed.

"Marvellous!" Markham rallied him. "That, of course, convicts Spotswoode."

"Tut, tut! But it helps substantiate my theory of the crime." He walked to the dressing-table and sniffed at a tiny silver atomizer. "The lady used Coty's *Chypre*," he murmured. "Why *will* they all do it?"

"And just what does that help substantiate?"

"Markham dear, I'm absorbing atmosphere. I'm attuning my soul to the apartment's vibrations. Do let me attune in peace. I may have a visitation at any moment—a revelation from Sinai, as it were."

He continued his round of investigation, and at last passed out into the main hall, where he stood, one foot holding open the door, looking about him with curious intentness. When he returned to the living-room, he sat down on the edge of the rosewood table, and surrendered himself to gloomy contemplation. After several minutes he gave Markham a sardonic grin.

"I say! This *is* a problem. Dash it all, it's uncanny!"

"I had an idea," scoffed Markham, "that sooner or later you'd revise your deductions in regard to Spotswoode."

Vance stared idly at the ceiling.

"You're devilish stubborn, don't y' know. Here I am trying to extricate you from a deuced unpleasant predicament, and all you do is to indulge in caustic observations calculated to damp my youthful ardor."

Markham left the window and seated himself on the arm of the davenport facing Vance. His eyes held a worried look.

"Vance, don't get me wrong. Spotswoode means nothing in my life. If he did this thing, I'd like to know it. Unless this case is cleared up, I'm in for an ungodly walloping by the newspapers. It's not to my interests to discourage any possibility of a solution. But your conclusion about Spotswoode is impossible. There are too many contradictory facts."

"That's just it, don't y' know. The contradict'ry indications are far too perfect. They fit together too beautifully; they're almost as fine as the forms in a Michelangelo statue. They're too carefully co-ordinated, d' ye see, to have been merely a haphazard concatenation of circumstances. They signify conscious design."

Markham rose and, slowly returning to the window, stood looking out into the little rear yard.

"If I could grant your premise that Spotswoode killed the girl," he said, "I could follow your syllogism. But I can't very well convict a man on the grounds that his defense is too perfect."

"What we need, Markham, is inspiration. The mere contortions of the sibyl are not enough." Vance took a turn up and down the room. "What really infuriates me is that I've been outwitted.

And by a manufacturer of automobile access'ries!
. . . It's most humiliatin'."

He sat down at the piano and played the opening
bars of Brahms's *Capriccio* No. 1.

"Needs tuning," he muttered; and, sauntering to
the Boule cabinet, he ran his finger over the mar-
quetry. "Pretty and all that," he said, "but a bit
fussy. Good example, though. The deceased's aunt
from Seattle should get a very fair price for it." He
regarded a pendent girandole at the side of the cabinet. "Rather nice, that, if the original candles hadn't
been supplanted with modern frosted bulbs." He
paused before the little china clock on the mantel.
"Gingerbread. I'm sure it kept atrocious time."
Passing on to the escritoire, he examined it critically.
"Imitation French Renaissance. But rather dainty,
what?" Then his eye fell on the waste-paper basket, and he picked it up. "Silly idea," he commented, "—making a basket out of vellum. The ar-
tistic triumph of some lady interior decorator, I'll
wager. Enough vellum here to bind a set of Epicte-
tus. But why ruin the effect with hand-painted gar-
lands? The æsthetic instinct has not as yet invaded
these fair States—decidedly not."

Setting the basket down, he studied it meditatively
for a moment. Then he leaned over and took from it
the piece of crumpled wrapping-paper to which he
had referred the previous day.

"This doubtless contained the lady's last purchase
on earth," he mused. "Very touchin'. Are you sentimental about such trifles, Markham? Anyway, the
purple string round it was a godsend to Skeel. . . .
What knickknack, do you suppose, paved the way
for the frantic Tony's escape?"

He opened the paper, revealing a broken piece of corrugated cardboard and a large square dark-brown envelope.

"Ah, to be sure! Phonograph records." He glanced about the apartment. "But, I say, where did the lady keep the bally machine?"

"You'll find it in the foyer," said Markham wearily, without turning. He knew that Vance's chatter was only the outward manifestation of serious and perplexed thinking; and he was waiting with what patience he could muster.

Vance sauntered idly through the glass doors into the little reception-hall, and stood gazing abstractedly at a console phonograph of Chinese Chippendale design which stood against the wall at one end. The squat cabinet was partly covered with a prayer-rug, and upon it sat a polished bronze flower-bowl.

"At any rate, it doesn't look phonographic," he remarked. "But why the prayer-rug?" He examined it casually. "Anatolian—probably called a Cæsarian for sale purposes. Not very valuable—too much on the Oushak type. . . . Wonder what the lady's taste in music was. Victor Herbert, doubtless." He turned back the rug and lifted the lid of the cabinet. There was a record already on the machine, and he leaned over and looked at it.

"My word! The *Andante* from Beethoven's C-Minor Symphony!" he exclaimed cheerfully. "You know the movement, of course, Markham. The most perfect *Andante* ever written." He wound up the machine. "I think a little good music might clear the atmosphere and volatilize our perturbation, what?"

Markham paid no attention to his banter; he was still gazing dejectedly out of the window.

Vance started the motor, and placing the needle on the record, returned to the living-room. He stood staring at the davenport, concentrating on the problem in hand. I sat in the wicker chair by the door waiting for the music. The situation was getting on my nerves, and I began to feel fidgety. A minute or two passed, but the only sound which came from the phonograph was a faint scratching. Vance looked up with mild curiosity, and walked back to the machine. Inspecting it cursorily, he once more set it in operation. But though he waited several minutes, no music came forth.

"I say! That's deuced queer, y' know," he grumbled, as he changed the needle and rewound the motor.

Markham had now left the window, and stood watching him with good-natured tolerance. The turn-table of the phonograph was spinning, and the needle was tracing its concentric revolutions; but still the instrument refused to play. Vance, with both hands on the cabinet, was leaning forward, his eyes fixed on the silently revolving record with an expression of amused bewilderment.

"The sound-box is probably broken," he said. "Silly machines, anyway."

"The difficulty, I imagine," Markham chided him, "lies in your patrician ignorance of so vulgar and democratic a mechanism.—Permit me to assist you."

He moved to Vance's side, and I stood looking curiously over his shoulder. Everything appeared to be in order, and the needle had now almost reached the end of the record. But only a faint scratching was audible.

Markham stretched forth his hand to lift the sound-box. But his movement was never completed.

At that moment the little apartment was filled with several terrifying treble screams, followed by two shrill calls for help. A cold chill swept my body, and there was a tingling at the roots of my hair.

After a short silence, during which the three of us remained speechless, the same feminine voice said in a loud, distinct tone: "*No; nothing is the matter. I'm sorry. . . . Everything is all right. . . . Please go home, and don't worry.*"

The needle had come to the end of the record. There was a slight click, and the automatic device shut off the motor. The almost terrifying silence that followed was broken by a sardonic chuckle from Vance.

"Well, old dear," he remarked languidly, as he strolled back into the living-room, "so much for your irrefutable facts!"

There came a loud knocking on the door, and the officer on duty outside looked in with a startled face.

"It's all right," Markham informed him in a husky voice. "I'll call you when I want you."

Vance lay down on the davenport and took out another cigarette. Having lighted it, he stretched his arms far over his head and extended his legs, like a man in whom a powerful physical tension had suddenly relaxed.

"'Pon my soul, Markham, we've all been babes in the woods," he drawled. "An incontrovertible alibi—

my word! If the law supposes that, as Mr. Bumble
said, the law is a ass, a idiot.—Oh, Sammy, Sammy,
vy worn't there a alleybi! . . . Markham, I blush
to admit it, but it's you and I who've been the unutterable asses."

Markham had been standing by the instrument
like a man dazed, his eyes riveted hypnotically on
the telltale record. Slowly he came into the room and
threw himself wearily into a chair.

"Those precious facts of yours!" continued Vance.
"Stripped of their carefully disguised appearance,
what are they?—Spotswoode prepared a phonograph
record—a simple enough task. Every one makes 'em
nowadays——"

"Yes. He told me he had a workshop at his home
on Long Island where he tinkered a bit."

"He really didn't need it, y' know. But it facili-
tated things, no doubt. The voice on the record is
merely his own in falsetto—better for the purpose
than a woman's, for it's stronger and more penetrating. As for the label, he simply soaked it off of an
ordin'ry record, and pasted it on his own. He
brought the lady several new records that night, and
concealed this one among them. After the theatre he
enacted his gruesome little drama and then carefully
set the stage so that the police would think it was a
typical burglar's performance. When this had been
done, he placed the record on the machine, set it
going, and calmly walked out. He had placed the
prayer-rug and bronze bowl on the cabinet of the
machine to give the impression that the phonograph
was rarely used. And the precaution worked, for no
one thought of looking into it. Why should they?

. . . Then he asked Jessup to call a taxicab—everything quite natural, y' see. While he was waiting for the car the needle reached the recorded screams. They were heard plainly: it was night, and the sounds carried distinctly. Moreover, being filtered through a wooden door, their phonographic *timbre* was well disguised. And, if you'll note, the enclosed horn is directed toward the door, not three feet away."

"But the synchronization of his questions and the answers on the record. . . ?"

"The simplest part of it. You remember Jessup told us that Spotswoode was standing with one arm on the switchboard when the screams were heard. He merely had his eye on his wrist-watch. The moment he heard the cry, he calculated the intermission on the record, and put his question to the imagin'ry lady at just the right moment to receive the record's response. It was all carefully figured out beforehand; he no doubt rehearsed it in his laborat'ry. It was deuced simple, and practically proof against failure. The record is a large one—twelve-inch diameter, I should say—and it requires about five minutes for the needle to traverse it. By putting the screams at the end, he allowed himself ample time to get out and order a taxicab. When the car at last came, he rode direct to the Stuyvesant Club, where he met Judge Redfern and played poker till three. If he hadn't met the Judge, rest assured he would have impressed his presence on some one else so as to have established an alibi."

Markham shook his head gravely.

"Good God! No wonder he importuned me on

every possible occasion to let him visit this apartment again. Such a damning piece of evidence as that record must have kept him awake at night."

"Still, I rather fancy that if I hadn't discovered it, he would have succeeded in getting possession of it as soon as your *sergent-de-ville* was removed. It was annoyin' to be unexpectedly barred from the apartment, but I doubt if it worried him much. He would have been on hand when the Canary's aunt took possession, and the retrieving of the record would have been comparatively easy. Of course the record constituted a hazard, but Spotswoode isn't the type who'd shy at a low bunker of that kind. No; the thing was planned scientifically enough. He was defeated by sheer accident."

"And Skeel?"

"He was another unfortunate circumstance. He was hiding in the closet there when Spotswoode and the lady came in at eleven. It was Spotswoode whom he saw strangle his erstwhile *amoureuse* and rifle the apartment. Then, when Spotswoode went out, he came forth from hiding. He was probably looking down at the girl when the phonograph emitted its blood-chilling wails. . . . My word! Fancy being in a cold funk, gazing at a murdered woman, and then hearing piercing screams behind you! It was a bit too much even for the hardened Tony. I don't wonder he forgot all caution and put his hand on the table to steady himself. . . . And then came Spotswoode's voice through the door, and the record's answer. This must have puzzled Skeel. I imagine he thought for a moment he'd lost his reason. But pretty soon the significance of it dawned on him;

and I can see him grinning to himself. Obviously
he knew who the murderer was—it would not have
been in keeping with his character had he failed to
learn the identities of the Canary's admirers. And
now there had fallen into his lap, like manna from
heaven, the most perfect opportunity for blackmail
that any such charmin' young gentleman could desire. He doubtless indulged himself with roseate
visions of a life of opulence and ease at Spotswoode's
expense. When Cleaver phoned a few minutes later,
he merely said the lady was out, and then set to
work planning his own departure."

"But I don't see why he didn't take the record
with him."

"And remove from the scene of the crime the one
piece of unanswerable evidence? . . . Bad strategy,
Markham. If he himself had produced the record
later, Spotswoode would simply have denied all
knowledge of it, and accused the blackmailer of a
plot. Oh, no; Skeel's only course was to leave it, and
apply for an enormous settlement from Spotswoode
at once. And I imagine that's what he did. Spotswoode no doubt gave him something on account and
promised him the rest anon, hoping in the meantime
to retrieve the record. When he failed to pay, Skeel
phoned you and threatened to tell everything, thinking to spur Spotswoode to action. . . . Well, he
spurred him—but not to the action desired. Spotswoode probably met him by appointment last Saturday night, ostensibly to hand over the money, but,
instead, throttled the chap. Quite in keeping with
his nature, don't y' know. . . . Stout fella, Spotswoode."

"The whole thing . . . it's amazing."

"I shouldn't say that, now. Spotswoode had an unpleasant task to perform, and he set about it in a cool, logical, forthright, businesslike manner. He had decided that his little Canary must die for his peace of mind: she'd probably made herself most annoyin'. So he arranged the date—like any judge passing sentence on a prisoner at the bar—and then proceeded to fabricate an alibi. Being something of a mechanic, he arranged a mechanical alibi. The device he chose was simple and obvious enough —no tortuosities or complications. And it would have succeeded but for what the insurance companies piously call an act of God. No one can foresee accidents, Markham: they wouldn't be accidental if one could. But Spotswoode certainly took every precaution that was humanly possible. It never occurred to him that you would thwart his every effort to return here and confiscate the record; and he couldn't anticipate my taste in music, nor know that I would seek solace in the tonal art. Furthermore, when one calls on a lady, one doesn't expect that another suitor is going to hide himself in the clothes-press. It isn't done, don't y' know. . . . All in all, the poor johnny was beaten by a run of abominable luck."

"You overlook the fiendishness of the crime," Markham reproached him tartly.

"Don't be so confoundedly moral, old thing. Every one's a murderer at heart. The person who has never felt a passionate hankering to kill some one is without emotions. And do you think it's ethics or theology that stays the average person from homicide? Dear no! It's lack of courage—the fear of being found out, or haunted, or cursed with remorse. Observe with what delight the people *en masse*—to wit, the state—put men to death, and then gloat over it in the newspapers. Nations declare war against one another on the slightest provocation, so they can, with immunity, vent their lust for slaughter. Spotswoode, I'd say, is merely a rational animal with the courage of his convictions."

"Society unfortunately isn't ready for your nihilistic philosophy just yet," said Markham. "And during the intervening transition human life must be protected."

He rose resolutely, and going to the telephone, called up Heath.

"Sergeant," he ordered, "get a John-Doe warrant and meet me immediately at the Stuyvesant Club. Bring a man with you—there's an arrest to be made."

"At last the law has evidence after its own heart," chirped Vance, as he lazily donned his top-coat and picked up his hat and stick. "What a grotesque affair your legal procedure is, Markham! Scientific knowledge—the facts of psychology—mean nothing to you learned Solons. But a phonograph record— ah! There, now, is something convincing, irrefragable, final, what?"

On our way out Markham beckoned to the officer on guard.

"Under no conditions," he said, "is any one to enter this apartment until I return—not even with a signed permit."

When we had entered the taxicab, he directed the chauffeur to the club.

"So the newspapers want action, do they? Well,

they're going to get it. . . . You've helped me out
of a nasty hole, old man."

As he spoke, his eyes turned to Vance. And that
look conveyed a profounder gratitude than any
words could have expressed.

CHAPTER XXX

THE END

(Tuesday, September 18; 3.30 p. m.)

It was exactly half past three when we entered
the rotunda of the Stuyvesant Club. Markham at
once sent for the manager, and held a few words of
private conversation with him. The manager then
hastened away, and was gone about five minutes.

"Mr. Spotswoode is in his rooms," he informed
Markham, on returning. "I sent the electrician up
to test the light bulbs. He reports that the gentleman
is alone, writing at his desk."

"And the room number?"

"Three forty-one." The manager appeared perturbed. "There won't be any fuss, will there, Mr.
Markham?"

"1 don't look for any." Markham's tone was
chilly. "However, the present matter is considerably
more important than your club."

"What an exaggerated point of view!" sighed
Vance when the manager had left us. "The arrest
of Spotswoode, I'd say, was the acme of futility. The
man isn't a criminal, don't y' know; he has nothing
in common with Lombroso's *Uomo Delinquente*. He's
what one might term a philosophic behaviorist."

Markham grunted but did not answer. He began
pacing up and down agitatedly, keeping his eyes ex-

pectantly on the main entrance. Vance sought a comfortable chair, and settled himself in it with placid unconcern.

Ten minutes later Heath and Snitkin arrived. Markham at once led them into an alcove and briefly explained his reason for summoning them.

"Spotswoode's up-stairs now," he said. "I want the arrest made as quietly as possible."

"Spotswoode!" Heath repeated the name in astonishment. "I don't see——"

"You don't have to see—yet," Markham cut in sharply. "I'm taking all responsibility for the arrest. And you're getting the credit—if you want it. That suit you?"

Heath shrugged his shoulders.

"It's all right with me . . . anything you say, sir." He shook his head uncomprehendingly. "But what about Jessup?"

"We'll keep him locked up. Material witness."

We ascended in the elevator and emerged at the third floor. Spotswoode's rooms were at the end of the hall, facing the Square. Markham, his face set grimly, led the way.

In answer to his knock Spotswoode opened the door and, greeting us pleasantly, stepped aside for us to enter.

"Any news yet?" he asked, moving a chair forward.

At this moment he got a clear view of Markham's face in the light, and at once he sensed the minatory nature of our visit. Though his expression did not alter, I saw his body suddenly go taut. His cold, indecipherable eyes moved slowly from Markham's face to Heath and Snitkin. Then his gaze fell on Vance and me, who were standing a little behind the others, and he nodded stiffly.

No one spoke; yet I felt that an entire tragedy was somehow being enacted, and that each actor heard and understood every word.

Markham remained standing, as if reluctant to proceed. Of all the duties of his office, I knew that the arrest of malefactors was the most distasteful to him. He was a worldly man, with the worldly man's tolerance for the misfortunes of evil. Heath and Snitkin had stepped forward and now waited with passive alertness for the District Attorney's order to serve the warrant.

Spotswoode's eyes were again on Markham.

"What can I do for you, sir?" His voice was calm and without the faintest quaver.

"You can accompany these officers, Mr. Spotswoode," Markham told him quietly, with a slight inclination of his head toward the two imperturbable figures at his side. "I arrest you for the murder of Margaret Odell."

"Ah!" Spotswoode's eyebrows lifted mildly. "Then you have—discovered something?"

"The Beethoven *Andante*."

Not a muscle of Spotswoode's face moved; but after a short pause he made a barely perceptible gesture of resignation.

"I can't say that it was wholly unexpected," he said evenly, with the tragic suggestion of a smile; "especially as you thwarted every effort of mine to secure the record. But then . . . the fortunes of the game are always uncertain." His smile faded, and his manner became grave. "You have acted generously toward me, Mr. Markham, in shielding me from the *canaille;* and because I appreciate that courtesy I should like you to know that the game I played was one in which I had no alternative."

"Your motive, however powerful," said Markham, "cannot extenuate your crime."

"Do you think I seek extenuation?" Spotswoode dismissed the imputation with a contemptuous gesture. "I'm not a schoolboy. I calculated the consequences of my course of action, and after weighing the various factors involved, decided to risk it. It was a gamble, to be sure; but it's not my habit to complain about the misfortunes of a deliberately planned risk. Furthermore, the choice was practically forced upon me. Had I not gambled in this instance, I stood to lose heavily nevertheless."

His face grew bitter.

"This woman, Mr. Markham, had demanded the impossible of me. Not content with bleeding me financially, she demanded legal protection, position, social prestige—such things as only my name could give her. She informed me I must divorce my wife and marry her. I wonder if you apprehend the enormity of that demand? . . . You see, Mr. Markham, I love my wife, and I have children whom I love. I will not insult your intelligence by explaining how, despite my conduct, such a thing is entirely possible. . . . And yet, this woman commanded me to wreck my life and crush utterly those I held dear, solely to gratify her petty, ridiculous ambition! When I refused, she threatened to expose our relations to my wife, to send her copies of the letters I had written, to sue me publicly—in fine, to create such a scandal that, in any event, my life would be ruined, my family disgraced, my home destroyed."

He paused and drew a deep inspiration.

"I have never been partial to half-way measures," he continued impassively. "I have no talent for compromise. Perhaps I am a victim of my heritage. But my instinct is to play out a hand to the last chip—to force whatever danger threatens. And for just five minutes, a week ago, I understood how the fanatics of old could, with a calm mind and a sense of righteousness, torture their enemies who threatened them with spiritual destruction. . . . I chose the only course which might save those I love from disgrace and suffering. It meant taking a desperate risk. But the blood within me was such that I did not hesitate, and I was fired by the agony of a tremendous hate. I staked my life against a living death, on the remote chance of attaining peace. And I lost."

Again he smiled faintly.

"Yes—the fortunes of the game. . . . But don't think for a minute that I am complaining or seeking sympathy. I have lied to others perhaps, but not to myself. I detest a whiner—a self-excuser. I want you to understand that."

He reached to the table at his side and took up a small limp-leather volume.

"Only last night I was reading Wilde's 'De Profundis.' Had I been gifted with words, I might have made a similar confession. Let me show you what I mean so that, at least, you won't attribute to me the final infamy of cravenness."

He opened the book, and began reading in a voice whose very fervor held us all silent:

"'I brought about my own downfall. "No one, be he high or low, need be ruined by any other hand than his own. Readily as I confess this, there are many who will, at this time at least, receive the confession sceptically. And although I thus mercilessly accuse myself, bear in mind that I do so without offering any excuse. Terrible as is the punishment inflicted upon me by the world, more terrible is the ruin I have brought upon myself. . . . In the dawn of manhood I recognized my position. . . . I enjoyed an honored name, an eminent social position. . . . Then came the turning-point. I had become tired of dwelling on the heights—and descended by my own will into the depths. . . . I satisfied my desires wherever it suited me, and passed on. I forgot that every act, even the most insignificant act, of daily life, in some degree, makes or unmakes the character; and every occurrence which transpires in the seclusion of the chamber will some day be proclaimed from the housetops. I lost control of myself. I was no longer at the helm, and knew it not. I had become a slave to pleasure. . . . One thing only is left to me—complete humility.'"

He tossed the book aside.

"You understand now, Mr. Markham?"

Markham did not speak for several moments.

"Do you care to tell me about Skeel?" he at length asked.

"That swine!" Spotswoode sneered his disgust. "I could murder such creatures every day and regard myself as a benefactor of society. . . . Yes, I

strangled him, and I would have done it before, only
the opportunity did not offer. . . . It was Skeel
who was hiding in the closet when I returned to the
apartment after the theatre, and he must have seen
me kill the woman. Had I known he was behind
that locked closet door, I would have broken it down
and wiped him out then. But how was I to know? It
seemed natural that the closet might have been kept
locked—I didn't give it a second thought. . . . And
the next night he telephoned me to the club here. He
had first called my home on Long Island, and learned
that I was staying here. I had never seen him before
—didn't know of his existence. But, it seems, he had
equipped himself with a knowledge of my identity—
probably some of the money I gave to the woman
went to him. What a muck-heap I had fallen into!
. . . When he phoned, he mentioned the phonograph, and I knew he had found out something. I
met him in the Waldorf lobby, and he told me the
truth: there was no doubting his word. When he
saw I was convinced, he demanded so enormous a
sum that I was staggered."

Spotswoode lit a cigarette with steady fingers.

"Mr. Markham, I am no longer a rich man. The
truth is, I am on the verge of bankruptcy. The business my father left me has been in a receiver's hands
for nearly a year. The Long Island estate on which
I live belongs to my wife. Few people know these
things, but unfortunately they are true. It would
have been utterly impossible for me to raise the
amount Skeel demanded, even had I been inclined
to play the coward. I did, however, give him a small
sum to keep him quiet for a few days, promising him

all he asked as soon as I could convert some of my
holdings. I hoped in the interim to get possession of
the record and thus spike his guns. But in that I
failed; and so, when he threatened to tell you everything, I agreed to bring the money to his home late
last Saturday night. I kept the appointment, with
the full intention of killing him. I was careful about
entering, but he had helped me by explaining when
and how I could get in without being seen. Once
there, I wasted no time. The first moment he was
off his guard I seized him—and gloried in the act.
Then, locking the door and taking the key, I walked
out of the house quite openly, and returned here to
the club.—That's all, I think."

Vance was watching him musingly.

"So when you raised my bet last night," he said,
"the amount represented a highly important item
in your exchequer."

Spotswoode smiled faintly.

"It represented practically every cent I had in the
world."

"Astonishin'! . . . And would you mind if I
asked you why you selected the label of Beethoven's
Andante for your record?"

"Another miscalculation," the man said wearily.
"It occurred to me that if any one should, by any
chance, open the phonograph before I could return
and destroy the record, he wouldn't be as likely to
want to hear the classics as he would a more popular
selection."

"And one who detests popular music had to find
it! I fear, Mr. Spotswoode, that an unkind fate sat
in at your game."

"Yes. . . . If I were religiously inclined, I might talk poppycock about retribution and divine punishment."

"I'd like to ask you about the jewellery," said Markham. "It's not sportsmanlike to do it, and I wouldn't suggest it, except that you've already confessed voluntarily to the main points at issue."

"I shall take no offense at any question you desire to ask, sir," Spotswoode answered. "After I had recovered my letters from the document-box, I turned the rooms upside down to give the impression of a burglary—being careful to use gloves, of course. And I took the woman's jewellery for the same reason. Parenthetically, I had paid for most of it. I offered it as a sop to Skeel, but he was afraid to accept it; and finally I decided to rid myself of it. I wrapped it in one of the club newspapers and threw it in a wastebin near the Flatiron Building."

"You wrapped it in the morning *Herald*," put in Heath. "Did you know that Pop Cleaver reads nothing but the *Herald?*"

"Sergeant!" Vance's voice was a cutting reprimand. "Certainly Mr. Spotswoode was not aware of that fact—else he would not have selected the *Herald.*"

Spotswoode smiled at Heath with pitying contempt. Then, with an appreciative glance at Vance, he turned back to Markham.

"An hour or so after I had disposed of the jewels I was assailed by the fear that the package might be found and the paper traced. So I bought another *Herald* and put it on the rack." He paused. "Is that all?"

Markham nodded.

"Thank you—that's all; except that I must now ask you to go with these officers."

"In that case," said Spotswoode quietly, "there's a small favor I have to ask of you, Mr. Markham. Now that the blow has fallen, I wish to write a certain note—to my wife. But I want to be alone when I write it. Surely you understand that desire. It will take but a few moments. Your men may stand at the door—I can't very well escape. . . . The victor can afford to be generous to that extent."

Before Markham had time to reply, Vance stepped forward and touched his arm.

"I trust," he interposed, "that you won't deem it necess'ry to refuse Mr. Spotswoode's request."

Markham looked at him hesitantly.

"I guess you've pretty well earned the right to dictate, Vance," he acquiesced.

Then he ordered Heath and Snitkin to wait outside in the hall, and he and Vance and I went into the adjoining room. Markham stood, as if on guard, near the door; but Vance, with an ironical smile, sauntered to the window and gazed out into Madison Square.

"My word, Markham!" he declared. "There's something rather colossal about that chap. Y' know, one can't help admiring him. He's so eminently sane and logical."

Markham made no response. The drone of the city's mid-afternoon noises, muffled by the closed windows, seemed to intensify the ominous silence of the little bedchamber where we waited.

Then came a sharp report from the other room.

Markham flung open the door. Heath and Snitkin

were already rushing toward Spotswoode's prostrate body, and were bending over it when Markham entered. Immediately he wheeled about and glared at Vance, who now appeared in the doorway.

"He's shot himself!"

"Fancy that," said Vance.

"You—you knew he was going to do that?" Markham spluttered.

"It was rather obvious, don't y' know."

Markham's eyes flashed angrily.

"And you deliberately interceded for him—to give him the opportunity?"

"Tut, tut, my dear fellow!" Vance reproached him. "Pray don't give way to conventional moral indignation. However unethical—theoretically—it may be to take another's life, a man's own life is certainly his to do with as he chooses. Suicide is his inalienable right. And under the paternal tyranny of our modern democracy, I'm rather inclined to think it's about the only right he has left, what?"

He glanced at his watch and frowned.

"D' ye know, I've missed my concert, bothering with your beastly affairs," he complained amiably, giving Markham an engaging smile; "and now you're actually scolding me. 'Pon my word, old fellow, you're deuced ungrateful!"

There's More to Follow!

More stories of the sort you like; more, probably, by the author of this one; more than 500 titles all told by writers of world-wide reputation, in the Authors' Alphabetical List which you will find on the *reverse side* of the wrapper of this book. Look it over before you lay it aside. There are books here you are sure to want—some, possibly, that you have *always* wanted.

It is a *selected* list; every book in it has achieved a certain measure of *success*.

The Grosset & Dunlap list is not only the greatest Index of Good Fiction available, it represents in addition a generally accepted Standard of Value. It will pay you to

Look on the Other Side of the Wrapper!

In case the wrapper is lost write to the publishers for a complete catalog